COMING UP IN THE SPRING

Conjunctions:48
FACES OF DESIRE

Edited by Bradford Morrow

"Desire, for hire, would tire a shire," Joyce wrote in *Finnegans Wake*, though it's likely the shire'd be tired even if desire weren't hired, but just happened along on its daily rounds.

Of all emotions, desire is the prime engine. Desire informs all that we do, sparks everything from the smallest gesture between two people to relationships between cultures. When it establishes residence in the heart, it becomes a tireless agency of will. Desire, quite often, is deeply undesirable, a contentious and electric foe. Burning desire can skew a soul way out of shape. It motivates good and evil by turn and is as ancient as breath itself. Now sexual, now religious, now charitable, now greedy, now thoughtful, now callous, desire runs as deep as belief or shallow as a whim.

In *Conjunctions:48, Faces of Desire*, several dozen of contemporary literature's most provocative and adventurous writers will explore the tricky terrain of desire in essays, fiction, poetry, and memoirs. The many diverse contributors to this special issue include Donald Revell, Mei-mei Berssenbrugge, Carole Maso, Brian Evenson, Robert Kelly, Tova Reich, and Rosamond Purcell, among others.

Faces of Desire offers an exuberant look into one of the most mysterious, complex aspects of human life.

Subscriptions to *Conjunctions* are only $18 for more than eight hundred pages per year of contemporary and historical literature and art. Please send your check to *Conjunctions*, Bard College, Annandale-on-Hudson, NY 12504. Subscriptions can also be ordered by calling (845) 758-1539, or by sending an e-mail to Michael Bergstein at Conjunctions@bard.edu. For more information about current and past issues, please visit our Web site at www.Conjunctions.com.

CONJUNCTIONS

Bi-Annual Volumes of New Writing

Edited by
Bradford Morrow

Contributing Editors
Walter Abish
Chinua Achebe
John Ashbery
Martine Bellen
Mei-mei Berssenbrugge
Mary Caponegro
Elizabeth Frank
William H. Gass
Peter Gizzi
Jorie Graham
Robert Kelly
Ann Lauterbach
Norman Manea
Rick Moody
Howard Norman
Joanna Scott
Peter Straub
William Weaver
John Edgar Wideman

published by Bard College

EDITOR: Bradford Morrow
MANAGING EDITOR: Michael Bergstein
SENIOR EDITORS: Robert Antoni, Peter Constantine, Brian Evenson,
    Micaela Morrissette, David Shields, Pat Sims, Alan Tinkler
WEBMASTER: Brian Evenson
ASSOCIATE EDITORS: Jedediah Berry, J. W. McCormack, Eric Olson
ART EDITOR: Norton Batkin
PUBLICITY: Mark R. Primoff
EDITORIAL ASSISTANTS: Jessica Loudis, Daniel Pearce, John Sinaiko

CONJUNCTIONS is published in the Spring and Fall of each year by Bard College, Annandale-on-Hudson, NY 12504. This issue is made possible in part with public funds from the New York State Council on the Arts, a State Agency. NYSCA

SUBSCRIPTIONS: Send subscription orders to CONJUNCTIONS, Bard College, Annandale-on-Hudson, NY 12504. Single year (two volumes): $18.00 for individuals; $35.00 for institutions and overseas. Two years (four volumes): $32.00 for individuals; $70.00 for institutions and overseas. Patron subscription (lifetime): $500.00. Overseas subscribers please make payment by International Money Order. For information about subscriptions, back issues, and advertising, call Michael Bergstein at (845) 758-1539 or fax (845) 758-2660.

Editorial communications should be sent to Bradford Morrow, *Conjunctions*, 21 East 10th Street, New York, NY 10003. Unsolicited manuscripts cannot be returned unless accompanied by a stamped, self-addressed envelope. Electronic and simultaneous submissions will not be considered.

Conjunctions is listed and indexed in the American Humanities Index.

Visit the *Conjunctions* Web site at www.conjunctions.com.

Cover design by Jerry Kelly, New York.

Available through D.A.P./Distributed Art Publishers, Inc., 155 Sixth Avenue, New York, NY 10013. Telephone: (212) 627-1999. Fax: (212) 627-9484.

Printers: Edwards Brothers

Typesetter: Bill White, Typeworks

ISSN 0278-2324
ISBN 0-941964-63-9

Manufactured in the United States of America.

TABLE OF CONTENTS

CONJUNCTIONS:47
Twenty-fifth Anniversary Issue

EDITOR'S NOTE

IT WAS THE YEAR of the Rooster. The year Ronald Reagan was inaugurated fortieth president of the United States. Back then the national debt was only a trillion, and the highest-grossing film was *Raiders of the Lost Ark*. Britney Spears was born that year and Bob Marley died. Prince Charles married Lady Diana Spencer at St. Paul's Cathedral. Luke married Laura on *General Hospital*. The USSR tested nuclear weapons that year. So did France. So did the United States. Olivia Newton-John's "Let's Get Physical" topped the charts. Pete Rose surpassed Stan Musial's National League record of 3,350 hits, and Billie Jean King was outed by her ex-lover. Nelson Algren died that year. Paris Hilton was born and Elias Canetti won the Nobel Prize. It was the year Augusto Pinochet began his second term as president of Chile in the same month Isabel Perón, ex-president of Argentina, was sentenced to eight years in prison. The Dodgers beat the Yankees that year, and Israel annexed the Golan Heights. Rubik's Cube was Toy of the Year. Lech Walesa was *Time*'s Man of the Year. Pigmeat Markham died. President Reagan resumed production of the neutron bomb. Males-only draft registration was upheld as constitutional by the Supreme Court that summer, the summer Sandra Day O'Connor was confirmed as its first female justice. Mohammad Ali Rajai, the president of Iran, and Mohammad Javad Bahonar, Iran's prime minister, were assassinated in bombings that August. Twenty-five years ago, MTV first went on the air with the Buggles' "Video Killed the Radio Star" and Bill Haley, best remembered for "Rock Around the Clock," died. Nineteen eighty-one was the International Year of Disabled Persons. President Reagan was shot and wounded by John Hinckley Jr. in an assassination attempt. Pope John Paul II was shot and wounded by Mehmet Ali Agca in an assassination attempt. America's first test-tube baby, Elizabeth Jordan Carr, was born that year, the same year Walter Cronkite retired and Dan Rather became anchor of *The CBS Evening News*. On April 12, Columbia became the first space shuttle to orbit the earth. *Dynasty*'s first episode was aired that year. Joe Louis died. Eugenio Montale died. Natalie Wood drowned. Anwar Sadat was gunned down while reviewing a military parade. Iran released fifty-two American hostages who had been held for 444 days. In a televised interview during the summer of 1981, Barbara Walters asked Katharine Hepburn, "If you were a tree, what kind would you be?"

Editor's Note

This was the climate into which *Conjunctions* was launched, a climate which even the most diehard optimist would agree has only worsened. In the literary province of the culture it has occupied for twenty-five years, *Conjunctions* has always spoken up for itself. All of its writers have together with me voiced its purpose and helped navigate its direction. I hope we will continue to do so. Anniversaries are looking-back moments, but I prefer to stay sighted in the other direction. I do remain these years later just as stubborn as ever in my belief that the written word, the imaginative agencies of poetry, fiction, plays, and essays, are necessary to the enrichment, indeed the survival, of the human spirit. Literature has always been, for me, the most profound way to ask and try to answer our most difficult questions. Nearly a thousand writers in *Conjunctions*—which I continue to think of as a living notebook—have explored the human experience, and many thousands of readers have traveled with them. I, for one, have been deeply grateful to be on the journey.

So many people helped and inspired me over the years. A catalog would fill pages. I'm deeply grateful to all of them. A few in particular—Kenneth Rexroth, my cofounder; James Laughlin, a paradigm; Henry Geldzahler and Arthur Lambert, who kept the rent low in those early years; Martine Bellen, who worked beside me through the most difficult of times; Bill White, Pat Sims, and Michael Bergstein, sine qua non; Leon Botstein and Dimitri Papadimitriou, who believed and believe in the value of *Conjunctions* and have nurtured it for most of its life, along with all the good people at Bard College—I thank from the bottom of my heart and hope the debt of gratitude remains manifest in the many volumes themselves.

—Bradford Morrow
October 2006
New York City

Their Back Pages
Jonathan Lethem

PAGE ONE, PANEL ONE, the island. A dense atoll in a wide barren sea peppered with sharks' fins. Palm trees, sandy shore, pale lagoons, distant smoldering volcano, etc. Interior rain-forest cloaking caves, freshwater springs, shrieking inhuman trills, a nest of ferns where bleached skeletons embrace, who can say what else.

Page one, panel two, the plane. A bolted turnip with wings, now aflame.

Page one, panel three, porthole windows of plane. In first class, the Dingbat Clan. Father Theophobe Dingbat, mother Keener Dingbat, son Spark Dingbat, daughter Lisa Dingbat. In coach, Large Silly (a clown), Poacher Junebug (a hunter), C. Phelps Northrup (a theater critic), Murkly Finger (a villain), Peter Rabbit (a rabbit), King Phnudge (King of the Phnudges), C'Krrrarn (a monster). Large Silly and C. Phelps Northrup are in black & white, all others are in color. All gaze downward, terrified, except C'Krrrarn, who plays computer solitaire.

Page one, panel four, splashdown. The plane's wings curl inward to cover its windshield as it crashes into the lagoon. The wings have fingers, and the doomed pilot and doomed copilot peer from between the fingers like eyeballs.

FROM THE JOURNALS OF C. PHELPS NORTHRUP

July 14

On this fifth day of our desolitude I fear our little compact of necessity has fractured. Mr. and Mrs. Dingbat have refused Poacher Junebug's sagacious notion that we depart the beach for the caves of the interior, insisting that salvage is imminent and in trepidation of the rumored wolverines and bandicoots roaming the deeper groves. However, despite his intrepitude and riflery, Poacher Junebug has succeeded in bagging nothing, which circumstance neither allays our fears nor stocks our larder. The hunter also continually alludes, in snide asides, to the possible deluxe repast to be made of Peter Rabbit. Hence, much dissension, resulting in parturition of our ranks; Peter

9

Rabbit now savors protection within the circled wagons of the Dingbat Family, on the sand where we first crawled ashore, while Poacher Junebug, Large Silly, King Phnudge, and I have undertaken to conquestify the interior. Murkly Finger has, too, stayed behind and entrenched on the beach, in a fragment of the airplane's darkened hull, within which he hoards untold provisions. Only King Phnudge has managed penetration of Finger's lair (King Phnudge has no arms and so perhaps represented no threat to Finger's cache) but his vocabulary was inadequate for conveying to us any sense of the inventory he'd espied there: "Creamy dreamy breamy—hip hurdle hoo!"

C'Krrrarn has of course from the first gone his own way. He was sighted again by the brainy little Dingbat girl, early this morning, posed atop the volcano. Lisa summoned us all to see him there, still as sculpture, foreclaw beckoning to the new sun.

PRENOSTALGIA CLEARANCE SALE!!!
LIMITED EDITION DINGBAT SODA
REDUCED
FUTURE COLLECTORS' ITEMS???
T. DINGBAT'S BEER COLA (nonalcoholic)
KEENER'S LITE ICE TEA
LISA DINGBAT'S CHERRY-ROOT BREW
SPARK'S FIZZUM (caffeine reduced)
GONE BUT NOT FORGOTTEN???
TWENTY DOLLARS PER CASE
DINGBATS WE MISS U!!!

Ten-year-old Spark Dingbat wandered the beach at midday, wearing an inverted bowl of woven palm fronds, a sun hat fashioned by Keener, his mom. Spark had left his family and Peter Rabbit at the campsite they'd improvised, a ring of crappy lean-tos encircling a presumptive fire that his dad, Theophobe, had serially failed to light. His sister, Lisa, having forged a twee, cooing alliance with the terrified hare, Spark was left somewhat on the outside. Now, obstinately solo, he strolled at the shell-strewn beach's exact margin, where the wiper blade of surf just dyed the pinkish sand a wetter hue, where his eight toes were teased by a fringe of bubbles.

Rounding the top of a rocky knoll, a view unfolded below, of an inlet sheltered from the harder surf of the surrounding beaches. Two fat figures splashed there, Large Silly and King Phnudge. Spark clambered past the spit of rock and eased down the sand embankment, to stare from the inlet's grassy ridge. The clown had removed his shoes and clothing, all but his jet black underwear. His feet were enormous, his white body both fleshy and firm, like the ripest fruit. King Phnudge remained fully dressed, or perhaps he was painted. His crown and beard seemed to flow into his collar, and his collar seemed to be one with his belt and his boots, less accoutrements than fancy outcroppings of his smooth, pudgy whole. Armless, he splashed excitedly side to side in water that came to what should have been his knees, while beside him the clown beat maniacally in the water with a large, forked stick, a dowser who'd discovered the sea. The two made a natural pair in Spark's eyes. Their other strong resemblance was to his father, but Spark suspected no one among the islanders would ever remark on it. His father was famous. Large Silly and King Phnudge were nobodies.

"What are you doing?"

Large Silly and King Phnudge wheeled, completely surprised.

"What's it look like, boy? Poacher said he saw some sea bream in this pool."

"Fishy splishy wishy hup huzzoo!"

"How are you going to catch them?"

"With nets of vapid questions and sarcasm. In our teeth. With that headgear of yours—hey, there's a notion. Cough up the fedora, lad."

"Use the king's crown."

"Crowns, if you hadn't noticed, have a hole in the middle. Besides, I don't think it comes off."

"Stuckity pluckity pizzazz—hooble hoo!"

Spark sighed and passed his hat to the eager clown, then watched as it was thrashed to fragments in the hopelessly clumsy attempt at fishing. Spark never saw evidence of a fish. If there had been any, king and clown had certainly frightened them off. Keener's meticulously woven palm fronds were borne off with the seaweed and foam in the pool's gentle tide.

C'KRRRARN   TEARS OFF THE TOP OF A PALM TREE AND FEEDS!!!
C'Krrrarn is staying within himself.
C'KRRRARN TEARS OFF A CORNER OF THE VOLCANO AND FEEDS!!!

11

C'Krrrarn is staying within himself.
C'KRRRARN TEARS OFF A CHUNK OF THE OCEAN AND DEVOURS IT!!!
C'Krrrarn sits perfectly still and tries to empty his mind.
C'KRRRARN SLURPS THE BLOOD OF THE DINGBATS!!!
Long study has demonstrated to C'Krrrarn that the other person is himself.
C'KRRRARN TEARS OFF A PORTION OF THE HORIZON AND DEVOURS IT!!!
C'Krrrarn gazes into the horizon and the horizon gazes into C'Krrrarn and each is calm and free of desire.

FROM POACHER JUNEBUG, AN INDEX

Island, Accursed, *panel 4044*
Island, Confounded, *panels 3176, 3189, 3204n, 3226, 3573, 3564, 3888, 4002, 4036*
Island, Consarn deviltry of, *panels 3344–45, 2455, 3988n, 4012*
Island, Dadburned critters on, *panels 3224, 3656, 3813, 4009*
Island, Dingblasted Fools on, *panels 3208, 3225, 3457, 3800-01, 4009*
Island, Durned, *panel 4129*
Island, Goshforsaken, *panels 3185, 3765*
Island, Riddiculush, *panels 3345, 3679, 4088–9*
Island, Terrible, *panels 3899, 4034, 4067, 4122*
Island, Woeful, *panels 3550, 3823, 4129*
Island, Wretched be this, *panels 3944, 4191*

FROM THE JOURNALS OF C. PHELPS NORTHRUP

July 27
Decline sets in. Tempests wreak havoc on our poor dwellings every third day. Between, corrosive sunshine. Despondent over prospects of rescue. We find little and less to eat. Eighteen days and we come to know some of our companions too well, others not at all. Murkly Finger roams the shore at night, cackling. In sunlight he retracts like a rodent to his hole, around which he has erected an array of sharpened sticks dug in pits of sand, disguised with flimsy leaf cover and more sand, and which would collapse inward at a footfall. The clown floats on his back in the spring where we would drink, moaning

snatches of merry song, muttering wry punchlines without any jokes to them. He has forsaken his hygiene, enclothed in only his undergarment and a purple island hyacinth, its stem wended in his loopy tufts of hair. His feet are rotting. Poacher Junebug, I now understand, catches nothing, fulminates only. The rabbit is in no danger, except from himself. Like the derelict clown, the hare has abandoned clothing, shedding his red waistcoat and bow tie. He now goes on all fours, heeding some natural call. Lisa Dingbat, that former exemplary tot, follows him everywhere, and she too presently goes *au naturel*. I tried to confabulate with her one recent afternoon and she only sniffed and nibbled at the air, issuing a rabbity wheezing sigh, perhaps believing herself a sibling to Peter. The other Dingbats remain largely hidden from view. They must be hungry.

One seldom thinks of C'Krrrarn these days.

King Phnudge, unexpectedly, makes good companionship. We frequently embark on foraging walks together, gleaning nothing of consequence or edibility but nonetheless conveying if only to one another a heartening tone of decorum and kinship. King Phnudge alone, besides myself, retains the outward dressing of his former self (I should say: apart from my top hat, which was stolen and presumably devoured by a monkey). He cleaves to good cheer at all times and acts as though bounded, as we all once were, by the strict gutters and panels of decency. Despite his gormless patois, I find myself understanding his highness better and better.

PHNUDGESONG

> Fear and rage it shakes my soul
> I say only *Poorly Moorly—deedle dole!*
> I want to fuck and eat and strangle you
> I say only *Starving Carving—hoodle hoo!*
> Shit hole shit hole shit hole
> I'm sick of myself—*hup hizzole!*

"I'm better than this. I'm better than these people. I don't belong here!"

"Try this on, dear."

"I don't want to try anything on. I don't need another hat. I want my family, nobody's even listening to me. Where are the children?"

"It's not a hat. Lisa's playing with the rabbit, and Spark is out exploring the island."

"Quit crafting stuff out of palm fronds and frog skins and pond scum, Keener. Nobody needs that shit."

"Just see if it fits, Theo."

"How could they send me to a place with monsters and hunters and clowns and theater critics? The clown and the theater critic, they're not even in color and I want to go home! They make me feel old!"

"Nobody sent you, honey. Our plane crashed."

"It's a setup. It's always a setup. What were we even doing on a plane with those types? What is this, some kind of wicker hockey mask? I can't breathe through this thing."

"Oh, that looks silly. It's not for your face. Put it down . . . there."

"You wove me a thatched codpiece?!?!?"

"I'm working on breastplates and a helmet. The samurai often wore wicker armor, you know."

"What good is wicker armor on an island?!?!"

"I'm just trying to get you prepared for a new life, lover."

"!@&$%#! I don't want a new life! I want my old life!"

"You'll eventually have to lead this island, Theo. Nobody else is going to do it. Peter Rabbit isn't going to do it. The black-and-white characters aren't suited for it. Poacher Junebug's discredited himself. King Phnudge, well, he's just not right. And Murkly is a villain."

"That's another thing, I don't want to go around there anymore, I don't like the way he looks at you!"

"He can't help himself, Theo. I just wanted to bring him a sun hat."

"Did he let you into his little hiding place?"

"Yes, we sat and had a very nice talk."

"I don't want you to have a very nice talk!!!!"

"Yes, dear. I won't in the future."

"How can I lead the island when I can't even keep tabs on the Dingbats?!?!?!"

Spark Dingbat ascended the volcano easily. It had steps. Near the top he passed a small pyramid of skulls in various shapes and sizes—a skull duck with giant ovoid eyes, a skull robot with antenna ears, a skull pig with a tiny bone beret incorporated into its cranium.

C'Krrrarn perched at the rim of the volcano, seeming bigger than he had in the plane, looming like an outcropping of the rock itself. As the tiny beret was to the pig's skull, so C'Krrrarn was to the volcano. Beyond C'Krrrarn Spark saw trickles of steam seeping from between burnt umber rocks, the undersides of which glowed orangely, like enormous briquets. Seagulls massed on C'Krrrarn's brow and shoulders, their dried liquid droppings striping him in the manner of a jailbird character, perhaps some crow or weasel standing before a parole board of bulldogs.

"I hope I'm not bothering you."

C'Krrrarn did not speak.

"You didn't look like you were doing anything."

C'Krrrarn did not speak.

"Are you waiting for something?"

C'Krrrarn did not speak.

"My mom says you could just probably swim off this island any time you wanted, or else maybe walk along the ocean floor, but then where would you go, because it's not like you have a home somewhere, and maybe in a way this island is as much like a home as you've ever known, and maybe we even crashed here because you were sort of attracted to the island from the airplane, like you felt some kind of geomagnetic tropism or maybe you glanced down and it reminded you of your mom and dad, do you think that might be right?"

C'Krrrarn did not speak.

"Are you going to kill us all? Just kidding."

C.D.N.S.

"How can you sit like that in the same position for so long? Don't your legs or your butt fall asleep?"

C.D.N.S.

"My mom is weaving you a tatami mat out of all this crud from the beach. Do you know what a tatami mat is? She said you would."

C.D.N.S.

"Do you mind if I sit here for a minute?"

Note to artist: Everywhere along the bottom gutters of the pages now, muddy footprints, rabbit droppings, and Dingbat spoor (*ed. What does that look like?*), forming an abject trail of smeary pictograms spelling out an unknown future.

15

Page forty-two, panel one, King Phnudge, alone in the woods. The island's sole monkey has approached him from underneath a fern. The monkey carries a hand-cranked music organ and wears a top hat. King Phnudge raises his eyebrows in delighted surprise.

Page forty-two, panel two, a campfire in a clearing. Large Silly and Poacher Junebug and King Phnudge and C. Phelps Northrup devour shreds of the monkey, whose scorched remains hang from a spit over the fire. The monkey's carcass still clutches the organ. Northrup wears the top hat.

Page forty-two, panel three, in the brush at one side of the clearing, Peter Rabbit and Lisa Dingbat stare wide-eyed at clown, hunter, king, and critic as they eat the monkey. The rabbit and girl are unseen by the others.

Page forty-two, panel four, moving on all fours, the rabbit and the girl silently slip into the woods, where they resume nibbling on ferns.

Page forty-two, panel five, night, the campfire, now abandoned by the others. Theophobe Dingbat tiptoes up to the extinguished fire, where he locates a charred monkey rib. He sucks at it thoughtfully.

Page forty-two, panel six, Murkly Finger. He crouches in his cavernous shard of airplane hull, reading a comic book, which is opened to a splash page showing C'Krrrarn towering over an alpine village.

From where he sat beside C'Krrrarn, Spark Dingbat could see into the island whole, as if he sat within a camera obscura. He saw his mother, now outfitting Poacher Dingbat and King Phnudge and C. Phelps Northrup in thatched armor, adjusting the palm-frond breastplates over their torsos while they stood at awkward attention, trying not to disappoint.

He saw Large Silly covered in baked mud, with dried grasses stuck to his arms and legs, sitting beside the creek masturbating.

He saw his sister and the rabbit hiding in the grass watching Large Silly.

He saw his father standing on the beach angrily punching his agent's number into a wicker cell phone and listening for a signal.

As though with X-ray vision he saw, too, into Murkly Finger's lair. Murkly Finger sat surrounded by suitcases from the wrecked plane. Alongside the clothing Murkly Finger had laid out as a pallet on the ground was a neat row of reading materials. Among them was Spark's own collection of *Dingbat Family Cavalcade* and *Dingbat Collectibles Catalog*. Murkly Finger also had a set of limited-edition clothbound *Tennyson Trolley Sunday Pages,* taken from C. Phelps Northrup's luggage, a Dover paperback of *The Seventh Voyage of the Phnudges,* a copy of *The Oxford Treasury of Comic Strips,* and a stack of *HORRENDOUS TALES OF C'KRRRARN!,* issues number one through thirteen, sealed in plastic sleeves.

He saw the grave his sister and the rabbit had dug for the blackened skeleton of the monkey.

He saw the island's birds and bugs.

He saw himself, too, seated beside C'Krrrarn on the rim of the volcano.

Spark Dingbat saw the island whole.

POEM

Say, Keener Dingbat, I wrote you a poem
On a funny old island where much has gone wrong
Sit right back and you'll hear of my love
For your coiled scribbled hair and your spidery legs
Not so spidery though as the giant spider I killed
To protect you, my love, but should I have let it eat
Your husband and kids and that wretched vile clown?
Oh, Keener Dingbat, you're haunting my days
I seek you in the pale lagoon and at the hidden spring
I seek you like a sheriff hunting a walnut oh shit
I stole that line, I can't help myself, I steal everything, I am
Your Villain,
Murkly

FROM THE JOURNAL OF C. PHELPS NORTHRUP
August 12

Rustling in our armor like a flock of pigeons we stormed Murkly Finger's lair at dawn. We all partookipated—I mean, all able-bodied adultish manlike characters, even the dissolute clown, with the sole exception of Theophobe Dingbat, who declined command of our sally, leaving that to his spouse. The scoundrel Finger proffered no resistance—rather, welcomed us inside, so it was we at last unearthed his secret: not the yearned-for stockpile of nourishing provisions, but the histories of our earlier selves, the panels and pages of our lives precursive to banishment on this island. Each of us retreated initially to various corners of the island, to mull on that from which we'd been distranded. Before he secreted it from my meanderish eyes, I glimpsed a sample of the earliest appearances of Poacher Dingbat, in *Frontier Follies*—once a much less squat and feral figure, Poacher at his first flush had the stature and equipoise of a young Dan'l Boone. And how King Phnudge must miss his queen and Phnudglings! I myself mourned an earlier self, the dapper gadabout wit who'd mercilessly shuttered theatrical kerfuffles with his encaustic pen.

By evening we'd received the first reports of the clown's escape. It was the female Dingbat child who alerted us, the first we'd heard her speak aloud in weeks. We searched the isle from stem to stern, but found no sign of him. With Poacher I even ascended the terrifying volcano, where C'Krrrarn and Spark Dingbat keep their enigmatical watch. They refused our questions with resounding silence, but it was plain enough there was no sign of clown there, unless he'd disintegrated in the bubbling melt. It was not until the following morn that he reappeared, on the pebble beach, contentedly munching a word balloon.

Large Silly seemed happy enough to show us what he'd done: clambered backward into his own panels, using the gutters as rungs on a ladder into the past. A trick, the clown told us, that he'd learned from a duck. With practice, he implicated, we might learn it, too.

Page eighty-eight, panel one, the cove. A large pile of antique black-and-white furniture from *Tennyson Trolley* is afire. Poacher Junebug and C. Phelps Northrup turn a spit on which five word balloons have been impaled. The edges of the balloons are gently browned. Junebug and Northrup both salivate greedily, their eyes like full moons.

def. *Flotsam:* flot-sam *n*
1. wreckage, debris, or refuse from another character's panels, found abandoned on the beach or floating in the water
 See also: jetsam
2. characters who live on the margins of cartoon lore, such as clowns, hunters, critics, monsters, children, or animals (*considered offensive in some contexts*)

def. *Jetsam:* jet-sam *n*
1. cargo or equipment that either sinks or is washed ashore after

18

being thrown overboard to lighten the load of a cartoon in distress
See also: flotsam
2.   cartoons that have been discarded as useless or unwanted

"... and then, as shown on pages five through seven in issue forty-seven, Keener failed to make me a ham-and-eggs breakfast in the manner to which I have become accustomed, on the morning before I was supposed to go onstage with the Rolling Stones, causing me to eat Pop-Tarts and therefore to completely fnargle the gig—hey, are you getting this down?!?!"

"Sorry, yes, if you could just go a little slower, Mr. Dingbat."

"I'm paying you twenty-five clamshells a day to take dictation on my memoirs, critic, not to surreptitiously nibble on those crispy word balloons you've got ineptly hidden in your palm-frond satchel!!"

"Most sorry, Mr. Dingbat, but you really should taste this one, Poacher acquired it in *C'Krrrarn*, Issue #7, 'The Caverns of Despond,' it has something of the dank savor of a truffle mushroom—"

"Give me that!!! Mmmm, crunch, slurp, crunch, slurp ..."

"Now, try this one, it was spoken by a fair lass from, ahem, my own adventures, and makes a perfect tonic, if I may be so bold, a counterpoint to the first ... it has the bite and tangicity of a Vermont apple, perhaps a Pink Lady or a Red Delirious ..."

"Ahhh, crunch, munch, glug, glub ... ah, this is hopeless, we're never going to write my memoirs!!!"

From his place where he sat beside C'Krrrarn, Spark Dingbat saw his sister running in the woods with the rabbit. His sister had grown fur and a small tail.

From his place where he sat beside C'Krrrarn, Spark Dingbat saw his father swimming joyfully with the clown and the critic in the surf. Their three pudgy bodies resembled dolphins and it was hard to tell one from another.

From his place where he sat beside C'Krrrarn, Spark Dingbat saw his mother in a tower she'd painstakingly constructed out of plywood made from the woven-together heat and stink and motion lines salvaged from the panels of the other characters. She was in the upper room of the tower, humping Murkly Finger, who still wore his cape and hood.

From his place where he sat beside C'Krrrarn, Spark Dingbat saw King Phnudge commanding his army of slave Phnudges as they carried his castle forward, brick by brick (bricks balanced on their miserable heads because they had no arms) and reassembled it on the far side of the island.

From his place where he sat beside C'Krrrarn, Spark Dingbat saw Poacher Dingbat with his bamboo spear and his wicker sack full of word balloons, returning from another successful expedition.

From his place where he sat beside C'Krrrarn, Spark Dingbat saw Spark Dingbat in his place where he sat beside C'Krrrarn. They sat on two tatami mats, a large and a small, woven specially by Spark's mom. Each subsisted, for the time being, on thought balloons, which they swallowed as soon as they arose, without opening their mouths. It was enough.

Realm of Ends

Ann Lauterbach

1.

Francis turns. He has something to say. He has an
announcement. He says, "Snow in summer" and falls silent.

A single egg in the nest. Francis turns.
It is not metaphysical; it is merely distraction.

Time passes. The nest is empty.
The snow, bountiful. A girl dedicates her last weeks

to a show of force. She writes gracefully about force.
Francis turns. He seems weak and small and without volition.

Thus the bird lands on his head.
Thus there are radiant seconds.

Is it reliable? Not the garden. Not the bed.
The streaming elocution is more or less prosaic.

The bird lifts up onto the bare branch.
The tree, an elm, is dying, almost dead.

Francis is indifferent but the bird, a cardinal,
shines on the barren branch.

Tit tit tittit tit hovers the weary pragmatist.
It is hoped, by Francis and the rest, that she

cannot know heartbreak, not
the melodrama of the nest's margin of error.

2.

All day in the fir trees, night remains.
Time passes. Francis is immobile, bereft.

He has recalled the condition of stone.
He has resumed his incalculable origin.

And so the second comes too quickly,
follows too quickly upon the first.

Others, mobile and incidental and lush,
attest to the perishable variety at large:

shark, polar bear, other political incidents
having little in common with the immobility of Francis.

A fence and an alarm, a cat and a cradle,
these also are not acceptable, not progression.

3.

The day has become abstract; I cannot know it.
It spits and complains as if it were real

but it is only a matter of time.
How, for example, forgetting

becomes opaque.
As if, dark on dark, an inert stone.

Francis is only a sentimental stone.
Francis is impoverished and mute.

Francis is a fiction of the glare, turning
into the Tuscan sun, under the juniper, among flowers.

Doves perch on his head and shit on his sleeves.
This is an example of natural observable fact.

Yet the day is opaque
despite recurring flags in the graveyard

lending their gala strophe to the forgotten;
despite the fantasy of the Tuscan saint

turning in his soiled robes
under the heavy lemon trees, the ornamental

beds: roses, lavender, creeping thyme.
Along the path the lovers come

through the thrash of sunlit leaves,
the heavenly scents of lemon and rose.

The day is a tide of sensual foreboding
in the salty sweat of their backs

riding on white linen
in a luminous small room

in the taste of cool wine on their swollen lips.
The day, for the lovers, heaves with potential.

4.

The reverie stalks the real; it stretches abstraction
to its limit, deposited at the feet of Francis.

But given the impermanence of birds,
the cardinal's nest on the deck,

given the domestic and the spiritual
the utilitarian and

the forgotten, given
these cold mercurial shapes, arbitrary

hinges, islands, perpetual desires
and their advocacy among the least entitled,

given that one falls in love
with the condition of hope

and falls out of love with its
cruel replacement, hope,

so that what is valued is not the same
and the shape of the body in the window

is foreign, the picture of the woman,
her body and face

at odds with their person, at odds with her
curiosity, her pertinence.

In a dream of the girl and the lover,
now forgotten as the day, inevitably, is forgotten,

there is a difference between being forgotten
and being among the dead, but

given these episodes,
their proof turns to night and stone.

5.

The ears are ordinary, the feet
distorted. The girl has a condition

not announced in the green room
but nevertheless leaked to the press.

Biography has its compulsions, its regrets.
It could be the materiality of opaque gold

and the severity of promises,
their promiscuous gift,

oaths made on pillows between lovers.
There, in the eventide,

a strangling usurps the petty comma,
staggers from rejection to confirmation to murder

institutionally foretold. O Francis!
Are you standing for the cold, the cruel,

the bargain between such desire and such trust?
Take no prisoners. Let the homily endure.

The holidays are adept at the spectacle of divorce.
They specialize in silence, gala silence.

Masterpieces of the still life
make their way onto tables of the celebrants.

Holy! Holy! Holy! intones the priest.
Things are given and taken away.

Here is a token of my affection.
Here is my child.

6.

Turning the figure away, removing it
leaves its replica shadow

to shift with the gloating wind.
Later, the sculptor

pieces together poor bits of fabric,
copies from memory the shape of the lips.

The original remains vocable,
escaping the dream's

unscripted solitude, conceiving night's
blind, its familiar embrace.

Francis is silent. He has taken a vow.
Suffering unfurls its performance,

elicits revenge. On a ladder,
the man turns to address the public.

He has imagined strangling the woman.
He imagines his future in a nest.

From The Pesthouse
Jim Crace

EVERYBODY DIED AT NIGHT. Most were sleeping at the time, the lucky ones who were too tired or drunk or deaf or wrapped too tightly in their spreads to hear the hillside, destabilized by rain, collapse and slip beneath the waters of the lake. So these sleepers (six or seven hundred, at a guess; no one ever came to count or claim the dead) breathed their last in passive company, unwarned and unexpectedly, without any fear. Their final moments, dormant in America.

But there are always some awake in the small times of the morning, the lovemakers, for instance, the night workers, the ones with stone-hard beds or aching backs, the ones with nagging consciences or bladders, the sick. And animals, of course.

The first of that community to die were the horses and the mules, which the travelers had picketed and blanketed against the cold out in the tetherings, between the houses and the lake, and beyond the human safety of stockades. They must have heard the landslide—they were so close and unprotected—though it was not especially bulky, not bulky enough, probably, to cause much damage on its own. In the time that it would take to draw a breath and yawn, there was a muted stony splash accompanied by a barometric pop, a lesser set of sounds than thunder, but low and devious nevertheless, and worrying—for how could anyone not know by now how mischievous the world could be? The older horses, connoisseurs of one-night stands when everything was devious and worrying, were too weary after yet another day of heading dawnways, shifting carts, freight, and passengers, to do much more than tic their ears and flare their nostrils. Even when, a moment later, the displaced waters of the lake produced a sloshing set of boisterous waves where there had not been any waves before, the full-growns would not raise their heads. But the younger horses and the ever-childish mules tugged against their ropes, and one or two even broke free but hadn't the foresight to seek high ground in the brief time that remained.

What happened next was almost silent. The landslip had hit the deepest side of the lake and, therefore, took some moments to reach the bottom, ten man heights from the surface, and then took some moments more for the avalanche of stone, earth, swarf, and ancient buried scrap to show how heavy it was and squeeze the life out of the gas-rich sediments, the volatile silt and compacted weeds, the soda pockets, which had settled on the bed through centuries and were now ready—almost eager—for this catalyst. Shaken up and shaken out in one great flatulence, the water fizzed and belched until all the gases were discharged, to form a heavy, deadly, surface-hugging cloud, not as high as the pines but higher, certainly, than animals. There wasn't any wind that night to thin the suffocating vapors and no longer any rain to wash the poison from the air, but there was gravity to direct them down, beyond the rapids and cascades, along the valley, past the tetherings, past the secret wooden bridge, past the metal fields, past the stone footings of the one-time shoe factory and tanning works, to seep between the palings of the pine stockades and settle on the town at the river's crossing point where almost everyone was sleeping and dreaming of the ruined, rusty way ahead and all the paradise beyond.

Too near the lake and not sleeping was the boy called Nash, whose job that night was to protect the animals from cougars, wolves, or thieves—or bush fish such as rattlers, possibly—though there'd be nothing he could do but shout and draw attention to himself if any of these many perils did approach the tetherings. He'd been too cold and wet even to doze, but not as cold and wet as usual. He huddled round his stove stones—which following the midnight downpour produced more smoke than heat—in his new and somehow terrifying coat. He'd traded it only that day (with a man half his height again and three times his weight) for a good supply of dried fruit, some pork twists, and a leather water bag, hardly distinguishable from one another in taste or texture, and a flagon of apple juice that the giant, like a giant, had dispatched on the spot. So when the boy heard the landslip and the waves and stood to hear them better, should they come again, his coat spread out around him on the ground like chieftain robes intended for display but—at least for anybody as short as he was—not ideal for walking.

Now Nash spotted the two loose mules and hurried out into the night to picket them again. He was not surprised when the coat snagged round his ankles and feet and brought him down. The coat had already toppled him several times that night. He didn't hurt himself—boys bounce—but he felt more winded than made sense, more dislocated than he should, and stayed on the ground for a few moments to catch his breath and find his balance. His coat of farm goatskins and hair was as good as a bed and thick enough to keep the moisture out for a while. He'd have to shorten it, he thought. He'd have to cut off half a goat and turn the trimmings into belts or gloves, turn the trimmings into profit, actually. When he had time.

But for the moment, unaccountably, he was too comfortable to move. He had no time or energy for anything, not even sleep. He lost himself in the hairs and skins, forgot the nighttime and the mud. He did feel sleepy, finally, but not alarmed. Too lost to be alarmed. The air was weighty, and its smell was stupefying—somewhere between the smell of mushrooms, eggs, and rotting, clamped potatoes. He'd stand up in a moment, shuck off his dreams of belts and gloves, remove the coat, and catch the mules. He'd be in trouble otherwise. A mule was wealth. But though his dreams soon ended, he never caught his breath and never caught the mules and never found out what had happened at the lake. This wasn't sleep oppressing him. He dimly recognized as much himself. He was the victim of magic, possibly, or fever—there was already fever in the town, he had heard— or a curse, the sort that storytellers knew about—or else some dead air from the grave, encouraged by the rain, had come to press its clammy lips on his. He'd tasted it. His lungs were rigid, suddenly. He was in the gripping custody of hair and skins. He'd been a fool to trust a giant. It must have seemed the coat had always meant to smother him, was trained to kill. This was a homing coat that now would flee, as loyal and cunning as a dog, to rejoin the tall man who had traded it and, no doubt, would trade it many times again, exchanging death for apple juice.

Down in Ferrytown, not sleeping, either, were two passengers from ten days west, a beauty boy—no beard—not twenty yet, and his slightly older wife. They'd found a berth in the lofts of the dormitories, against the guesthouse rules that naturally put the women behind locked doors in different quarters from the men, but two-a-bed nevertheless. It was less comfy and colder than those first-floor beds where his parents and his sisters were, but more private and consoling. These newlyweds didn't have to share their air with anyone. No wonder they'd been making love, as usual. Moving on each day and spending every night in some new space was oddly stimulating, they'd found, as was having sex as quietly as they could in sleeping company, against the rules. But now that lovemaking was concluded, they were quarreling in whispers, despite the likelihood that everything they said could be heard by strangers. The consolations of lovemaking don't last long when you are fearful, regardless of the massive hope beyond the fears. How many days would it be before they reached the ocean and the ships? The beauty boy thought one more month. He'd not pretend that things were better than they were. The far side of the river was an odd, perplexing place, he'd heard, haunted, wrecked, and hard underfoot, with prairies of rubble where people had once lived in bastions and towers. The way ahead would be hard beyond imagining. His wife did not believe such stories. She was uncompromisingly optimistic, hopeful beyond reason. The rain that night had been more salty than she'd expected. When the rain tastes like tears, the sea is close. She'd seen a white bird ("That's a sign"), and she'd heard another passenger say they'd reach the shore—the mighty river with one bank—in just three more days. Then the future could begin. So much for rubble, bastions, and towers. Her husband was too easily impressed. She drifted off to thoughts of boarding ship in three days' time, and no more quarreling. . . .

Not sleeping and on the verge of calling out for the busy couple in the lofts to keep quiet was a woman who had strained her back. She'd been too eager earlier in the day to help her horse negotiate the steep descent into the valley and had fallen awkwardly. She sat up in her cot and flexed her spine, hoping not to wake the woman at her side. The pain shot down the outside of her left leg and cramped her toes. She crossed her fingers, willing it to go, and in a while the pain had disappeared. . . .

Not sleeping was the ferryman who, having heard the rain, knew that he would have to drag himself from bed too soon, call his four sons, and go down to the crossing to fasten the raft more securely and further in to the shore before the water surge. Not sleeping was the baker and his daughter who had just got up to start preparing flat bread, ash cake, and pea loaf for the morning, enough dough and cornmeal for at least one hundred and sixty passengers who'd need to eat before they were ferried on the raft to the east bank of the river and yet another day of lugging to the coast. . . .

Not sleeping was a woman who had been alarmed by travel and by travelers—all her life—and was not much liked by anyone she met, but had been much more terrified of staying put, where she was born, while all her family and neighbors emigrated east, fired up by boredom, hope, and poverty. Now she was sick from too much wayside grain and drinking sullied water for more than a month. She'd rather breathe her last than gag any more. She'd told her husband, "I should have stayed at home." He'd said, "You should have."

She pulled her knees up to her chest and tried to belch the colic out. . . .

Not sleeping was a tall man from the plains—not quite a giant, except to boys—who had to go out, barefooted, in the cold to the town palisade for the second time that night to urinate. He would have worn his goatskin coat if he'd not traded it that day. He was standing with his trousers down and pissing apple juice when what had come out of the lake with such a show just moments previously arrived without a sound and almost without a shape to overwhelm whomever it could find, the wakeful and the slumbering.

This used to be America, this river crossing in the ten-month stretch of land, this sea-to-sea. It used to be the safest place on earth.

1.

Franklin Lopez had not been sleeping in Ferrytown, though he'd wanted to. He'd not been sleeping anywhere, in fact. Couldn't sleep. He'd weathered such pain the day before that he'd been forced to consider what anyone (other than his brother) who'd seen the wincing recoil in his limp or examined his inflamed leg had already told him, that he shouldn't walk another step. Certainly he shouldn't walk downhill on such a long and hazardous gradient, unless he wanted to damage his knee beyond repair and put paid to any hopes of getting to the coast and boarding ship before the worst of the fall storms. He and his brother, Jackson (named for their parents' small hometown on the plains), had left the journey rather late as it was. Too late, perhaps. The prairie tallgrass had already whitened and buckled. Apart from nuts and mushrooms, there was little free food to be gathered at the trackside. The first rains had arrived and soon the winds and snow would get to work. Traveling would become more hazardous and then impossible. Only the ill-prepared, the ill-fated and the ill-timed were still strung out thinly along the previously busy route, hoping to make the final sailings before ice and squalls shut down the sea and, anyway, made shore-to-ship or ship-to-shore impossible. The wayside going east was already littered with the melancholy camps and the shallow graves—soon to be torn up by wolves—of those whose bodies couldn't take the journey, those who had been fatally chilled by wading through rivers, those who had starved and weakened, those who had been thrown by their horses or poisoned by their suppers, those who had been crushed between the fears of going forward and the dread of going back.

31

So Franklin understood that he could not readily afford to waste much time nursing such a slight injury. But neither could he afford the purchase of a horse or passage on a wagon where he could rest his leg. What should he do then? Cut a stick and limp down to the coast? "Just put up with the pain," as Jackson advised? Carry on regardless, let nature take its course? He'd tried the stick, the putting up with pain, he'd trusted nature's course. His knee got worse. So finally he conceded. He'd have to find shelter and stay exactly where he was, high in the ridges, to sit out the swelling. It was an exasperating setback and something that he was slow to tell his brother. But what other choice was there? His knee was too bloated to bend and too painful to take any weight. The flesh between his ankle and his thigh was sausaging with every step he took. The skin was stretched and cloudy. One more afternoon of walking could lame him for a month. A day or two of rest might rescue him. Besides, this injury was not a failure that he should feel ashamed of, no matter what the stiff expression on his brother's face seemed to suggest. He'd done better than some to get so far—more than sixty testing days of walking from the battered, weather-poisoned village of his birth—without much damage beyond the usual aches and pains, the usual broken skin, and this damned knee, he told himself. He'd be a fool to take any chances now if he wanted to enjoy the undulating rewards of the sailboat deck, and then to put ashore this year in the other place, whatever that might be, with his pith intact enough to make a good start.

"It'd be crazy to take the risk, Jacko," he told his brother at last, coloring with self-consciousness as he spoke. He was still prone to being seized by sudden, girlish reddeners whenever he least wanted it.

"Only the crazy make it to the coast," was the older man's reply. Yes, that was the wisdom of the road: you had to be crazy enough to take the risks, because the risks were unavoidable. "Well, then, Franklin Lopez . . . ? You say."

"I've said."

"So say it again."

"Well, do what you want, if you're the crazy one. I'm staying here till it's good enough, my knee."

"How long's 'till'?"

"Three days, four days, I guess."

"I guess a month!"

Franklin knew better than to argue with his volcanic brother. He did not even shake his head. He watched Jackson mull over their problem for a few moments more, his eyes half closed, his lips moving, his fingers counting days. "That knee'll snare us here a month, if not a month then half a month. Too long," Jackson added finally. "By then the winter'll be on us like a pack of wolves. You hear me, little brother?" Little brother? Less in everything. "You sit down now, then that's the end of it. We're carrion."

This was their final argument, the last of many, with Franklin daring to protest that his "crazy" brother should press on to the coast without him (but not meaning it—who'd want to be abandoned to the winter and the woods, to be buried, along with the trail, beneath layers of mud, leaves, and snow, even if it meant a few days free of bullying and censure?) and Jackson insisting that he'd stick by his infuriating, timid, blushing sibling till the last if he really had to (but resenting his physical weakness, his infuriating, girlish laugh that seemed to buckle his whole body, his dreaminess, his hypochondria, and saying so repeatedly—"That bitching knee's not half as bad as you make out," and "Where'd we be if every time you got a touch of charley horse you wanted three days' rest?"—until Franklin said, "Ma's hearing every word you speak").

Now the brothers had to face the prospect of some nights apart— the very thing that Ma had said should not occur—while Jackson went ahead to sell his labor for a day or two and obtain some food. He'd leave his brother with their knives, the leaking water bag, the spark stone, the pair of tarps, their change of clothes and make do trading with his strength and overcoat. That heavy, much-loved overcoat that his mother had stitched together from four farm goats would have to go despite the colder days ahead. It was the one thing that the brothers had that, though it had not quite been admired, had certainly been noticed by strangers. Being noticed might prove to be a handicap as they got closer to the lawless coast. So trading on the goats would be advisable. With any luck, Jackson would soon return with provisions and possibly the part share of an onward-going horse or at least the purchase of a cart ride among the women, the children, and the old for his unmanly brother. Once in Ferrytown, if the worse came to the worst, they could pass the winter in relative safety. For the time being, though, Franklin would have an uncomfortable few nights on the mountainside; Jackson would have a proper bed. The best that Franklin could hope for was a mattress of pine cones.

Franklin might not be on his own entirely. Already he could hear the chirring of insects, the whistle of the quails, and barking deer. And there was a boulder hut—evidently occupied, though possibly by lunatics or bandits, Jackson warned, amused to alarm his brother—on the edge of the tree line a hundred paces off, where a large but unmaintained bald had been burned clear by hunters. There was no movement from within, so far as they could tell, just smoke. "Keep your distance. That's best."

And Franklin would not be entirely out of touch with his brother and their shared hopes. Despite the pain in his knee, he had succeeded in reaching the final woody swaggings in the sash of hills where there were almost uninterrupted views to the east. His hopes of getting free from America could be kept alive by a distant prospect of the lake, the town, and the longed-for river crossing, after which, they'd been told, the going was less hilly though punishing in more unusual ways.

It was late afternoon when his elder, tougher, taller brother shook his hand and set off down the track, promising to come back to the swaggings within three days. The dusk was already pushing daylight back into the sun. Jackson would barely reach Ferrytown before dark. But he was fit and well, not injured yet, and, unlike all the other travelers still on the descent with their carts and sledges, their mules and wheelbarrows, he was unencumbered by anything other than his coat. Unlike the mule trains, with their whistle-nagging masters and the packhorses with their bridle bells foretelling all the merriments ahead, he descended silently down the twists of Butter Hill, as it was known locally. (A hill so tortuous and uneven, they claimed, that any milk carried up or down it would be jolted and churned into butter.) You could not miss him, though, even in that gloaming. He was so much taller than the rest and hurrying like a man who was counting on a hot supper, and walking even taller than himself, actually, catlike and stretched (while Franklin walked shrinkingly, his shoulders bunched). The pinto patterns of the goatskins marked him out as someone of account, the sort of man who should be welcome and respected anywhere he went.

Once he'd lost sight of his brother and the last few stragglers doing their best to negotiate the steep route through the rock chokes and the willow thickets down to the houses and a good sleep, Franklin made a cocoon of the two rolled tarps on a mattress of tinder-dry leaves and pine cones, and settled down for the night in a grassy bay with his back sack for a pillow. His knee was painful, but he was tired enough to sleep. He spoke the slumber verses to himself, to drive away regrets (the certainty that he would never see his ma again, would never walk their stead), and cleared his head of any thoughts of home or hungry animals or the comforts he was missing.

In what remained of the slanting light, Franklin Lopez tried to sleep while facing east, downhill. The closeness of Ferrytown was a comfort to him: from his high vantage point, he had seen the busy little lanes and yards, and watched the ferry, its raftboards packed with the day's last emigrants and their suddenly weightless possessions, as it was let out on its fat ropes to drift downstream, never quite capsizing, until the four helmsmen dug in their great oars and poles to bring the craft ashore in the shallows of the deeply graveled landing beach. He had seen the emigrants unload with hardly a wet rim, foot, or hoof and set off on a boardwalk of tied logs—their burdens heavy again—across the flood meadows, steaming with mist. Soon the first of them reached the outer river bluffs and then—the last of the mountains safely at their backs—they began the long haul through what seemed to Franklin from his vantage point to be a green, oceanlike expanse of gently undulating flats and plains, stretching, swell upon swell, so far into the distance that his eyes ran out. He had then watched the ferry, unladen but now set against the river, being towed back upstream by a team of oxen on a winch and beached for the night at the moorings. He had seen the first lamps lit and heard what sounded like a song. Surely Franklin could not wish for a prospect more reassuring or more promising than this.

Once the moon came up above the leaden volumes of clouds, augmenting what was left of day, the lake in the valley—hidden up till then in mist—was like a silver pendant, with the river as its glinting chain. Franklin had not seen so much standing water before. Perhaps the sea would be like that, flat and safe and breathtaking.

2.

The boulder hut on the far side of the bald, well out of danger's way, too high for that night's heavy vapors, was occupied by Margaret, the only stub-haired person in the neighborhoods. Red Margaret. Or the Apricot, as she was called by local men, attracted by her color— and her plumpness—in a land where nearly all the other heads were black, and then were gray or white. Her grandfather, as any parent would, had condemned her coppery tresses to the flames as soon as he had suspected that she was suffering the flux. She'd vomited all day, she'd had diarrhea, she'd shivered like a snow fly but was hot and feverish to touch, she'd coughed as drily as a jay, there were rashes on her face and arms, her neck was rigid and painful, and the onset of her problems had been cruelly swift, though not as swift as the news of her illness, which had raced around the houses as fast as sound—the sound of her mother weeping—and, once again, turned their compound of dwellings into a place to avoid. *Once again,* because only three months previously, in the high heat of the summer, her father, just as she had done the night before, had gone to bed healthy, sweet, a little overweight, red-haired, and woken up soft, battered, and darkened. He'd died of flux, the first of seven towns-people to die and who knows how many unnameable travelers on their journeys to the boats who'd reached the far bank of the river and were out of sight and out of memory before they started shivering.

The flux was carried in and carried out by travelers, or by their goods, or by their animals, or in their bedding or in their clothes. The illness was an intermittent visitor, unwelcome but well known. So what else could be afflicting Margaret except that self-same flux that must have hidden like a demon in their house since Pa had died, biding its time while choosing someone else's bed to share? And what choice had they but to carry out the rules and protect Ferrytown from her?

Her grandpa—repeating what he'd already done too recently for his son, her father—had shaved her skull, removing all the ginger drama from her head with a shell razor, and then called the closest women in the family, two sisters and her ma, to take off Margaret's body hair, snapping it out to the roots, the last of it wherever it might be—from her eyebrows and, most painfully, her lashes; from her nostrils, even; from her lightly ochered forearms and her legs; elsewhere, the hidden hair—and massage her scalp with pine tallow until she was as shorn and shiny as a stone and smelling like a newly readied plank.

Everybody in the land must know what shaven baldness signified. No one could mistake her for a safe and healthy woman now. Not for some time. Not for a tress of time. She should not expect a welcome anywhere with that alarming head. But if she were that rarity—a sufferer who could defeat the flux—the regrowth of her hair, once it had reached her shoulders anyway, would prove that she was truly safe again.

They burned her clippings on the outside fire, full thirty-one years of growth reduced in moments to a brittle tar. It smelled like blacksmith's shop, like horses' hoofs, like carcasses, as you'd expect from such a pestilence. With any luck the venoms of the flux would now have been destroyed by fire and Margaret would survive her illness, like trees survive the winter if they shed their leaves. At least the flux could not be drawn back into her body through her hair now that she was almost bald. The signs were good, they told her, hoping to believe these baseless reassurances themselves. No bleeding yet, no body smell. Her father had bled from his mouth and nose. She'd be more fortunate than him. If there were any justice in the world, she'd have the good luck denied to Pa, her mother said.

But still, like him, she'd have to go up to the little boulder Pesthouse above the valley for ten days or so—unattended and unvisited—to see if she recovered or was lost. There was no choice but to be hard-hearted. If any of the travelers were ill, they were thrown out of town at once. No bed or sustenance for them. But if the victim was a Ferrytowner, the Pesthouse was the only option. Margaret would have to take the westward route up Butter Hill against the side of history.

The women had already rid themselves of wool and fur and dressed in their safest waxed clothes—garments that were too slickly fibered, they hoped, to harbor any pestilence. They chewed tobacco as protection. But, nevertheless, they were unwilling to resist this final risk and their last chance, probably, of making their farewells. They kissed Margaret on her cheek. And the men shook hands with her. Then—when she had gone to pack her bag with her three things and her brother had been sent to prepare the horse—they all washed their fingertips and lips in vinegar. You don't take chances with the flux.

Her grandpa led her on the horse up into the hills that same morning, three slow and ancient travelers, it would seem, the old man taking care with every step as if his bones were as fragile and as flaky as log ash, the woman slumped across the horse's neck, too weak to sit straight, the mare itself so displeased with the unresponsive weight and the loose stones on the butter-churning climb that it would stop and try to turn whenever the leash was slackened.

Margaret had never been into the hills before. There'd been no need. It was unwise and, indeed, against the community conventions for a local woman to go beyond the palisades unless she was unwell. Time was too precious for useful bodies to wander aimlessly in the neighborhoods. Margaret, like all the other women without husbands or children, was kept busy helping out in the guesthouse where there were nearly always more than a hundred meals to serve each evening and beds and breakfasts to make next day.

Her grandpa hadn't been up into the hills very often either. Until the ascent with his ailing son three months previously he hadn't been up to the summit of Butter Hill in many years, not since the travelers, drawn to the river's shallow crossing, had made his town rich. All the more ambitious huntsmen and fishermen had turned to making their fortunes out of farming for the table, ferrying, hospitality, and charging everyone for doing anything: crossing charges, passage fees, stabling costs, piloting, provisioning, protection tax, and levies just for wanting to go east.

It was astonishing how wealthy a little hospitality could make the locals. This fertile valley of which it used to be boasted that you had only to flick a booger on the ground for a mushroom to grow overnight was now fertile in even less taxing ways: stretch a rope across the road and travelers would pay you with their jewelry, their cloth, their inheritances just to be allowed to jump over it; toss a rag across a log, call it a bed, and they'd be lining up to sleep in it; shake a chicken's feather at a pot of boiling water and you could make your fortune out of soup.

The only problem was that travelers bring problems of their own and ones beyond control. Stockades and palisades could keep marauders at bay. The lock-up jail beyond the tetherings with its no-bed and its no-light could hold and quiet down the troublemakers and those who couldn't settle bills in this *Stay-and-Pay or On-your-Way* community. But illnesses, like bats and birds, were only visible too late, when the damage had been done. The toughest maladies have wings. There are no fees or charges high enough to deter the flux, no palisade is that tall.

It was, as usual, busy on the road. Margaret and her grandpa stepped aside and hid from every descending emigrant they passed, every string of horses, every cart or barrow, every band of hopefuls that made its way downhill.

Her head was covered in a heavy blue scarf, so her shorn, white scalp was out of sight. That would not draw any comment from strangers. Even at that time of the year, all travelers with any sense would protect themselves against the sun and midges with hats, handscarves, veils, or hair. The sun occasions modesty. It disapproves of flesh. But Margaret's face, if shown, would certainly betray the dangerous and appalling truth. What little of her skin wasn't raised and scarlet with rashes was gray with exhaustion.

It was uncomfortable—unbearable—to wear the heavy scarf around her hot and nagging head. She tried to lift it, push it back and off. But she could not allow herself to be seen, her grandpa told her—it would be too damaging for business if word got out that even just one person in the valley had the symptoms of the flux. A hundred meals, a hundred beds, would go to waste each day. Nobody would dare to spend the night with them.

"Turn your head, Mags, if you can," he instructed her. "Pull your scarf across your face, let them mistake you for . . ." He couldn't think that she resembled anything, except a woman at death's door riding in the wrong direction with her back turned to the sea. He did his best to hide her from the stares and even from the necessary greetings. He pulled the horse into the thickets whenever he heard voices coming or the sound of carts and bridle bells. He made her duck into impasses of rock until the path was clear. And if anybody happened to get close to them or called, wanting directions or news, he answered for the two of them, trying not to draw attention to himself by either being too unfriendly or too welcoming. If anybody asked he'd claim his granddaughter was simple, not bright enough to speak: "Best let her float in her own company," he'd say.

So Margaret and her grandpa took half a day to reach the nearest woody swaggings in the sash of hills, where the rocky scrubland of the ascent relaxed into softer meadows and clearings of grass and highland reed, before the darkness of the woods and the distant, snowcapped mountain pates. The view was wasted on them. They hardly bothered to look back. The old man had to get home, while Margaret wanted nothing more than to sleep. She'd rather die than undertake another climb like that. So for her, the first sight of the Pesthouse at the edge of the hunter's bald was a relief.

Unlike the tree-trunk barns and cabins in the valley, the hillside hut had not been built for comfort. It was at core a woodsman's soddy, constructed out of sun-dried turfs, fireproof and wind protected, much loved by mice, but easily collapsed. Indeed, it had collapsed from time to time, in those far regretted days when it had little use, but since that healthy time, that time of remedies and cures, the Pesthouse had been strengthened by an outer wall of boulders, dry built and sturdy. There was a sleeping bench inside, a hearth and chimney stack, a leather bucket and some pots.

Margaret hid in the undergrowth to empty her bowels—no blood, good luck—and then collapsed into the grass while her grandpa set to work. He swept out the soddy with snapped pine brooms, beat the stones with sticks in case any snakes had taken up residence, and set the fire in the stone grate with kindling and a striking stone. Provisions and a water bag were hung from roof branches above the fire, where they'd be marinated in wood fume and safe from little teeth. He gathered bracken and country corn for Margaret's bed. She rested her three lucky things on her chest—a silver necklace that was old enough to have been machined; a square of patterned, faded cloth too finely woven to have been the work of human hands; some coins from the best-forgotten days inside a cedar box—and lay down on the bed, with Grandpa's help. He placed an unfired pot of cough syrup made from onions mashed in sugar on the floor at the side of her bed: "Watch out for ants, Mags." He touched her forehead with his thumb, a finger kiss. "I'm ashamed to leave you here. I hope it grows. Thick and long." He wiped his hands again on a vinegary rag, then he and the horse were gone and she was sleeping.

When she woke, somewhat revived, it was already evening. The trees were menacing—they wheezed and cracked. Bats feasted on the early moths. The undergrowth was busy with its residents, and Margaret, Red Margaret, the Apricot, the drained and fragile woman in the hills, that applicant for unexpected death, felt shocked and lost, bewildered and unloved. Why had she been singled out? Why had the archer released his arrow into her? Such misfortune was too much to face alone—the pestilence, the pain, the degradation, and the restless meanness of the night that she must spend on her own father's deathbed, breathing his last air. She coughed, a friendless cough, and had to listen to the trunks and branches coughing back, like wolves, too much like wolves for her to dare to sleep again. She'd never feared trees before. In daylight, trees had let her pass, ignored her almost, pretended not to notice her. But now that the moon was up, the forest seemed to be alert and mischievous.

The Pesthouse occupant took comfort from her talismans that night. She passed the necklace through her fingers, recognizing and remembering the contours of each engraved link; she rubbed and stroked her piece of cloth; she smelled the cedar in the little box. Finally, she weighed the coins in her hands, the pennies and dimes and quarters that she had found among the pebbles on the river beach. She fingered all the images in the dark and tried to recognize the heads of people from the past, mostly short-haired men, one with a beard, "In God We Trust," one with a thickish ponytail bouncing on his neck, one heavy chinned and satisfied. Was that the eagle she could feel? Where were the leafy sprigs and flaming torch? Was that the one-cent palace with the twelve great columns at the front? She dragged her nail across the disk to count every column and tried to find the tiny seated floating man within, the floating man who, storytellers said, was Abraham and would come back to help America one day with his enormous promises.

3.

Franklin had not expected so much rain. Anyone could tell from how brittle the landscape was that, in these parts at least, it had scarcely rained all season, and what clouds there'd been that day had been horizon clouds, passersby, or overtakers, actually, for they were heading eastward, too—but hardly any time had gone before the last light of the day threw out its washing water, splashing it as heavily as grit on the brittle undergrowth and setting free its long-stored smells, part hope and part decay. The rain was unforgiving in its weight. It meant to stay and do some damage and some good in equal parts. It meant to be noticed. It meant to run downhill until it found a river and then downstream until it found a sea. "If you're looking for the sailing boats, just follow the fallen rain" was the universal advice for inexperienced travelers.

Franklin couldn't sleep through this. He couldn't even sit out such a downpour. He'd have to find some better shelter. He shook out the leaves from his bedding, wrapped the two already damp tarps around himself, and limped as best he could onto a rocky knoll from which he could peer into the darkness and through the rain from a greater height. He hadn't noticed any caves or overhanging cliffs or any forest thick and broad-leafed enough to offer hope of staying dry for very long. This was the kind of rain that wouldn't rest until its job was done.

Now Franklin considered the little boulder hut on the fringes of the clearing, with its gray scarf of smoke. It was the sort of place where inexperienced or incautious robbers might have made their den, well positioned for picking off stragglers even though anyone with any sense would give it a wide berth. But Franklin would take the risk—despite Jackson's warnings, but also because of his brother's stinging accusation earlier that day that "Only the crazy make it to the coast"—and see if he could bargain any shelter there. He'd lost his bearings in the storm and in the darkness, though, and couldn't quite remember where he'd seen the hut. On the forest edge, for sure, but where exactly, how far off? What residue of light remained was not enough to spot its chimney. He sniffed for wood smoke but sniffed up only rain. He'd have to stumble in the dark and trust to luck, and still take good care not to wake any hostile residents, though the chances were it was just a woodsman's cabin or some hermitage, a no-choice place to rest his knee and stay dry for the night.

No matter where he stumbled, he could not see the outline of a roof, as he had hoped, or any light, but he was old enough to know where anyone would build a hut if there was free choice. Not entirely under trees, for a start, and not in earthy shallows where bogs might form. But half in, half out. Not too exposed to wind or passersby. But looking south and on flat ground, preferably face on to a clearing.

It was her coughing that led him to her, finally—the hacking, treble cough of foxes, but hardly wild enough for foxes. A woman's cough. So now Franklin knew the place, and where it stood in relation to the far too open spot where he had rolled his cocoon. He took his bearings from the coughing—waiting for it to break out, then subside, and then break out again—and from the heavy outlines of the woodlands and the hillside. He shuffled through the soaking grasses, taking care not to snap any sticks, listening for beasts below the clatter of the storm, until he could hear the telltale percussion of the rain striking something harder and less giving than the natural world, something flat and man-made. And now indeed he could hear and see the black roofline of a hut and a chimney stack. Then, between the timbers of its door—but for a moment only—he caught the reassuring and alarming flicker of a candle flame, just lit from the grate. He knew exactly what that meant: whoever was inside had heard him creeping up. They had been warned and would be ready.

Franklin hung his back sack on a branch, pulled off his tarps, and took out his knife, its blade still smelling of the meadow onions they had found and eaten raw earlier that day. The lighted candle meant that the occupant (or occupants) was nervous, too. So he grew more confident. Now he made as much noise as he could, trying to sound large and capable. He called out, "Shelter from the rain?" and then when there was silence, "I'm joining you if you'll allow." And finally, "No cause for fear, I promise you," though he was more than a little fearful himself when there were no replies. The boulder hut was big enough to house a gang of men in addition to the coughing woman, all armed, all dangerous. A man with a knife, no matter how tall he was, could not defend himself in the dark against missiles, or long pikes, or several men with cudgels. He tried again: "I'm a friend. Just say that you'll welcome me out of the storm, or else I'll step away." A test of hospitality. Some coughing now, as if the cougher had to find a voice from far away, and then, "Come only to the door. Don't open it." The woman's voice. A youngish voice. Already he was blushing.

For a door, the hut had little more than a barricade of rough pine planks. Franklin said, "I'm here." He peered between the planks and could just make out the dark form of one person, resting on one elbow in a bed, backlit by a wood fire in a grate. Nothing to be frightened of. Nothing physical, at least. Some traveler, perhaps, who just like him was suffering from knees and needed shelter for a while. "I'm going to drown unless I come inside," he said. She coughed at him. No *Stay away*, no *Come*.

Franklin pulled the door aside with his left hand, resting his right hand with the knife on the low lintel at his chin height. She held her candle out to get a better look at him and in a sudden guttering of light they saw each other for the first time: Red Margaret was startled first by the size of him, two times the weight and size of her grandpa, she thought, and then by what she took to be a face of honesty, not quite a handsome face, not quite a beauty boy, but narrow, healthy, promising, a face to rescue her from fear if only he would dare. Franklin saw the bald, round head of someone very sick and beautiful. A shaven head was unambiguous. It meant the woman and the hut were dangerous. He stepped back and turned his head away to breathe the safer, rain-soaked air. He was no longer visible to her. The door frame reached only his throat. He put the door back into place and reconciled himself to getting very wet and cold that night. "A pesthouse, then," he said out loud, to show—politely— that he understood and that his curtailed friendliness was sensible. Too late to call his brother back, though calling out for Jackson was Franklin's first instinct, because if there was disease in the pesthouse, there could well be disease down there, among the inhabitants of Ferrytown.

Now the woman was coughing once again. Her little hut was full of smoke, he'd noticed. And her lungs, no doubt, were heavy with pestilence, too. Dragging his tarps behind him, he crashed his way back through the clearing and undergrowth into the thickest of the trees, where the canopy would be his shelter. He had been cowardly, he knew. He had been sensible. Only a fool would socialize with death just to stay warm and dry for the night. He found a partly protected spot among the scrub oaks just at the top of Butter Hill where he could erect a makeshift tent from his stretched tarps and protect himself a little. His decision to stay up in the hills to rest had clearly been a foolish one. Jackson had been right as usual. A crazier, more reckless man would have faced the risks of pressing on, injury defied, and enjoyed the benefits of a warm bed, surely better for a limping emigrant than sharing a stormy night with bald disease, no matter how eye-catching it might be.

Franklin's knee had worsened in the rain and during his latest stumbles through the sodden undergrowth. Its throbbing tormented him. It almost ached out loud, the nagging of a roosting dove, *Can't cook, cook, cook.* Even when, in the early quarters of the night, the storm had passed, and the moon, the stars, and the silver lake had reappeared, he could not sleep. Her face was haunting him, her face in candlelight (that celebrated flatterer) with its shorn scalp. He might have touched himself with her in mind, despite his pain, had not the valley raised its voice above the grumbling of his knee and the hastened beating of his newly captured heart. The dripping music of the woods was joined by lowland drums. There was the thud and clatter of slipping land, a sound he could not comprehend or recognize—he knew only that it was bad—and then the stony gust, the rumbling, the lesser set of sounds than thunder that agitated the younger horses and the ever-childish mules out in the safety of the tetherings.

On Butter Hill, above the river crossing where west was granted access to the east, Franklin Lopez sat alarmed, entirely unasleep, in his wet tarps, the only living witness when the silver pendant shook and blistered—a pot, a lake, coming to the boil.

4.

Jackson had taken a liking to the modest town, with its smoke and smells and the clamor of voices, livestock, and tools. Even though he had arrived at its boundary fences a little after dark, there were still a few trading stalls set up, warmed and lit by braziers and lanterns, where he was greeted by dogs, his palms and tongue inspected for infection by gatekeepers, and told at once what the tariffs were—how much he'd have to pay to cross their land, the cost of food and shelter for the night, the onward ferry fee. He would be welcome as a guest if his face was free of rashes, if he wasn't seeking charity, if he didn't try to win the short-term favors of a local woman, and if he put any weapons—and any bad language—into their safekeeping until he traveled on. Weapons, rashes, charity, and short-term favors of any kind were "off the menu," he was told. But, otherwise, they had good beds, fresh bread, sweet water, and easy passage to the other bank "for anyone prepared to keep the peace and pay the price." What had he to offer in return? He had only his coat to trade, he told them, and any labor that they might require of him during the few days that it would take his brother, Franklin, to recover from his exaggerated laming.

All the traders at the gates seemed interested in his piebald coat and gathered round him, admiring his mother's stitching and marveling at its immodest pattern. But their interest was mostly an excuse to question their oversized visitor and stare at him. None would purchase the coat, though, no matter how little he wanted in exchange. It was too grand for them. Nobody they knew was tall or outlandish enough for such a garment anyway, they explained, and there was little likelihood that another man of such height and in need of protection against the cold and rain would pass through their community. But, nevertheless, the traders were careful and flattering in their dealings with Jackson Lopez, as strangers always were, he'd found. His height and strength earned him promises of work in exchange for lodgings: there were sacks of grain to stack and store for winter in the dry lofts and, as ever, there was wood to cut and sewage to be carted out, all familiar tasks. They even promised him a single bed. For once he wouldn't have to share his body space with Franklin.

Jackson need never sleep with his brother again. He was free to stop just one night in Ferrytown and then move on alone the next day, unencumbered. He was tempted to, or certainly he'd played out the idea as he'd come down the hill still irritated by the unwelcome waste of time.

His brother had been a constraint, even before his knee had let them down. Younger brothers often are. They're the sneaks who tell your parents who it was who broke the bowl or lamed the mare or stole the fruit. They're the ones who hold you up, pleading caution, wanting home. They're the ones who'd choose to go roundabout Robert to avoid danger rather than to smell it out and face up boldly—and unblushingly—(as Jackson always would) to the argument, the snake, the bear, the cliff face, or the enemy. And older brothers have no privacy, unlike older sisters for whom privacy is considered fundamental. No, the firstborn males are expected to share their blankets with all the younger ones, and share the work, and entertain each other in the evenings with the light of just the single candle, and travel—even migrate!—in a pack, as if no future was possible, except in each other's company. It certainly was dead right, that traditional warning to anyone with itchy feet, that there is no better way of getting to resent a friend, whether it's a brother or a neighbor, than by traveling with him.

"You take good care of him," his mother had instructed every time they'd left the farm buildings for a day of work, all the way through his childhood and adolescence. And those had been almost her final words to Jackson when her sons had set off toward the boats less than two months previously. "You take good care of him." She still saw Franklin as a boy who needed to be tied by ropes to someone bigger and more trustworthy. She hadn't said, "And you take good care of yourself." Perhaps he ought to start. Walking down the hill alone, at his own pace, had been an unexpected pleasure that he might happily prolong, on this side of the water and beyond. He'd sleep on it. He'd make his mind up once he'd tested the local hospitality and found someone to trade with him. No matter what he decided—return to Franklin and that maddening laugh of his (as seemed dishearteningly inevitable) or hurry on (the thrilling fantasy)—he had to freshen his or their supplies of food.

As it happened, while Jackson was walking in past the tetherings toward the guesthouse, savoring his recent freedom and the prospect of his first good meal for many days, the boy called Nash was on his way to begin his night of caretaking with the local and passage animals. He was wheeling a smoking barrow with a cargo of glowing stove stones from the family grate bedded in earth to keep him warm. He had pushed some sheets of thin cloth up the back of his shirt as well, but he still expected to be cold, especially in the period just before sunup, and—on that night at least—he expected to be wet. He could smell the coming rain, and the bats—always trustworthy forecasters of a storm—were out unusually early in search of rain-shy insects.

So when the immense man in the surprising coat asked him to point out the roof of the guesthouse and where the clothing broker lived, an opportunity was spotted and a deal was soon struck. Jackson parted with the coat, and Nash set aside his wheelbarrow and hurried briefly to his family yard to provide the dried fruit, the pork, the leather water bag, and the apple juice that he had traded with this astounding visitor, who seemed less astounding, shorter even, as soon as he pulled off his outerwear, kissed it farewell as if it were a friend, and draped it round the boy's narrow shoulders. Nash set off for the tetherings again but slowly. The coat—twice too long—was a greater hindrance even than the heavy wheelbarrow of earth and stones. Nevertheless, these were joyful moments for a ten-year-old— except that he felt anxious. He'd been overeager to win the good opinion of the giant and exchanged too many useful things for something inexplicable. Inexplicable to his parents and neighbors, at least. He'd been selfish, too. A coat serves only its owner—although in this rare instance, four small boys and their dogs could easily find shelter under it. Nash would have to spend the night perfecting his excuses. But for the moment he was glad of the opportunity, as the final strangers of the day passed by, to parade his new encumbrance.

Jackson felt the evening chill at once, but he was liberated, lighter in himself. He'd left his ma behind at last and distanced himself a little from his brother. The coat had been her manhood gift to him. In richer times. They'd feasted on four sibling goats with all the other families and she had scraped and tanned the hides to make his gift, which she said—too frequently—would last him a lifetime. It would outlast him. Jackson was certain that if she were to imagine him now and wonder how he and Franklin might have fared, the coat would be a sure part of it. Now he was beyond imagining—and glad of that.

The meal that night was not as grand as he had hoped, although the usual country protocols were followed closely before the food was served, raising expectations. Everybody had to wash their hands at the canteen door in water that after passing through two hundred hands, dirtied by the journey, smelled of horse hair, sweat, and rope, and looked as brown as tea. And for at least the second time that day (for news of Margaret's illness had made the Ferrytowners vigilant and fussy) everybody was inspected for rashes or livid spots before they were allowed to take their places. The women had the best benches, on the wall side of the tables. The men sat in the central gangway with nothing to support their backs. Their children and any adolescent boys too young to grow a beard gathered on their haunches, on mats to the side of the fires and were forbidden to move or speak above a whisper. No dogs. Hats off. And sleeves rolled up, in optimistic readiness.

Jackson was given a low stool at the head of the shorter table so that he could stretch his legs and use his elbows without fear of braining a neighbor. It suited him to take this mostly practical and cautious placement as a mark of respect not only for his size but also for his bearing, which he considered dignified. The candlelight made all the faces seem rudely healthy and animated, and soon new friends were being introduced and stories told. Jackson, though, stayed mostly silent, partly because he had no direct eye contact across the table, partly because his immediate neighbors were too old and tired to draw his attention, but largely because he was taciturn by nature, prepared to express a short opinion but not eager or even able to prattle. Besides, his head was full of awkward possibilities.

When the food itself was served, it was clear that the hosts had gone to no expense. It was hog and hominy with corn bread, they said (though it was later claimed by one of the travelers—possibly a joke—that he'd pulled a yellowish raccoon hair from between his teeth. "I've never seen a ring-tailed hog before!"). Hardly anybody failed to clear their plates, however. Anything was better than the travel pantry that had provided yesterday's meals.

The meat was followed by oatmeal and molasses, offered without the benefit of silverware, so eating it by hand was a noisy, self-conscious business. The adults felt obliged to extend their little fingers respectfully as they ate, using their fores and indexers as spoons and reserving the smallest pinky for dipping into the dishes of salt and for scooping pine nut mash onto their molasses. Such good manners seemed excessive for that quality of food but necessary in the company and under the scrutiny of strangers.

Nobody was truly satisfied. This was not the meal that they'd been dreaming of on the journey, when they'd been making do, at best, with brushjack stew and feasting on the skeletal corpses of packhorses and mules, or on carrion. A chicken's egg, some milk, some recent, cultivated fruit, true bread, and mutton would have served them better.

Despite the quality of the food, however, Jackson could have eaten twice as much again. At least his stomach was half full for once, and sweet. And eating in the company of so many other emigrants had been a kind of nourishment as well, even though he had not spoken yet. But when the elderly woman to his right offered him her unfinished oatmeal and some untouched quarters of bread he felt required, once he had cleared his board, to set aside his dignity, provide his name, and say a word or two about his journey east. He had listened to the travel tales of his fellow diners with little interest. So much disaster and regret should not be spoken of when it was over, Jackson thought. What was done was dust, as far as he was concerned.

Such rapes and robberies and injuries and deaths, so many bolting horses, snapped axles, wagon fires, and sudden floods did not fit his experience. His account would tell of uneventful days marked out by boredom and hardship and livened only when the weather or the landscape played its trick of exposing travelers to mud or drought or, when the route had not been notched or blazed on tree trunks by preceding travelers, luring them into valleys that had no exit at their farthest ends. He told his story in a sentence, one that did not mention his brother.

"We could use a pair of shoulders like yours," the old man said, nodding at his wife for her approval. "Our cart's too heavy and we've lost a horse. We're moving out tomorrow if you'd appreciate the ride. Pay your fare with your muscles, when the going's poor." Jackson nodded. Yes, he'd sleep on it and let them know. He'd be sleeping on a lot of things that night. His single bed would be crowded with temptations.

In fact, it was not at first easy for anyone to sleep that night. What they'd eaten crept around inside their guts, foraging with its nocturnal snout. And then the storm arrived, beating against the rest-house walls, keeping everyone awake to wonder what state the route ahead would be in and whether they should rest up in the town for another day, allowing the mud some time to crust. The men called out in the deafening darkness from their shared beds, exchanging advice and providing their versions of the likely route ahead. No two versions were the same. The liars and the teasers could exaggerate as much as they wanted to. The worriers could share their greatest fears without shaming themselves. They were only faceless voices in the night. And they could safely list their various adversities—the beatings and the robberies, the time that they were stoned by bears, the five nights drifting on a lake, the treachery of so-called friends, the toil and drudgery, the hunger and the thirst, the murderous temperatures that they'd survived—from between warm coverings and underneath a decent roof.

The optimists among them believed that once the river had been crossed, something of the old America would be discovered, the country their grandpas and grandmas had talked about, a land of profusion, safe from human predators, snake free, and welcoming beyond the hog and hominy of this raw place, a place described by so many of their grandparents in words they learned from *their* grandparents, where the encouragements held out to strangers were a good climate, fertile soil, wholesome air and water, plenty of provisions, good pay for labor, kind neighbors, good laws, a free government, and a hearty welcome. A plain and simple ambition, surely.

Here were men who'd come from places with flat and functional names like Half-day Bridge, Boundary Wood, Center Island, and—yes—Ferrytown, but within a day or two they expected to travel on the Dreaming Highway that led, so they believed, through Give-Your-Word Valley to Achievement Hill and a prospect of The Last Farewell, with its long views from the far shore of America. On the journey the country would be flat, they'd heard, with surfaced tracks as hard as fired clay. "Not flat," someone corrected them, "but downhill all the way, sloping to the sea. The wheels do all the work. That's why it's called the Dreaming Highway. The country lets you sleep." The journey to the boats, he said, would be an easy and a speedy one. "A hog could roll there in a sack."

But there were doubters in the darkness, too, men who'd heard less comforting reports. Rivers too wide and wild to cross. Forests so impenetrable and gloomy that nothing grew at ground level except funguses—and little moved except wood ants and blind lizards, both as white as snow, and rats that hunted for their prey by smell alone and so had noses longer than their tails. Great dusty, waterless plains. Ridges sharper than a knife, that tore your clothes. Others spoke of brackish swamps that could be crossed—in twenty days, if you were strong and lucky—only by travelers who dared to leave their horses and their carts behind and drag themselves across the mire on wooden rafts.

And were there any people, beyond the river crossing? A multitude, yes. Everyone who'd ever headed east to catch the boats. There were no boats. Or else it was a land where no one lived and there'd be not a soul to provide, once in a while, a good dry bed or any hog and hominy. "You'd be glad to dine on raccoon then." Or otherwise the people were all unwelcoming, or they were naked cannibals, or they were dwarves "smaller than a prairie dog, but uglier."

"But furrier!"

"And very tasty on a slice of bread!"

By now the laughter in the room was louder than the rain. Indeed, the rain had relented somewhat as had their indigestion. Now they could fall asleep more easily, apprehensive but amused. "Watch out," one of the men whispered, wanting to be the final voice, after all his companions had fallen quiet. "There's folk out there, one day ahead of Ferrytown, who are as handy with their toes as with their fingers. They can wipe their butts, scratch their noses, poke your eyes out, and pick your pockets, all at the one time."

But there was still another man simmering to speak. "From what I've heard tonight," said Jackson from his single bed at the far end of the hall, too softly to be heard by many of his fellows, "there're at least a hundred different lands beyond the river. And none of them strike me as likely. Maybe all of us should only wait and see what we'll find when we've planted our feet on the actual earth ahead of us." He wanted to say out loud what he was hoping for within—that if he advanced his shoulders to the couple with the heavy cart and left his brother to take care of himself, then he could square it with his conscience only if the way ahead for Franklin would prove to be an easy and a kindly one. He fell silent for a little time, judging his words, and wondering, too, whether he could ignore the pressure in his bladder from the flagon of apple juice he had traded and drunk, before adding, "I'll tell you something. For free. This afternoon, I walked down the very same hill as all of you and I looked ahead and used my eyes. I saw the view. Nobody missed the view, I'm sure. And what I saw ahead of me was land and sky just like the land and sky we've always known. Tomorrow you can see it for yourselves." Tomorrow, he was thinking, as he fell asleep, will be like yesterday.

Vincent, Homesick for the Land of Pictures

Peter Gizzi

Is this what you intended, Vincent
that we take our rest at the end of the grove
nestled into our portion beneath the bird's migration
saying, who and how am I made better through struggle.
Or why am I I inside this empty arboretum
this inward spiral of whoop ass and vision
the leafy vine twisting and choking the tree.
O, dear heaven, if you are indeed that
or if you can indeed hear what I might say
heal me and grant me laughter's bounty
of eyes and smiles, of eyes and affection.

To not be naive and think of silly answers only
nor to imagine answers would be the only destination
nor is questioning color even useful now
now that the white ray in the distant tree beacons.
That the sun can do this to us, every one of us
that the sun can do this to everything inside
the broken light refracted through leaves.
What the ancients called peace, no clearer example
what our fathers called the good, what better celebration.
Leaves shine in the body and in the head alike
the sun touches deeper than thought.

O to be useful, of use, to the actual seen thing
to be in some way related by one's actions in the world.
There might be nothing greater than this
nothing truer to the good feelings that vibrate within
like in the middle of the flower I call your name.
To correspond, to be in equanimity with organic stuff
to toil and to reflect and to home and to paint
father, and further, the migration of things.
The homing action of geese and wood mice.
The ample evidence of the sun inside all life
inside all life seen and felt and all the atomic pieces too.

But felt things exist in shadow, let us reflect.
The darkness bears a shine as yet unpunished by clarity
but perhaps a depth that outshines clarity and is true.
The dark is close to doubt and therefore close to the sun
at least what the old books called science or bowed down to.
The dark is not evil for it has indigo and cobalt inside
and let us never forget indigo and the warmth of that
the warmth of the mind reflected in a dark time
in the time of pictures and refracted light.
Ah, the sun is here too in the polar region of night
the animal proximity of another and of nigh.

To step into it as into a large surf in late August
to go out underneath it all above and sparkling.
To wonder and to dream and to look up at it
wondrous and strange companion to all our days
and the toil and worry and animal fear always with us.
The night sky, the deep sense of space, actual bodies of light

the gemstone brushstrokes in rays and shimmers
to be held tight, wound tighter in the act of seeing.
The sheer vertical act of feeling caught up in it
the sky, the moon, the many heavenly forms
these starry nights alone and connected alive at the edge.

Now to think of the silver and the almost blue in pewter.
To feel these hues down deep, feel color wax and wane
and yellow, yellows are the tonality of work and bread.
The deep abiding sun touching down and making its impression
making so much more of itself here than where it signals
the great burning orb installed at the center of each and every thing.
Isn't it comforting this notion of each and every thing
though nothing might be the final and actual expression of it
that nothing at the center of something alive and burning
green then mint, blue then shale, gray and gray into violet
into luminous dusk into dust then scattered now gone.

But what is the use now of this narrow ray, this door ajar
the narrow path canopied in dense wood calling
what of the striated purposelessness in lapidary shading and line.
To move on, to push forward, to take the next step, to die.
The circles grow large and ripple in the hatch-marked forever
the circle on the horizon rolling over and over into paint
into the not near, the now far, the distant long-off line of daylight.
That light was my enemy and one great source of agony
one great solace in paint and brotherhood the sky and grass.
The fragrant hills spoke in flowering tones I could hear
the gnarled cut stumps tearing the sky, eating the sun.

The gnarled cut stumps tearing the sky, eating the sun
the fragrant hills spoke in flowering tones I could hear
one great solace in paint and brotherhood the sky and grass.
That light was my enemy and one great source of agony
into the not near, the now far, the distant long-off line of daylight
the circle on the horizon rolling over and over into paint.
The circles grow large and ripple in the hatch-marked forever.
To move on, to push forward, to take the next step, to die.
What of the striated purposelessness in lapidary shading and line
the narrow path canopied in dense wood calling
but what is the use now of this narrow ray, this door ajar.

Into luminous dusk into dust then scattered now gone
green then mint, blue then shale, gray and gray into violet
that nothing at the center of something alive and burning
though nothing might be the final and actual expression of it.
Isn't it comforting this notion of each and every thing
the great burning orb installed at the center of each and every thing
making so much more of itself here than where it signals.
The deep abiding sun touching down and making its impression
and yellow, yellows are the tonality of work and bread.
To feel these hues down deep, feel color wax and wane
now to think of the silver and the almost blue in pewter.

These starry nights alone and connected alive at the edge
the sky, the moon, the many heavenly forms
the sheer vertical act of feeling caught up in it.
To be held tight, wound tighter in the act of seeing
the gemstone brushstrokes in rays and shimmers.
The night sky, the deep sense of space, actual bodies of light

Peter Gizzi

and the toil and worry and animal fear always with us
wondrous and strange companion to all our days.
To wonder and to dream and to look up at it
to go out underneath it all above and sparkling
to step into it as into a large surf in late August.

The animal proximity of another and of nigh.
Ah, the sun is here too in the polar region of night
in the time of pictures and refracted light
the warmth of the mind reflected in a dark time
and let us never forget indigo and the warmth of that.
The dark is not evil for it has indigo and cobalt inside
at least what the old books called science or bowed down to.
The dark is close to doubt and therefore close to the sun
but perhaps a depth that outshines clarity and is true.
The darkness bears a shine as yet unpunished by clarity
but felt things exist in shadow, let us reflect.

Inside all life seen and felt and all the atomic pieces too
the ample evidence of the sun inside all life
the homing action of geese and wood mice
father, and further, the migration of things.
To toil and to reflect and to home and to paint
to correspond, to be in equanimity with organic stuff
like in the middle of the flower I call your name.
Nothing truer to the good feelings that vibrate within
there might be nothing greater than this
to be in some way related by one's actions in the world.
O to be useful, of use, to the actual seen thing.

56

The sun touches deeper than thought
leaves shine in the body and in the head alike
what our fathers called the good, what better celebration.
What the ancients called peace, no clearer example
the broken light refracted through leaves.
That the sun can do this to everything inside
that the sun can do this to us, every one of us
now that the white ray in the distant tree beacons.
Nor is questioning color even useful now
nor to imagine answers would be the only destination
to not be naive and think of silly answers only.

Of eyes and smiles, of eyes and affection
heal me and grant me laughter's bounty.
Or if you can indeed hear what I might say
O, dear heaven, if you are indeed that
the leafy vine twisting and choking the tree
this inward spiral of whoop ass and vision.
Or why am I I inside this empty arboretum
saying, who and how am I made better through struggle
nestled into our portion beneath the bird's migration
that we take our rest at the end of the grove
is this what you intended, Vincent.

Heaven and Hell

Joanna Scott

ON A JULY DAY IN 1919, beneath the blue dome of the summer sky, the guests watched from the base of a hillock as a young woman was joined in marriage to the man she thought she'd lost forever in the war.

Do you—
She does.
Do you—
He does.

Lazy waves lapped and sucked at the rocks below. Seagulls floated on tilted wings over the gazebo, where a five-piece band was waiting to play. A dog down at the far end of the beach plunged into the water to retrieve a stick thrown by a boy who had grown bored with the ceremony and wandered away. A soft breeze rustled through the dry leaves of hawthorn bushes.

After the exchange of vows, the bride and groom stood unmoving in front of the pastor for such a length of time that some of the guests began to wonder if the young couple knew what to do next. Then the bride reached for the groom's hands, together they lifted the lace veil, and, as they turned, their lips met perfectly, pressing together in a kiss that two years earlier no one would have thought possible. That this kiss almost didn't happen was enough to draw the assembled guests together in shared relief. At last, Gwendolyn Martin and Clive Crawford were husband and wife.

Unfortunately, Tom Martin, father of the bride, was missing the great event, his absence a result of bad luck so typical that he almost relished his despair, since it reinforced his sense that he couldn't help what he did. The fact that he wasn't where he wanted to be at that moment would eventually become an addition to his long list of mishaps, his entire life being a sequence of contests with fate that he kept losing, but not without a struggle. To prove that he didn't give up easily, he slammed the weight of his whole body against the bathroom door. But the door was made of sturdy oak, and with the newfangled bolt irreparably jammed, Tom was stuck inside the bathroom, rubbing the darkening bruise on his shoulder while his only daughter married her true love.

Seated on wooden chairs arranged in rows along the relatively flat part of Madison Point, the guests were happy to watch for as long as the kiss would last, which with the bride and groom clamped greedily together was turning out to last longer than the usual kiss to mark a union, longer than any wedding kiss anyone had ever witnessed, longer than it had taken the couple to say their vows, and, at this rate, longer than the entirety of the preceding ceremony.

The pastor, rotund Father Gaffner, kept his head slightly bent, his posture suggesting infinite patience, making it impossible to wonder how long it would take until he intervened. Apparently, he saw no reason to intervene. He would let the bride and groom go on kissing for as long as they pleased while the guests watched with growing awe that any kiss could last this long—long enough to turn the remarkable event into something that would become the stuff of legend. Gwen and Clive had begun kissing and would keep kissing. In that other dimension where the miraculous future of their love had been born, they would never stop kissing.

Keep kissing, Gwen's Uncle Hugo wanted to urge. Break the record of kissing. Kiss through the day, dear Gwen and Clive. Kiss through the night. Kiss for as long as it will take cause and effect to be reversed and all the damage that has ever been done to be undone. Kiss away Clive's blindness. Kiss away the memories of war. Kiss away death. Keep kissing until the end of the world, or at least until the arrival of Tom, that scoundrel of a younger brother who had made Hugo's life difficult for all of his fifty-one years.

Where was Tom? Not where he was supposed to be, of course. Tom had never been where he was supposed to be. When he was a boy, he could be counted upon to drift from whatever game he'd started to play. As a man, he drifted from job to job and woman to woman. And as a father, he had just drifted away.

Hugo couldn't know that his brother had spent the morning locked in the bathroom of a seaside inn, where he was treating himself to a hefty dose of self-pity. If he were a better man, Tom thought, he'd accept that the only thing left for him to do was put the revolver to his chest and pull the trigger. Click. If only he had a revolver. He had a toothbrush and Arm & Hammer paste. He had Pepto-Bismol. He was ready. No, he wasn't ready and wouldn't be ready until he'd been given the chance to improve his predicament. Even if he were entirely blameless for everything that had gone wrong, he knew himself as well as Hugo knew him and would have readily admitted that he was a selfish man. He was also sunken-eyed, yellow-haired, white-whiskered, and hungry for meat after being locked in the bathroom in room number four of the Tuckett Beach Inn for hours—days, it seemed to Tom, or at least long enough to miss his daughter's wedding.

No one except Hugo would have cared enough to wonder at his absence. The bride didn't even suspect that her father had been invited. To Gwen, Tom was the strange man with tufted ears and a ridiculous handlebar mustache who appeared in her life no more than once a decade. She didn't pretend to feel any familial attachment to him. It was fair to assume that while Gwen stood there kissing Clive, there was no one farther from her thoughts than Tom.

The kiss went on and on. The guests stared, their amazement making them simultaneously tense with expectation and confident that such a kiss could only be a deserved reward. The scene was marvelous, unending, and unrepeatable. Just to witness the kiss gave each guest an expansive feeling of worthiness.

And yet it appeared that Tom Martin had decided he had someplace better to be than at Madison Point on this fine summer day. Unless Tom had simply forgotten how to get there. He had last visited the estate when Gwen was eleven, the event preserved by Hugo with his Kodak Brownie in a photograph of Gwen perched on the seat of a bicycle and Tom standing by the front wheel looking as if he'd just realized he'd taken the wrong road and was hopelessly lost.

Damn that Tom. Hugo had even wired money for his brother's train fare from St. Louis. But Tom had probably used the money to travel in the opposite direction. Instead of coming to his daughter's wedding—to begin at noon, *promptly*, Hugo had added on the invitation to his brother—Tom was probably hundreds of miles away, heading nowhere in particular and inadvertently attaching himself to some new, doomed scheme.

Down on the beach, the dog, a Newfoundland, emerged dripping from the water, the stick clamped between her jaws. The dog's quick shudder was familiar to the boy, who leaped backward to avoid being soaked as the dog shook herself dry. The boy's laughing shriek, though muted by the shushing wind, startled the guests, who weren't ready to be reminded that life was continuing beyond the circle of their assembly. Though none of the guests made any visible move, a rippling unease traveled forward through the rows, passing from one person to another until it finally reached the bride and groom, provoking them to bend slightly away from each other, their minuscule separation dramatic enough to suggest that they were preparing to bring their kiss to an end. The guests continued to stare, savoring this culminating vision of love. The bride and groom had kissed a wonderful kiss and were about to be done, or so the guests thought—mistakenly, as it turned out, for in the next moment the couple fell back toward each other, mouths latched eagerly, for after all they had been through they deserved to kiss and would go on kissing no matter what.

Uncle Hugo admired their defiance. But he had enough foresight to know that eventually the world would intrude. If only he could predict what form the intrusion would take, he'd try to prevent it. Gwen and Clive deserved to kiss for as long as they wanted to kiss. And if they kept on kissing, sooner or later Tom Martin would have to show up.

But Tom couldn't show up unless someone opened the door and let him out. Here he would stay, alone with his thoughts in this tomb of a windowless bathroom, a tub for a coffin, water dripping with torturous irregularity from the faucet. What could he do to improve the situation? His boss at the furniture store in St. Louis would have advised him to make a mental list of ten positive outcomes and ten things that brought him joy. Also, he would have warned Tom to avoid chocolate, white sugar, mushrooms, and foods that had been preserved, reheated, and fermented. And Tom definitely should avoid thinking about the wedding he was destined to miss.

It was a wedding as lovely as the guests had predicted it would be. But no one had expected it to be as transfixing as a dream, as deliciously unpredictable. Time itself seemed to have broken from its normal pace and had taken to swooping in reverse then swirling forward like the cottonwood seedlings that blew about in the breeze. In the grip of their fascination, the guests wouldn't have exclaimed if nymphs and satyrs had cavorted across the lawn.

A baby, set down by her mother to crawl between the rows of chairs, chortled happily. Bees flitted in the honeysuckle vines woven through the gazebo's trellis. Down at the beach, the boy wrestled the stick from the jaws of the Newfoundland. Women enjoyed the sunshine that warmed their shoulders through silk shawls. Men enjoyed the way the breeze rippled the linen of their wide trousers. Even the lemony, thick scent from the mudflats to the south was something to savor, especially when mixed with the perfume of honeysuckle and driftwood and salt. The only melancholy element

61

was the vague sympathy that some guests felt for those who hadn't been invited.

Tom Martin had been invited. It could be, Hugo considered, that Tom had planned to attend but was running late. Though ordinarily Tom couldn't be roused to run. He preferred to walk. Hugo's brother Tom was never in a hurry and considered any commitment an inconvenience.

It seemed that Tom Martin didn't care enough to tolerate the inconvenience of his daughter's wedding. But Hugo cared. He hoped that simply by being present at this important event, Tom would set in motion what was sure to be a long and difficult process of reconciliation, made more difficult because the two people involved were content with their estrangement. Wasn't it always easier to forget rather than forgive? When Tom had left Carol, Gwen's mother, for another woman, he hadn't even known that she was pregnant. After Gwen was born, it had taken Hugo three months to locate his brother, who was hiding out in Cleveland, and tell him that he had a daughter, an effort that he would allow himself to regret from time to time, though only in secret, along with the agonizing love he secretly felt for Carol, dear Carol, who was never more than grateful to Hugo for offering her and Gwen a haven.

Beyond the point, whitecaps wrinkled the dark surface of the sound. Seagulls continued to wheel silently overhead. On the beach, the boy waded into the shallow water after the dog. The baby, sitting up in the grass, found an empty nymphal shell of a cicada and fingered it gently. Still standing humbly in front of the kissing couple, Father Gaffner tightened his jaw in a subtle grimace, as though he were suppressing a burp or a chuckle. And buzzing in jerky exploration among the buds of the honeysuckle, the bees kept at their single-minded work.

Tom, in contrast to the bees, was an expert at doing nothing. He could sit on the edge of a filthy blue tub staring at a blue toilet bowl, the air in the bathroom like an August afternoon in St. Louis. He could play the part of the vagabond his brother thought him to be, a man with his slouch hat rolled up in his suitcase, who was never in a hurry. Or he was rarely in a hurry. Well, sometimes he was in a hurry. Sometimes he got hungry for his breakfast. He was hungry now. Someone, let Tom Martin go! Free him from the prison of his soul, redeem him, make him innocent again, lift him up, open the door to this stinking bathroom, give him beef jerky, ten cents for a pack of cigarettes, and a ride to Madison Point. Believe it or not, he wanted to attend the wedding of his daughter, even if she didn't want him there and greeted him with those icy blue eyes, blaming him for being who he was. But really, as he sat in the sapping warmth of the bathroom, it had begun to seem possible that he was not necessarily equal to his actions. Even if he couldn't undo what he'd done he might be able to avoid repeating his mistakes, his worst mistake being leaving that crackerjack Carol, the first of the many lovers he'd left behind and the one who died before she learned to stop loving him. Carol, Gwen's mother, never enjoyed the luxury of indifference. For the pain he'd caused her, Tom was sorry—sorrier now than ever. With no one but himself for company, he couldn't be distracted from wondering how things might have been different if he'd taken Carol with him when he'd left twenty-three years ago.

Hugo could have told his errant brother what would have been different. If Tom had taken Carol with him, Hugo wouldn't have had the chance to raise Gwen and escort her down the aisle on her wedding day. After all they'd been through together, from Gwen's scarlet fever, her childish tantrums and joys, to her engagement to Clive, the war, Clive's disappearance in France, his blindness and slow recovery in a military hospital in Nyons, their reunion, their marriage, Hugo could only be glad that Carol had stayed when Tom left, and that he'd kept his love for her a secret until the end, and beyond. He never had to ask her what she felt for him—he could see in her eyes that he was like a brother to her. If she'd known he'd wanted to be more than that, she would have left Madison Point. He would have lost not just her but Gwen and everything that followed, and his life wouldn't be culminating now, despite his brother's absence, or perhaps because of it, in this record-breaking kiss on a perfect July day in 1919, with the guests mesmerized, the seagulls floating like angels overhead, a boy splashing in the water down at the beach, a baby lifting the shell of a cicada to her mouth, and one lone honeybee diving into the roses of the bride's bouquet.

The scene being exactly what Tom was trying not to imagine in the bathroom of the Tuckett Beach Inn. He didn't have to be a genius to guess that his daughter's wedding would include equal parts of beauty and guilelessness, acceptance, risk, ferocity, and resistance. All in the name of love. The daughter of crackerjack Carol wouldn't marry a man she didn't love. Right, Carol? Carol? It was only out of boredom that Tom called Carol—first in a whisper, then with a murmur, then with a shout. But don't think that Tom Martin believed in ghosts. He didn't need metaphysics to be certain that death is the end

63

of life, period. Still, Carol, you could do Tom a little favor and unlock this door, or, short of that, talk to him. He could use the company. Carol, are you there? Carol!

Hugo could have told Tom that it was useless to call Carol, since even if she did exist as a singular entity in the spirit realm—a possibility that Hugo, like his brother, didn't entertain for a moment—surely she wouldn't have left her daughter's wedding just to open the door for a man who had abandoned her twenty-three years ago. Tom was stuck, and Carol was the last person on earth—or elsewhere—who would help him come unstuck.

Yet Hugo knew that it would be just like Tom to lay the fault of his absence with Carol. Go ahead, blame a dead woman for the fact that Tom was missing this kiss of all kisses, love making the burden of expiation as light as a feather, with the guests restored to their primeval nobility by the advantage of their presence here at Madison Point. What? Simply put, Hugo was thinking that this must be similar to paradise—layers and layers of pure happiness, like pages in a book.

Given the transfixing quality of the scene, it wasn't surprising that no one noticed when the baby, balanced on her pudgy rump between the forest of legs, put the shell of the cicada in her mouth. No one noticed that the seagulls abruptly flew away, one after the other, in the direction of a fishing boat on the horizon. And no one noticed when the boy, who had waded up to his thighs after the Newfoundland, slipped off the edge of a sandy shelf and disappeared into the deep water.

What the guests did notice was the bee. While Gwen and Clive kissed, the bee that had been exploring the bouquet rose from the flowers slowly, like a spider on a thread, hovering for a moment near the bride's shoulders and then rising toward the buttery sheen of her cheek. Its thorax vibrating hungrily, the bee seemed to be searching Gwen's skin for a good place to pierce it. Gwen and Clive continued kissing, oblivious, but the guests, along with Uncle Hugo, watched with concern.

Someone had to stop the bee from stinging the bride, Hugo thought, leaning forward, privately trying to reason his way free of his reluctance to intrude. Wasn't there anyone who could help, someone who could intervene without being noticed?

Neither Tom nor Hugo would ever know that they were similar in one essential way: when they needed help, they thought of Carol. Watching the bee buzzing near Gwen, Hugo thought of

Carol. Stuck in the bathroom of the Tuckett Beach Inn, Tom thought of Carol.

"Who's Carol?" asked the maid after opening the bathroom door with her skeleton key. She addressed Tom with the frankness of a child half her age. He noticed that her brown eyes slipped off center as she stared. Her unkempt hair was more orange than red. There was a canker scab on her chin, and her cotton dress fell loosely over her hips.

She was too pretty to look so awful, Tom thought. And she was too forward with a strange man standing before her wrapped only in a white bath towel.

"You were calling for Carol," she persisted. She squatted to take a better look at the lock.

"She was my wife," Tom lied.

"Was?"

He answered with an impatient snort.

"Bless you," she said, as though he'd sneezed. She turned the lever of the bolt back and forth until it jammed again. "Not a day goes by when something doesn't go wrong," she announced, without exasperation. "I need a screwdriver." When she stood, her odd gaze alighted on one side of Tom's face. Without thinking, he moved his hand through the air as if to bat away a mosquito. She started visibly, teetered as if she'd been struck in the face. For a moment Tom thought he had hit her inadvertently, and he was seized by terrible, feverish guilt. He wanted to fall down on his knees and apologize. But she smiled at him as if to indicate that an apology really wasn't necessary, especially from a man dressed in a bath towel. Go on, she seemed to tell him, lifting her chin and looking toward the room where he'd left his suitcase. You're free.

While he gathered his clothes, the girl warned him not to shut the bathroom door, and she set off to find a screwdriver. Tom scrambled into his suit, combed his mustache, snapped the buckle of his suitcase, and left in such a hurry that he forgot to pay his bill.

Out on the road in front of the inn, he waved down a dairy cart being pulled by a round-bellied mule. When the dairyman heard that Tom wanted to go to Hugo Martin's estate at Madison Point, he said he'd take him there himself. Coincidentally, he had a wheel of cheddar in back to deliver to the wedding reception.

"Does that ol' mule go any faster?" Tom asked.

The dairyman looked at him askance, not unlike the way the maid had looked at him.

"You want my Rascal to go faster?"

"Yes, please."

"Real fast?"

"Sure."

The dairyman tipped his cap, revealing the youthfulness of his face. He couldn't have been older than seventeen, Tom thought. Leaning toward the mule as though he meant to grab its tail between his teeth, the dairyman gave a short laugh, warned Tom to hold on, and cracked his whip in the air. The mule flattened its ears against its head and took off, trotting faster than Tom had ever known a mule to trot.

Tom Martin was somewhere between Tuckett Beach and Hugo's estate when the wedding guests first noticed the bee rising from the bride's bouquet. Their attention couldn't have been any more intense at this point; what changed with the bee was the unity of their responses. One man coughed into his hand in warning. A woman whispered audibly enough for her husband to hear, "Oh no." And the mother who had set her baby on the grass glanced down and noticed the shiny tip of an insect shell sticking out from the baby's grinning lips.

A mere few yards offshore from the narrow stretch of beach, the boy, submerged in the murky saltwater, was holding his breath. Though he didn't know how to swim, he'd taught himself to hold his breath during bath time. Once he'd even held his breath for as long as it had taken him to count in his head from one to twenty-five.

He began counting silently. As he counted, he wondered if it was possible to learn to breathe underwater. He tried to propel himself by pulling at the water in the same way that he'd pull himself up to the next branch when he was climbing a tree. Five, one thousand, six. When he relaxed his arms and legs, he felt himself turning a somersault, and when he stretched out again he couldn't tell which direction was up. Nine, one thousand, ten. It was strange that he couldn't see the sky. He was glad, though, to have the chance to feel brave. Feeling brave was the best feeling in the world, better even than the sleepy feeling when his mother kissed him goodnight on the tip of his nose. She would think him very brave when he told her what had happened, though she'd be angry that he'd gotten his clothes wet. Twelve, one thousand. Or had he reached thirteen? It was frustrating to forget how far he'd counted. He'd been hoping to make it past twenty-seven. If he'd been counting straight, he might have already reached twenty.

He felt his shirt suddenly tighten around his chest. In the next moment a tugging force caused him to turn on his back, and his face broke through the surface of the dark water. It was good to see the sky just where'd he'd left it. And it felt good to loosen his collar with two fingers and take a deep breath. He felt a little disappointed that he hadn't been given the chance to count to thirty underwater, but he was glad to be floating on his back, with that big black friendly dog dragging him toward shore by his shirt as though he were one of the sticks he'd thrown into the water for the dog to fetch.

In their chairs around the hillock, the guests couldn't have reliably said how much time had passed since Father Gaffner had declared Gwen and Clive husband and wife. Some believed in hindsight that the kiss hadn't lasted longer than a minute. Others were sure that at least half an hour had passed. But to Hugo Martin it was as long as he could have wished, for just as the bee dove through the narrow opening below the chins of the bride and groom, a mule pulling a dairy cart came trotting along the sandy track leading to the gazebo. Even before the cart had stopped, Tom Martin jumped off.

"Was that fast enough?" the young dairyman asked.

"That was plenty fast," Tom assured him as his gaze turned toward the mound where the bride and groom were standing and kissing. Despite his nearsightedness, Tom could see the couple clearly enough to tell that there was something willfully permanent about them as they kissed, as if they were trying to turn themselves into statues.

It took Father Gaffner to finally break the spell. Father Gaffner, who had once nearly died in an anaphylactic response to a sting, noticed the bee for the first time when it passed to his side of the bride and groom.

In the seventh row of guests, the mother pulled what was left of the cicada shell from her baby's mouth. Down at the beach, the boy climbed up on the Newfoundland's back and rode the dog through the few remaining yards of shallow water. At the base of the gazebo, Tom suddenly remembered that the name of his daughter's husband was Clive. And since Hugo had swiveled around to watch Tom, he didn't see Father Gaffner frantically shake a hand to wave away the bee, his gesture causing the bride and groom to separate with a sucking sound that one man would later describe as water going down a drain—evidence that tongues were involved, he would insist in a conversation similar to others that would go on through the banquet. What actually happened? How long had the kiss really lasted? The guests weren't sure, and their uncertainty would only increase, every new exchange adding details that confused them more until there was nothing left to do but drink too much champagne and dance.

How I Lost My Religion
Valerie Martin

ANNABELLE'S MEMORABLE REMARK

I WONDER NOW HOW MOTHER persuaded my father we needed a maid. He was away at sea most of the time, we lived in a four-room apartment, there was only my sister and I, Mother didn't have a thing to do, and money was tight. She must have complained of the ironing, for that was mostly what Annabelle did. In those days, before the invention of clothes driers and wash-and-wear fabric, ironing was the most tedious and invariable chore of the housewife.

Nor do I know how Mother found Annabelle, but it may have been through her friend and hairdresser, Zeline, a talkative, tough, and generous divorcée who ran a beauty salon out of her house a few blocks from our apartment. I spent fascinating hours on the red-and-green linoleum floor of this establishment, perusing salacious magazines and getting into weepy altercations with Zeline's three spiteful daughters, who were spoiled and fiercely territorial. Mother considered Zeline her social inferior; she was to have these oddly dismissive yet dependent relationships with hairdressers all her life. Sometimes my sister and I were left in Zeline's care, and often of an evening, when Mother arrived from wherever she had gone, we all sat around Zeline's kitchen table while her latest boyfriend cooked something he'd shot or trapped or pulled out of the Gulf of Mexico. The adults drank beer and talked into the night, the laughter of the women sudden and dangerous, like flashes of lightning amid the low rumbling thunder of the conversation, the atmosphere increasingly charged with sex. I practiced the art of being invisible. I have no memory of ever speaking or being spoken to during these long dinners. I fell asleep on the floor or on the carpet in Zeline's living room, where it was always quiet and cool. No one had air-conditioning then, but every house was equipped with a contingent of heavy, serviceable oscillating fans, strategically deployed to rotate the liquefying heat through the rooms.

By the time I began to record the world outside myself, Zeline's shop, the fans, and Annabelle were all solidly in place. There was an exhaust fan in the window of the kitchen where Annabelle stood over the ironing board, patiently pulling the iron back and forth across our line-dried clothes. I liked to watch her, and she did not appear to dislike my company. I knew she had two daughters of her own—so many daughters in our steamy little world—both older than me, but I was never to see her with her children. She was probably the same age as my mother, early thirties, but she seemed ageless to me and alien. At the end of the day she left our apartment and took the bus that delivered her to the planet of Negro domestics. Sometimes, if it was raining in the morning, Mother took me with her to pick Annabelle up at the covered bus stop surrounded by cemeteries, the first stop these domestics passed through on the way to their jobs in our solar system. They huddled together there while the rain poured off the awning in a solid sheet, one eye out for their employer's car, bantering as cheerfully as children in a schoolyard. As we pulled up, Annabelle separated from her compatriots, leaped through the cascading rain, and landed gracefully on the seat beside me. There was not much in the way of greeting as it was early in the morning and Mother had been obliged to get up, so she was in a foul humor. When we got back to the apartment and dashed through the rain to the door, Mother preceded us up the stairs, heading, without comment, straight back to bed.

What did Annabelle look like? Though she spent one day a week in our house for eight years, I don't think I would recognize her if I saw her today, even if she looked as she did then. I know that she wasn't heavy—Mother would never have hired a fat person—that she was taller than Mother, and that her skin was dark brown, as were her eyes. I remember watching her hands, which fascinated me, spreading the shirts out across the board, lifting the iron. Her knuckles were darker, almost black, the palms lighter, pinkish, but the variations from dark to light were as seamless as a watercolor sky.

I can call up her hands, but not her face. I was not a child who noticed adult faces. I was ten or so before I stopped confusing my father with the few other men who visited us—my uncle, my mother's cousin, a friend who was the director of the community theater where Mother occasionally tried out for parts. Burned in my memory is an exchange that took place between my parents when I was five. My father was in residence, taking up a lot of space in the living room, and I wanted him to swing me by my arms. "Swing me, swing me," I demanded, dancing before him. He gave me an incredulous look, backed away as if from a muddy and insouciant puppy, and said, "What are you talking about?"

"You know," I pressed on. "Hold my hands and swing me around like you did before."

My father was a small man who gave orders to recalcitrant sailors near his own age and twice his size, and his ability to send out a fiercely repressive vibration was legendary in our family. I felt, though I did not see it, the sharp blade of the look he gave my mother flash out over my head. "You must be thinking of somebody else," he said.

I dropped my hands, wandered away. I knew he was right, but I couldn't think of who that other man might have been. I remembered that he had taken my hands and swung me round and round, then set me down on the carpet, where I reeled with pleasurable dizziness. Mother hadn't disapproved; she might have laughed. When I could stand up, I'd said, "Do it again," and to my delight, the man had held out his big hands to mine and off I'd gone, faster and faster, flying through the humid air like a trapeze artist. Later I understood how unlikely it was that this man could have been my father, who rarely touched any of us and disliked all displays of high spirits. When he had to sit through a dinner at Zeline's, where five little girls romped underfoot, shouting, weeping, complaining, spilling Coke across the table, showing one another the food in their mouths, my father clung to his glass of Scotch on the rocks as if it were a life preserver and he a drowning man. Mother's friends and relations were a trial he bore willingly, for they all adored him, but he breathed a sigh of relief when we got up from the table to go home. Mother had a high school girlfriend she kept up with, Muriel, who was married to a gloomy, deeply corrupt young lawyer. This couple invited us all to their French Quarter apartment regularly, and when my father was home he went without complaint, but I knew he thought Muriel ridiculous and her husband a sorry drunk. He didn't much like our landlord, who lived downstairs, or any of our neighbors.

But he liked Annabelle. He never said he did, but I knew it, and she liked him. They were both taciturn and stoical by nature and what they liked about each other was that they could be in the kitchen together and not talk. This was in the morning when Mother was still asleep; she rarely rose before eleven unless there was some pressing necessity. My father would greet Annabelle, fix his coffee and toast, then sit at the table reading his newspaper while

Annabelle dragged the iron back and forth over the shirts and pants, dresses and sheets, sprinkling the wrinkles with water from a Coke bottle fitted with a rubber sprinkler top. I didn't notice faces then, but I was a barometer for emotional atmosphere, and the pressure in the kitchen on these mornings was so low, the air so fresh and positively charged, that I was drawn from wherever I was hiding into the kitchen. If I could keep still and quiet, my father would fix me a slice of toast carefully spread with butter and strawberry preserves, cut into triangular quarters and presented on a plate with a glass of juice. Annabelle sometimes took a cup of coffee too, which she drank standing at the board, not hurriedly, but meditatively, her iron set to one side. She didn't smile at me or express her pleasure in any measurable way, but I knew she was enjoying the coffee, that she was not, for the moment, working. She worked hard, I knew that, though Mother maintained that she was lazy, and she didn't waste a break when it came her way. The kitchen was quiet, shaded by plaintain trees; the air limpid, still, and cool; Mother was asleep. It was as good as it got in my world. I took Annabelle's example to heart and enjoyed the hell out of my toast.

Annabelle's memorable remark was made one chilly afternoon when we were alone in the kitchen together. I was sitting on the floor watching her as she transported clean dishes from the rack to the cabinets. When the rack was empty, she pulled the garbage bin from under the sink and took up the brown paper bag by its handles. This was always her last duty of the day, taking the garbage down the concrete stairs off the kitchen and out to the can in the shell alley behind the garage. The bag came free of the bin and, as I was in a position to observe the bottom of it, I noticed that it was shiny, and sagging perilously at the center seam. "That bag is all wet," I said. Annabelle set it down quickly, tilting it to one side to confirm my observation. "Lord," she said. She took a bigger bag from alongside the refrigerator, placed it over the top of the hazardous bag, and skillfully flipped the whole enterprise over so that the garbage went into the dry bag and the slick bottom was now on top. She ran a damp mop over the wet spot on the linoleum, took up the new bag, and went out the door. In a few minutes she was back, pulling on her cloth coat and chuckling to herself. Then she addressed me, as she always did, as an equal. "I surely have to thank you for telling me about that bag," she said. "If it had bursted on those steps, I believe I would have lost my religion."

Fifty years later I can still feel the complex set of emotions—

wonder, pride, pleasure, curiosity, anxiety—that washed over my childish consciousness in the wake of this marvelous remark. I think it must have been my first recognition of myself as a creature possessed of the highly touted "free will," capable of effecting change for good or ill in the world around me. First there was the wonder of being thanked by an adult, which went through me like some golden shaft of the gods, from my bony chest to my toes, a busy, tingling sensation as if flies were swarming through my blood vessels. That this expression of gratitude was not casual or dismissive, that there was nothing offhand about it, that indeed Annabelle had gone down the stairs and up again thinking kind thoughts about me, this touched me as nothing had before. Then there was the pleasurable rush of pride: I had done a good thing! If I had not spoken, which had naturally not occurred to me, a very bad thing would have happened to Annabelle. I pictured the moment when the bag burst, spewing its sodden, odoriferous contents, the limp lettuce and soggy tomatoes, the meat scraps, the globs of oatmeal and mashed potatoes, the open tin of fat skimmed from chicken broth, all cascading down the steps—surely some of it would have landed on Annabelle's shoes—and then the slow, painstaking process of picking it all up, rebagging it, finally taking out the mop and bucket to wash down the steps. Doubtless she would have missed her bus. Because I was small and enamored of lolling about on the floor, I had been in a position to save Annabelle from a dismal fate. Observation was power. Perspective was important. There were several ways of looking at every situation, and one, too often neglected by big people, was from the underside.

A final consideration was the curious content of Annabelle's remark. She didn't say I had saved her from a nasty bit of work, she said I had saved her from losing her religion.

I had a dim idea of what religion was. We attended the ugly orange brick Episcopal Church on Canal Street most Sundays, where I sat trying to determine the provenance of the big toe protruding from beneath the tablecloth in the mural of the last supper over the altar, and I knew it was my mother's opinion that church services brought out the devil in my sister and me. Religion had to do with Jesus, that incomparable dinner host, who loved children and sheep. At church there were impressive displays of flowers, men in colorful robes, and glazed doughnuts on offer in the assembly hall where the congregants congregated after the service. What was there in all this that could be lost?

I had no one to consult about this question. It was a mystery to be pondered, and I filed it away among others of its kind: the suspicious three-pronged tracks scattered among the roots of the willow in our yard that might have been left by Martians, the accumulating evidence that my dog, Shep, could read my thoughts. Religion, like a coin or a child in a department store, had some intrinsic value and could, in certain dire circumstances, be lost. Such a loss was to be guarded against. I shuddered at this prospect. Was the intensity of my anxiety proof—even then, before I understood the rules—that I knew religion was a devilish test, one I was already doomed to fail?

PARADISE

Our apartment was in a section of New Orleans called Lakeview (now a ghost town of gutted houses, each with a brown waterline above the door) though no part of it came anywhere near Lake Pontchartrain, the beautiful, brackish, tidal, natural wonder that tops the crescent of the Mississippi River like a pot lid, making an island of the city. The lake was lined by a stretch of beach where we were occasionally taken to frolic, but Mother preferred the less raucous, contemplative pleasures of sitting on the seawall. Both of these appealing destinations were in the aptly named Lake Vista. Years later, when I was in high school, an elderly nun with an intact memory told me that there had been a time when Lakeview lived up to its name, and the lake waters came right up to the convent door. The pricy, more elegant Lake Vista had been created by enterprising real estate developers who looked across the shallow waters and saw miles of houses, big houses, with flat green lawns, accessed by a wide, curving boulevard beyond which was a thin patch of green and a concrete seawall. To realize this vision they had dumped acres of river sand into the water. Like everything else in our city, Lake Vista was sinking, but in the meantime one could sit on the seawall and look out at the sailboats. The stairs, which led down beneath the undulating surface of the water, thrilled me. When the tide was out, the lower steps were covered in a dangerous, slippery green slime.

The water we could actually view in Lakeview was in a wide canal that ran down the middle of our street. In the spring or in the fall, when hurricanes came through, this canal overflowed its grassy banks, sending legions of disgruntled crawfish scuttling along the sidewalks. Lakeview was popular with families of modest income because it was close to two schools, one public and one parochial, as well as the vast public park, home of the museum, the Dueling Oaks, and various WPA gardens and statues. Most Lakeview residents owned their plain brick concrete slab houses. The concrete slab was a recent innovation, rapidly replacing the old raised piers that made houses like my grandmother's in the Ninth Ward so irresistible to children and dogs because of the cool understory where no grownups ever intruded. Building lots in Lakeview were small, the houses were close together, but the neighborhood was dotted with verdant empty lots where the grass was as high as my chest, and the impressive roots of old oaks, magnolias, and weeping willows crisscrossed the hard ground like ship ropes tossed out in all directions, creating leaf-strewn and moss-upholstered couches big enough for a child to sprawl upon comfortably in the heat of the day.

The tree roots were inviting, but they couldn't compare with the exhilaration of scrambling up among the rough, graceful branches that lifted me skyward like friendly hands. I knew all the trees that sported makeshift tree houses, platforms patched together from bits of scrap board and nailed right into the tree branches, constructed and abandoned at some earlier period by those strange, belligerent creatures—boys. I could stay in the trees for hours, drinking sugar water from a Girl Scout canteen I'd inherited from my sister, watching bugs and scratching mosquito bites. It was there, in the treetops, that I experienced the first tentative intimations of immortality.

The floor taught humility, patience, observation, but in the trees I had the not original sensation that I was part of something big, and I entertained the possibility that God was in nature in much the same way I was in the world of grownups—invisibly. Like me, animals, trees, grass, rocks, all might have a world of feelings about what was going on, but they had decided to keep quiet about it.

Just how natural is a child's pantheism? How much of it proceeds from a sense of wonder and how much is simply a reflex of self-defense? My passion to be in the trees was not delight; I was not Wordsworth's sturdy babe trailing clouds of glory from his diaper, who rushes into nature in search of "the visionary gleam," though like that boy I felt the shades of the prison house threatening to close about me in our apartment and in the schoolyard. It wasn't a dimly remembered heaven I sought, but rather a haven, not joy, but surcease of anxiety. It seemed to me that if I was not somehow part of the astounding beauty and complexity of nature, I was an exile, as surely as Adam and Eve, once the gates clanged shut behind them, were exiles, doomed to homelessness for eternity.

I knew about Adam and Eve; we'd heard their awful, demoralizing story in Sunday school, where I had volunteered the information that because they had children they must have been married, which observation caused my classmates to titter in a way that left me red with shame. Adam and Eve had had it all: they could talk to animals, the weather was always good, they adored each other, no quarrels, no in-laws, blissful ignorance, one forbidden tree. And then because a snake suggested there might be something worth knowing, because Eve was curious, the Creator was so outraged that the whole human race had to suffer for it forever, cast out of his garden, but not out of his sight, not out of his mind. And they must suffer, suffer, suffer, for generations; men must toil to find food and shelter, women must endure the agony of childbirth. An important feature of this story, in my childish imagination, was the immediate cancellation of the animal language fluency compact. On one side of the gate Adam and Eve could talk with animals, on the other they could not. For some reason animals behaved differently after the expulsion as well, the lion and lamb no longer lying down together. The food chain must have come into being in that literally fatal moment, man and beast hurled into the wild, scrambling over one another to get to the top.

Everything about this story is hateful, yet I absorbed it as most children do, as if it actually explained something about the world I was living in. It was a fallen world; disobedience and curiosity of a rather minor order were what God could not tolerate. Once we had lived in paradise, also called Eden, which was an earthly garden where we had been innocent, ignorant, and happy, but now there was no possibility of going home. Jesus, by his suffering and death, had opened new gates to a heavenly mansion, which was not paradise, though the same word was sometimes applied to both. Heaven is a kind of paradise, but the lost, the original paradise is never conflated with heaven, because, for one thing, Jesus wasn't in the Garden of Eden. His presence, as well as things like streets of gold and ranks of angels, now made heaven the more desirable option.

This was problematic to me. Lying in my tree house, watching a cardinal like a fiery dart streak from one branch to another, making a roly-poly bug curl up with the lightest touch of my finger, catching a vivid green anole, which squirmed itself into a dull brown in my hand, listening to the buzz of the natural world all around me, I knew that if given the choice between the Garden of Eden and heaven, I would take Eden. There are no trees in heaven, and no animals. The sound of angelic voices is unceasing, but one never hears the rain.

I was a timid child, much too anxious to formulate any notion of rebellion or even impatience with the received ideas of the adults who controlled my world. I didn't think to ask why God, who reportedly loved us, would be so unbending, so vengeful and cruel. It didn't occur to me to think, well, then, I don't like this God. I only wished, with all my heart, that I among all others could find a way back to the Garden of Eden. I thought there must be a way, a secret path, perhaps through one of the vacant lots, or down a rabbit hole, or that I might find a cave dripping with silver stalactites at the back of which was a gate. I was always on the lookout for keys. There was nothing in the story to suggest that the garden had gone out of existence. I believed that animals, so evidently beyond reproach and so much more comfortable in the world than people, knew where it was, that if they chose to, they could direct me to Paradise. I still believe this.

Any serious contemplation of nature will lead to the conclusion, as even Wordsworth came to admit, that however much we might wish it so, nature is not a loving mother, or even a very safe environment for a creature without fur. One day while I was climbing an unusually tall, straight tree trunk, which some previous enthusiast had equipped with ascending strips of wood, the handhold pulled loose and I fell from a considerable height for what felt like a long time onto the hard ground, where I lay for many moments unable to draw a breath into my burning chest. I gazed up into the sparkling, lush green of the indifferent treetop with the certain knowledge that I had been betrayed. How could the natural world reject such a loving, faithful child, a good child, who was incapable of killing even a roly-poly bug, who talked to trees every day of her life?

Eventually I got up, brushed myself off, and went in search of a tree I knew to be child-friendly. One tumble didn't do it, but I'd had a glimpse of the void that was available for full-time contemplation if Romanticism ever failed me and I understood why—though their movement was doubtless lateral rather than horizontal—when Adam and Eve were kicked out of the garden that event was described as "the fall."

Valerie Martin

HELLFIRE

When my mother married, she left the Catholic Church and became an Episcopalian, thereby erasing the popish taint that must have horrified my father's staunch midwestern parents, who were lifelong adherents of the Church of England. Mother's conversion was, in her view, a step up socially, a consideration evidently of more consequence to her than the fact that in the eyes of the church she left behind she was now on an elevator straight to hell.

Her parents, whom I called Nana and Papa, didn't share the same religious convictions, so there was a precedent for her defection. Papa had been a German Lutheran, but early in his marriage he had achieved the singular distinction of being excommunicated from the solace of the sacraments. The story was that his pastor had come to dinner and been horrified by Papa's grace before the meal, which comprised the waggish quatrain "We can live without God / we can live without books / but the civilized man / cannot live without cooks."

Nana was a devout Catholic, given to novenas and daily mass. She had raised three children in the church without opposition from her godless husband, whose principal interest in life seemed to be reading the morning paper until the evening paper arrived. Papa didn't object to his wife's rosary, curled enticingly in a glass dish on the nightstand in their bedroom, or to the pictures of Jesus and Mary hanging on the opposite wall, which would have been the first faces he saw every morning of his long married life. I was fascinated by these pictures. They were fabricated of blue and yellow butterfly wings, which gave them a heavenly iridescence. The loving mother and her divine son smiled blandly from the confines of the ebony frames, each pointing at his/her flaming heart. Jesus's heart was wrapped in what looked like barbed wire; Mary had a sword thrust through hers and it was wreathed in puffy clouds. I had seen Jesus hanging from the cross in our church, which was disturbing enough, but this vision of the opened chests, the barbed wire, the sword and flames, the blissful smiles, the extended index fingers commanding the viewer to contemplate the wounded hearts, the eerie serenity in the presence of what should have been mortal agony, all this struck me as both terrifying and appealing.

There were no pictures of Christ's mother in our church, rarely any mention of her in Sunday school, and nothing about the condition of her heart in the liturgy. Jesus, hanging from his cross before the altar, looked pensive, but he didn't appear to be suffering. There was, presumably, agony in hell, but this was never a subject much touched upon in the homilies of Father Clayton, a dapper, white-haired, endlessly cheerful man whom my mother admired; he was her idea of what a clergyman should be—unmarried, charming, a serious gourmand. I spent my time during the service sliding around on the kneeler and lining up the prayer books in the rack so that the black alternated with the red, but now and then I tuned into the sermon and got the good news that there was virtually no one Jesus didn't love, nothing he wouldn't forgive. Santa had a list and an agenda, but Jesus didn't even want us to suffer for the sins we had actually, verifiably committed. He had died so that we wouldn't have to pay that righteous debt. About the only way one could miss going to heaven was to refuse to believe this last bit, that Jesus loved us so much he had been willing to die to spare us eternal suffering.

I liked Jesus for this. I failed to wonder who it was that demanded his sacrifice. The thought that I might be in any danger of eternal perdition didn't occur to me; everyone agreed that Jesus loved children most of all. I was free of anxiety about the next world until I was in second grade, when I was invited to attend church with a school friend who belonged to a very different sort of congregation.

That I had a friend who wanted to spend time with me was something of a miracle, as I was hopelessly inept at striking the right note with the other little girls at my school. I was so nearsighted I had to take my notebook to the front of the room to copy down the foot-high letters on the blackboard. I cried a lot, which put everyone off, including my teachers. My mother gave me my lunch money in the morning and invariably I dropped it somewhere on the four-block walk to school, so that when the teacher called my name to collect it, I looked about myself in horror and burst into tears. This problem was eventually solved by having the three nickels tied up in a handkerchief and pinned to my skirt, which made me the subject of ridicule by those eager to ferret out weakness, so at lunch money–collection time, as I sat at my desk solemnly untying the knot of my shame, I still cried. There was always, daily, some fresh failure, some humiliation, some mild criticism that would send me into a fit of weeping. I cried when another little girl's picture of a bluebird was chosen over mine to decorate the bulletin board. I cried nearly every day on the playground, because I was not chosen for games. I cried every week at my piano lesson. The only place I didn't cry, as my mother observed in a tone rich with the approbation of stoicism that was the hallmark of my family, was at the dentist's, where I sat patiently beneath the drill, my mouth open as wide as I could get it, while my cavity-prone teeth were packed with iron.

Gail, for some reason—perhaps she was sadistic and enjoyed watching me cry—was not put off by my weeping. I don't remember how or why I came to think of her as a friend. I was invited to her house, which was near our apartment, on my way home from school, where her mother served us Oreos and milk. Then she came to our apartment and my mother, caught up in the novelty of it all, actually baked chocolate chip cookies and waited upon us at the kitchen table. There was an overnight at our house, which included a visit to church. That was when Gail told me she was a Baptist and I gathered that being allowed to attend our church was something of a stretch for her parents. After the service, as we munched our doughnuts in the assembly hall, I asked Gail what she thought of the proceedings. "Too much kneeling," she said. "I thought I was going to faint."

Reciprocity being in the definition of friendship, I was forthwith invited to spend the night at Gail's and to join her family at their church on the following morning. Nothing in this overnight left an impression upon me. I have only a dim memory of Gail's unremarkable parents; her house was like all the others, though I suspect it was pathologically clean. Gail herself lives in my memory as curly haired, pushy, confident. The dinner was probably Salisbury steak, that rubbery staple of the fifties; the car, in which we were driven to the Baptist Church, roomy and stolid, a Plymouth or a Dodge.

Mother had told me that I would find the church service very different from that with which I was familiar. "I don't care for it," she said. "It's all hellfire and brimstone." She didn't explain how she knew this; it seemed to be a statement of common knowledge, and her observation was so offhand that I didn't register it as a warning.

As we entered the unimposing white frame building that housed the church, I was more curious than apprehensive. Inside, everything was bright, salubrious rather than sinister. There was no stained glass and the sunlight streamed through the tall windows so forcefully I could see the dust motes whirling in the air. The floor was a light wood, varnished to a warm glow. There was a cross at the front, but Jesus wasn't on it and, oddest of all, there were no kneelers between the plain pine pews. We took our seats nearer to the front than my mother would ever have agreed to sit, and after some cheerful conversation among the congregants, who drifted in and found their places, the priest, dressed in an ordinary suit and tie, unannounced by a choir, unattended by altar boys, appeared upon the altar and the service began.

There were prayers, not the ones I knew, a hymn I'd never heard before. Money was collected by the passing around of wooden ewers, just as in our church. My mind wandered, as it always did. I tried not to look at Gail, who sat primly at my side, her hands folded in her lap. The priest, who was not, I later learned, called a priest but a preacher, stepped up behind the podium. He breathed in haughtily, as if testing the air for suspicious odors. He read a passage from the book on the lectern, pressing his index finger hard into the page, stressing certain words, lingering over this one, bearing down on that one in a way that struck me as silly, like playacting. I felt a strong desire to get farther away from him, but that was impossible. He closed his eyes and bowed his head over the open book. Then he cleared his throat and launched into his sermon.

What was the import of the tirade he poured out upon his audience? There was talk of Christ's suffering, of the blood "gushing" from his wounds and pouring down over his eyes, blinding him, so that "all he could see was blood." Blood was a two-syllable word, a scary word. The notion of our unworthiness was introduced, of the likelihood that our faith was weak, and there was a long description of the torment that awaited us unless we changed right now, this minute, turned from our wickedness, opened our hardened hearts, cleansed our souls, which were rotten with sin, stinking in the Lord's nostrils, and accepted our savior.

I knew that adults were capable of sudden, inexplicable anger; it was not the first time anyone had yelled at me. But I had never seen a man in such a prolonged rage, and it was incomprehensible to me that the congregation did nothing to stop him. My palms were damp, my back wet where it was pressed against the pew, as if I were being blasted by a hot wind. The preacher's face reddened, his eyes bulged, his mouth contorted, spitting out the words with such vehemence that he lifted up onto his toes and clung to the podium for balance. I sneaked a look at Gail, who was fiddling with the sash of her dress, and at her parents, who attended to the fury of their spiritual leader with bright interest, like good students. A dull terror suffused my senses and I went under, allowing the rest of the sermon to flatten me like the one-ton weight that fell on the cat in the Tom and Jerry cartoon I'd seen at the movies. I thought it would never end. It was very like the hell the preacher threatened us with, a place where we would thirst and burn for eternity—did we know how long that was? Eternity, he warned us, was without end, without time; as much as we might try to imagine a million years and multiply it by a million times a million, eternity was much longer than that. By that time eternity would have hardly gotten started, our sufferings would have barely commenced.

Mercifully we weren't yet in eternity. The preacher reached his peroration and even those of us who were damned got a temporary reprieve. He closed his book, folded his hands, and invited us to join him in the safe harbor of bland recitation.

Afterward, when we were back at Gail's house, she asked me what I thought of the service. "It was all hellfire and brimstone," I said confidently. She took this comment in silence and the morning passed uneventfully. My mother came to pick me up; there was an exchange of pleasantries at the door. Off we went, back to the apartment.

The church visit had been disconcerting, but the repercussions of it turned out to be truly harrowing. When I approached Gail the next morning in the school foyer where the little girls all gathered before the bell to best each other in fiercely competitive rounds of jacks, she turned her back on my greeting and walked away. It was the first time I had ever been publicly "cut," but the cut was so firmly and skillfully executed that I knew it would be pointless to pursue her. At recess I tried again, halfheartedly, to engage her in a stroll to the oak near the fence where another set of Martian footprints was available for inspection; again she turned away. At the end of the day I went to our usual meeting place, the last pole on the covered walkway, but she wasn't there. I looked across the wide avenue where our chain-smoking traffic guard herded the skittish, gaggling flocks of children between the yellow lines. I spotted Gail's pink jacket, her termagant curls, already on the far sidewalk. She was laughing at some remark, doubtless about me, with Lauri Damity, a girl everyone agreed was popular, fun to know. I waited until Gail was out of sight, joined a few late stragglers at the curb, and walked home as I had been accustomed to do before those heady weeks of having a friend, by myself.

I was mystified by Gail's quixotic rejection of me, but I did not, at first, connect it to anything I had said or done. She had dropped me, I concluded, for reasons as impervious to comprehension as those for which she had taken me up. I had wanted to please her and failed, just as I wanted to please anyone who showed an interest in me—my teacher, my classmates, my parents, my piano teacher, my dog—and I had failed with Gail as I failed with all the others—except my dog. This failure with Gail was regrettable, but I didn't feel particularly hurt, as I understood it to be in the nature of things. In truth, being friends with Gail had been a tremendous strain. As I walked along the familiar sidewalk, my poor brain, which wandered in a kind of waking dream when unencumbered by the compulsion to please someone, went on a tear. I was back in the luxurious hum and throb of the natural world, more creature than little girl, unconcerned with the past or the future, dawdling comfortably in the present.

For a few days Gail's sudden absence from my limited scene went unnoticed, but it was my turn for the milk and cookies and by the end of the week my mother noticed that I had made no mention of the obligation. I didn't think Gail could come, I said, wishing that would be the end of it, but of course it wasn't. If I'd had any sense I would have said I didn't really like Gail, but that never occurred to me and, after some persistent questioning, I revealed that Gail no longer spoke to me, that she didn't want to be my friend.

For some reason this annoyed my mother. She didn't doubt that I had done something wrong. With the skill of an inquisitor she probed the vulnerable chinks in my pathetic defenses and concluded that I had said something rude about Gail's church. I tearfully denied this charge, but ultimately, pressed for my exact words, I gave in and confessed that I had repeated what Mother herself had observed, that the service had been "all hellfire and brimstone."

Mother was appalled. How could I have been so stupid? Didn't I know how sensitive people were about their religion? It was no surprise that Gail wanted nothing to do with such a dolt as me. Mother only hoped Gail had not reported my outrageous comment to her parents.

For a long time I refused to believe that my remark was really the cause of Gail's rebuff. I couldn't imagine anyone being so petty and oversensitive. After all, she had told me my religion required "too much kneeling" and I had not thought a thing about it. When school was out I found another friend, a neighbor named Karen, who lived only a few doors from our house. With a great deal of encouragement Karen even summoned the courage to join me in my treetop adventures. One day toward the end of summer, as we shared a butter-and-sugar sandwich in our leafy bower, the subject of Gail came up and I expressed my incredulity at the abruptness of our breakup. Karen, having heard the story from the girl who was now "best friends" with Gail, knew all about it. "Gail was real upset," Karen explained, "because of something you said about her church."

In the fall Gail was not in my class and I ceased caring about her, but the impression left upon me by the enraged preacher didn't fade. It was his Herculean effort to describe the duration of eternity that troubled me. He hadn't thought it sufficient to say that the pain or pleasure that awaited us in the next world would last forever, or even forever and ever, as the Kingdom, the Power, and the Glory were said to last in the Lord's Prayer. He had felt the need to demonstrate to his congregation that they could not calculate how long eternity would last, that it was beyond arithmetic, beyond comprehension, beyond reason. Though our offenses to the divine will were committed in real time, which had a limited duration—a hundred years or so was something I could imagine—we would pay for these crimes for eternity. This world was transitory, but the next one was not.

I didn't know the word transitory, but I knew what a bus trip was and it seemed to me that, in this preacher's scheme, we were all on one together, those bound for paradise and those bound for hell, and only the driver knew which passengers were going where. Once a week I took a bus to my piano teacher's house in the company of my sister, a trip of about two miles down Canal Boulevard, another misnamed street, as there was no canal anywhere near it. My sister always handled the fare, so there was no anxiety about losing it. The windows were open; the bench seats were dark blue vinyl, wide and comfortable. I liked the bus. One of my running fantasies was that there would be a prize for the best-behaved child and this would, of course, be me. Sometimes the bus was crowded with black women, domestics going home from their jobs. There was a movable sign with wooden dowels on either end, designed to fit into holes in the rail at the back of each row of seats. This sign read FOR COLORED PATRONS ONLY. Anyone, black or white, was free to move the sign back or forth, but I knew we were always to sit in front of it. Sometimes the sign moved steadily forward as we made our stops, until we were sitting across the aisle from people of color, but as long as we were still in front of the sign on our aisle, this was allowed. I imagined the heaven/hell–bound bus might have a similar arrangement, a constantly shifting designator of those God loved and those he condemned to perdition. It occurred to me that near the end of the line a battle might break out among the passengers, everyone fighting for a seat on the right side of the sign. This was the contest I pictured whenever I heard the expression "all hell will break loose."

Trial of the Satellite
or
How My Great-great-great-grandfather Almost Lost His Virginity on His Fifteenth Birthday

Robert Antoni

WILLY'S MIND TRAVELED BACK across the sea to England, to the day of his fifteenth birthday—7 May 1845—the day of his family's excursion to Oxfordshire for the first trial of the Satellite. Since his father had been sacked at the paper manufactory several months before, normally his mother woke his three sisters at Dyers' first bell, and they were dressed and out the door an hour before Willy and his dad even stirred from their beds. But this morning it was his father who roused them all at the dawn, singing with excitement—*Merzeedotes and dozee-dotes!*—which the rest of the family listened to with a mixture of pleasure and mild revulsion, everybody hustling to get ready. Today was a self-declared half holiday for all members of the Tropical Emigration Society. It felt like Boxing Day!

The event had already been postponed three times. For the enthusiastic members of the new society, the delays were unbearable. Yet Mr. Etzler remained perfectly calm and unconfuffled. His machine had already proved itself in the purest of languages: mathematical calculation. What need of a trial? To pander to the insecurities of suspicious, boorish blockheads? unreasoning blabbermouths? Those men and women guilty of nothing less than mental sloth, the foulest sin to afflict the human race since Adam and Eve were expelled from their Garden. Mr. Etzler challenged all English people to examine before they judged, lest they pass up the greatest opportunity ever presented to them for some other less-deserving nation to seize upon. Lest they be labeled fools and idiots. Mr. Etzler challenged anyone to find an error among his observations and computations. He defied them. Experience, observable facts, could not be questioned. Numbers, unlike slippery words, did not lie.

Due to the unflagging energy of his principal devotee, Mr. Stollmeyer, Etzler's Satellite and Naval Automaton (his universal water machine, which harnessed the immense power of our ocean's waves) were now patented in five countries: Great Britain, the United States, France, Belgium, and Holland. Mr. Etzler had no time for such trifling matters himself. He had no need for personal gain, want of self-protection. His ideas were freely given. They were offered up unflinchingly to the whole of humanity without a single thought or hope of recompense, since any gratification in the unsavory ways of *this* world—monetary reward—would surely sully the magnitude of his grand gesture. What Etzler offered to every English man and woman was Free Entrance to the Lost Garden. Not the flawed Biblical Garden of our first ancestors. But a Perfect Paradise transformed by the powers of Nature—ordered, subdued, stripped of all wildness and danger. A return to innocence *and* knowledge, where Science alone—not privilege or birthright, want or fear of want—dictated the destiny of human beings. But only to those who chose to follow in his lead. Only for those who sought to save themselves. It was all so easy, simple, clear. Let them *believe!*

Willy's mother, Elizabeth, had sewn large egg-shaped patches of a particularly gaudy gold-plaid material over the knees of his church trousers. Because he'd ripped a hole in the right elbow, she'd stitched matching patches onto the elbows of his jacket as well. She'd made him a gold-plaid cap that Willy detested, but felt he had to wear out of obligation. As he dressed himself, including his celluloid collar and tie, Willy couldn't decide if he looked more like a scarecrow or a clown. His sister knocked on his door and entered with an exasperated expression on her face. Georgina retrieved her only pair of high-heel shoes, the ones she wore to church, which she found hidden beneath his bed. A second later Mary charged in, smiling like a hyena, and she got down on her knees to reach beneath his mattress and rescue her pink bloomers.

She ran out giggling—

"Georgie *said* they was under there!"

Breakfast was tea with milk and honey and a package of shortbread biscuits they'd all been eyeing on the shelf now for three days, purchased by his father. Willy knew the biscuits were an extravagance that did not exactly meet with his mother's approval. But she said nothing. And this morning, despite herself, she was smiling with the rest of them—all crowded around the kitchen table lit by a single candle—busy picking up crystals of granualted sugar and shortbread crumbs from her plate with the moistened tip of an index finger.

Neither was Willy's mother pleased to see her husband get up from the bench and take a pint bottle of whiskey out of the cupboard, obviously purchased in anticipation of the day's event, too, which he tucked into a pocket of his jacket. But she said nothing.

"Liz," he reasoned, "the gin palace'll milk us at double price."

"Then you'll have no reason to visit it." She looked at him. "*D'accord!*" she said, slipping into her native French.

His father awarded Amelia the extra biscuit, which she divided between her two sisters and Moffie, her rag doll, who came along for the trip to Oxfordshire, too. Tucker senior blew out the candle. The family got up and gathered their belongings. They followed him single file, up the stairs to the street, into the gray morning light.

As they filed past their borough's ancient oak tree and the vagrants lined up before it, each waiting his turn, little Amelia pinched her nostrils at the stench. Willy watched his father pause and turn long-ingly toward the tavern across the street. Men had begun to gather in the yellow gas-lit warmth inside. Willy recognized a handful of them as his father's friends, also Chartists and members of the society. He heard the raspy excitement in their sleepy voices. Suddenly Willy could taste the faintly nauseating, smoky sweetness of whiskey in his mouth—but surely his father would never allow him to drink alcohol in front of his mother and sisters? In any case Elizabeth, her brow furrowed, had already taken hold of her husband's shoulders to turn him around, shoving him gently in the direction of the station.

They'd take the local to Victoria, where they'd meet up with Mr. Powell and the Whitechurches, then the Oxfordshire line to Bicester. *The Morning Star*, official organ of Etzler and the TES—now a biweekly journal in its seventh number—had printed diagrams, descriptions, and explanations of the Satellite and its seemingly supernatural capabilities. The journal also detailed the machine's "connective apparatus," a series of ropes and rods by which the power would be transferred from some fixed place or "prime mover"—the crank of a "perpetual artificial reservoir" consisting of windmill-driven water buckets poured over a wheel or, preferably, a thundering tropical waterfall or river. This apparatus communicated with a "central drum" of three meters in diameter in the middle of the Satellite's "orbit," about which the ropes were wound and con-nected in turn to the machine's main vibratory beam, shifting it to and fro, to and fro; this oscillatory action driving (by way of a ratchet and "universal sprocket") the machine's single front wheel or shaft of 2.5 meters in length, armed with giant pyramid-shaped daggers that protruded and pierced sharply into the ground: thus the Satellite advanced inexorably over the earth.

Etzler had provided for every foreseeable detail. Even friction and sagging: "The ropes from the prime mover to the central drum travel upon pulleys and rollers to diminish friction and abrasion, and from the drum to the Satellite they are held suspended in the air by specialized cars with poles of bammboo [sic], so that they may be extended to a very great distance, yet still keeping from the ground."

For the purposes of the trial, however, the power to drive the Satellite would be supplied by a steam locomotive of twenty-seven horses' power graciously loaned to the TES by Dr. Edward King of Blackhorn, a speculative capitalist won over by Etzler to his cause. This small locomotive had, until recently, been in service transporting light goods and produce between the outlying boroughs and central London. Dr. King also made available to the society his estate located near Bicester, a property of eleven square acres—appropriately christened, three months previously in the *Star,* as "Satellite Field." The journal had reported the progress, over the past months, of the Satellite's construction by Mr. Franklin Tedium, the engineer contracted by the society. Also of the various difficulties met by Mr. Frank (as he was popularly known) in interpreting Etzler's plates and instructions. This, in particular, caused distressing setbacks, since each time the engineer ran into a roadblock he would have to wait several days, or in some cases weeks, for an indignant and piqued Etzler to return from some distant place in England or Europe where he had gone to lecture on the advantages of tropical emigration, then to clear up "Frank Simpleton's silly little conundrums."

Needless to say, a number of fiercely heated rows had erupted between the two headstrong men, with many bruised sentiments, causing further delays. In fact, it was due to the good-natured intervention of Willy's dad and Mr. Powell that the two gentlemen still spoke to each other a-tall.

Because of his extensive knowledge and practical experience in a number of areas—including the cultivation of food crops from his years spent as a farmer on the Isle of Wight, and the general principles of engineering after his years overseeing production at the paper manufactory—Willy's dad was enlisted as the enthusiastic, officially appointed assistant to Mr. Frank. For this reason he traveled almost daily from their home in the outskirts of south London to Mr. Frank's shop in Bicester. This assistance, of course, Willy's dad offered to the society gratis. On some of his trips to Bicester he was accompanied by Mr. Powell. On some of them, Willy's dad did not return home for three days in succession. Then he'd fall into bed in a kind of exhausted delirium, only to sleep without interruption for another three days—a circumstance that caused a certain amount of friction between Willy's parents. Until his mother decided to make an investigative journey to Bicester herself, unannounced, where she discovered the doors swinging on their hinges and the shop vacant, the disassembled Satellite like a heap of scrap iron abandoned and left to rust, and Willy's father, Mr. Powell, and Mr. Frank stone drunk in the pub down the street. This very nearly put an end to his father's participation in the construction project, and it certainly prevented Willy's mother from granting permission for him to accompany his father to Bicester.

During those intervening months since Willy and his dad had gone with the Whitechurches to Manchester to attend Mr. Etzler's lecture to the ironmongers, and to meet him and Mr. Stollmeyer for the first time, Willy's hormonal imbalance had threatened to overspill its zenith. He sought new ways to enhance his pleasures, inexplicable even to himself. That same night, on their train journey home from Manchester, Willy had stolen Mrs. Whitechurch's copy of the inaugural issue of *The Morning Star*. He intended to study its pages further, and he did pull them out and leaf through them absentmindedly from time to time. But suddenly one evening, in a vaps (the journal had sat untouched with the dustballs beneath his bed for over a week), he nailed the *Star*'s cover page with Mr. Etzler's image to the wall at the foot of his bed. Willy discovered a distinct satisfaction in perfecting his aim.

The other things that occurred during those months seemed, by Willy's own admission, even more strange and incomprehensible, and he could not say how in particular they related to Mr. Etzler. Willy took to pilfering his sisters' undergarments—Georgina's brassiere, Mary's bloomers with the little pink bows at the hips. He ransacked his mother's trousseau and stole her tattered "French" garter and a pair of moth-eaten silk stockings from her wedding gown. Willy borrowed Georgina's only pair of high-heel shoes, the ones she wore to Sunday Mass. He pinched a bit of Cashmere powder, some rouge, a broken lipstick. Hidden in his room, with the aid of a flickering candle and his mother's tiny makeup mirror, his hand trembling with excitement, Willy would paint his face. He'd don the stolen undergarments. Then he'd whack off.

Willy's frenzy seemed to grow in intensity with each occurrence. Again, Georgina was the first intruder.

Willy was meant to be studying for a maths exam. But with the growing inevitability of his family's sailing for the island of Trinidad at the shortest notice, counted among the first history-making "pioneers" of the new society (whether they'd cross the Atlantic by conventional "hollow" ship or be whisked across in three or four days' time on one of Mr. Etzler's "floating islands" was not yet clear), the little fervor he had once mustered for his studies now waned altogether. What could his schoolbooks or his masters possibly say that would in any way relate to the world that awaited him? What had they experienced beyond the ancient and exhausted shores of England? Had any of *them* eaten a banana?

His sister entered Willy's room quietly one evening to call him to dinner, just in time to dodge the carefully aimed, arching projectile of his youthful jism. This time she found no open books spread dutifully on the bed around him. This time it was not the disproportion of the toetee held in his hand that so startled Georgina. She stood at the foot of his bed, breathless, eyes wide as saucers.

"Fuck Jesus, Joseph, and Mary!" she swallowed. "My brother's a flaming poofter!"

Georgina's eyes shifted from the spectacle of Willy's six-foot, severely bony body clad in nothing more than her own brassiere and high-heel shoes, Mary's pink-bowed bloomers, and a tatty garter and stockings he'd gotten from who knows where—his hideously painted face—to the frightful image nailed to the wall beside her:

◈

Victoria Station was pandemonium. Willy's family followed his father's lead, squeezing each other's hands (including Amelia's rag doll, Moffie), so as not to lose one of them on the crowded platform. They weaved their way like a string of squid, back and forth among the excited, shouting passengers, everybody moving toward the Bicester train. Meanwhile Willy's father searched in vain for Mr. Powell and the Whitechurches.

According to the most recent issue of the *Star*, the TES expected extensive crowds to be on hand for the trial. Two large grandstands of scaffolding and wood benches had been erected for the spectators at Satellite Field, as though for a parade. The *Star* promised all comers a "rural feast," with ample "creature comforts." There were sure to be food and drink stands (including, according to Willy's dad, the gin palace and several beer booths). Mr. Etzler could not be present himself for the trial (he was at that moment in Scotland attending to more important business—lecturing to the society's recently formed branch in Aberdeen, where, astonishingly, several hundred new shares had already been taken up). But he did send his advices in a hand-delivered memo to Mr. Stollmeyer—printed, perhaps by oversight, in the *Star*—who would indeed be present to supervise the event. Mr. Etzler suggested that with a bit of ingenuity, the trial might be turned into a "lucrative money-making venture," which he agreed to split "fifty-fifty with the society."

He suggested charging an admission price of sixpence for all spectators coming on foot, and at least a shilling for those rich enough to arrive by carriage. Etzler was vehement that "even members of the society could and should be made to pay the full price to see my Satellite in action" (regardless of the fact that the members legally *owned* the machine, as it had been constructed with the society's funds). The use of the Satellite to perform "work," he stipulated, as agreed upon in the bylaws drawn up by the TES, was a very different matter from the "spectacle of a demonstration for pleasure purposes." In any case, regardless of the questionable legality of the situation, Mr. Stollmeyer printed up a number of placards on his press at the Strand office. He posted them himself in Bicester, and Bradford, and throughout the Oxfordshire area, as well as in other places where they would draw ample attention, including Victoria Station.

Willy was the first to notice one of these very placards, posted just beneath the #3 of the Bicester platform:

NOTICE TO THE PUBLIC:

The mighty "Iron Slave," or **SATELLITE,**
invention of Mr. J.A. Etzler,
will be seen in full operation,
on May 7th at 8:30 AM in "Satellite Field" at Bicester,
capable of performing these & more
extraordinary & here-to-for unheard-of feats:

1. PLOWING
(1 acre in 4 minutes; 360 acres per day)
2. RIPPING OUT GIANT TREES
BY THEIR ROOTS
3. INSTANTLY PULVERIZING BOULDERS
(of 3-5 tons)
4. MOWING DOWN HILLS & MOUNTAINS
5. SAWING TIMBER, STONE & STEEL BEAMS
6. DIGGING TRENCHES, CANALS & LAKES

ADMISSION:
sixpence for pedestrians
1 shilling for those arriving by horse

REFRESHMENTS WILL BE SOLD!!!

A handful of TES members, who had at some point belonged to the military, dressed themselves in full regalia and brought along their rusty muskets so that a volley of shots might be fired to announce the "takeoff" of the Satellite. Another group, dressed also in unrelated military garb, formed a band that included a large bass drum, a couple of snares, a tuba, cymbals, flute, trombone, several bugles, a French horn, and a triangle played with great concentration and delicacy by an obese former member of the Royal Guard. According to rumor, they had met at the Crossed Sabers Tavern, near Victoria, early the previous evening. They had just left this facility, having spent the entire night "synchronizing." Needless to say, the majority of them were having difficulty not only blowing into their instruments, but remaining on their feet. The "Satellite Ensemble," as they dubbed themselves, happened to ride in an open car adjacent to the one the Tucker family traveled in for their journey to Bicester.

The ensemble provided a welcomed distraction for Willy's sisters, who went forward to listen. And as the train departed the station with a loud cheer, Mary led Amelia in a waltz, much to the enjoyment of the ensemble and several onlookers. Meanwhile, in their compartment, Willy's mother dozed, despite the grating music and the noisy locomotive. This enabled Willy and his dad, both smiling mischievously, to sneak a few furtive nips of whiskey. Until Mr. Powell arrived, red faced and smiling, and his father collected up his papers, which included several oversized, dog-eared illustrations of the Satellite, tied in a roll with a piece of twine. The two men left for some other part of the train to examine the drawings and discuss the day's event, and no doubt to polish off his dad's bottle.

The Satellite Ensemble broke into another waltz that was so speeded up, it sounded like a polka.

For a time Willy found himself sitting alone with his mother. She no longer slept. In her lap she held a wicker basket containing the cheese-and-tomato sandwiches she'd made for their lunch, since the victuals offered at the food venues were sure to be priced out of their range. Willy suspected that she could smell the alcohol on him. He held his breath, his face reddening.

Suddenly Willy produced a loud, whiskey-smelling belch—

"*Berrrupt!*"

His mother looked at him—

"I'm expecting decent manners from you today, William," she was practically shouting to make herself heard over the band and the chugging train. "You're advised *not* to model your behavior after these gentlemen, including your father, *comprend?*"

Willy nodded.

The ensemble ended their waltz with a great bash of cymbals.

"Ah, *finalement!*" His mother shifted her basket to the seat beside her. "I'm going to check on your sisters."

Now, despite the overcrowded train, Willy had the compartment all to himself. His intention was to move aside his sisters' coats and bags and other belongings, the basket of sandwiches, and stretch out on the seat—maybe he'd catch a few minutes' sleep before they arrived in Bicester?—when the small bottle of whiskey tumbled out of his father's jacket, neatly folded over the armrest.

In a matter of minutes it was half empty—Willy could not be sure how much he and his father had previously consumed—when he decided the safest thing was to recork the bottle and tuck it into his own jacket, buttoning the pocket securely.

The ensemble started in to some species of military march—

um-pa-pa um-pa-pa

Willy stretched himself out on the seat. He shut his eyes, smiling, content, waiting for the whiskey to take over. Before long, despite himself and his situation, involuntarily, Willy began rubbing his hard toetee beneath the crotch of his trousers.

For inspiration he tried to picture Georgina's budding tot-tots, beneath her thin nightgown, which he had caught a glimpse of that morning as she bent down to reach under his bed. But what Willy now envisioned looked terrifying—like a rack of medieval torture. For a moment he imagined himself stretched out across it:

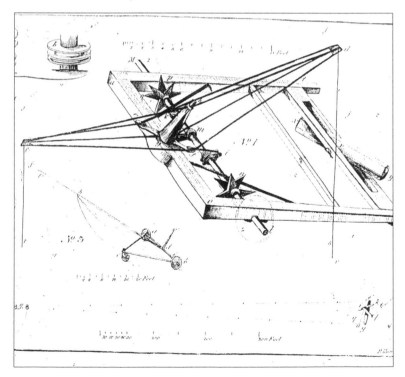

◈

Suddenly Willy felt the compartment door bang open against his leg.

"Here's a healthy lad!"

Mrs. Whitechurch entered wearing a brightly colored cloak and bonnet, despite the relatively warm weather. She looked to Willy like Little Red Ridinghood, though Mrs. Whitechurch was her grandmother's age.

"I can see we've caught you in the midst of your morning exercise!"

Willy sat up—startled, embarrassed—but not by Mrs. Whitechurch. He blinked his eyes, unsure whether he was sober or drunk, awake or dreaming.

"Willy," said Mrs. Whitechurch. "Please make the acquaintance of my dear niece, Juliette. I told you all about her, remember?"

He nodded.

"The two of you have got *so* much in common," she said. "You're going to get along splendidly, I've no doubt a-tall!"

Willy struggled to order his thoughts. Though absurd, Mrs. Whitechurch still believed that he was "mildly retarded," thus the anticipated camaraderie with her niece. So far as he recalled, Mrs. Whitechurch's niece was thirty years of age; she'd been born with the "downs." Both of which might be perfectly accurate, though Willy could detect no disagreeable *physical* signs of the latter, at least not yet: on the contrary, he had never in his life encountered a woman more strikingly handsome than the one sitting on the bench before him. Not excluding her healthy tot-tots—fairly bursting from the neckline of her sky blue silken blouse—which Willy was compelled to notice as Juliette reached into the crevice of her brassiere to remove the tiniest book, covered in mother-of-pearl, with a similarly sized white pencil tucked into a special pocket of its binding.

Juliette slid out the pencil and dabbed the lead against her tongue. She scribbled something into her book, which she turned toward Willy, smiling—

auntie said you were no mere schoolboy

Willy stared at the page, then up at Juliette, uncomprehending. She flipped the page of her little book, dabbing the pencil—

I was referring to horsie

She nodded toward his lap.

Willy became aware of himself for the first time since Mrs. White-church and her niece had entered his compartment, his toetee standing up unmistakably and rudely against his crotch. He buttoned his coat over it.

"Much obliged," said Mrs. Whitechurch. "Now, I'm going to leave Juliette in your care for a moment, while I go and extract Mr. White-church from the company of your father and Mr. Powell. They're making a pretense of studying their drawings!"

With that, tiny Mrs. Whitechurch shoved herself off the seat. She straightened her bonnet and scampered out the door.

In some ways Willy was less embarrassed by his vulgar display, a moment before, than by the miserable state of his appearance. He deeply regretted the gaudy patches on his tatty suit—a couple of inches too short at his wrists and ankles, pulling at the shoulders, baggy around his chest and waist—inherited from his father. He could feel the silly cap sitting crookedly on his head. Suddenly Willy felt ashamed of the gaping hole in his right boot, with his great toe, clad in its white sock, like a dirty eyeball peering through—those boots had been passed down from his father also. Willy sorely wished he'd have at least polished them.

Juliette's perfume smelled of lavender, though Willy could not have named the flower. He knew only that as he breathed it in, he felt the distinct sensation of tumbling backward through the air. Juliette sat holding her little mother-of-pearl-covered book, its gold tassel to mark the page, neatly in her lap. Her legs were crossed at the knees so that Willy could detect a delicately stockinged calf, caught between a cream-colored ankle boot and the hem of her skirt, a thick mauve weave. She wore a matching cream-colored belt of kid leather around her waist and, draped over her silky sky blue shoulders, a lilac shawl. Her hair was all blond ringlets, gathered loosely with a ribbon behind her neck. Her jaw and cheeks and brow were strong boned, but her full lips and amber eyes seemed to Willy perfectly soft and delicate. Her nose was long, and straight, and strong.

Unlike her aunt and uncle, Juliette was exceptionally tall, and Willy would discover that in her short boots she stood only a couple of inches beneath his own six feet. Later he would detect a jostling limp as they walked together, her arm through his—as though she couldn't quite judge the rise of the ground to meet her left foot.

For a long minute they sat staring at each other, both oblivious to the rocking, chugging train, the rasping *um-pa-pa* of the Satellite Ensemble.

Eventually Juliette dabbed the lead of her pencil against her tongue and scribbled into her book, turning it up for Willy to read—

I want to kiss you too

For several days Mr. Frank, Willy's dad, Mr. Powell, and a number of assistants had been busy setting up for the trial. Mr. Stollmeyer had arrived only the previous afternoon from Bingley. There he had lectured to animated crowds of five to six hundred, demonstrating models of Mr. Etzler's machines. One hundred and fifty new shares of the TES had been instantly grabbed up by the Bingley branch: all was eagerness to depart a wretched republic, enthusiasm for their new and superior tropical home! Yet, despite his fatigue, Mr. Stollmeyer traveled directly from Bingley to Oxfordshire—even bypassing the bank in London, his pockets bursting with cash and coins. And as the first drops of rain began to fall on Satellite Field, he made a detailed examination of all the equipment, declaring everything to be in perfect readiness for tomorrow's trial.

The two grandstands and the food and drink booths had been erected well over a month before. The more important business at hand dealt with the Satellite. Mr. Frank's first and perhaps most arduous task had been to transport the machine—weighing in at slightly more than three tons now that it was fully assembled, without including any of its numerous prescribed attachments—from his mechanic's shop in Bicester to King's field in the outskirts of town, a distance of a mile and a half. Etzler's plans called for "detachable wheels" at each corner of his machine, so that it could "very easily be shifted from place to place with the minor efforts of a single man." But there had been neither sufficient funds nor time to design and make them. Needless to say, without these wheels, the job of moving the obzockee Satellite was somewhat like trying to roll a dead cow, and ten strong men, all straining together, could not budge it. The formidable task was accomplished by hoisting the machine onto a reinforced flatbed car, laying some extra rails, and utilizing Dr. King's small locomotive—the same steam engine that would supply the Satellite's power—to lug it onto the field.

Once the Satellite was moved into position, Dr. King's locomotive was similarly hoisted from its rails. It was then fixed stationary to the ground on a selected spot 120 yards away and at right angles to the "central drum," with the Satellite equidistant on the other side of the field. The earth beneath the two driving wheels of King's engine was dug out so that they turned freely in the air. Then the two half-inch-thick ropes stipulated by Etzler were connected to a crank on each of the wheels. The ropes were then stretched out and wound numerous times around the drum—one clockwise, the other counterclockwise—after which they were suspended another 120 yards and made fast to each arm of the Satellite's main vibratory beam.

The diameter that the machine would travel in a perfect and uninterrupted circle around its "satellite" (the prime mover itself *or* the drum(s), fixed at the exact center of each orbit, depending on how the configuration was laid out) could be varied from twenty yards to sixteen thousand feet, in accordance with how short or long the ropes were made. (One orbit comprised seventy-seven acres; eighteen orbits comprised one "circuit," consisting of fourteen hundred acres; and fifty-five circuits made up a single "dominion," eighty thousand acres in area, which the Satellite would plow—it could simultaneously sift, weed, prepare, and plant if desired—in exactly 206 days.) There was a steering mechanism at the back of the Satellite that Mr. Frank would control with his feet, stepping and applying weight to one side or other of the "rudder," in this way altering the Satellite's course. Attached to the "nose" of the machine were two ropes that Mr. Frank would grasp in each hand to steady himself, rather like a jockey mounted upon his racehorse.

In sum, the genius of Mr. Etzler's highly imaginative theory had been wed to Mr. Frank's sound and dependable practicality:

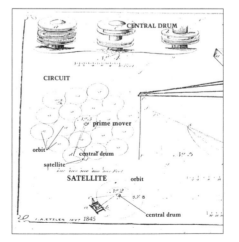

PRACTICAL DEMONSTRATIONS:

UNIT	AREA IN ACRES		TIME REQUIRED (for Satellite to plow & c.)
	1		4 minutes
	15	60/4 =	1 hour
"Orbit"	77	77/15 =	5 hours
	360	15 x 24 =	1 day
"Circuit" (18 Orbits)	1,400	18 x 5 = 90/24 =	3.75 days
"Dominion" (55 Circuits)	80,000	55 x 3.75 =	206 days

Hardly had their lips met when the conductor began clanging his bell, signaling their arrival at Bicester. Willy's three sisters burst into the compartment and began collecting up their belongings, so excited to get off the train that they did not notice their brother and Juliette.

"Willy's got a girl," Amelia said, hurrying toward the landing.

"Don't be silly," Georgina answered.

"But they were kissing," she said. "I know they were!"

"I assure you," Georgina said seriously, "Willy does not have a girlfriend."

"Not if she's wearing a *dress!*" Mary laughed.

Fortunately for all concerned, the uninterrupted rains of the previous night had ceased early that morning for the trial. There were even a few rays of sun sneaking out from behind the clouds as the enthusiastic members of the TES swamped the little country station at Bicester. They spilled shrieking and shouting and *um-pa-pa*ing onto a gravel and sycamore-lined King's Way. By the time the spectators gathered on a pristine, dew-sparkling Satellite Field—swarming from all directions like bees to the hive—they numbered well over eight hundred.

Seeing the enormity of the crowd, and suddenly fearing a revolt of unrestrainable proportions (also taking into consideration that many of the laborers had been drunk for twelve hours already), Mr. Stollmeyer raised to his mouth the large pasteboard cone he'd constructed specially for the occasion. He announced in a loud voice that the entrance fee advertised for the trial would henceforth be dispensed with. His message was answered with a tremendous cheer, accompanied by the firing of several muskets from the volley team who believed, mistakenly, that the Satellite had already taken off.

Women and children filed into the spectator's stands, eager to claim seats while there were some available. They arranged themselves in little groups, spreading blankets across the benches and unpacking their picnic baskets. Counted among these poor, laboring women were even a number of fashionably dressed members of the gentry, accompanied by servants who busied themselves unpacking their mistresses' hampers. Several of these wealthy women had brought along their opera glasses, which they used more to spy on their husbands at the gin palace than to observe the proceedings of the trial. (It was not exactly clear that day whether the Satellite was "the great leveler of society" claimed by Etzler, or the alcohol.) Most of the men, including the volley team and the ensemble, rolled up their trousers and sludged directly onto the still-wet field to inspect the Satellite. Otherwise they hurried over and joined the long queues that had already formed before the palace and the beer booths, the proprietors of which did manage a rip-roaring business, until later in the afternoon when the patrons became so drunk and unruly they tore into the stands with their bare hands and began helping themselves, wrecking one of the beer booths entirely.

Due in part to his nervousness, in part to the whiskey he had consumed, Willy's knee joints seemed to come unfastened the moment they disembarked the train. Coupled with Juliette's limp—the two walking arm in arm, assisting each other—they were quickly left behind by the eager spectators. The pair arrived at Satellite Field a good half hour after the festivities had already reached full swing. But they did not join the others. It was Juliette who spied a private place beneath one of the grandstands, which she directed Willy toward. It was like a secret cave: not only concealed and cozy and relatively dry, but removed from the crowds—all of their shouting and raucous behavior seemed very far away despite the fact that the spectators were perched only a few feet above their heads.

Juliette removed her shawl and spread it on the yellowed grass for them to sit on. Willy wanted to take his jacket off also. Not simply to spread it on the ground in a similar fashion, but suddenly he felt unbearably hot and sweaty. Yet for some reason he felt embarrassed by the half-drunk bottle in his pocket, more so than by his toetee pressing up rudely against his crotch beneath the jacket—though

Juliette would have detected them both long ago. He kept his jacket buttoned up tight.

They sat on Juliette's shawl and she loosened Willy's tie. She carefully unclipped the celluloid collar that constricted like a serpent around his neck. Juliette removed from her purse a silk kerchief that she used to wipe his dripping temples. She kissed him again. Then, with a teasing smile, she took out her little book and wrote—

I've a surprise for you when you get inside

⟡

Although Mr. Stollmeyer deemed it unnecessary, Mr. Frank insisted on disconnecting the ropes from the cranks and checking the locomotive's operation in its new position, before applying power to the Satellite. And with good reason. The engine was stoked and Mr. Frank set the driving wheels slowly into motion. But with the first burst of steam, the spectators on the field, unaware of this preliminary check and believing it to be the official launch of the Satellite, took off running en masse toward the machine—accompanied by a round of shots and a burst of music from the ensemble. When they became aware that the Satellite was unmanned and disconnected, somewhat confused, they took off running again, this time in the direction of Dr. King's locomotive, crowding thickly around it. During this time, however—due to the rains of the previous night and the freshly loosened ground—the moorings fixing the engine in place had become loose, and the machine began to vibrate. It threatened to run out of control, eventually slipping backward from its hold into the trench dug beneath its wheels, by now a fairly deep mire. As a result, a great torrent of mud was churned up and spewed high in the air by the freely spinning wheels, drenching the majority of the crowd head to toe, before Mr. Frank could possibly blow off the steam and shut down the runaway locomotive.

Now the disgruntled, mud-soaked spectators, seeing that there would be a substantial delay before the engine could be remoored and restoked, cursing among themselves, moved off in the direction of the booths and the gin palace.

⟡

It was not yet 10 a.m. when the sun appeared full and strong above Satellite Field. This was fortuitous as it immediately began to dry the sodden grass. Most of the laborers had taken a half-day holiday for the trial, and were required to return to their jobs in the manufactories by noon. At first it had appeared hopeless that the Satellite could be demonstrated in the short time remaining, especially after the initial slippage of Dr. King's engine. But a number of the men quickly removed their jackets and rolled up their shirtsleeves (they were covered in mud anyway), and they set themselves to the task of lifting the locomotive out of its trench—coordinated by the "heave-ho's" called out by Mr. Stollmeyer through his pasteboard cone. The engine was remoored in a new position measured out and decided upon by Mr. Frank and Willy's dad, and in a matter of minutes the laborers dug a fresh trench beneath the locomotive's driving wheels, this time on higher and drier ground. Mr. Stollmeyer put down his cone and descended into the trench himself, and with a bit of improvised ceremony, he fixed the two ropes of the connective apparatus to each of the cranks. Meanwhile Mr. Frank and Willy's dad restoked the engine.

Now the three men took their positions: Mr. Frank at the back of the Satellite wearing a jockey's leather cap and special protective goggles, a rope of the "reins" grasped securely in each hand; Mr. Stollmeyer with his pasteboard cone positioned just behind the drum at midpoint; and Willy's dad with his hand on the gear of King's locomotive. At the predetermined "ready" signal from Mr. Frank, Mr. Stollmeyer called out to Willy's dad so that he could apply power (of the three men only Mr. Stollmeyer had a clear view of Satellite, central drum, and prime mover simultaneously, as Willy's dad and Mr. Frank performed their operations blind to each other).

Of course, with the first blast of steam from the locomotive, several members of the volley team (those still on their feet) shot off their muskets. A burst of music erupted from the ensemble, and the crowd of spectators rushed screaming onto the field again. As agreed, Willy's dad applied the locomotive's power *cautiously.* He watched the two lines of the connective apparatus draw taut and the central drum rotate smoothly several times, back and forth, clockwise and counterclockwise. Several of the onlookers, including Mr. Stollmeyer, actually witnessed the main vibratory beam above Mr. Frank's head jerk roughly back and forth, two or three times, the entire machine lurching forward—as though roaring into life.

This is what Mr. Stollmeyer—by this point beside himself with excitement, his free hand waving madly and long beard blowing in the breeze—attempted to communicate through his cone to Willy's dad, over the mayhem of the spectators. Willy's father, however, misinterpreted Stollmeyer's message and—somewhat overwhelmed by his own emotions—he applied full power.

Now the Satellite gave such a tremendous jolt that Mr. Frank lost his footing at the back of the machine. He was instantly tossed fifteen feet into the air, coming down on the still-vibrating main beam—which he managed to wrap his arms and legs around, hugging the beam like a bear—fighting for his life to hang on. At this same moment a rope of the connective apparatus caught in one of the half-inch pulleys set between the prime mover and the central drum (Mr. Etzler's plans clearly specified pulleys of *one inch,* as he would disdainfully point out later); the rope was instantly severed, whipping past the central drum, and due to all of the excessive coiling, wrapping itself around Mr. Stollmeyer's leg. The rope then began to drag him full pelt on his backside across the still-damp grass, in the direction of the prime mover. Of course several of the laborers, including the obese triangle player from the Satellite Ensemble, seeing Mr. Stollmeyer in danger, threw themselves bodily on top of him as he slid past, hoping to bring him to a halt. As a result not only Mr. Stollmeyer, but an additional three or four men, were dragged half the length of Satellite Field, while Mr. Frank clutched for dear life to the wildly oscillating main beam, before Willy's dad could successfully blow the steam off King's locomotive.

Hidden beneath the stands, Willy and Juliette lay naked in each other's arms, peacefully asleep. She had removed each article of his clothing with the utmost delicacy. But by the time Juliette had gotten to the buttons of Willy's trousers, unfastening them one by one and slipping her warm hand inside to caress it—overwhelmed by his own self-consciousness—Willy's toetee had shrunk to the size of a stumpy fried potato.

Juliette had written then in her little book—

try thinking about something else

Willy had fought to focus on the proceedings outside, but the only thing that came to mind was his rack of torture.

Juliette undressed them both completely, their clothes scattered around them on the yellow grass. She had attempted to soothe his rattled anxieties with the whiskey, until the bottle lay empty beside him. Juliette had tried any number of techniques to coax Willy into a state of relaxed excitement. She had placed one of her tender nipples in Willy's mouth for him to suckle upon. She had taken his stumpy potato wedge between her own warm lips until, in bitter anguish, Willy had begged her to stop.

❁

After another considerable delay, the severed rope was rewound and spliced, the engine restoked, and once again the three men took their positions. Mr. Stollmeyer's cone had been crushed beyond all possible use, so at the signal from Mr. Frank he cupped his palms around his bearded mouth and called out to Willy's dad. The response of the volley team and the ensemble was, this third time around, somewhat delayed, since by now the laborers still remaining into the late afternoon had grown sluggish and drowsy. Nevertheless, before the vibratory beam above Mr. Frank's head could oscillate three times successively, the machine was packed in on all sides by excited, cheering spectators.

Everyone, however, had learned a valuable lesson from Mr. Stollmeyer's buttocks slide earlier in the day, and despite their inebriated state, they were careful to stay clear of the ropes. Willy's father gently applied more power; the central drum rotated smoothly back and forth, clockwise and counterclockwise, and the oscillations of the vibratory beam caused the Satellite's fiercely armed front shaft to turn and rip up the ground.

All were ecstatic, none more than Mr. Stollmeyer, who would recall those exquisite thirty seconds for the rest of his life!

For a half minute the Satellite was even able to achieve its maximum velocity of not quite three miles an hour. But despite the fact that Etzler's long chains of numbers—always growing longer and longer until they threatened to run off the page—had created in the minds of most of the onlookers a fantasy of great *speed*, in reality the machine hardly appeared to make any progress a-tall. On the contrary, a lame donkey could outrun it! So that within a few seconds, perilously, even the most inebriated of the spectators had left the Satellite behind.

Now Mr. Frank, holding tight to the reins (and still frightened out of his wits by his previous catapult and wild ride on the vibratory beam), peered through his goggles at the crowd of drunken, cheering, waving spectators: they had gathered in a thick mob directly in front of him. Exactly in the path of his three-ton machine, its fiercely spiked shaft churning away—threatening to mow them down and grind them to sawdust like so many sturdy oaks! Mr. Frank closed his eyes behind his protective goggles, whispered a quick prayer, and he pounced with all his weight on the right side of the rudder. As a result, the Satellite veered sharply to the left, one of the ropes immediately kinked and snapped, and a thoroughly demoralized Mr. Stollmeyer called out to Willy's dad to blow off the steam.

By the time Willy and his father exited the small neighborhood station in their south London borough to begin their short walk home, the streetlights had been extinguished and it was past midnight. His mother and sisters had returned to Dyers at noon, they'd worked a seven-hour shift, and were now asleep in their beds. Willy carried Juliette's lilac-colored shawl loosely under his arm, though he would not have let it go for all the world. He had awoken still lying on the shawl—naked, cold, and tragically alone—but then he had discovered the tiny slip of paper tucked into his palm—

I shall convince auntie to bring me to the tropics too

Dazed, Willy had dressed himself and stumbled out onto a wrecked Satellite Field, littered with bottles and rubbish. The sun had almost disappeared completely behind the distant line of trees. Only his father, Mr. Powell, and Mr. Frank remained on the field. They were crouching around a flickering lantern in the semidark, still discussing the results of the trial. Willy took a seat beside his father, and he sat there on the trodden grass for a long time, hours it seemed, hugging the shawl against his chest, while the men talked, interrupting their conversation occasionally for one of them to roll out a large dog-eared diagram, take up the lantern, and point out something to the other two. Willy was not listening, and in truth he had no idea whether the trial had been a success or not. The men did not seem upset, though the jubilation they had all exhibited that morning had clearly subsided. Eventually the men got to their feet. Thoroughly exhausted, they collected their jackets and papers and other paraphernalia, and set off in the dark for the country station at Bicester. Willy followed at a short distance.

◈

His father put his arm around Willy's shoulders as they walked home. They did not talk, each taken up by his own thoughts, which were very different. Willy stood with his father before the bar of their local tavern for several seconds before he even realized that they had entered the premises together. Tucker senior made a sign to the proprietor, and two shot glasses of whiskey appeared before them. Willy's father waited for his son to raise his glass. They touched them together, swallowed them back together.

When they stepped out of the tavern, Willy's dad led him across the street to the small triangular park with its ancient oak, approaching the great trunk from behind. The oak's dusty leaves were stirring gently in the breeze, and with the dim light of an unseen moon, they cast faintly mottled shadows across the ground and the two men's backs, father and son. There were no vagrants lined up on the other side of the tree at this hour, yet the odors rising from the gurgling gutter beside them were tremendous. Father unbuttoned his fly, bent forward slightly at the waist to remove himself, then began splashing warm urine against the trunk, a faint smoke rising up, caressing the bark. Son followed suit. The two peed together for a long minute.

Then they stood in silence, another minute, before Willy's father spoke—

"It'll never work," he said distractedly, "this Satellite. I've known it from the beginning. And after today I am more certain than ever."

Something in the way he pronounced *ever*, drawing it out, told Willy that he had not finished.

"It matters not," his father said. "What's important is that we have something to believe in—anything. An *illusion!* What matters is that it's fervent enough to get us someplace else."

Willy's dad stood staring up into the shadowed leaves, pensive, toetee still in hand.

"I haven't forgotten," he said at last. "Happy birthday, Willy."

He looked down at the base of the oak's trunk, then across at his son, smiling for the first time all evening. What his father said then would return to Willy for the rest of his life, a tender sweetness, bitter sting—

"Imagine, son, a year from now, all of us together, we'll celebrate your birthday in the tropics!"

Two Stories
Lydia Davis

REDUCING EXPENSES

THIS IS A PROBLEM you might have someday. It's the problem of a couple I know. He's a doctor, I'm not sure what she does. I don't actually know them very well. In fact, I don't know them anymore. This was years ago. I was bothered by a bulldozer coming and going next door, so I found out what was happening. Their problem was that their fire insurance was very expensive. They wanted to try to lower the insurance premiums. That was a good idea. You don't want any of your regular payments to be too high, or higher than they have to be. For example, you don't want to buy a property with very high taxes, since there will be nothing you can do to lower them and you will always have to pay them. I try to keep that in mind. You could understand this couple's problem even if you didn't have high fire insurance. If you did not have exactly the same problem, someday, you might have a similar problem, of regular payments that were going to be too high. Their insurance was high because they owned a large collection of very good wine. The problem was not so much the collection per se but where they were keeping it. They had, actually, thousands of bottles of good wine. They were keeping it in their cellar, which was the right idea. They had an actual wine cellar. But the problem was, it wasn't good enough or big enough. I never saw their wine cellar, though I once saw another one that was very small. It was the size of a closet, but I was still impressed. But I did taste some of their wine, one time. I can't really tell the difference, though, between a bottle of wine that costs $100, or even $30, and a bottle that costs $500. At that dinner they might have been serving wine that cost even more than that. Not because I was there but because of some of the other guests. I'm sure that very expensive wines are really wasted on most people, including me. I was quite young at the time, but even now a very expensive wine would be wasted on me probably. This couple learned that if they enlarged the wine cellar and improved it in certain other specific ways, their insurance premiums would be lower. They thought this was a good idea, even though it would cost something initially, to make these improvements. The bulldozer and other machinery and labor that I saw out the window of the place where I was living at the time, which was a house borrowed from a friend who was also a friend of theirs, must have been costing them in the thousands, but I'm sure the money they spent on it was earned back within a few years or even one year by their savings on the premiums. So I can see this was a prudent move on their part. It was a move that anyone could make concerning some other thing, not necessarily a wine cellar. The point is that any improvement that will eventually save money is a good idea. This is long in the past by now. They must have saved quite a lot altogether, over the years, from the changes they made. So many years have gone by, though, that they have probably sold the house by now. Maybe the improved wine cellar raised the price of the house and they earned back even more money. I was not just young but very young when I watched the bulldozer out my window. The noise did not really bother me very much, because there were so many other things bothering me when I tried to work. In fact I probably welcomed the sight of the bulldozer. I was impressed by their wine, and by the good paintings they also owned. They were nice, friendly people, but I didn't think much of their clothes or furnishings. I spent a lot of time looking out the window and thinking about them. I don't know what that was worth. It was probably a waste of my time. Now I'm a lot older. But here I am, still thinking about them. There are a lot of other things, important things, that I've forgotten. I haven't forgotten them or their fire insurance. I must have thought I could learn something from that.

BURNING FAMILY MEMBERS

First they burned her—that was last month. Actually just two weeks ago. Now they're starving him. When he's dead, they'll burn him too.

Oh, how jolly. All this burning of family members in the summertime.

It isn't the same "they," of course. "They" burned her miles thousands of miles away from here. The "they" that are starving him here are different.

Wait. They were supposed to starve him, but now they're feeding him.

They're feeding him, against doctors' orders?

Yes. Yesterday we said, let him die. The doctors advised it.

He was sick.

He wasn't really sick.

He wasn't sick, but they wanted to let him die?

He had just been sick, he had had pneumonia, and he was better.

So he was better and that was when they decided to let him die?

Well, he was old, and they didn't want to treat him for pneumonia again.

They thought it was better for him to die than get sick again?

Yes.

Then, at the rest home, they made a mistake and gave him his breakfast. They must not have gotten the doctors' orders. They told us, "He's had a good breakfast!" Just when we were all prepared for him to start dying.

All right. Now they've got it right. They're not feeding him anymore.

Things are back on schedule.

He'll have to die sooner or later.

He's taking a few days to do it.

It wasn't certain he would die before, when they gave him breakfast. He ate it. They said he enjoyed it! But he's beyond eating now. He doesn't even wake up.

So he's asleep?

Well, not exactly. His eyes are open, a little. But he doesn't see any-

109

thing—his eyes don't move. And he won't answer if you speak to him.

But you don't know how long it will take.

A few days after that, they'll burn him.

After what?

After he dies.

You'll let them burn him.

We'll ask them to burn him. In fact, we'll pay them to burn him.

Why not burn him right away?

Before he dies?

No, no. Why did you say "a few days after that"?

According to the law, we have to wait at least forty-eight hours.

Even in the case of an innocent old professor?

He wasn't so innocent. Think of the testimony he gave.

You mean, if he dies on a Thursday, he won't be burned until Monday.

They take him away, once he's dead. They keep him somewhere, and then they take him to where he'll be burned.

Who goes with him and keeps him company once he's dead?

No one, actually.

No one goes with him?

Well, someone will take him away, but we don't know the person.

You don't know the person?

It will be an employee.

Probably in the middle of the night?

Yes.

And you probably don't know where they'll take him either?

No.

And then no one will keep him company?

Well, he won't be alive anymore.

So you don't think it matters.

They will put him in a coffin?

No, it's actually a cardboard box.

A cardboard box?

Yes, a small one. Narrow and small. It didn't weigh much, even with him in it.

Was he a small man?

No. But as he got older he got smaller. And lighter. But still, it should have been bigger than that.

Are you sure he was in the box?

Yes.

Did you look?

No.

Why not?

They don't really give you an opportunity.

So they burned something in a cardboard box that you *trust* was your father?

Yes.

How long did it take?

Hours and hours.

Burn the professor! What a festival!

We didn't know it would be cardboard. We didn't know it would be so small or so light.

You were "surprised."

I don't know where he has gone now that he's dead. I wonder where he is.

You're asking that now? Why didn't you ask that before?

Well, I did. I didn't have an answer. It's more urgent now.

"Urgent."

I wanted to think he was still nearby, I really wanted to believe that. If he was nearby, I thought he would be hovering.

Hovering?

I don't see him walking. I see him floating a few feet off the ground.

You say "I see him"—you can sit in a comfortable chair and say that you "see him." Where do you think he is?

111

But if he's nearby, hovering, is he the way he used to be, or is he the way he was at the end? He used to have all his memory. Does he get it back before he returns? Or is he the way he was near the end, with a lot of his memory gone?

What are you talking about?

At first I used to ask him a question and he would say, "No, I don't remember." Then, he would just shake his head if I asked. But he had a little smile on his face, as though he didn't mind not remembering. He looked as if he thought it was interesting.

He seemed to be enjoying the attention. At that time he still liked to watch things. One rainy day, we sat together outside the front entrance of the home, under a sort of roof.

Wait a minute. What are you calling "the home"?

The old people's home, where he lived at the end.

That is not a home.

He watched the sparrows hopping around on the wet asphalt. Then a boy rode by on a bicycle. Then a woman walked by with a brightly colored umbrella. He pointed to these things. The sparrows, the boy on the bicycle, the woman with the colorful umbrella in the rain.

No, of course. You want to think he's still hovering nearby.

No, I don't think he's there anymore.

You may as well add that he still has his memory.

He would have to. If he didn't, he would lose interest and just drift away.

I do think he was there for three days afterward, anyway. I do think that.

Why three?

All the Modes of Travel
Robert Kelly

The wind grows little hairs
that shiver sideways when the wind
hurries forward pulling things along
into the traveler.
                Tendrils,
the traveler thinks, wisps
of difference between words,
after all all words are breath
all breath is wind, right?
A forest is utterly vernacular,
violence but no lies in it.

Things tell us to be true.
De vulgari eloquentia.
Now imagine writing down the wind.

The young nun bends forward
she is not mean or hasty like the others,
he feels her cool breath
on his lips, on his upper lip
as she instructs him, *my mouth
another's breath* he feels
but doesn't think. Thinking
comes later. She bends close
to him, he sees she has eyes,

he dares himself to see them
for a moment: calm, amused,
assured, words come later,
now they are only a color
and are close, the color is like
green with no green in it,
or amber with no brown
and so much light. She bends
closer to him, she knows
what she knows, she knows
he doesn't see well, she speaks
clearly, the way we speak
to the blind, she speaks the wind
onto him calmly, no haste,
I already forgive what you will do
she tells him, the wind
blows so we can see the little hairs
on her arm, fine hairs
on the nape of his neck
moving from the same wind,
the wind is a wedding, she bends
close to him, there are distinctions,
she explains, words and meanings
are all we have, and touches him
like this, such as these.

Then she is gone
from his close face,
moved back
against the blackboard
to which she turns to write:

exile   nomad   pilgrim   wanderer

Now what are these? Explain the difference,
she says and smiles at him,
alone in the immense classroom.

An **exile** is one who has gone out
from his country, sent out by the king
or hearkening to some inner voice
like Abraham our father.

                    He is not
your father, little boy. You have no father,
you are an exile: what are you?
I am what they used to call a wretch,
Old English *wræcca*, outcast, exile,
I am a privative, defined
by what I'm not, I have no home,
I come from somewhere that doesn't want me
and go where I am not known,
a blind man married to a pretty girl
and every hand is turned against me.

That is right, little boy. But if you were a nomad
what would you be then?

A **nomad**
is a kind of businessman who sells the distances
alone, he travels and he has no home
but the road he knows. But here's the thing:
he knows the road, the road takes him
from grass to grass, and all his sheep
walk along the weary way but the way

is like the hallway from the bedroom to the kitchen,
a nomad is the opposite of an exile,
a nomad is at home all along the way
because every place is full of his advantage,
the economies of wind and water
make his sheep fat, the sunshine
shows him where to go, and night
is a wolf that knows to keep his distance,
a nomad is a bourgeois on the road.

Very good, industrious little boy,
I have seen you going from desk to desk
like a scholar from book to book
looking for the place that has a place in it
for you, you are a nomad, that is so,
unprofitable so far, singular, sheepless
but your day will come. Till then
suppose you were a pilgrim?

O a pilgrim

is a sudden thing, a going towards
and always onward, no thought
of where to come from or of where
I am right now, o I am a pilgrim,
it's in my mind to travel
all the way to where you are
because I have seen your eyes
and smelled the sweet chalk of your clothes
I know you are holy, holy,
and a pilgrim always goes
to what is holy, a pilgrim knows
nothing but *the quality*
of his destination, nothing of what she

to whom he travels really is,
just that divinity of sheer seeming,
and so he goes and so I rise
from this shabby personage I am
and travel toward you
my goal, my dusty flower, my lost Eden,
the only good I really know.

O forward little boy, bold and ignorant,
all your knowing will take you
only as far as my knees, and what then,
what will you do then, my princeling,
my impossible scholar
who has lost his little book
and has to make the words up
as he goes along, is that you,
will you try to travel in me,
will you be my wanderer?

A **wanderer** I am
I was trying to understand it
it sounds so glamorous, like water
running over grass and rock,
like the moon in barren apple trees,
like a dog asleep by a ruined house
but now you've said my name
for all I know is what comes to mind
and apple blossoms happen of pure chance
and what am I, I am nothing
and all I say becomes my road
and I have nothing anywhere but road.

Scissors-in-Window. July 2002. Photograph by Emma Norman.

Scissors-in-Window
Howard Norman

I WAS HIRED BY the Canadian Folklife Archive to collect folktales in Nova Scotia, transcribe life histories, record skip-rope songs, write monographs. It was good to be employed. But the director, Mr. Karjanian, said, "If you want to work on a more permanent basis, you'll need to further your education." So I enrolled in the Folklore Institute at Indiana University. "When you obtain that degree," Mr. Karjanian said, "come see me." In 1971–72, while earning my MA in folklore, I had a job bussing tables at the campus dining room reserved for faculty and administration. It was a work-study position and allowed me to pay my rent. My housemate was Dadati Okura, who was village royalty in Ghana, simply the handsomest man I had seen or have seen yet. Dadati was writing a thesis on African proverbs and moral aphorisms. I'd answered his ad on the bulletin board at the institute. When I would come back from working the dinner shift, around nine o'clock, I'd smell curry, rice, lamb, fish, one of Dadati's inventive and unsurpassable stews. There was always enough left, so that, as Dadati said, "You don't have to eat that shit where you work." More often than not, he'd be sitting on the sofa with a beautiful young woman, a student, sometimes a young faculty member; they were of many races and colors and ages. Before escorting his friend into the bedroom, where they stayed, or didn't, the night, he would always say, "We're going to disappear now." But first, being a thoughtful, sympathetic man, he would put a Moroccan, South African, or Ivory Coast album on the turntable, an accompaniment to his "disappearance" and to my trying to study *The Morphology of the Folktale* by Vladimir Propp. I remember that Dadati owned mysterious recordings of North African desert nomad music ("bootlegs from Paris") done by the novelist and ethnomusicologist Paul Bowles and could discourse brilliantly on them. His thesis came to 877 pages. I have a copy. After graduate school we kept in touch by letters and the occasional telephone call. He always put at least one postage stamp depicting a bird on his envelopes. In time he became a schoolteacher. He sent photographs of his school,

119

which was a typical open-air wattle-and-daub construction. Inside were slat benches, a blackboard, boxes of chalk, a crate marked UNICEF. Every spring he'd send a portrait of his twenty or so students, though one year he had upward of thirty. In each portrait Dadati towered proudly at the center, wearing shorts, sandals, a brightly colored shirt. Smiling that infectious smile, like the one he'd smile before saying, "We're going to disappear now." In December of 1980 I received a letter at my Toronto apartment from Dadati's sister, Mariata-Mary, describing how Dadati's body had been found "along a road" so mangled and burned he could scarcely be identified. His assailants had shot him, doused his clothes with gasoline, and lit him on fire, but not before taking his hiking boots, which he'd purchased at Seal's Army-Navy Surplus in Bloomington, Indiana. There was a "political dispute" of some sort, as Mariata-Mary put it. Did I want my letters returned? Did I want any of his phonograph records? If so, please send a postal money order for shipping.

Dadati's favorite aphorism was: "The best music can melt ice and drown fire—the best musicians don't sleep alone." Our first evening in the house in Bloomington, it was very humid, "not the dry heat of my home," he said. In hideous syncopation, a sound befitting a B-movie attack of giant insects, cicadas whined loudly from what seemed like every tree in the neighborhood. You could go mad. I made lemonade. We chewed on the ice cubes. Dadati told me he had spent his scholarship money on seeing African musicians play every night in Paris, en route from Lagos to New York. "Spent it all in a month," he said. "But do I look unhappy?" I've never seen a man look less unhappy in my life.

I was thinking of Stravinsky's phrase "the weight of an interval." In the context he presented it, a lecture in London on composition, he meant that the silence between notes serves to echo the emotion of the preceding note and to set up a tense anticipation of the note to follow. I think about that. Because now and then, feeling the sodden weight of an interval, almost a respiratory alarm, as if the next breath might not arrive, I experience a sudden freeze-frame of memory: I visualize Dadati Okura loping across the campus—he was six feet six inches tall—humming, "Soul Traveler," by the Messeners, a funk-blues band out of Chicago who'd played a concert at Indiana University in the student union. Then, in the merciless synapse of imagery, the bane of thinking narratively, sentences from Mariata-Mary's letter come alive: ". . . a jeep stopped next to my brother. The men in the jeep had on camouflage uniforms. He was just being a schoolteacher."

*

One other vivid memory from 1972 was seeing the Hungarian musical genius Janos Starker, nearly bald, with a wonderfully intense face, leather valise in hand, walking across the campus on his way to meet his Thursday morning master class. I sat in the concert hall during just about every one of those sessions, hidden in the shadows of the back row, and watched and heard his pointillist instructions to his five students. I wondered if there were always only five students.

Two years earlier, while I was researching a documentary film for Films Canada—yet another freelance employment—in Halifax, Nova Scotia, my landlord, Mrs. Everett Gibbs, introduced me to Bach's suites for cello, playing them on an old Grundig Majestic turntable in the sitting room of her bed-and-breakfast on Robie Street. Mrs. Gibbs had a childhood notorious for the double suicide of her parents; they had leapt from separate ferries running between Halifax and Dartmouth across Halifax Harbor within two hours of one another, and, according to Mrs. Gibbs, the reasons for this remained a mystery. She was raised by an aunt in Halifax, and had eventually taken over that aunt's bed-and-breakfast.

Her recording was by Janos Starker. I purchased my own copy in Toronto. I've since listened to renditions by Rostropovich, Yo-Yo Ma, and others; I consider Starker's to be inimitable. This is scarcely of importance, but I listened to it, exclusively, while writing my first novel, *The Northern Lights,* and all through the writing, again exclusively, of *The Bird Artist,* my second. While writing *The Museum Guard,* I listened to Satie and Chopin nocturnes, but halfway through switched to the Bach suites for cello (which may account for a bifurcated cadence in the prose between the first and second sections, the last being epistolary), and while writing *The Haunting of L.* and my new novel, *Devotion,* returned to the suites for cello. Music and writing, then. My favorite writer, Akutagawa Ryonosuke, wrote: "What good is intelligence if you cannot discover a useful melancholy?" In writing, melancholy, calibrated as exactly as possible, seems the desired condition. Every writer is different. For me, I suppose music must be more than background or accompaniment, but an intensifying element. The patient construction and artful provocations of a composition—whether Bach, Satie, or Chopin— must formally sponsor the deliberateness of writing a sentence, paragraph, novel. Music must transport one to the necessary level of engagement with the writing itself, make fluid the boundary between joy and despair, dreaming and waking, or any other emotional counterparts. Like a watercolor painting, a spectral maritime landscape, a storm just touching land, the light seemingly pulled into the clouds, in late autumn in Nova Scotia. I still listen to Starker's *Suites for Unaccompanied Cello* as if hanging on for dear life.

While watching Starker's master students, their contorted postures of adoration over their instruments, their passionate concentration, even their proximity to such genius as Starker was, I recall thinking, "I wish I could be one of them." From the get-go I realized that Starker's recording of the Bach suites—along with his performance, on another album, of Kodaly—might, if I listened to it often, allow me to come to some new knowledge of myself. I knew this music could be *persuasive.* I should have thrown myself at Janos Starker's feet on the campus one day, like a supplicant monk suddenly overwhelmed with gratitude. Those master classes, replete with Starker's reprimands, exasperation, and praise, always ended with the students choosing a piece, and playing it with Starker for their own edification. I don't exaggerate—those classes helped me organize my emotions; to what extent, I don't exactly know, but they did. In effect those six cellists got me through a year of acute homesickness, love sickness, difficult seminars, waiting tables, studying to all hours, killing time, life too packed with enervating endeavor. I proved only an average student. I forgot to get a haircut for seven months. I got walking pneumonia. I spilled coffee on a provost. But Dadati set me up with a lovely, talkative woman named Amy Rainwater, who had dark red hair and was taking a degree in business administration ("wholesale and retail," she said, "I'm into management"); that went swimmingly, for a week. Our final dinner together—spaghetti and wine on the porch—afforded her the opportunity to try some of the vocabulary useful, I imagined, for her future profession, as well as ending a relationship: "You're just not delivering the goods." (She was married three months later in the chapel on campus; wed, in fact, the campus chaplain, who had graduated from Indiana University in theology.) Still, solitary autumn drives in the country were nice. I'd brought a black claptrap two-door Ford convertible, though no mechanic seemed able to properly balance its wheels. There were, for instance, pileated woodpeckers an hour south in heavily wooded Brown County that, through binoculars, looked like miniature archaeopteryx, enormous birds, leaving vertical texts of braille on tree after tree, and one could hear them for hours, quite close by, while reading a book or writing a letter at a picnic bench. What more could a person ask? Maybe a cup of coffee. Oh, I forgot to mention, Dadati got me to try absinthe.

To prove that I was somewhat "in over my head" with academics, or was at least diminished in my ability to distinguish and prioritize ideas, by late October I had underlined all but a few sentences in *The Morphology of the Folktale.* I looked at my old copy of the book recently; it's so marked up, annotated, filled with scarcely legible marginalia, it appears to be an art project, each page a canvas of queries, exclamation points, coded references, and asides.

*

"Of course," Mrs. Gibbs said one evening, after showing me a photograph album replete with newspaper clippings, one whose headline read MAN AND WIFE LEAP FROM DIFFERENT FERRIES (as if it was a coordinated daredevil stunt), "it couldn't have been happenstance now, could it? Still, I continue to believe in God, but his works that day have caused me lifelong pain. I don't forgive him. In fact, my unforgiveness is testimony to my belief he exists, or else why bother, forgiveness or unforgiveness, either or? I was only ten. And to think how both my mother and father would walk me down to the harbor to watch the ferries at night. That was all the entertainment a young girl needed, along with an ice cream cone. Sounds terribly quaint— sickeningly quaint, I suppose. But it's the truth. The newspaper articles don't mention it, but did you know their bodies were discovered not twenty feet from each other, the same part of the wharf? Oh, look, I've darkened your evening, haven't I? Actually, I have very, very fond memories of my mother and father. Do you know what? They told me everything they did on the day I was born. I was born nearly at midnight. They'd spent the entire day together, August 16, 1903, then I was born nearly at midnight. You know the poet Emily Dickinson? She said that to travel, all one needs do is close one's eyes. Sitting here some nights, I close my eyes and travel back, back, back, and am delivered at my parents' feet, look up, and see their smiling faces. Then again, I don't—not ever—visit the wharf."

*

"A photograph," Josef Sudek said, "has the capacity to put the soul on a deeper incline." My daughter, Emma, took a photograph in Elizabeth Bishop's childhood house in Great Village, Nova Scotia.

It depicts a scissors holding shut the slant-on-slant (as they're called up there) window in the cramped room Bishop slept in. Some biographical facts: Bishop was born in Worchester, Massachusetts, in 1911. Her childhood was peripatetic. After her father's death, she moved with her mother to Great Village, along the Bay of Fundy. From April 1915 into 1917 they lived with Elizabeth's paternal grandparents in this house, which was transported from the village of Mount Pleasant in the 1860s. Elizabeth returned to Great Village each summer from 1919 to 1930. The Elizabeth Bishop House is now a historical property owned by the Elizabeth Bishop Society. Its volunteer custodian is Sandra Barry, a poet, memoirist, and biographer of Bishop's childhood, who lives in Halifax. The modest house itself is located right in the village, along a stretch of Route 2 that includes Upper Economy, Economy, and Lower Economy, which parallels the Bay of Fundy, famous for the outlandishly violent hydraulics of its Tidal Bore, lobster boats, and shore birds, and the mythological gazetteer of Mi'kmaq Indian place names chronicling the eventful life of the giant culture hero Glooskap. On the second floor of the house itself is the master bedroom, the tiny makeshift bedroom with a scissors locking closed the window, and a third bedroom. But the master bedroom is where Bishop's mother became unhinged, signaling her breakdown with a scream. Bishop chronicles this in her story "In the Village," which begins: "A scream, the echo of a scream, hangs over that Nova Scotia village." Soon after, Elizabeth's mother was installed in the Nova Scotia Hospital in Darmouth, which today still seems a draconian edifice, across the harbor from Halifax, and Elizabeth never saw her again.

A scissors in a window. Simple enough as a utilitarian artifact, except it's not exactly simple. In fact, it's anything *but* simple. At different times between 1975 and 1979, long before I'd ever stepped foot in the Elizabeth Bishop House, when I was still scraping together a living as a folklorist, I collected a number of extended anecdotes about, and references to, "scissors-in-window," a sort of category of superstition. This motif was not my essential focus, yet after I'd heard my first scissors-in-window story, I specifically began to ask about others. Most memorable, to me, at least, among the dozens I heard, concerned a certain grave marker in a small cemetery near Advocate, Nova Scotia. For all intents and purposes, the words chiseled into this marker compose a kind of earthly retribution. An indicting voice from the grave, if you will. The epitaph reveals a long-harbored secret from World War One. And after a week of research, folklore detective work, as it were, consulting church records, newspaper files, mostly just talking to people, I discovered that the epitaph reprised a quite complicated incident, a small novel in and of itself. Mrs. Annie Dewis will tell the story here. But first, let me present the epitaph, written on a rectangular slab of gray granite approximately four feet in height and eighteen inches wide, an archipelago of moss on its surface, pocked, weathered, and unkempt, at the south end of the cemetery:

> *In France it was I saved*
> *my brother Donald McMillian's life*
> *not vice-versa.*
> *It was I carried him*
> *back to the trench.*
> *God as my witness.*

Donald McMillian and his older brother, Henry, both served in the same Canadian infantry unit in France. Their family had close friends in the Dewis family, who lived a few miles away in Advocate Harbor. In late July of 1977, I transcribed the following explanation for the epitaph, from Mrs. Annie Dewis, age sixty-one, whose parents were friends of the McMillians, and who remembered the actual incident "like it was yesterday."

"Donald McMillian simply couldn't live down the shame of it—
"it ate away at him
"that he'd lied all those years about it being him who saved his
"brother Henry's life
"Henry, who by the way, suffered the mustard-gas cough
"whereas Donald breathed freely.
"In 1926 Henry McMillian drowned in the Bay of Fundy.
"He drowned angry at his brother Donald.
"There was good reason for this, because, truth be told, Donald's the
"one drowned him.
"Some say it was just drunken carelessness one night at the wharf.
"Those who say that are fools, too much faith in mankind.
"You know the types, they're everywhere, not just in Nova Scotia.
"Rarely but now and then murder visits our province.
"As for who did what to whom, here's all the proof I ever needed:
"First, shortly after Henry drowned, Donald married Henry's wife,
"Evie,

"Within a week after the funeral, they got married in Peggy's Cove,
"not at home
"they just came back and announced, 'Well, we're now married!'
"How about them apples?
"Listen up, this is important—
"when Henry McMillian was buried
"the fellow who carved words on the grave marker—I forget his
"name—
"was authorized by law
"to carry out the exact wishes of the last will and testament of the
"deceased
"if the deceased mentions what he wants written
"and Henry did
"and paid for it in advance!
"When everyone first read those words you could have knocked
"them over
"with a feather.
"Henry McMillian had kept his brotherly heroic act to himself
"all those years.
"They say no good deed goes unpunished.
"The very day after Henry was buried—according to Evie—
"Donald secured a scissors-in-window
"in the attic of the house
"that she and Henry formerly shared together
"the house in which Donald was now her husband.
"You better believe
"that Donald prayed nightly
"the scissors worked.
"Scissors-in-window—want to know what that's about?
"Well it has directly to do with ghosts.
"A scissors placed to keep a window shut
"keeps the unwanted ghosts
"out,
"the wanted ghosts
"in.
"Wanted-unwanted.
"The scissors lets the house
"enforce the distinction.
"Tell me, why would anyone lie on their own gravestone?"

From Utopia, or, My Pleasure
E*die* M*ei*d*av*

HIGHWAY 5
2008

> *Those same people who once said God was dead,*
> *a long time ago? Well. Now the FACTS are IN.*
> *These folks have to face some pretty incontro-*
> *vertible evidence. They might have to finally*
> *ADMIT that it's THERAPY that IS DEAD. I am*
> *swearing to this.*

IN HIS LINO-COVERED concrete cell one floor above the guard, the prickle of talk-radio static below signals that soon the breakfast tray will fall into the rack. The guards push it through the slotted-metal door that keeps Lana's father from the corridor. Do they offer their gruel toward or against his nausea? Don't they know what meds do to a man's stomach? Lana's father won't trouble himself too much with the breakfast offering. He's busy with a logic exercise in an out-dated SAT book, trying to complete final preparation for an exam.

He'd entered academia in a different era, when one could be brilliant and never have passed through any American status-endowing meat-grinder. Had never finished his BA in any manner a university would recognize. Had never entered any American university as a student, and understood this stood against his case.

As if he'd thought he was exceptional, outside the usual laws all along. He was like Rimi Bukovy at Harvard or like Vann Methel at Stanford; like so many academics who in their student years had never given the academy the time of day.

He's made a turn, returned to the cause of self-betterment. Half-hearted, sure, but there's hope that this particular upward spiral will be fully documented. It would help if it were. If he showed he was someone who obeyed rules. Because there exists a possibility he could transmute his charges, get released.

In the X-rays, his lung cancer looks like a friendly black fist. Defanged old man, this line of reasoning goes, whom could he hurt?

Let the guy out. Let him die of cancer in peace.

But a new governor's in business, has to prove something to the cronies who helped get him elected. A showcase is a showcase, business business, get the sizzle on, the Brevital flowing.

Problem is, it doesn't matter what any of the various activist groups mobilizing for or against his release think. Not the Women Against Violence Against Women who'd like him to stay in the rage cage. Not the No Death Penalty People who'd like him to be released on medical grounds.

He knows he's everyone else's pingpong ball and there's a curious relief in being another's pingpong ball, freed from his own neural firings. If this most recent appeal ends up being rejected, one into which he'd put his heart, the state of California or governor or both think he's worth only ten more days of life. Ten more days before eight hundred milliliters of Brevital injected at two venipunctured points of entry make him exhale the desire to breathe (venipuncture is probably preferable but he doesn't want to think about it) or before they release him on grounds of the sneaky fist.

(And at first they'd thought he'd been making it up but the medics have confirmed him.)

He rasps over the logic problems. The prednisone helps contain the black fist, though it also endows him with a whole raft of other questions.

> A cherry is to a cherry tree as a gem is to a:
> 1) mine, 2) jewelry store, 3) jewelry setting, 4) jeweller, 5) all of the above, 6) none of the above

FROM WHOSE LOINS

Years ago this had happened:

Lana usually didn't go to his readings and this time she had brought Shula. Sophomore year of high school, early on, their second year of friendship. Lana's father was giving one of his Berkeley readings, which always spelled trouble: legions of fans. She'd never actually been to one of his readings but she'd heard about them. And there stood her progenitor, from whom she had sprung, Mahler rumpled in a business suit but eyes burning under the heavy brow, his profile the sharpest hatchet. Corduroy patches at his elbows and wrinkles in his suit contained the vortex only somewhat, given that all lines of energy pointed at him.

A crowd, spilling in to the second floor of the bookstore. Hanging off the edges of the staircase listening to the loudspeaker. A bouncer hovering, anxious despite his muttonchop sideburns and the extremely large metal belt buckle under his navel, signifying a tail-biting snake. A *failed local poet,* her mother whispered.

Mahler had read in a deep, portentous voice from his latest book, *Firing the Love Hole.* Had said: I'm ready for your questions.

And a woman stood up to say:

> For years I have been very interested in extraterrestrial visitations. I have long considered the relation between holes in certain varieties of cheese and the concept of holes in the moon, along with the drain at the bottom of the bathtub, and wonder if you feel there's some biomorphic resonance happening with all this, and how you might relate it to the way the counterculture relates to the larger culture. Is it centrifugal or centripetal, basically? I come originally from a Wisconsin dairy farm and that's a way of saying I really enjoy this book and the whole idea of wormholes and portals through which all sorts of things can enter.

And Mahler had nodded, genially, an old European courtesy in his nod. When a costumed man whom Lana hadn't seen before pushed forward, Lana had pinched her friend Shula, seated on her other side, Shula trying to hold back her hebephrenic giggles. A man in a white polar bear outfit, holding a transistor and a giant white phallus, said, choked with emotion:

> I am appearing here as a manifestation of Hermes, the messenger, and just want to say, Mahler, you urge us all to follow one kind of life, you preach about BIOLOGICAL BIRTH-RIGHT VS. CHOICE and SELF-CREATION, about SELF-MYTHOLOGIZATION beyond the determinism of neurons and then Mahler! Man! You live the most predetermined life possible, a tenure-track bourgeois professor's life. I mean how clichéd does it get? You have your lovely wife and kid and vintage Porsche and ivy-covered North Berkeley house, which, if these are not received icons, right? if they are not about choice but just about perpetuating the bourgeois status quo, I'm Hermes, so what's with that, man?

—and the bouncer, the failed local poet, made as if to move the man out. At which Mahler raised a cordial hand. Don't worry, he said wearily. I know this man. He was the emperor! He paused and began again with care:

129

> No one knows with greater pain that I do the disparity be-
> tween what my work suggests and the way I lead my actual
> life.

Which filled Lana with a passion for her father. He was honest, not
thrown by criticism, a father who knew how to handle everything.
Distant, maybe, but capable of inspiring such odd loyalty among his
fans.

If only they knew about his temper, she did think.

For a second she could see her father as he was loved, reflected in
the eyes of what they called his shaggies. How could it not make her
love him more? She was his Moppy, though he only called her that
in good moods, when smoking his Cuban cigars. For a second she
loved him fully.

Two women up front began waving their arms in a genial
paroxysm.

Yes? he said, pointing to them.

> I just want to say, in response to whatever the Hermes guy
> said, that your first book really gave me great permission to
> follow my muse all these years.
> It gave us all sorts of freedom.
> And we both really want to thank you for it.

Which was when Lana had realized the two women sat on the
metal chairs naked but for the pansies bedecking their hair.

She nudged her mother, on the other side of her. What's *that?* she
had asked, for want of anything better. Shula kept giggling on the
other side of her.

It's OK, said her mother. A new sort of shaggy. You know your
dad's work—it attracts certain followers.[1]

Lana had looked at her mother then, noted the slight tremble of
the lower lip and the way she'd lingered on the idea of *work,* their

---

[1] Only two years later, 1984, Lana in college would be struck with guilt, her bound-
aries porous, permeated with regrets about family. At such moments she'd place a call
home. You never knew in what state you'd catch him. Dad? she'd say, faltering on the
last part, so that she would have uttered one full note followed by a series of semi-
quaver grace notes, all decrescendo and prelude to nothing, especially because the name
had never felt right. Lana had never really known what to call her male progenitor,
and when her mother spoke of their father, Mary often said things like Your Father as
in Your Father wants you to switch to the bilingual French school or Your Father
would like us to eat dinner early tonight as later on he's in some kind of symposium.

family's holy flag. She'd studied her mother: the nervous brown hands crossed like the well-bred Midwestern schoolgirl she remained at heart despite early childhood on the reservation and her papers on the ills of western thought as represented in ethnographic representations of women—

and again Lana had made her favorite vow *I'll never be like her.*

2008

Hope Springs
South of the Grapevine
Southern California

You continue long enough in life, you'll find that what you call hope, some call amnesia, others nostalgia. A woman enters a sulfurous open-air spa just south of California's navel. The place happens to be called Hope, and despite the carvings and general mutterings of the place, she will learn that the name of the place does not come from some ancient tribe. If once there had been prayer grounds, they now lie beneath the place where feet—brown red black white—pad toward one of three pools. In her head she hears the refrain *Kansas she said is the name of her star.*

The hot pool is kept at 116 degrees Fahrenheit. When you first get

---

The progenitor and seed.

Your Father.

And in such moments Lana could tell her mother reveled more than slightly in her father's fame, and also that his fame had replaced any last eroticism between her parents, his repute the equivalent of a lingering touch, a scent around the two of them in their matrimonial capsule. She had read in a paper of her father's once that part of the primal hindbrain of men valued a woman by how obviously other men valued her. And that in this way a circle of cavemen could sense which woman was fertile, touchable. But her mother had her own version of this: the more her mate Vic was valued by the world, the more Mary cleaved to him. In Lana's view of things, the more Mary suffered the effects of such worldly valuation, the more she was stuck for life.

The central mystery of her parents' lives: how could her mom have known what her father would achieve? When they'd met, signing themselves up for a life together, for the production of a daughter and a few miscarriages, for weathering sabbaticals in other countries, her father, from the evidence of photographs, had not been much more than a callow undergraduate student from Liechtenstein, passably handsome, hair slicked back in the fashion of the times, chin determined as the cowlick, the brow studious, and the eyes a little easier to find back then under that brow. A boy with promise, a shy smile. Would you guess his intensity, the people he would inspire? Maybe from the stance, shoulders hunched forward as if to hide any message that might emanate from the chest but some kind of surprising jut forward of the hips.

131

in, you feel you have scalded your epidermis and purification has already begun: they're going to scalp you of your prior self.

The woman—Lana—tells herself she is glad not to meet anyone's eyes though secretly she wants them.

Someone will soon tell her that the warm pool is kept at a decent ninety-six degrees. Most people stand neck-deep, leaning against walls, with a clear religion about the avoidance of gazes. Some float on backs, toes hooked under the guardrail, absorbing healing minerals, a whale-like breast or groin occasionally surfacing. Some help others float so they may deprive the senses. A few sit in dead seriousness facing each other, whispering, still enough to be having sex at least tantric. Push the senses forward or back: these are the two goals. Be in the body or try floating out of it in dead-man's pose. These are people taking a break from the stress of the rest of the world. This is a retreat center + site for soul expansion, as the catalog instructs.

The cold pool is at thirty testicle-sucking, nipple-hardening degrees. You are to plunge into this immediately before or after the hot pool. In a different area, partitioned away from the adults' reconnection with their inner beings, two small kidney-shaped baths await phantom kids. Meanwhile, everyone is naked, everyone knows the exact temperature of the pools.

I am dying, the woman is thinking, as many have thought before her, heat working at least ninety-nine strands of her past out into the waters. She is making certain vows about her future. Her hair

---

And why should it have fed Mary so, when Mary clearly had her own accomplishments, her own fans and scholarship, her own abstracted velcrolike brilliance, piecing together odd facts, synthesizing them? Lana didn't know if her mother had just a retentive or an original mind but in academia the difference didn't seem to matter all that much. Both Vic and Mary had carved out a good life together and their daughter would never be able to reach its peaks: she was the product made extraneous by cofactors. Lana would feed Mary's scones to all the shaggies camped out on their front lawn but in her bedroom could spend hours drawing huge charcoal circles on paper taped to the wall, wondering when she herself would ever say anything that could be of use to others.

Following this logic, she'd gone to college as far away as she could, shooting like a poolball away from too much intimacy with her parents' private life, the postprandial-French-cheese system that had kept all three of them running for so long. She'd grab any available American myth about inventing yourself in places of extreme pressure. Every inch and action of her would refute her father's stodgy values: that was what counted. Every time she threw the tarot cards or the I Ching coins or looked at her astrology chart, she would actively undo her father's belief in the hardwiring of neurons, his religion about neurons crafting an individual's ability to feel and hence follow his freedom and bliss. Alas, was her inability to undo his religion her neural birthright and hence her destiny?

waves, pools, swirls upon itself. She pulls it up, ties it in a knot. It is December 8.

Tomorrow the thirty-three-year birthday celebration of this place is due to start, attracting all sorts of people wanting to let go, let it out, let God. There will be rehearsals, gatherings, reunions, all culminating in a final performance. At no point will anyone mention the death penalty. Why should politics sully a place like this?

Nearby, a man in a railroad cap sweeps mulberries off the path. Does he also study the back of her neck?

Rules are posted everywhere around Hope Springs, taking on a tone familial or punitive, sometimes both. No breakables in the pool area. Plus no cell phones, drugs, pets, or children in the adult pools. No talking in the pool area, only whimpering (the *S* in whispering has melted a bit).

Checkout is at twelve, and please don't be so gauche as to take room towels to the pools. No meat, fish, poultry, or nudity allowed in the cook-it-yourself kitchen area, unlabeled food will be thrown away, round-top coolers in the fridge are prohibited. No use of residents' shelves, no staying past your parking permit's time of ejection. No lateness to yoga classes. The ethos of the group dance night at Hope Springs was love like you have no fear, dance like nobody's watching, live like you have died a million times.

The folksy but ungrudgingly peremptory signs go along with the free Q-Tips, cotton balls, lavender lotion and soap. All part of utopia's noblesse oblige. But no blaming the place if something goes wrong and you get lost on one of the sixteen hundred acres of hiking trails or a mountain lion snags you because you crouched and didn't throw rocks and spoke in a high voice or you end up getting Lyme disease from a tick bite since you did sign that release when you entered oblivious and hopeful through the big metal griffin gate. Bell's palsy, depression, memory loss: a few of the symptoms you could get from a tiny bug.

Meanwhile, some hundred-plus miles north, the governor tries to find his face in the mirror, having a hard time locating it this morning.

It takes lots of rules to keep utopia running on par, Lana keeps thinking.

People come from all zones with every breed of idea so rules become linkage and religion. *Uptight,* she thinks, one of the few words her father borrowed from the argot of his day. He thought it a useful neologism. Uptight, Lana, is a useful metaphor. But *groovy,* no.

Radical as bland ubiquitous praise, no.

The word uptight in her head while the pool does its job and heats her up. She knows from other zones she has been in that some people gladly volunteer themselves to be enforcers, while others find delight in breaking rules. The signs bear witness.

NO UNINVITED SEXUAL ADVANCES OR ACTIVITY IN THE POOLS.

NO SEXUAL ACTIVITY IN THE SAUNA—SECURITY WILL BE CALLED.

IF YOU'RE IN A HURRY, YOU'RE IN THE WRON PLACE.

She reads it all, oddly relieved by explicitness. The sum total of these signs is innocence: nothing can be covered, all gets washed away.

No matter the weekend, water draws them. Everywhere you go, people carry around little bottles of the stuff. They lean over the tap next to the waterfall by the warm pool, slurp it or lavish it over bodies, bounce like nude eternal kurort children to a destination along the wall, arms aloft, bearing unbreakable tinted bottles, offering private rites to the local god.[2]

This is fertile valley in what otherwise would be unbroken desert along Highway 5, south of Bakersfield and north of Los Angeles, just below the Grapevine. Apart from the fields, the prison is the main institution in the greater underpopulated county, positioned some hundred miles north of them, and by a quirk of real estate, the current governor's residence is planted only some twenty miles north of that. What is nice about the desert is that mileage signs are well maintained: along the interstate, no matter how isolated you might feel among tumbleweed, broken barbed-wire posts, and dead-dream

---

[2]To release yourself from the world's shackles, you must first embrace them: according to the teal-colored pamphlet, this was the first tenet of the December workshop. I just said, enough with the desk job! Did I sign up somewhere to die on the cross? one woman asks a friend, the sauna making her wax contemplative. The man on the bottom heating rack rolls over on his belly to look up at them, but only glimpses the luminescent promise of their thighs. How do you get between such things?

Head first for the kundalini pool, where all inhibitions and syndromes are disappeared, gesundheit. Along with rising mortgage rates, crammed PTA meetings, briefcases, and colleagues of the martyrological disposition, disappeared along with unused jogging clothes and mildewed yoga mats and lost gloves, torn nylons and friends who don't understand your tone, along with too-tight jeans and spotted ties, silk scarves and T-shirts boasting atrophied attention-deflecting slogans for utopian parties long since disbanded. For only $35 a day base admission, here's the Hope Springs premise: let demons be banished from the premises, gone, and this time please God let the cleansing stick, let freedom stay, om shanti namaya, om shanti shanti om.

Life is a river, change only happens when you embrace the problem, you got to be with what is, every crisis is an opportunity, every opportunity could lead you to enlightenment, being in the moment is all we've got. Right?

oil pumps, at least you know where you are, in your car, free in the USA, speeding north or south.

Cowboy legacy continues in the Hope Springs oasis, in that showers with swinging saloonlike doors tease the viewer, revealing shampooed heads and, below, bare legs, while more contemporary *pleine-aire* showers let you see everything. Everything anyway mostly gets seen. Between pools, some people wear towels or bathrobes, a sophisticated effacement. Usually, however, big or small, fat, thin, thinner yet, people wear nudity covered over by bliss or focus, two useful veils over intermediate layers of solipsism or narcissism. Some people, younger women and older men, tend to wear shame or its cousin brazenness as a cloak over all other affects. Some stare at everyone else, a preemptive strike against being looked *at.*

But nothing really hides. People may pretend not to look but bodies—a potpourri of bodies, a rainbow, a cornucopia—are seen here that beg surveillance, bodies never depicted in any magazine or Renaissance painting or African sculpture or specialist Internet porn site.[3]

---

[3]Sink of the tattooed and cockringed, of pierced or natural, Asian African Anglo Latino, bellies tight or multiple, breasts tiny or tripled, red brown yellow pink white orange, buttocks furry or denuded. Some bodies belong more to the fourteenth century's fields and child-bearing and early mortality than to our space-age vitamin-capsule eternity of the twenty-first, but they are all here. Long-testicled or long-clitorised, siliconed or liposuctioned. Exercise-addicted or lenient and unfetishized. All bodies a testament to denial or indulgence. How have you treated time? How has time treated you? Don't ask. Bodies rushed through meals and cars or bars, through lunchtime walks and ischemia risk and into Sufi dancing or Mommy & Me classes. No matter what, each turn reveals tree rings, or, more morbidly, the charts: which hour will be yours to die in?

Not to mention the men with penises that are tiny surprises resting on a crepuscular sack. Or those of corporate girth who follow their bellies around in bewilderment, their heads distinguished and well groomed. Older women with smooth self-aware buttocks. Younger women Brazilian-waxed, their crinkly labia coupling with the equipment of young men with sincere eyes and handlebar moustaches and pierced noses. Those of skin clear or pocked and multitufted. The puffy-labial and cluster-nutted. The hermaphroditic, paganist, and/or transgendered. Hunched and erect, males or females with genial clumps of beard, long thick hair floating in the water. All bodies crying out the story, to anyone who will listen: leisurely physical self-fulfillment or slow martyrdom.

Homo sapiens in every contemporary type comes to Hope Springs to be shed of shields like coffee-cup sleeves and kids' doctor appointments and making a living, shed of ailments and annoying colleagues. Shed of portable music players and chamber music subscriptions and aging parents and clothes in the new black and the old, freed of nepotism and cronyism and bad politics. Liberated from powerful roommates and controlling neighbors. (Ostensibly free from race and class but preferably never gender). Free from absentee mates or alcoholic parents. Raised from their helplessness in the claws of syndromes: carpal tunnel to overworked mother to acquired immunity.

Edie Meidav

The woman gets out of the pool and into the warm pool, where an older man is saying to a younger girl: Today is the first day of the rest of your life, and the younger girl laughs as if the cliché breaks newly upon the dawn of her consciousness. Does this count as the signs' idea of sexual advance (verboten), or would this be merely affable exchange?[4]

---

[4]Beyond how to manage grief (*Witnessing Your Emotions, workshop #89, spring of 2006*), there is no perfect evacuation scenario here.

No decent earthquake survival scenario.

December 10, the plan is to account for this soon and post more signs.

Liquid lavender-scented soap (made from flowers grown in the surrounding meadows and crushed near the cob-bale temple) flows out from opaque teats stationed around the sinks and showers around Hope Springs. Thus everyone starts to smell the same, a combination of lavender and earthgut sulfur and iron piped into the hot pool (the peroxene filter keeps the whole thing clean, fifteen hundred gallons of water pumped through, catching any inorganic material, allowing through only H_2O and Na and Su and Pb).

Lavender brings out sulfur's low notes and iron's high notes, while also tranquilizing the amygdala, the brain's efficient center for both trauma and pleasure.

You can't walk that death penalty beat forever, the guy who used to work at the max-security penitentiary up the highway is saying to his new friend. Twelve years I was there. Then it got to me.

No kidding, his friend says before submerging himself. When he reemerges, he says: How about snagging some lunch?

Water flows from the hot pool into the warm pool, so a special hot oasis happens near the stairs. There is also an arsenic footbath near the entrance to the warm pool but the catalog promises the arsenic comes in trace amounts, not at all poisonous.

Sometimes white flakes of calcium precipitate form on the surface of the warm pool and the pilgrims get alarmed, imaginations and self-awareness already highly aroused and hypochondriacal, yet the flakes just mean the pool is crowded, that the spa works its wonders, each person having acted as a human ice cube, cooling the earth's magma-warmed waters: the calcium becomes like sugar condensing in cooled tea. The hot pool is in something resembling an elf's cave, while the cold pool exposes itself to the elements.

This sameness of nudity and scent makes sex a greater plausibility. How many veils are there between your floating member and someone else's floating hole, your wet hole and someone else's wet member? Thus, people's faces work to hold up new veils by the minute: the all-time favorite is dignity, as is the visage of sex-transcending enlightenment, a new kind of spiritual chastity armature. Bliss always works. Sometimes, a naked couple will seem clothed by sole virtue of each one's pride in their mate's naked body when displayed to cold air and hot water. In couple's faces, one spots the courtship story and mutual attraction, while their discrete bodies tend to evanesce.

The men's dormitory flanks the women's dormitory. You can get private rooms with shared or half or full bath, dorm living or tent camping out in the meadow past the half-constructed cob-bale temple still awaiting a donor for work to be finished.

There is also the sauna. No matter the lavender soap used as a disinfectant, the sauna never stops smelling of the sweat of thirty-five years of wet and prone bodies. Oak soaked with a sweat gone archival, a legion of Finns and Swedes and everyone else having shed toxins so deep into the wood that no one's new sweat has a fighting chance. One breathes in the heated old sweat and at the same time *history*, the Hope

The woman—Lana—is perturbed by how familiar certain details feel. The mulberries, for one. Why do mulberries seem so familiar? How did she learn these are mulberries? They fall slowly, get caught on branches, end up smashed into the pavement next to the pools so the concrete bears a splotched map of regret.[5] No squirrels thrive near the pools of Hope Springs—all fruit-gathering hopes would be squandered.

Springs into which one humbly enters one's own body as a worldly petitioner, a stressed-out nutcake, a beggar for the sacrament of cleansing, healing, as close to immortality as one can get in this life, youth and renewal sans mildew.

Some song plays on the radio in the guard station: Cal-I-Forn-I-Cation.

Statistics would state that clever conversation doesn't occur much at Hope Springs, and that political conversation is barely tolerated. What does always unfold, no matter the residents, is a curatorial discussion re: choices and consumption. Consumption of regimes ecological or psychological or digestive, career minded or habitat specific.

A parade of bruises brings on a parade of cures. Sacred sexuality as a weekend practice combined with being a Web-site manager and renovating condos in one's spare time? The conversation consumes everyone. Ways to overcome psychological trauma by holding versus selling. The benefits of Pilates versus yoga versus NIA. Gestalt versus transpersonal versus meditation. Zen versus Vipassana versus Mahayana versus surfing. Stay in the relationship or leave? Twelve steps versus transcending the literalism of the step? Committing to Amerika instead of leaving for Asia or Europe or Latin America? No matter their ostensible import, all conversations reduce to this: the attainment of greater health whether in one's muscles, mood, spiritual plane, or colonic hygiene.

Say that spiritual materialism seems an oxymoron but here it thrives: here the belief is that one can attain perfect psychological security plus health, passion, creative fulfillment plus enough money, equaling bliss.

December 10, day one of the Surrendering Grief workshop, the beginning of the EnlightenBreath experience. At the break, a clump of men sunbathe on the cramped spot of sun on the deck. They lie on their sides, of womanish hip, their stomachs sliding a bit, reading. Some are not lazy. They do leg lifts and abdominals, their sex falling this way and that way, Peter Rabbit and Jemima Puddleduck, childishly vulnerable, pierceable, blushing, a confession of boyhood. Some may be ex-felons or even feds—but who cares? Under the sun, one nation innocent. To each individual let there be all over again the simple birthright of body.

[5]When they'd still been in the car with their mother, roaring south, plugged into the DVD, Sedge and Tee had watched as all the kids fell in the lake when the boat with Maria capsized as they approached the estate, and the newly arrived second-fianceé baroness swallowed her derision under a polite smile and a how-do-you-do. Sedge and Tee weren't happy about this idea of ending up at Hope Springs, surrounded by naked people, a fact their mother had glossed over a bit. On the way south, a hundred miles before Hope Springs, their mother had not admitted much to them, including that they were driving by the prison whose walls would be the last her own father will ever see.

The countdown before Christmas, so people had driven with greater frenzy. This is desert that last saw a white Christmas somewhere around 1959, the year when much of the consciousness of the land had frozen. A year before people used the word *consciousness* so freely.

That afternoon she'd checked into the room that would belong to them, to her and her new beau, Dirk, the new resident guru of Hope Springs. Like a honeymoon suite: ruffled swag, floral bedprint, heart-shaped soap, fluffy towels. Next to the room for her twins. Down the hall from where Dirk would receive supplicants.

Lying for the first time on her bed, she had wondered about mulberries and squirrels, but also this: why did the looping yellow-rose wallpaper remind her so much of something?

Sometimes you open a suitcase and glimpse a ghost leaving: your hopes for this journey or your past journeys, all the beings you may have traveled with. In much the same way that, driving down here with the boys, the telephone poles had bounded like colts into her rearview and then stayed, impassive, sentinels passing judgment. She'd been so caffeinated she'd jumped each time a pole appeared, like a judgment from on high, there in the desert plain heading toward the Grapevine. The boys hadn't noticed her jumps, because to make them avoid noting their loss—leaving the north coast of Yalina and the house they'd known since they were tiny, their grandparents' land, the whole bit—she'd plugged them into watching *The Wizard of Oz*, playing only to them in the backseat.

A gong sounds to bring all the participants into the fold of the Big House where zafus and zabutons and special healing mats are arrayed in a big circle. Those who are not partaking in the EnlightenBreath workshop watch enviously as others cinch together, a perfect purse for the containing of communal awareness.

I am going to kill myself if he doesn't admit that you can't live in a lie, one woman tells her friend.

When people first work here they are called candidates. Most have come from places like Wisconsin or Somerville or Westchester or Hamden, though many have come from Cape Town and Bath, from Munich or Lyon or Cleveland, from Vallejo or Tarzana or Paso Robles, possessing names, mostly self-endowed, like Kodiak and Sierra and Love, Hrimaty, Chandrika and Nalini, Shashi and Satya, Lincoln and Gandhi and Nelson and Raoul and Yoko. No Madisons, Nixons, Irvings, Courtneys, Stanleys, Michikos, or Richards. Some Melissas and Britneys, many Lindas and Christophers and Jonathans. Some are bodyworkers, some work in the office, some teach yoga, some clean bathrooms and sweep steps, standing naked in the warm bath in the morning wearing a railroad work cap in order to signify a connection to a holy lineage of working while they scrub with full mindfulness the calcium precipitate off the ledge, watched by all eyes in the pool. Lore surrounds every element of Hope Springs, even the mulberry trees, even the scrubbing, even the naked but spottable multibillionaires.

Sometimes people in the warm pool are overcome. You see only their faces, leaning back, in some paroxysm of sudden grief and memory or possibly orgasm. Muscle memory works that way, each person an onion, each layer holding some good or bad memory. As the waters work their magic, many layers are shed.

A horse of a different color! she heard the taximan in Emerald City saying, and then later: I am Oz, the great and powerful, and later Judy Garland's response: I am Dorothy, the small and meek. And finally, her favorite line, the wizard, discovered by Toto: Pay no attention to that man behind the curtain.

There was also the promise Lana had made, that she would go on this adventure with an open mind. So she had tried to ignore certain things.[6]

For one, the extent to which her boys had been as skeptical about this new man as they'd been about any of the others. But this one was different. First time she'd been with an older man. Such an older man—in his early fifties—and besides, he had a desire to do something beyond his own brute ambition. Because Dirk wanted to involve people in a collective project to transform the world's consciousness, and had been invited to Hope Springs for an indefinite residency, to help heal masses drawn to these waters. Plus, she'd accepted the liberty of confinement for so long, now she needed to shake things up a bit, find the liberty of actual liberty.

First off: she'd see about a good school for the twins. It would be good for them to have a break from studying up north among the fresh-faced but secretive children of pot growers with all their well-rehearsed scripts about Daddy's job. Instead, here they'd study with California's other grandsons and granddaughters. The spawn of Indians and ranchers, of Mexicans and migrants and cowboys, those who stayed put and who moved through, all workers and heirs and truckers half settled into the valley riven by the great highway.

---

[6]The woman who didn't want to be looked at still doesn't want to be looked at. She stops at the table for late registrants to the Getting Over Grief session. Try it, says another woman sitting nude, wearing long dark braids at the little table, innocent, more a naked little girl selling lemonade. See if you like the morning session, the girl-child says. If you want, I can sign you up for the afternoon and evening sessions later. The woman who didn't want to be looked at, who clutches a yellow towel around her, signs her fake name: Lana Wagner.

The braided girlchild studies Lana's handwriting. You're all about the future, she says, and then picks up a card from a deck and reads like a bad actress from it: You are blessed, and waits, almost growing annoyed.

Lana realizes she's supposed to echo the affirmation, and blurts it back—*I am blessed*—surprised that her throat clenches, that for just a second she could cry. Don't be silly, she tells herself.

Go enjoy the pools. You'll hear the gong when it's about to start, says the braided lemonade girlchild. It's all there for you.

LANA

didn't appreciate that her boys weren't taking well to the new beau Dirk. She could hear them through the thin stucco talking about the guy.

He's creepy, man. That laugh of his is so fake, Tee said, attempting a poor facsimile.

He's almost as creepy as that guy who runs this place.

Hogan?

Yeah, but Hogan has a terrarium, Sedge was saying. Anyway, Hogan doesn't run the place, he manages it.

Big diff, said Tee.

You know Hogan said he'd let us see the tarantula, said Sedge.

No way.

Tee had severe arachnophobia, and Lana wondered that her sensitive, sweet boy Sedge would bring up tarantulas. Since they'd come to Hope last week, Sedge had been acting out.

Ow! Sedge moaned jokingly, his sensitive self revealed again.

I didn't kick you hard.

OK.[7]

How long will Ma be with this guy? Tee asked, tending to rely upon his twin's greater social instinct.

I don't know—Sedge made it into at least three syllables. Kno-oh-oh.

Hey, just asking.

You want a medal or a monument?

---

[7]The pure eternal of a kid's heart: Sedge, hugging her as he approached three—and why did such sweet memories come from that period?—talked often of circumcision. Why was it necessary to clip skin off boys, and not girls? They cut mine off?

Not all of it, honey. Just part. It's cleaner.

What religion are we?

They sew it up, she said, wondering if her understanding of anatomy was wrong. Just like when Daddy got his bunion removed. They sewed it up, right, and then they took the thread out.

Like the mice in Cinderella?

Right, sewing like that. Like once I had a bike accident, she said, and I fell under a bike, an older girl who'd been on the back fell on top. I got a hole in my chin and it had to be sewn up. See the scar?

Sedge started to cry: I don't want Mama ever to have booboos.

But that was back then, honey.

Not even back then, I don't want Mama ever to have booboos. Not Poppy either.

Well, sometimes we have booboos and then we heal.

But I don't want Mama ever to be hurt.

She didn't want to hear it, their mock-casual twin-prattle, their fakery of adults, a way of making everything OK, a discourse like wet mortar that helped shore up their days. Things flowed and then became Sedge and Tee stories. They always had this prattle whether joyous or angry or feeling sorry for themselves in their completely different ways.

What did she have libido for? Earplugs. She couldn't find them. If she one day wrote a memoir of her life during this period, she would put a giant fluorescent orange earplug on the cover. This must be the necessary price of being with kids: a being made of earplugs, removable occasionally. Sometimes you had to tune things out because your self needed that room. No one had told her about this self-and-self question of motherhood. Easy to forget yourself in, say, putting toys away—wooden or plastic, that question had engaged her for a long time until she had just surrendered to the tsunami of petrochemical toys that is American upbringing in the twenty-first century. Easy to engage in talk of superspy space robots with your sensitive son. And then, as if you were surprised by an uninvited guest, you'd see a shade of your old self, some glimmer of prekid time, and it would strike an odd subjunctive note. A doppelgänger showing up, saying essentially: excuse me, did you really *mean* to abort me? Tell me you didn't mean it.

She had asked the twins to take an afternoon nap because she needed one and now instead they were piping in poison music, their twin prattle into her bedroom. The stucco walls really must be thin for her to hear them so clearly.

She wondered if you could make a sculpture out of earplugs. How would you get them to stick together?

Her hand crawled across a pillow, looking for just one soft little orange-and-yellow-striped earplug. And got what she wanted. Even when she squeezed it in (but had it hurt her hearing, having children and then having earplugs, all that fluid stuck in her ear, the blessing of children taking away a portion of its endowment?) she could still hear the music of their speech. Imagining what they were saying was almost worse than hearing it.

I give up, she said to her pillow. A highly unmuscled pillow. Forget about napping today.

Dirk was out convening with the people who ran the place. It's true she didn't know him all that well but early signs had been promising. She liked that he made a big show of talking equally to the groundskeepers and the owners, Doreen and Albert, or DorAlba as they were affectionately called around here.[8]

Though her boys liked the head groundskeeper, Hogan, because of his terrarium, Dirk had found that guy a bit unsettling, though he probably understood some of his future survival depended on him. This guy Hogan was really in cahoots with DorAlba, that much was clear. And Dirk's own goal was to turn this residency into something more than just a residency. He was in his fifties, at least (she hadn't pressured him to tell her exactly, allowing him this jot of male vanity) and he knew it was time to begin to find a following for the movement that had come to him in a flash after years of being just a garden-variety transcendental meditator leading private groups in dance and emotional management. His work, as he called it, was partly dance continuum and partly contact improv but it went beyond movement to become an all-encompassing theory/praxis. It's all about the slash, he'd intoned.

Her own goals were hazier. She'd thought it would be great if she could get back to writing songs, and had even brought her own guitar, or maybe she would paint a bit, though there'd been some concern from Dirk about this when she'd asked where she could set up a painting studio. He'd pointed out the ecological nature of Hope Springs, and that pigment carried in any toxic media might not be the best thing for the local watershed if they hoped to make a good impression, given that he was coming with a family *entourage,* which, if you thought about it, hadn't been part of his original arrangement with DorAlba.

Entourage: Lana and her twins. When had they become a family entourage, additions to the main roadshow?

And that whole idea of *where would she wash the paintbrushes* started to occlude her consciousness so much that it started to seem almost nonsensical, a child's nattering. Why had she even wanted to paint here? Did she have some myth that she'd be Georgia O'Keeffe? Was she going to paint the twitch and dangle of all these naked people?

The desert makes many human enterprises start to seem foolish, or conversely, all too necessary for survival.

---

[8]Who were DorAlba, according to Dirk? Two MENSA types who had shot out of early brain experiments of the sixties and skidded through Kinsey-assistant-land only to land, Doreen in a muumuu, Albert in a sarong, in the beginning of the twenty-first century, leaving the management of their grounds to their trusted aide Hogan.

For instance, Lana tries hard to remember what had led her toward Dirk when she'd met him, there on the dance floor of that rain-spattered Catholic church four months ago: the sign being her womb opening, the walls falling away, and when they'd walked on the cliffs outside, the stories she'd chosen to tell him, when she half knew that certain stories you told men functioned like a universal Turing machine, creating few responses, opening a portal in the male psyche, making most surrender fear in order to make a move if said move was up for question. Concerning:

1) times you'd been raped or almost raped
2) times you'd worked as a go-go dancer
3) to certain men, you could tell the story about using heroin in Paris

This had to do with the circle jerk of aggression, the method in which testosterone acted in certain neural loops, evinced by her favorite scene in *Last Exit to Brooklyn*, and she told Dirk these stories with inarticulable instinct: he'd then spoken of his past in costume, many minutes before he knew whose daughter she was.

Wow, she'd said to Dirk on the cliff. You were the polar-bear guy?

Hermes, he says. It was a phase. I had to carry a message to people. I stalked Mahler, basically. For the first time, Dirk's grin turned goofy, embarrassed, wrinkled.

Now he realized, a beat late, that she had said *the* polar-bear guy, and that she must have seen him in the Hermes guise. You were, what, in high school?

How old are you anyway? she asked.

Polar bears don't age, he said. Anyway, why does it matter?

So Mahler.

You see why I'd be interested.

Not really.

I was one of his first real followers.

I don't even get that part. Why so many followed him, she said, with unusual passion, remembering the shaggies.

He looked at her walking along the cliffs, felt a first flare. They called him the Pied Piper, he said.

Her expression stayed fixed, like a ladder back, but how?

She didn't see his gaze; she'd watched her feet on the damp flattened sea grass. Really, what little girl could forget all of the shaggies camped out on her front lawn? Who could forget her own mother putting out scones and jam for the followers on Sundays? Their hippie gratitude for such humane touches, smitten by the mother as part of the Mahler myth. Transubstantiation! Hands that had touched Vic's privacy had crafted these banal scones and now extended the plate to dirty-nailed hands. Could the ubiquity of these shaggies have played a factor in her mother's death? Lana had never considered the possibility.

Back when Lana had been ten or so, suffused with the desire to be a nun in order to heal the world, a quick phase, she'd asked her mom: Can't we have the shaggies come and live in our wine cellar? This was a hard idea to explain, a harder one to win. Later Lana saw how patently absurd her idea was: the shaggies living in her parents' French-cheese-eating house among all the sociological tomes advocating equality?

I studied with Mahler in an undergrad class, Dirk was telling her. I went to find him in his office and waited with everyone else slumped in the halls. Then when I got my shot at the king I said I'm starting far behind, because that was my delusion at that time, that reading books made a person better, so I said to him how can I get ahead in reading books, you know, when I'm so far behind? and I swear the guy looked through me, I'm not kidding, and finally said: You shouldn't even be in school, you're a maverick, you should just go and live in Mexico, you'd learn more. Now, said Dirk, can you see how that just set me on this whole different path?

Not really. She was struck by how, when Dirk was speaking of her father, the light of youth came into his eyes, his language shifted so that she could see the passion and hurt boy that had been hiding behind his mantle of preternatural enlightenment, his rhapsody over natural beauty. This was a quality she sometimes liked in a man, what she'd liked in her boys' father, Kip. The hurt boy in dialogue with the grown, capable man, arguing with him; and then in bed the boy and the man would try to traverse the distance between the two by their passion for her. Then her body and being did become a ladder, as if she were a healing nun of sex.

When I got into school, Dirk was saying, Mahler basically stepped into the Jesus-shaped hole in my psyche. Like the guy really saw through me, I thought: God, the guy might as well have fathered me.

So you followed his advice?

Look, what can you do if someone really *knows* you?

He let the remark stay in the air, saw the unforeseen gift of it gathering all sorts of romantic grit and dirt he hadn't fully intended.

It's a gift, he said. You can't take that away from the guy. You know, news travels slowly. I heard he'd killed his wife, I gave up. I cut my hair, went straight, came back up north, got into contact improv in San Francisco, and now I'm here today.

They were circling the ruins of the burned hotel, turned in on themselves. Hey, he said. His face was bright in the dark. You were great on the floor today. Your spirit was so open. What just happened?

Can we not talk about it?

Like a shadow.

It wasn't a choice. It wasn't like choosing whether or not to tell a rape or go-go story. He'd compelled it out of her. She would tell him.

You know what? I'm Mahler's daughter.

The missing daughter of Mahler?

Lana Mahler.

Man. Dirk looked returned out of the smoothness of the 2000s to another era's jargon. He was happy, exultant, filled with the glory of return. Lana Mahler!

She doesn't really remember what else they talked about that night. Only his face: a riffled pack of cards, calibrating, some of the cards glowing. He turned back to talking about it. The justice of finding Mahler's daughter here in this nowhere coast town of Yalina. How amazing was that? All signs fit. Dirk had turned his life over to a crazy man, having fallen in with a whole Mexican group of liberationists because of him, and then the corrections system would never let Dirk visit Mahler. He's probably written you, though, right?

Then he said the thing about her mind and pussy. By this point, she had brought him to the porch swing, outside the house of her children's grandparents. We're not in touch, she said. Look, my kids are going to wake up.

I'll whisper. Anyway.

Later in bed he stuck fingers in every possible place and it was impossible not to come because it felt like a million slave Lilliputians had tied a string around her clit and were trying to push a giant stone attached to the string away from it—slow, tiny but resolute struggles toward freedom—and then the stone broke free of the string, boomeranged enough to liberate all the little slaves. When only the previous week she had made some inner resolve that she wouldn't be vulnerable with someone for a while, give herself over to the love craving.

*

When she made the decision to go south on 5 with him to Hope Springs, they had known each other four months. *Je t'aime jusqu'a la mort* was playing on the tinny local radio station. She would have to sell the plan big-time to her kids, because the kids stayed loyal to the myth of their great lost dad, a bursting brilliant flower too great for Lana, according to at least one of the myths sown in their seedbed by their grandparents. She had decided you couldn't really escape anyone's stories forever, but you could at least sidestep a few of the nasty ones, the kind that came too soon and tended to overstay their welcome.

Five Poems
Clark Coolidge

LEGACY OF THE PLUG

The pup is gone   want an amoeba?
or an orange thing?   a "schizophrenic"?
it's marginal but we'll play along
the same vocabulary only fun this time

I saw the roaring rush past the clock towers
not even the starlings tried to hold on
a breach of flying objects just the same
to end it all you drop   understand?

Tape ripped from the sides of scrapers with resounding smack
they developed special lamps from the building fund
after supper we made a little model to help us
think it's all vanilla or nougat at this point?

These light boxes kept on strafing our neighborhood
father came out all struck dumb from the bushes
he was a replacement we realized after
the habitual bulks had been hauled away at last

We made our peace with the director of the piece
a professional masochist named Rama Lama Dingdong
then the credits caught fire lighting the beach
goodbye to anything within reach

THE NORMAL IS

She's like talking to a plate of lemon ice
leads to nothing but sheared streets and Shetland sweaters
the eyes won't track properly   there's
something happening over there too   Jay Gatsby
hung on a pier   I'd rather go to Peru
get my heart broke in Cuzco for the elevation
as if I somehow just popped up   I knew it
raised a monster but didn't turn out right
all you do is shove somebody   go away
screw your head on right reason for example
oodles of confusion and addled high times
usually parks her car on my dime   why
do you think of stripes here?   there's no point
talking off the top of this nation of mistakes
whole hills of burlap and beaverboard plus other
tons of so far unlabeled whatever   all the shades of vitriol
witness to the fall of youth and its dumbass regularity
the worst part of growing up is the rest of your life

FAR OUT MIDWEST

I had a red outfit too one time
then the aliens appeared   they showed me
some miraculous products   artistic
bath appliances   bare spots on bedroom walls
where something once   don't need to knock to enter
the edge of a piece of paper not empty   I could
go on . . . why doesn't anyone?   meanwhile
out at the source of the circus tent
I burned my suit   after that the world
smelled of velvet right to the cheek
the closet   the settee   a photo of nothing
we all should have been bred better and now
there's always something wrong   insects   well
what do you want?   insects   in a blue moon
someplace jazz is being made   beds rented
I have news   buttons to push   which is which?

eyeballs to fiddle with   knocks that sound like laughs
they're coming and you mustn't mention me!
these things mean to be taken seriously
in a yellow cab back to Illinois I suppose
all right let's have it
pumpkin rises in deserted pond

A STORY CALLED MISTY

Do you promise to laugh?   the one about
the five thousand priests and the nine hundred dolls
probably have that one on the wall of your office
up all night with the realization   Tumbling Dice
world without price   born a double palomino
see you in the headlines probably the breadlines
I can hardly see at all   the minutes seem to crawl
most of our cereals come from Virginia the Piedmont
the Delta some bishopric or other   are you
my mother?   this is an homage to Williams to Stevens
to Doodad   Nimrod   Abracadabra and the Cooties
we met down on the farm   the foggy road to
speleogenesis   not good enough?   Elaine May
will save it in rewrite   secretly the snail
is in the mail   I recognized your name on the weapon
what no one else has dared to say: the sun sucks
the drill cores have been misplaced   never saw the results
we'll gather later at Trees Lounge for the music
alone   I feel Dizzy was almost removed from the show
replaced by Cool Jerk   by the next in line   by
the scoopful   an expensive leather tetherball
as a rule   tape your want list here
drop a dime on no one   topspin is permissible
always write your name in the center of the page

Clark Coolidge

A FEW WINDOWS PAST HARVARD

I remember when the world was three
the persons were not quite inhabitants yet
but they were sad   chortles in short supply
you'd think they'd learned to bend already
I watched them carry out some very clear operations
questions?   the morning when no different than
usual was invented   play me some Schumann
nothing was canceled due to rain
golf ball or even slaughter   no homes to go to
a slurry of a match useful at any rate
the Godz were out of town   someday they will find
a fossil with a serial number   forget the DNA
comes in tubes with a gravity drive
the Paleozoic starts with an overwrought thriller
ends as one too   what a universe   all details
determined by chance or necessity   one body
gets away and we have nothing   whatever
it will be found to be made of Ridiculum

Traffic and Weather
Marcella Durand

What acts as a mirror to a city? When it is a continuum how can a reflection be created? It continues itself but does not see itself, and will never see itself because it won't end. Or can reflections stop unchecked growth? If outside the city reflects the city, will the city look and stop? As the skyline across the shores reflects the skyline, will it then? To send in an imitation of itself. To confront situations it would rather not be in. A sort of reflection but more of a necessary recreation. How the city is like ourselves. The sound reminds us of rain. The rain simulacra begins. And surrounds us with reflective waters.

The skyscraper appears to breathe as light crawls over its reflective surfaces. From hundreds of windows people look out over the shores, rivers, and acres of grasses. I see it from a distance so can only guess at the buckling and distortion glare on its miles of aqua glass. And rooftop air conditioners, interior heating systems, engineered cross-shock dispensers. A faint wiggle of distortion at its very top: the venting apparatuses at work. A small flame burnt once . . .

and saw it from another office, this one blocked up or facing an air-shaft. Like a dream in which walls were prefabricated. Wall after movable wall brought out the door and fed into a trash compacter. The fine dust covers her each day as she walks by. And later she finds her desk and books covered in ash.

Like the tedious film they watched at the opening. It looped the same images, which weren't that interesting to begin with. Outside there was at least one construction project per block. A matter of permits. Too many of them. She thought she'd chronicle each project per day. It was a project on projects. But it doubled back on itself

151

and got nullified. That's what happens when everything in a city is documented.

It becomes opaque.

In every direction. It is written in a different space. So it is not *site specific*.

It arrives in an oblique green space.

That was what they were looking for. In the proposal. It had to adhere to the *area*. Engage the *location*. He writes site over sight as though it would be illuminating. Corners are not good enough on their own but must be enhanced. Or aggravated. Decoration everywhere and a sound like birdcalls from the ceilings. Inside the concrete warehouse were imitations of nature, including a magnetic fountain everyone found irresistible. Needles hung in a star shape facing inward. People kept pointing, moving their fingers closer and closer, but not touching. Outside, the sunset was somewhat obscured by low storage containers that should have been dismantled. Then clouds were only glimpsed between bridge lattices because, you see, we were directly underneath them. How unspeakable to see a bridge rise from the end of a street.

Later we reduced back to human scale and entered a chocolate shop in anticipation of dinner. The sun had already set and clouds were invisible in a navy-black sky. Only the bridges continued being illuminated. Those, and the skyline on the other side. Where we were returning again. Growing large and citylike.

> *Je suis un éphémère et point trop mécontent citoyen*
> *d'une métropole crue moderne. . . .*

I jingle coins in my palm as I stroll the streets of my unending childhood. I have never become a man. I have never let go of childish things. My discontent buds and blooms on a routine basis: often several times per day. I lack the softness that is developed by the ease of mechanical things. Unlike the echoes that surround me, I am both aware of and obtuse about sudden events. The unsteadiness of a man walking toward me alarms me; the distant sounds of explosions mean nothing. We walk together in the same direction, downtown. We return home at night together, uptown. Slightly southwest and then slightly northeast. We walk arm in arm, as the sidewalks were designed to accommodate. They were designed to accommodate four people walking abreast. They were designed for you, me, and two more friends. Or I weave around three others, four, five, six who fill and overspill the sidewalks. All the thousands who fill the sidewalks.

Rien de riche.—La ville!

Groups of people look at it; cars slow down. They forget about their destinations. Thinking about them might lead somewhere—else. As we climb down from the woods, the path grows less rocky; there are fewer fallen branches and vines. Then, abruptly, the path is cultivated: we are surrounded by lawn and garden. The grass is green and the undulations of the land are gentle.

le faubourg se perd bizarrement dans la campagne

Pockets of springs, every acre a spring. From primitive springhouse to fountain. Spouting out of horse mouths or over giant frogs. In a courtyard enfolded within an alley overhung with cultivated plants in another part of the neighborhood and shuttered windows and attic quarters. A gray light pierces through skylights in which the glass is wired, making small parallelograms. Or they sandblast the facade again. Years later, dust from the "event" still sifts in through closed windows. Later that day she returns to find her desk covered in ash.

153

It is not *site specific.* Every proposal has to find a way to make exploited areas meaningful again. Even surrounded by developments and land-usage plans and township restrictions, the proposal must be *site specific.*

To be *site specific:* Enhance your understanding of the area. Artistic intervention in a "specific locale." Rehabilitation of brownfields? Industrial park! Exploited, developed, "privileged sphere," doubt the artist, make the artist doubt herself, extracted, gentrified, strategic. Prairie park. Desert orchard. City monument.

A: Strategic site. Surveyor. He is: a surveyor.

I am going back to work and you ask directions. Let me tell you a story about giving directions. Two people of indefinable gender stopped to ask which way the old wall uncovered by recent transit authority construction on a cross-harbor tunnel was. He couldn't remember the historical significance of the street name so told them to look for large landmarks by which they could steer. They were so bundled up against the cold all he could see was their eyes. They wanted to know where the closest public library was and he had absolutely no idea, so he told them to continue twelve miles down until they came to the pizzeria, at which point they were to turn left and continue onto the bridge, even though dusk was falling.

More stories about giving directions: The sailboat was supposed to be a fun ride on a soft summer night, until ferries trapped it between a tanker and a barge. The couple walked so far they came to a mall. A mall, in a city! Even if they had taken books out of the library, they would never have been able to return them. He was pretty sure they had accents. And when they asked him to take a photo . . .

Well, and the old wall was covered with blue sheeting and plywood. Even now they're still looking for it.

Or ropes swinging outside the window. A bad sign, indicating scaffolding and facade sandblasting to come. They appear at night and wield blasters over the faux limestone exteriors. Then you return to find large chunks of decorative elements embedded in the sidewalks in front of the door. That's the hazard of a city. In high winds, metal takes off and flies. A crosshatched upward swirl of wind lifts napkins, wax paper, paper bags, and newspapers. They reach to the *nth* floor and then sail out into the harbor.

In the other space gray light comes in through the skylight. No view of skyscrapers, light falling across a facade, a faint glint of river, nothing. Just an oblique track of fluorescent light above the air conditioner. Pools of water in plastic, protecting against the dust. A space when you should be in the other space. You long for it. The place you want to be. Although if you were in that space, you would want to be in the other space. It's like that, equally divided. The wind fills one part of the sail while the current pulls at the other. Each space is almost imaginable in your mind. As though to be there was to commute and discover only a small playhouse. To commute via rail or flight, or walking twenty minutes to be in an extension of the same city, or another city. That's why the suburbs are unimaginable. The same street curves around in intentional design. Design by one person makes it unimaginable when you are not him or her.

A conglomerate of mutual designs, a hodgepodge, a chaotic street structure built one upon another makes it imaginable, or at least one can dream about it.

Je suis un éphémère . . .

It arrives in an oblique green space.

How amazing to witness all this construction in one year. The steam cranes pump the pilings into the ground, as wooden planks are inserted to hold up the dirt. Small piles of rock and soil are meager

155

from years away from light. Not everyone who walks by eyes it for arrowheads or small beads.

All of that was already taken, as when the original bargain was made.

All this construction in one year. A ladder crashes through the glass *histórico* and everyone exclaims. Luckily it was on the dark side of the street, so no one was walking there. The entire city often feels like a *balloon frame:* built on wood, flammable; if combustion begins we'll spread one to the other, we are here together and conduct construction like electricity. . . .

as though we are electrical creatures

shocking each other

and linked as though through outlets

conducting relative to one another

a network, a web

of our communal electricity

as though we are outlets

or currents

and combustible in a way

electricity is not combustible in itself

we electrify ourselves

with our own electricity

no levels of wattage, no buffers

but directly one to another

current to each other

as the city catches fire

and explodes

visible to the most distant suburbs and exurbs, and settlements
    after those

and dark outlying areas very far out

a column of electrical fires

and bridges opening

as though we were water

as though once more living here could become ecstatic

NOTE. The italicized text comes from Rimbaud's "Ville," "Métropolitain," and "Villes II" in *Les Illuminations*.

Two Poems

C. D. Wright

END THOUGHTS

In the beginning the usual dark dark of very dark
In a few years there appears a crack in the dark a very small crack
The crack as I said appears very small
      and jagged as cracks are

The temperature has already been adjusted
      by the state
Our obsolescence built into the system

When you use the ladies' room
      do not put your purse on the floor
When the civilian words are dispensed
      different meanings will be assigned
The new meanings will be fired
      at the head and groin area

For instance saying Can't a girl get anything to eat around here
would now signify Water with a stomach wound is fatal
or if you were to say The mariachis are coming
      it would be interpreted as Just open the f___g trunk

All extroverted activity will be suspended
      in residential zones
Absolutely no tea parties under the trees

Crying helps
Crying doesn't help

One wants to make oneself smaller than the mouse
under the icebox one wants to dry into invisible ink

One has a sense of something out there that needs saving
      and one ought to attach the buckle
to a heavy gauge wire and pull him through

Waking up knowing this much is not the hard part
nor lifting the head from its existential drift
      it's the sticking of one's foot off the edge
      lowering it to the cold floor

and finding the correct instrument
to work that crack into a big enough opening
      to venture forward

Before the fall no story after the fall the old story
After the fires floods along with serpents and bugs
After the floods years of drought
After drought just dusk which is when everything
      really begins to hurt

      and then there is the human dimension

LIKE THE GHOST OF A CARRIER PIGEON

In a couple of hours darkness will throw its blanket
over the scene   she will pretend to read a mystery
      the mower and hammering will cease

The bees leave the andromeda and then

So much has been spent constructing a plausible life
she did not hear the engines of dissent run down

Some still attempt to cover the skull with the wire of their hair
      others shave everything instead

A solitary relives the pleasure of releasing his bird

There is no sacrosanct version   there is only time

C. D. Wright

Even now   if someone yells Avalanche   she has one
thoughts shudder against the ribs and go still

Soon the son would be out running around in her car
with a sore throat   soon the decibels commence killing off hair cells

She checks to see if the phone is charged and then

The ones responsible for slaying the dreamer are mostly in the ground
but the ones responsible for slaying the dream

suffer only metabolic syndrome

Even now   that her supply of contact lenses has dwindled
                    she was refusing to sing the Wal-Mart song

The bees would be back and then

All efforts at reconciliation aside   even if everyone exchanged germs
                    happiness is only for amateurs

A dress worn only once before has been hung on the door
                    the mirror under the cloth receives its image

Crepuscule with Mickey
Christopher Sorrentino

I AM INVITING HE and his wife to come down here on account of my own familiar feelings. Kids, as they say, is a pain in the tuchis by trade, and while those belonging to others is something I ordinarily do not care to become involved with, and generally speaking I am greatly opposed to guys who stick their nose into the business of other families, as I grow older I find it a pleasure to extend my authoritativeness on account of longevity into realms I might have avoided in my youth.

This is despairing people we're mentioning. They come for help as people in such straits oftentime have.

I am meeting them at the airport because struggling you shouldn't have to do when one gets off an airplane, and a car waiting is always nice. The bus and taxi transportation is a laugh and despairing people I feel should be as relaxed as possible when having a sit-down meeting in which a favor is to be asked. I have Victor drive me in the Fleetwood. He is a big shtarker direct from the island of Sicily, and what with his Victor-type face I have so named him for my convenience and easy reference.

They are all like pets; I name them. Easier, it makes things. Walking beside me through the airport is Big Frankie. What moniker did Frankie's mother dub him on the day he dropped? Who knows.

It is a charter flight and they come off of it. She is a fine-looking dame, taking dainty little steps with her little feet and ankles just so. This is what I am informed and do believe are *class cues*. This is a phrase obtained from the sociology-type people who have from time to time had occasion to speak with me. Anyway, they are a big tell, the tiny feet growing out of those sculptured ankles, and those little footsteps just ringing out with class and the sort of upbringing that use to be rare before it became widespread. Believe me, it was easier on the eyes to look at him. Don't mistake: according to me, she is gorgeous. In a way she reminds me of a girl, that use to work at the Half Moon, that was also a class act. But, regards him, just that he is a much more restful person to take a gander at, just set in his relaxed

161

and sort of easy way. If I were a big dog type of person, which I am not, he would remind me of a golden labarador, with his relaxed bearing, a guy what does not care if his breakfast gets all over his cardigan, or what.

There is an exchange of handshakes all around. I grab her hand and give it a good wobble because you don't know what to do with a lady these days and she gives this look that also spells class to me.

"Come on," I says, "I got a car waiting. You must be tired after the plane ride."

"It's a very short flight," she says, as if what I said isn't just something you say to say something, "I'm sure we're all right."

"So, you're walking?"

This gets a laugh out of him. Not her. But mothers with missing girls, I extend credit in their direction. She is looking very stressful. In addition of which, a guy like myself is definitely outside her ken.

"Get the bags, Frankie," I says to take initiative. In my experience a person will follow their suitcase wherever it goes. Frankie takes hold of the bags and carries them to the trunk while Victor gets out to open the door for the two of them, holding out his hand to help her in though she high-hats him.

You could say that a limousine is a very unsociable vehicle with the blacked-out windows and the driver that is big, uncommunicating, occasionally carrying small arms, and in sunglasses of that aviator type which is now widespread. But to me it is a matter of discretion and of course once inside the Fleetwood it's a different story. Inside the Fleetwood you're obliged to pass the time of day, if only to say, "Look, you mind if I sit facing forwards? Because I get a little feeling in my stomach from facing in the wrong way." You make a conversation, in other words. Now that I am putting my mind to it, it is a lot like the way it is with a cellmate in stir. Anyway, it is clearly up to me to break the ice of our conversation we haven't been having yet and I look across at him gazing in his easygoing but somewhat traumatic way out the window and her crossing one tiny ankle across the other, the woman who weighs a hundred pounds, net, and most of it the hairs on her head, which stand straight up and look hard, like a lemon meringue pie.

The popular press says what I am is the heir to the gambling empire of Bugsy, which nobody called him anything but Ben, Siegel, which I do not care to dispute because it would involve splitting hair. Anyway the thing which always has bothered me is the allegations which they're contending "Mickey Cohen lives extravagantly" or "Mickey Cohen loves publicity." I live the way I always have outside of the prison walls and I am the first or at least in the top three persons to admit that I don't see any good coming out of personal discomfort. On the other hand there is publicity, but let me point out two things which is first that nobody is mobbing me at the airport—which in the city of Los Angeles in the 1970s is the well-known place for celeberities to arrive and depart at and for their fans to greet them hollering and with autograph books and cameras flashing—so how much in other words publicity could there be?; and also so tell me what is so wrong with publicity? Danny Thomas receives publicity. Eartha Kitt receives publicity. Victor Borge receives publicity. Dean Martin receives publicity. I am a law-abiding citizen that has paid debts to society and if I am committing some big sin receiving publicity in the city of Los Angeles then let he who lives in a glass house cast the first stone.

I point things out on the drive, the civic improvements. Because what is a person if he isn't proud of the accomplishments of his city?, plus also the quiet can get you in a car-sized space. The main thing, though, is impress them with the sense that they're with a real citizen. Don't ask me how but someone who can show a feeling for the finer things right off the bat has a shot at coming off like a real human being. She just shakes her head, though, then moves her hand out from under his.

He says, "We made our home here in Los Angeles for several years, Mr. Cohen."

"It's a big city," I says. And I'm thinking all of a sudden of this episode of a cop show I seen once, where a nice kid just goes haywire; drugs, hair, moving out from the house in Sherman Oaks to like Hollywood, like a total Fuck You. Not that they say this in the show, but the idea. And it makes me think: if I ever was thinking I didn't want to join out with them in finding their daughter, then my mind is changed, I definitely do want to lend them a hand. Because a child that looks in its father's face and goes, Well Go Fuck Yourself—that is a big heartache, and you rue the tongue biting, the cut-it-out-with-the-nagging you're always saying to their mother; you think of that little pile of cigarette butts what you found under the hedge by the pool, you said nothing; the mileage on the car that mysteriously shoots up by forty, fifty miles a clip, you keep it to yourself; the short phone calls she's taking on the extension in the other room you're not in, seldom a word out of you; all those things where you say: OK, a good head she's got on her. OK, maybe it's just a little maze she is going through. So who could say no? Rachmones, in other words, is what I got.

Over at my house he sort of just flumps down into a chair but he is up on his feet again when I offer up the suggestion maybe you want to help yourself to a drink? People like to make their own drinks, I notice. She is walking around the room taking things in, trying to catch me at what she would think of as a mistake, though one of the first things I educated myself to purchase with hard-earned money is other people's good taste, and the place I can assure you is decorated with the snazz of one of the better hotels. He is standing at the bar examining all the manner of bottles and decanters I have lined up over there, snuffing a little which can happen when you get off of a plane because of what I read about the breaths of all the passengers mingle in the ventilation and could cause a cold to develop, so I suggest to him a shot of rye whiskey, neat, which is popular for its ability to assassinate germs at once.

He takes one of the decanters and lifts the stopper and takes a sniff. He says, "I've got to confess that I'm not at all sure of why we're here."

She says, "Oh, really?" She says, "That's quite an about-face. Before, you were so certain that we had to drop everything and come down here immediately." She says, "Just spit it out, Randy. This isn't the time to be polite." She says, "We're wasting Mr. Cohen's time."

I says, "I got time." As to illustrate this fact I seat myself. Meanwhile, he makes himself this drink and it is a healthy one. Still not in a big hurry to unburden himself so while I naturally cultivate a sympathy toward the husband in the event of marriage, I am beginning to see her point of view. He says, finally, "Well, you see," and it is at this moment that the thought arrives; he is worried about insulting me. From this, I get a laugh. The thing of the easy-offended gangster is a fairy tale, because life sets out to insult the gangster. It is a lifelong enterprise from birth, not a college major such as journalism or basketball. Which is the way of saying, I'm use to it.

"Why are you laughing?" he asks me.

"Is something *funny*, Mr. Cohen?" she says.

So I place my hands up near my face and wave them around a little, like I am trying to rid myself of a school of bees.

"Something is funny which is that you flew all the way on a plane down here to talk to me and now you're not talking. So why not try me?"

164

"Mr. Cohen," he says, "one of our reporters at the *Examiner* had suggested that you might be of assistance to us. As you may know, we've fallen out of touch with our daughter and—"

"Who got snatched."

"Yes," he says slow. "She was kidnapped from her apartment in Berkeley. And it's causing us some, that is, we're anxious to—"

"They carried her out of there *naked*," she says. "Can you imagine how embarrassed she must have—"

"Excuse, but this is the *San Francisco Examiner*?"

"Yes, of course."

"The Monarch of the Dailies?"

"That's what we call it, yes." He is sounding a little doubtful. It is the sort of thing I throw in there from time to time to slow a person down in their speech, sometimes to a stop. I think he's understanding this. He does not look like a guy who is anxious to hear his wife talking about his daughter getting hauled naked into the street.

"Mr. Cohen. That's hardly pertinent. As I was trying to say, our daughter was carried, naked, from her apartment—"

"Hearst papers always had the best funnies. Nobody's actual father took the *Journal-American*, but you would try to find the *J-A's* funny papers whenever you got the chance. Or was it the *Daily Mirror* we loved?"

"Now, how could you confuse the two?" He laughs, sits down across from me, and he is ready to talk about this for a while. I mean the discomfortude is gone because who's got the touch?

"The old papers," I says. "Everybody loves the old papers."

"The tatterdemalion newsies."

"The thunder of the presses."

"The whiskey-voiced old newspapermen."

But I lamp her out of the corner of my eye and see she is overdue to start in again, saying, you know—carried, naked, street.

At a certain point I was obligated to enroll in a course for recidivistic offenders so called. It was entitled Crisis Intervention and one such technique is the heading off of the lengthy yammering of excited yentas, which are certainly a crisis in my estimation. Our Group Leader, which was by way of calling him the teacher, instructed us to *defuse* and *anticipate*, and it is apparently obvious that the defusing thing has not worked so that I should lay out her beef for her and the theory is that she'll shut it up.

"So your daughter is carried away in the night and naked into the bargain. It must have been very embarrassing. And for you, too. And now she is schlepping guns all over the place and calling you bad names in addition."

It is certainly safe to say that I am sympathizing in all sincerity. It is my own sweet child which told me to shove off, though never were there guns carried, or statements of the seditious variety—but in the end these are just the trifling details for I am the type guy who can spend happy hours crying and snuffling into his soup, toting up heartache, getting sick with it, hives and eczema, cold sweats and nausea, haunted by the impression of the hole they'd shove you in if they had half a chance—I mean, like, whoever—and so who is need-ing details to make you feel worse? So her specific case: naked, guns, nasty names. "Acknowledge their concerns," is what Group Leader said. "Repeat them back to them, acting as a verbal mirror."

"I got some daughter trouble, too," I says. "Trouble begins in dribs and drabs. One day she starts taking meals in her room. The room smells like tuna fish and sour milk and on everything there's cracker crumbs. One day you find the cerise chiffon gown you got her stuffed like an old shmatte into the bottom of her wastepaper basket. One day you find narcotics paraphernalia."

"*Our* daughter was *abducted*," she says.

He says, "Catherine. It's not a competition. I think Mr. Cohen is just trying to empathize."

Ordinarily by this point I would be delighted to urge some guests I'd just made the acquaintance of to refer to me by my first name, which is Mickey as opposed to Meyer which is a name I never had too much use for, but I am very unnaturally pleased to be addressed formal style, with title and sir-name.

"Empathize!" And she shoots me this look that tells me that all appearances to the contrary you can't fool her that my daughter wasn't born on the misfortunate side of the track.

"Relate," Group Leader said. "Don't debate!"

"I am relating to you that I understand your situation, that if a helping hand was extended in my basic direction when I needed it I might have found my daughter elsewhere than amid the stars of Hollywood Boulevard, which incidentally are covered with globs of spit and chewing gum and whatnot. Bringing her home again was like bringing home the dogfaced boy; whiney, scratching at the door, and we are like, 'Now this is how you sit in a chair like a human person. This is how you cut a piece of meat. This is how you put a fork inside of your mouth.' I mean like, this is how you engineer a human bite of food."

"Honestly," she says. She takes a cigarette out of a pack of them, and starts tap-tap, tap-tapping it on her lighter.

"Maybe for you it would be easier," I says.

"I'm *certain* it would be," and on this note she puts the flame to the end of her butt.

I says, "So, we agree." Genial, but still this appears to raise a hackle or two and after one puff the cigarette goes right into the ashtray.

"Not on very much we don't," she says. "Let me put it to you, since my husband seems incapable of doing so. My husband is under the impression that your criminal connections—"

A wince from him here. "Not at all the way I would have put, characterized it."

"—put you in a better position to get information concerning our daughter's whereabouts and well-being. My husband is also under the impression that it would be better, after receiving the information from you, to act upon it directly, without providing the information to the authorities. On this second point," she looks at him, "we vehemently disagree. I believe that if we are capable of locating Patricia, the best way to welcome her back would be with the proviso that she take full responsibility for her actions."

"We do disagree," he says. "I'm just interested in knowing that she's all right. If she doesn't want to come out of the underground then that's fine. If she needs our help in some other way, I'd like her to know she has it."

"Oh, ho. Ho ho ho ho ho ho ho." This giggle is like a series of fine little French-accent "o's," total high-pitched and floating along. I wish I could draw for you a picture of her fine little red mouth shaping itself up to come out with the laughing sound, sending him deeper into this like downshouldered slunch with each little laugh. What it'd be like, I wonder, to have that laugh laughed at me every day for the last thirty years, usually when things already weren't a big picnic to begin with.

Him and I go for a walk in the garden. Because at some point she sticks her fingers in the little space of forehead between that big lemon meringue of hair and issues forth a complaint apropos of a headache. So I send her into a bedroom to lie down with a couple of aspirins, or Datrils, or Darvons—her head, her choice. Though they have made it plain that they have other arrangements, I'm glad the room's getting a little workout. I have a Filipino lady, her name is

Rebecca which by me is not a Filipino name, and I had her make the room up. According to Rebecca this is an "extra." Everything I want from Rebecca is an "extra." That is how Rebecca works it, for the supplemental buck.

He is a big meditational guy and he is blinking in the sun as we walk. I have a bench in a gazebo. I have a wishing well that doesn't actually go anyplace but that looks nice on the lawn, with even the little windy thing you bring the bucket up with. I have a real pool in the shape of a kidney but this has actually been empty due to a problem with cracks lately, don't ask.

That room was my daughter's that she is lying down in.

He takes off his glasses and rubs his eyes. This is a guy who, if sleep is the issue, he isn't getting any.

"You know, what she is talking with her full responsibility is a number of years in a federal facility," I says.

"I know," he says. He puts his glasses on his face so they repose there a little bit crooked. "But Mrs. Hearst always has been concerned about appearances. It used to be funny. I suppose it still is. But I believe it makes her feel better; to insist that our reputation is the important thing, to worry over whether someone is thinking the less of us. That, she feels as if she can do something about. Which is a damned sight better than she was feeling those first weeks, when it was all worry and dread. We felt as if there was literally nothing we could do except wait, wait and follow instructions. Everyone assuring us that everything was under control. But I knew that they didn't have anything under control. I knew that they didn't care. Always did sound a little too damned much like a groundhog hunt for my taste."

He gives his head a shake (the glasses waggle), and I'm knowing it never occurred to him before all this to face the whole thing of Your Life Is Nothing, Your Family Is Meat. Which is the natural state, what you could spend your whole life working against, building to rise yourself up out of zero, nothingdom, so that in the event of duly constituted authorities tipping up their hat brims to take a good long look at you they actually see something. For me to establish myself as a person of this kind of substance it meant one tough series of tasks, and some persons have spoken of them in an ugly manner. And I will be swift to admit: ugliness was involved. The tasks involved some ugly behavior. But I had to figure it out as I went for I was working in like complete blackness: my father left me less than nothing in that respect as far as an inheritance, I am speaking of guidance in the ways and means of success. He figures he's born helpless, he might as well die that way. When finally he passes on, he passes on kvetching to God about the busted gas ring in the kitchen, or the toilet leaking upstairs into the apartment. He was a guy that when you looked at him you didn't see nothing.

Can you imagine living through the whole entire thing of your life and when finally you're summoning all the chutzpah you got to talk to God you complain to him like he is the superintendent?

It was maybe from myself and him that I was able to look ahead and get a gander at the troubles in the cards for my children. I mean I would not for one instant say that everything I put together I put together for her, but it was not for nothing. It was not for greediness. They say, "Mickey Cohen loves publicity, he loves the extravagant lifestyle," but what they are really saying is that maybe it would be more *correct*, more *proper* for Mickey Cohen to be another invisible person who when they remove him from his house to a federal facility nobody sees him go or hears his lawyer making a big impression on a judge or a jury. They are protesting me rising myself up out of nothingdom. They are saying that all this really shouldn't belong to me at all. But I put it all together. And when the time finally came, everything was there for to help her. She needed help and I had made sure to provide. And guess what: it didn't mean shit.

And that is what he is just figuring out, now.

"Anyway," he says, "to Catherine's way of thinking, that's the important thing to rectify. That's the thing we need to set right: make sure everyone knows exactly who it is that they're dealing with. Make sure that in the end everyone knows what she *really* stands for. In a sense Catherine dreads her return. She's worried about what she'll say and do, whether she'll make a mess of all the hard work of shoring up our honor."

I am undecided as to exactly who are all the "shes" in this. But I says, "Whatever makes her feel better."

He says, "It makes me feel worse, the way she feels better."

A child becomes sick, a child misbehaves. A child invents strange games that involve having a conversation with themselves in a whisper. A child steals coinage you leave lying around just for the purpose. A child makes friends who you would rather they did not. A child breaks a toy from sheer carelessness and then hides the broken bits behind the furnace. All of it could smash your heart. What are you hiding the broken pieces for? Of your papa you're afraid? Tsatskeleh, who could care about broken toys? Toys are for breaking! And besides, who has the time? Papa's squaring everything away like some squirrel with nuts stuffed in his jowls. Back at the house, the wife, maybe she drinks. Or she is on a diet plan which is involving the gospel of the New Testament. Or she takes dancing lessons from a Brazilian homo. Nuts in your cheeks, your paws scrabbling on the herringbone floor. The maid going for the supplemental buck, and slipping to your kid ethnic foodstuffs into the bargain. Go ahead and try to establish a legacy. Go ahead, provide for the future. What a joke. And then what?

I am feeling a very disconsoling feeling, remembering and considering. I want to assist a couple in the locating of their daughter; what I get is a man and a wife and the usual bunch of difficulties. How not? Already they found out they are not so important as they wanted to think. Now they find out they aren't even so important to each other. And that is something which it takes a lot to bring out into the light. How long can you hide it and pretend? *Long* is how long. I says to myself, *"Fix it* for them, Mickey. You can *fix it."* What can I tell you? That is the way I'm built. For years people come up to me, "Help. Fix. Mend. Patch up." You get use to it. People thinking that you have all this excess confidence you can just lay off on them.

I says, "Well, here is what I know. From my criminal connections." This is a statement with the intent for him to laugh at it, but he makes a weird face. I select not to inform him because it can be an embarrassment to be advised what emotion you ought to have.

What I tell him is about a guy named Rosenthal in Cleveland. Rosenthal at times can be a tedious guy because what he likes is he likes to bring his wife up, who is formerly a Cohen before getting married to him. And he insists upon informing you every time you find yourself with the pleasure of talking to him that just off the boat his wife's family changed the name to Cohen in order to grab a higher social rung on the ladder. The real name is, I don't know what. The thing that burns Rosenthal's ass is that it worked: the father goes to Princeton. Under this phony and purloined name of Cohen he is attending Princeton, and then in due course he is married at the Kane Street Synagogue, and then the daughter arrives, and then comes the textile factory on the shores of Lake Erie, and then sooner or later who blunders along but Rosenthal with questionable business practices and you might call undersupplied ethics but with this completely legitimate name of Rosenthal. And it has been burning his ass for ever since. He gets so tired of being high-hatted by phony-baloney Princeton Cohen that he finally just burns the guy's factory down on the spur of the moment. An incident of enduring ugliness. He always goes to me, "Now, you're the real Cohen, Mick, right?" Why he doesn't just change his name to hers when he marries her, I don't know. A meshugeneh. I think of the *real Cohen* my father standing there five minutes every morning trying to get the stove lit. A real leg up. But the point, which this is besides, is that what the information Rosenthal has is that the girl has been spotted in the Cleveland area.

He says, "Are you sure, Mr. Cohen?"

I says, "It's what I hear."

I says, "Arrangements can be made. Right here and now, we can make arrangements."

He says, "We'd better wake up my wife."

I says, "She ain't sleeping."

What happens is we come back in the house and like I figured the Mrs. is up and in the living room doing her little chatchka tour, her hands lifting up and weighing items like fingered scales, as if there is not enough proof of my good taste for her two eyes all by themself. Bigger dummies than me have good taste, is all I want to say, they have magazines that tell you how. Every month the Horchow Collection arrives in my mailbox direct from Dallas, full of crystals and pieces of grainy oak and the clocks with Roman numbers on them.

"All right," he says. "Mr. Cohen discussed his proposal with me further. I think you ought to hear what he has to say."

She says, "You have to make me sound so disagreeable."

"So, you're all ears?" I'm still making with a light sort of tone. Because sometimes that is the best way to set a person straight without actually giving them an opinion how they ought to behave which nobody ever likes.

"Yes," she says. "I am *all ears*, Mr. Cohen. I am always listening. I listen to what my husband has to say about what we ought to do about this. I listen carefully to the opinions and advice of Charles Bates with the FBI."

"Good man, Bates," I says. This is such a obvious bullshit comment that I'm still waiting for it to hit bottom because nobody says nothing.

"I am actually *always* listening to people, and more often than not agreeing to the ridiculous, inappropriate things that they propose, and when, as they inevitably do, these things bring matters to a pretty pass, and I belatedly put my foot down, it is always *my* fault. It will *always* be *my fault.* So please tell me your ridiculous, ill-advised plan that can only make matters worse so that I can have had too much of such ideas and my husband then can alternately berate me and ignore me all the way back to San Francisco. Please."

Well here is the plan in a sketchy vein: Rosenthal has two niggers he knows that are reliable enough considering that they are junkies and that can be persuaded to do many things for cash money which as is well known can be somewhat difficult to come by for Cleveland nigger junkies. Rosenthal also has an interest in a private ambulette service in Cleveland. What the idea is is that Rosenthal provides one of his ambulettes and uniforms and such to the niggers as well as some small arms and we are also dressing the Mrs. in the uniform of a nurse (which in my opinion suits her). We, meaning them, go to an address that Rosenthal is providing, bust in, and rescue Patty while she, the Mrs., sits tight in the ambulette. The back door is thrown open, there is the joy of a reunion (that's how I put it), and then the ambulance heads for a small airfield near some burg called Macedonia, sirens going the whole time. I mean, who is going to stop a squalling ambulance to lodge queries? In the Macedonia place Patty is trundled aboard a small plane and shipped back to California.

She says, "And how do we explain to the authorities that we recovered our daughter at gunpoint with the assistance of some shady ambulance service operator and two colored drug addicts?"

"Authorities?" I says.

"I think I've made it very clear," and here she takes a gander at her husband, not me, "how I feel about all of this. She'll have to own up."

"I am doubtful Rosenthal will go for that."

"It really isn't any of Rosenthal's business."

"Well but, it is. Because like you're saying, how you going to explain it?"

"We wouldn't have to mention Rosenthal's name."

You could be pretty surprised at what you feel like you ought to mention sometimes under questioning by officers of the law. But what I says to her is, "The very idea is something that makes a personality like Rosenthal balk."

"What about our hiring people and going in ourselves?" he asks.

"This would be smart if it were possible but it frankly ain't. Seeing as Rosenthal has solo possession of the address."

"But of course he'd have to give it to us. It would be illegal for him to withhold it," she says. "He could find himself in hot water."

"That, lady, is not the approach you take with a Rosenthal. Especially since he's got everything that you want and you don't got nothing that he wants at all. This is a favor he's doing, and he's doing me the favor, not you. I got kids. He knows I know how it is with kids and that it's me wants to help you. He couldn't give a fucking shit. Frankly." And this is the extent of the French speaking I do.

"Well," she says after taking a few seconds to do some self-composing. "Getting back to where we were before. That sticking point, telling the authorities. We simply wouldn't mention his involvement. We're people of our word. No one even has to know that we've spoken with *you*."

"Oh," I says, "they know already."

See, the thing of it is I am kept under a pretty close watch. I have a relationship with the cops that is not exactly giving each other Christmas presents but it's like I am familiar with their names and how many children and I had Rebecca give one of them an egg salad sandwich once (yeah, an "extra") when his lunch gets run over. Long story. And they are conversed with who comes in and who goes out and I am careful to restrict my telephone chatter to lawful conversations like how about that Steve Garvey and whatnot and when the time comes to mail personal correspondence I will sometimes drive hither and yon to pop it into the mailbox in North Hollywood or Toluca Lake. But this news seems to strike them like an anvil on the head or a grand piano with a broken rope, and they are real quiet for a longish time.

Finally, she says, "Well, I think it's all perfectly ridiculous. A *nurse's* uniform."

I says, "You could be a doctor if you wanted instead."

He says, "Mr. Cohen seems to be open to some give and take, Catherine."

"Are you trying to be funny?"

The room is starting to get dark. A real Filipino would right around now come in to light the lights but since Rebecca is not being paid an extra dollar or two to make it worth her while these are the kind of thing I do myself.

"I don't think," she says, "that this sort of arrangement will do at all."

"Maybe we ought to think about it," he says.

"Think about what? About taking the word of dishonest people? About involving ourselves in a harebrained scheme? About paying to charter a plane to fly us back to San Francisco? And what about this charter plane business, Mr. Cohen?" She gives me a look. "Is that your friend Rosenberg, too?"

He opens his mouth and then shuts it after making this groanlike sound that if it was the beginning of a word you couldn't guess what the word was.

Now in my house I am alone again. That guest bedroom looks as if a smallish person maybe gave the mattress a whirl but not much more than that. A paper cup is crumpled up at the very bottom of the wastepaper basket in the bathroom, but something about the kind of hospitality that you measure on the scale of a crumpled Dixie Cup gives me a sad, old feeling of being nothing.

I think of my girl, that face in the windshield as the car backed down the drive the last time, I am waving good-bye, everything will be OK. What I packed into that wave, like it was the most important message I was sending with my arm: everything will be OK, it will be you and me practicing walking together, me holding onto your hands; it will be a birthday cake for you to blow on all the candles of wearing an imitation straw hat, a what do you call them, a boater; what happened to Santa? what happened to training wheels? We can go through picture albums and laugh at the haircuts if she wants. That arm was saying, isn't it enough to know that I'm waiting for you, right here in this spot? Isn't it enough, the arm was saying, that you have a father's every confidence? And this was in spite of everything under the bridge so far, which was quite a bit. The car rolled down the drive and turned into the street and then it was gone.

Nowhere

Joyce Carol Oates

MY MOTHER, I WISH . . .

The first time no one heard. So softly Miriam spoke. In the din of raised voices, laughter. In the din of high-decibel rock music. She was into the beat, sweating with the percussion. Shaking her head from side to side and her eyes closed. Leaking tears but closed. *My mother, I wish someone would . . .* At the crowded table no one noticed. It was the Star Lake Inn, the deck above the lake. Music blared from speakers overhead. Had to be the Star Lake Inn though it didn't look familiar. The moon was rising in the night sky. She'd lost her sandals somewhere. Couldn't remember who'd brought her here six miles from home. Then she remembered: the boy from the marina driving the steel-colored Jeep. Not a local guy. He'd been flirting with her all week. Her heart skidded seeing him. Big-jawed boy with sun-bleached hair, had to be midtwenties, father owned one of the sleek white sailboats docked at the marina but Kevin wasn't into taking orders from the old man like a damn cabin boy, he said. Anger flared in his pale eyes. He was from downstate: Westchester County. Half the summer residents at Star Lake were from Westchester County. He'd thought Miriam was older than fifteen, maybe. Gripping her wrist not her hand helping her up into the Jeep. A stabbing sensation shot through her groin.

Had to be past 11 p.m. The moon continued to rise in the sky above Mt. Hammer. She'd gotten off work at the boathouse at 6 p.m. In the Jeep she'd called home on her cell phone. Left a message for her mother she'd run into friends from school, wouldn't be home until late.

Please don't wait up for me, Mom. Makes me nervous, OK?

The boy in the Jeep didn't know Miriam's brothers, hadn't known Miriam's father. *Orlander* meant nothing to him. Maybe to his father who owned one of the new A-frames on East Shore Drive *Orlander* meant something. In the Adirondacks there were local residents and there were property owners from downstate. If you

175

were a local male you worked for the downstate property owners: carpentry, roofing, plumbing, hauling away trash. You paved driveways, you exterminated vermin. You fenced off property to keep out deer hunters like yourself. The expensive new lakeside houses were always in need of upgrading: redwood decks, children's rooms, saunas, tennis courts. Les Orlander had been a roofer. His brother-in-law Harvey Schuller siphoned out waste from buried septic tanks and dug new septic fields. *Your shit smells sweet to me* was a joke bumper sticker Miriam's father had had printed up but Harvey kept it displayed in his office not on his truck. If you were a local female you might work inside the summer residents' houses: cooking, caring for children, cleaning. You served at their parties. You picked up after their drunken houseguests. Uncomplaining, you wore rubber gloves to retrieve from a stopped-up toilet a wadded Tampax or baby diaper someone had tried to flush away. You wore a nylon uniform. You smiled and hoped for a generous tip. You learned not to stack dirtied dishes from the dinner table but to remove each plate ceremoniously murmuring *Thank you!* as you took the plate away. *Thank you!* you murmured as you served dessert and poured wine into glasses. *Thank you!* mopping up spilled wine, on your hands and knees picking up shattered glass. Your employers called you by your first name and urged you to call them by their first names but you never did. Ethel laughed to show she thought it was funny, such bullshit. Not that she was a bitter woman for truly Ethel was not.

Beggars can't be choosers, right!

Miriam's mother thought this was an optimistic attitude.

Three years of his five-to-seven-year sentence for assault Miriam's father served at Ogdensburg Men's Facility and during those years of shame her mother worked for summer residents and for a Tupper Lake caterer. Often Ethel stayed overnight at Tupper Lake twenty miles away. It began to be said in Star Lake that she met men there, at the resort hotels. She took "gifts" from them. At this time Miriam was in eighth grade and deeply mortified by both her parents. Her father she loved and missed so badly, it was like part of her heart was locked away in the prison. Her mother she'd used to love but was beginning now to hate. *Wish! Wish to God something would happen to her.* When Miriam's oldest brother, Gideon, confronted their mother one day, Ethel shouted at him that her life was her own not her damn children's. Her "money life" and her "sex life" she said were her own business not some damn loser inmate's who'd let his family down. Shocked then by the fury of the words roiling from her,

Ethel had tried to laugh, saying it was a joke, some kind of joke, anyway isn't everything some kind of joke, the way life turns out?—but Gideon would never forgive her.

Quit roofing, moved to Watertown, and impregnated a woman he never married and a few months later enlisted in the U.S. Marines and got sent to Iraq.

Even when their father was paroled and returned to Star Lake to live, Gideon avoided the family. Every time Miriam came home she steeled herself for news of him: he'd been killed in that terrible place. Or for the sight of Ethel, disheveled, lying on her bed in the waning hours of the afternoon.

I wish. Why don't you. Why, when you're so unhappy!

"Looking lost, Miriam? Where's your rich boyfriend?"

Miriam was a girl to be teased. A hot blush rising into her face. Her eyes were warm glistening brown with something shrinking and mocking in the droop of the eyelids. Her hair was streaked blond-brown, the commonest color. Before meeting Kevin after work she'd hurriedly brushed out her hair, pursed her lips applying dark red lipstick to make her appear older, sexier. Now it was hours later and the lipstick was eaten off and her hair was in her face and so many guys looking at her, laughing at her, all she could do was shake her head, blushing and embarrassed.

Oz Newell, who'd been Gideon's closest high-school friend, was calling down the table: "What'd he do, the fucker, take a leak and fall in? Want me to break his head?"

Nervously Miriam laughed, shaking her head *no*. She was scared of something like this. Older guys relating to her like she was their kid sister, wanting to protect her and somebody getting hurt.

Her brothers had gotten into fights at places like the Star Lake Inn. Her father.

Star Lake Resident Pleads Guilty, Assault.

Reduced Charges Lead to 5-7 Years at Ogdensburg.

The kind of work men did here in the Adirondacks. A belligerent attitude was natural. Drunk Friday night was natural. It was sheer hell to take orders from foremen, bosses. Rich men from downstate like Kevin's father. "Manual laborer." By age forty-five you'd be limping. By age fifty your back is shot. Natural to want to break some fucker's head. Miriam thought, *I had fists like theirs, I'd feel the same way.*

Must've been Miriam had wandered past their table looking lost. Looking like a girl who's been dumped by her boyfriend, trying not

177

to cry. Also she's underage. Also she's never had sex. Also she's been sick feeling, gagging in the restroom in one of the smelly toilet stalls but nothing came up. Whatever he'd given her, *Baby, you need loosening up.* In the Jeep, a joint they shared that made her cough, choke, giggle insanely. At the Star Lake, vodka and cranberry juice for Miriam. She was confused where Kevin had gone, exactly where they'd been sitting, couldn't find the table, someone else had taken the table, but maybe Kevin was inside at the bar, maybe Kevin was looking for her? Cigarette smoke made her eyes sting and blur, she couldn't see. Somebody grabbed at her arm, grinning faces lurched at her: "Miriam? Miriam Orlander? What're you doing *here!"*

So she was sitting with them. Practically on Brandon McGraw's lap. Like she was their little-girl mascot. Maybe because she wasn't beautiful. She was fleshy, warm skinned, but not beautiful. These were older guys in their twenties who'd gone to school with her brothers or who'd worked with them. One or two of them might've worked with Miriam's father. And one or two of them with Miriam's uncle Harvey Schuller. Where their girlfriends and wives were, Miriam wondered. When she asked, they told her it was boys' night out. She figured they'd come to the Star Lake Inn immediately after work to begin drinking. In summers you worked late, until 7 p.m. Miriam's father and brothers worked even later. The table was strewn with dirtied plates, empty bottles. The remains of hamburgers, deep-fried shrimp, pizza crusts. Onion rings, cole slaw, ketchup. A grease sheen on the Formica surface. The table was outdoors, above the lake; still the air was heavy with smoke from their cigarettes. They were drinking beer, ale, whiskey. They were drunk, high, stoned. Miriam saw the red-rimmed eyes she knew to associate with drugs: speed, crystal meth. These guys weren't into smoking dope like the kids she knew. Beyond wanting to feel mellowed out and restful like they could love mankind. She shivered to hear: raw male laughter like a braying of coyotes. Their young faces were reddened, coarse and prematurely lined from outdoor work. Their shoulders, necks, upper arms were thick with muscle. Their hair was buzz-cut short, or straggling past their collars. Martin had worn his straggly hair tied back in a kind of pigtail. The loggers and tree trimmers, who worked with chain saws, were likely to be scarred or missing fingers. If Miriam got drunker/sillier she'd count how many fingers were missing from the table. Sex energy lifted from the men's heated skins frank as sweat. Most girls would be uneasy in the company of so many men but not Miriam Orlander, who'd grown up in a household with three older brothers she'd adored.

Well, mostly. Mostly she'd adored them.

And her father, Les Orlander, she'd adored.

"Drown the fucker in the lake, who'd know? His rich daddy can drag the lake for his corpse."

This was Hay Brouwet. The subject seemed still to be whoever it was who'd brought Miriam to the Star Lake Inn, then abandoned her.

"What d'you say, Miriam? Pick out which one he is."

Quickly Miriam said, "He isn't here now. I don't see him."

Hay cupped his hand to his ear, not hearing. The rock music was so loud. The braying at the table so loud. Miriam caught her breath, seeing the smooth-shiny stub of Hay's right forefinger. Hay was a logger, must've had a chain-saw accident. Miriam felt faint imagining having to kiss that stub. Suck that stub, in her mouth. *If he asks me to, I will.*

In the Jeep, in the parking lot, Kevin made some joke about Miriam sucking him off, but Miriam pretended not to hear. In the tussle she'd lost her sandals. He hadn't meant to hurt her, she was sure. *Hey, baby, I'm sorry: just joking.*

Except Hay was married, wasn't he? One of the older guys at the table, had to be thirty. Seeing Miriam's eyes on him, winking.

"You see the asshole, let me know, OK?"

It was pretty clear Hay was high on something. That mean-happy red-eye-glittering look and he'd sweated through his shirt.

Crystal meth. Each of Miriam's brothers had instructed her individually never to try it. Not ever! Miriam was scared but intrigued. She knew that Stan, who was twenty-three, had had something to do with a methamphetamine lab—a cook-shop, it was called—but he'd never gotten caught and now he lived up in Keene. Ice was for older guys, not a fifteen-year-old girl whose hope was to go to nursing school at Plattsburgh State. An immediate high, wired straight to the brain. Her brother Martin was back in rehab at Watertown. *Fries your brain like nothing else. Makes you shiny and hard. Why's that bad? What's better you got to offer?*

Ethel had slapped him, he'd been yelling and laughing and stomping in the house so hard the windowpanes shook like a army bomber from Fort Drum was passing too low over the roof. Martin had hardly felt the blow, only brushed Ethel away like you'd brush away flies.

A few minutes later they heard him outside. A noise of breaking glass.

"Miriam, what the hell? You crying?"

179

It was the smoke. Making her eyes water. Her eyeballs burned in their sockets. She was annoyed, shaking her head *no*, why'd she be crying? She was having a great time.

Her left wrist where Kevin had grabbed and twisted was reddened in overlapping welts. Half consciously she was touching the skin, caressing.

"He do that? Your wrist?"

"No."

Brandon McGraw's blood yellow eyes were peering at Miriam's wrist. His bristly eyebrows nearly met over the bridge of his nose, which was large, red flushed, with deep, stretched-looking nostrils.

A look of shocked tenderness in Brandon's face so you'd almost want to laugh. Like the look she'd seen once on her father's face as he squatted in the driveway to stare at something small, wriggling, dying, a fledgling robin blown out of its nest.

"Like hell, Miriam. This looks like a guy's finger marks."

"Really, no. I'm just clumsy."

Miriam drew her arm away. Shrank both arms against her chest.

How she'd got there she didn't know. Six miles from home. Too far to walk in the dark. Missing her shoes. She was drunk, she'd been sweating so. *Miriam! I've been sick with worry.*

She hated Ethel. Couldn't bear to see Ethel.

Alone. The two of them. In the house on Salt Isle Road. Ethel, Miriam. Where there'd been six people, now reduced to two.

These guys felt sorry for her, Miriam knew. Seeing her they were thinking *Orlander: bad luck.*

"He didn't hurt me. I don't care about him. See, I'm having a great time. I want to dance."

Dance! Miriam wanted to dance! Stumbling and almost falling. The floor tilted beneath her like was the deck a boat? Were they on a cruise boat, on the lake? choppy waves?

Through the speakers blared heavy metal rock. Maybe you could dance to it. Was anybody dancing? Miriam wasn't the girl this was happening to. Miriam wasn't the type. How she'd got here to the Star Lake, which was a biker hangout on the marshy side of the lake, she didn't know. Underage but looking eighteen at least. No one asked her for ID. The kind of place the bartenders stayed inside and there were no waiters. You pushed your way in, got drinks from the bar, pushed your way back out onto the deck. Lights on tall poles. Insects swirling around the lights like demented thoughts. Miriam's brothers had come here. She'd been eating cold french fries from one of the greasy plates. Hadn't eaten since lunchtime. None of this was remotely like Miriam Orlander. At the boathouse she was the girl who blushed easily. The girl who didn't flirt with men. Had not wanted to waitress so she worked in the store where she was the youngest salesclerk who got stuck with the hardest work like unpacking the merchandise, stocking the shelves. What embarrassed her was the female employee uniform she had to wear. Red T-shirt with white letters AU SABLE BOATHOUSE straining against her breasts. Worse yet the white cord miniskirt trimmed in red. The miniskirt rode up her thighs. Sitting, she had to keep her knees pressed tightly together. Walking, she had to tug at the skirt, uncomfortably aware of her thighs rubbing together. Men stared. Some smiled openly. Miriam was a healthy girl: five feet six, one hundred thirty pounds. Ethel had crinkled her face at the uniform. *Miriam! I don't think this is a good idea.* She'd wanted to come with Miriam to the boathouse to speak with Andy Mack, who'd hired Miriam and provided the uniform for his "girl" employees but Miriam had screamed at her and run out of the house.

Now Miriam was dancing. Wild and tossing her body like it's impaled on a hook she's got to wriggle, wriggle, wriggle to get free. Oz Newell was dancing with her and for a while Hay Brouwet. For such burly muscled guys, they got winded fast. Miriam laughed at them. Miriam loved how the music poured like something molten into her veins. The beat was so fast her heart raced to keep up. Maybe it was ice he'd given her, maybe this was the ice-rush and she loved it. Breathing through her mouth, panting. Bare feet, kind of pudgy-pale feet, toenails painted dark to match the sexy lipstick, she's picking up splinters in the tender soles of her feet from the raw floorboards but doesn't feel any pain. Not a glimmer of pain. No more pain! Maybe it doesn't matter if she isn't beautiful the way Oz Newell is looking at her. His eyes on her breasts in the tight red T-shirt, his eyes on her soft rounded belly, her hips and thighs in the tight white miniskirt trimmed in red. Rivulets of sweat trickle down Oz's sunburnt face. Oz does construction work for Herkimer County. Oz had some kind of disagreement with Gideon; they didn't part friends. Miriam is weak with sudden love for him. Laughs to think how surprised Oz would be, she slipped her bar arms around his neck and tongued his face, licked away the sweat droplets like tears. Oz is twenty-five or -six. Ten years older than Miriam. Gideon's age. Not a boy but a man. His hair is a blond buzz cut. Eyebrows and lashes so pale you almost can't see them. Gray eyes like pinwheels, spinning.

181

Hay Brouwet is back, and another guy, fattish and drunk-silly, grimy baseball cap on his head advertising WATERTOWN RACEWAY. The dancing, if you can call it dancing, is getting out of control. Hay is shaking his shiny stub-finger in Miriam's face, gyrating his hips like some stoned rock star, collides with an older man carrying beers, two beers in the stretched fingers of each hand, and the beers go flying, there's a comical scene like something on TV, Miriam is helpless, laughing, panting, and breathless and almost wets herself. There's a feeling like fire: wild fire. The guys' eyes on her, the heavy-metal vibrations thundering inside her head. Like, with a fire, the wind blows it in one direction and not another—it's the difference between somebody's property going up in walls of roaring flame and somebody else's only a few hundred feet away, untouched. There are controlled burns in the Adirondacks. You have to get permission from the county. And there are uncontrolled burns—lightning, campers' fires, arson.

Arson. There's times you are so angry, so bitten down, you need to start a fire. Toss a match, evergreens dead and dried from acid rain, it's like a fireball, exploding. Miriam remembers one of her brothers saying this. *Hey: just joking.*

Miriam's father had been a volunteer fireman for Au Sable township. There'd been years of the excitement and dread of hearing the siren, a high-pitched wail from the firehouse a mile away, seeing Daddy roused to attention, hurriedly dressing if it was night, running out to his pickup. Often they'd smelled smoke, seen smoke rising above the tree line, heard sirens. Those years Miriam had taken for granted would go on forever. But after Ogdensburg, Les hadn't rejoined the volunteers. Maybe there was a law against ex-convicts being volunteer firemen, Miriam hadn't wanted to ask.

Abruptly the deafening rock music stopped. For a moment Miriam didn't know where she was. Her eyeballs were burning as if she'd been staring stupidly into a hot bright light. Inside her tight-fitting clothes she was slick with sweat like oil. Damn miniskirt had ridden up to practically her crotch. Like a child Miriam wiped her damp face on her T-shirt. Somebody's arms came down heavy on her shoulders, somebody stumbling against her, a big guy, soft-fleshy belly, a smell of whiskey and heat pouring off his skin. Quick as a cat Miriam disentangled herself and backed away. Ran barefoot to the edge of the deck where, overlooking lapping water just below, it was quieter, smelling of the lake. Miriam recalled as if through a haze that she was at Star Lake: six miles from home. The way the moon was slanted in the sky, now east of Mt. Hammer, it had to be late. *Worried sick about you. You're all I have.*

Star Lake was dark, glittering by moonlight. Said to be in the shape of a star but, up close, you couldn't see any shape to it only just glittering water and opaque wedges of shadow that were trees and, on the farther shore, the east side, lights from the new houses, not visible from the shore road. Miriam had never been in any of these houses, she had no friends who lived in them, mostly these were summer people who kept to themselves. Their houses were architect-designed A-frames, split-levels, replicas of old Adirondack log lodges. The last months of his life Miriam's father had worked for a roofing contractor on several of those houses. He'd been disbelieving, the prices people from downstate were paying. *Like another world,* he'd said. *It's another world now.* He had not seemed especially grieving, that day. Quiet and matter-of-fact informing his daughter as if it's something she should know.

"Hey, baby. Where you goin'?"

A hand came down on Miriam's shoulder. Fingers kneading the nape of her neck beneath her damp crimped hair. Miriam felt a stab of panic even after she saw it was Oz Newell. Now the music had stopped, she wasn't so sure of herself. *I don't want this. This is a mistake.* Miriam managed to twist away from Oz, but grabbed his hand, as a girl might do, to pull him back to the others, to the table. Oz slung his arms around her shoulders and nuzzled her hair, called her baby as if he'd forgotten her name. Miriam felt weak with desire for the man, unless it was fear. "I miss Gideon. Damn, I miss your dad." Oz's voice sounded young, raw, clumsy. He had more to say but couldn't think of the words. Miriam murmured, "I do, too. Thanks."

Halfway back to the table Miriam saw the jut-jawed young man from the marina, weaving through the crowd. It was a shock to see him, she'd taken for granted he'd dumped her. Was Kevin his name? Was this Kevin? Miriam hadn't remembered him wearing a Yankees cap but she remembered the arrogant jut-jaw face, the streaked blond hair. He was walking unsteadily and hadn't seen her. Or, seeing her, had not recognized her. He was alone, appeared to be looking for someone. Miriam wondered if maybe he'd been in the men's room all this while, being sick to his stomach. His face looked freshly washed and not so arrogant as he'd seemed with just him and Miriam in the Jeep when he'd bragged of his father's sailboat and twisted Miriam's wrist. Miriam pointed him out to Oz: "That's him."

183

2.

Did it to himself.

This was a way of speaking. It was the way she knew they were speaking. It was a way of wonderment, and of accusation. It was a way of consolation. In Au Sable County and Star Lake and where Les Orlander had been known. A way of saying *Nobody else is to blame, no one of us. Nobody did it to him, he did it to himself.* Yet it was a way of admiration, too. It was a way of saying *He did it to himself, it was his free choice.* A way of acknowledging *He did it to himself, he had the guts for it and not everybody has.* In the Adirondacks, a man's guns are his friends. A man's guns are his companions. Les Orlander had not been a fanatic gun collector like some. Like some of his relatives and in-laws. Shotguns, rifles. Legal weapons. Les had owned only a shotgun and a rifle and these were of no special distinction. *Did it to himself, used his rifle* was a tribute to the man's efficiency. *Did it to himself, out alone in the woods.* A gun is a man's friend when friends can't help. A friend to protect him from shame, from hurt, from dragging through his life. A gun can make a wounded man whole. A gun can make a broken man stronger. No escape except a gun will provide escape. *Did it to himself* had to be the legacy he'd leave his family.

3.

You know I love you, honey. That will never stop.

He'd said that. Before he went away. Miriam was staring out the school-bus window. Her breath steamed faintly on the window. Her eyes were glazed, seeing little of the landscape: trees, fields, roadside houses, mobile homes on concrete blocks at the end of rutted driveways.

. . . come see me, OK? Promise?

There came the tall, clumsy Ochs girl lurching toward her. As the school bus started up, lurching along the aisle staring and grinning at Miriam. She was at least two years older than Miriam: fourteen, one of the special education students at school. Her face was broad and coarse and blemished in dull red rashes and bumps. Her small cunning eyes had a peculiar glisten. Lana Ochs wasn't retarded but said to have "learning disabilities." Her older sister had been expelled for fighting in the school cafeteria. On the bus, no one wanted Lana to sit with them, she was so large boned, fidgety, and smelled like rancid milk. Miriam's backpack was in the seat beside her. She was saving a seat for her friend Iris. Miriam stared out the window as Lana approached, thinking, *Go away! Don't sit here.* But Lana was hunched over her, grinning. She asked, "This seat taken?" and Miriam said quickly, "Yes, it is." For Iris Petko, who was in Miriam's seventh-grade homeroom, would be getting on the bus in a few minutes, and Lana Ochs knew this. Still she hung over Miriam, swaying and lurching in the aisle, as if about to shove Miriam's backpack aside. In a whiny, insinuating voice she said, "No it isn't. It isn't taken, Miriam." Miriam was sitting halfway to the rear of the bus. There were several empty seats Lana might take. In another minute the bus driver would shout back at her to sit down; it was forbidden to stand in the aisle while the bus was in motion. Miriam said, "It's for Iris. You can sit somewhere else." Her eyes lifted to Lana Ochs's flushed face, helpless. Lana's hair was matted and frizzed. Her lips were fleshy, smeared with bright red lipstick. Older boys on the bus called Lana by an ugly name having to do with those lips. Lana leaned over Miriam, saying in a mock whisper, "Hey Miriam: your father and my father, they're in the same place." Miriam said, "No, they're not." Lana said, "Yes they are. That makes us like sisters." Miriam was staring out the window now, stony faced. She was a shy girl but could be stuck-up, snotty. In seventh grade she had that reputation. Her friends were popular girls. She received high grades in most subjects. She'd had three older brothers to look after her and there had been a certain glamor accruing to the Orlander boys who'd preceded their sister in the Star Lake public schools. Now the youngest, Martin, a sophomore at Star Lake High, no longer rode the school bus but got a ride into town with friends. Miriam was vulnerable now, not so protected. She could smell Lana Ochs leaning over her, saying in a loud, aggrieved voice for everyone to hear, "You got no right to be stuck-up, Miriam. Your father is no better than my father. You think you're hot shit but you're not." Miriam said, "Go away. Leave me alone. I hate you," and Lana said, "Fuck you!" swinging her heavy backpack against Miriam, striking her on the shoulder. Now the driver, who should have intervened before this, braked the bus and shouted back at them, "Girls! Both of you! Stop that or you'll get out and walk." Lana cursed Miriam and swung past the seat, sitting heavily behind her. Miriam could hear her panting and muttering to herself. Miriam fumbled to open her math book: algebra. Her heart was beating frantically. Her face burned with shame. Everyone on the bus had been watching, listening. Some she'd thought were her friends, but were not. Wanting to scream at them, *Go away! Leave me alone! I hate you.*

At this time, Les Orlander had been incarcerated at the Men's Maximum Security Prison at Ogdensburg for just six days.

4.

Ogdensburg. Almost as far north as you could drive in New York State. And there was the St. Lawrence River, which was the widest river Miriam had ever seen. And beyond, the province of Ontario, Canada.

Miriam asked Ethel could they drive across the bridge to the other side someday, after visiting Les, if it was a nice day and not windy and cold, and Ethel said, distracted, glancing in the rearview mirror, where a diesel truck was bearing close upon her, on Route 37, "Why?"

It added something to the prison, Miriam wanted to think, that it had once been a military fort. Built high on a hill above the river, to confound attack. From the access road the prison was too massive to be seen except as weatherworn dark gray stone like something in an illustrated fairy tale of desolation and punishment. Beside the front gate was a plaque informing visitors of the history of the prison: "Fort La Présentation was built in 1749 by French missionaries. It was captured by the British in 1760 and its name changed to Fort Oswegatchie. After the Revolution, it was the site of several bloody skirmishes in the War of 1812. In 1817, its name was changed to Ogdensburg and in 1911 it was converted into the first state prison for men in northern New York State. In 1956—" Ethel interrupted irritably, "As if anybody gives a damn about history who'd be coming here." Miriam said, stung, "Not everybody is like you, Mom. Some people actually want to learn something." Miriam made it a point to read such plaques when she could. So much that was shifting and unreliable in her life; at least history was real.

It was a way, too, of telling Ethel: *You aren't so smart. You didn't graduate from high school. As I am going to do.*

Probably Ethel was right, though. Visitors to Ogdensburg had other things on their minds.

Everywhere were signs. PRISON PERSONNEL ONLY. RESTRICTED AREA. TRESPASSERS SUBJECT TO ARREST. VISITORS' PARKING. VISITING HOURS. PENALTIES FOR VIOLATION OF CONTRABAND RESTRICTIONS. A ten-foot stone wall topped with coils of razor wire surrounded the prison. Once you got through the checkpoint at the gate, you saw an inner electrified six-foot wire fence, angled sharply inward. Whenever she saw this fence, Miriam felt a clutch of panic picturing herself forced to climb it, like a frantic animal scrambling and clawing to twist over the top, cutting her hands to shreds on the glinting razor wire. Of course, she'd have been shocked unconscious by the electric voltage.

No one had escaped from Ogdensburg in a long time.

Ethel was saying with her bitter-bemused laugh, "Damn prisons are big business. Half the town is on the payroll here. Guards run in families."

Once you passed through the first checkpoint, you were outdoors again, waiting in line with other visitors. It was a windy November day, blowing gritty snow like sand. The line moved slowly. Most of the visitors were women. Many had children with them. Many were black, Hispanic. From downstate. A scattering of whites, looking straight ahead. *Like sisters*, Miriam thought. No one wanted to be recognized here. Miriam dreaded seeing someone from the Ochs family who would know Ethel. She hadn't told Ethel what Lana Ochs had said on the bus that everyone had heard. *Your father and my father. In the same place.*

Miriam didn't know why Lana's father was in prison. She supposed it had to do with theft, bad checks. Though it might have been assault.

It wasn't uncommon for men in the Star Lake area to get into trouble with the law and to serve time at Ogdensburg, but no one in the Orlander family had ever been sent to prison before. Miriam remembered her mother screaming at her father, *How could you do this, so ashamed, ruined our lives, took our happiness from us and threw it into the dirt and for what!*

Miriam had pressed her hands against her ears. Whatever her father had answered, if he'd shouted back or turned aside sick and defeated, Miriam hadn't known.

It was true: Les had taken their happiness from them. What they hadn't understood was their happiness because they'd taken it for granted, not knowing that even ordinary unhappiness is a kind of happiness when you have both your parents and your name isn't to be uttered in shame.

Les had been incarcerated now for nearly eighteen months. Gone from the house on Salt Isle Road as if he'd died. *Doing time.*

Miriam had constructed a homemade calendar. Because you could not buy a calendar for the next year and the next and the next, at least not in Star Lake. On the wall beside her bed she marked off the days in red. *Wishing-away time* was what it was. Miriam overheard her mother saying on the phone, *You wish away time, like wishing away your life. Goddamn if I'm going to do that.*

Miriam hadn't understood what Ethel meant. She'd understood the fury in her mother's voice, though.

Les Orlander's sentence was five to seven years. Which could mean seven years. Miriam would be nineteen when he was released and could not imagine herself so old.

"Move along. Coats off. Next."

They were shuffling through the second checkpoint, which was the most thorough: metal detector; pockets and handbags emptied onto a conveyor belt; coats, hats removed, boots. Ethel was flushed and indignant struggling to remove her tight-fitting boots. Each visit to Ogdensburg was stressful to her. She seemed never to accept the authority of others to peer at her, examine her belongings, query her. She was an attractive woman of whom men took notice, if only to stare at her, then dismiss her: a face no longer young, a fleshy, sloping-down body. Breasts, hips. Since her husband's arrest and imprisonment she'd gained weight. Her skin seemed heated. Her dark hair was streaked with gray as if carelessly. In the parking lot she'd smeared dark lipstick onto her mouth, which was now downturned, sullen. The black female security guard was suspicious of her. "Ma'am? I'm asking you again, all the contents of that bag *out*." Ethel's hands were shaking as she fumbled to comply. Miriam was quick to help. Under duress, she immediately became Ethel's daughter. She would side with her mother against others, by instinct.

Orlander, Ethel and *Orlander, Miriam* were checked against a list. A guard directed them into another crowded waiting room. Hard not to believe you were being punished. Related to an inmate, a criminal, you deserved punishment, too.

Everywhere they looked was glaring surfaces. Rooms brightly lit by fluorescent tubing. Linoleum floors, pale green walls. Where a surface could be buffed to shine, it shone. Miriam had never smelled such harsh odors. Disinfectant, Ethel said. "One good thing, there's no germs in this damn place. They'd all be killed."

"I wouldn't be too sure, Mom. We'd be killed before that."

"God, I hate it here. This place."

"Think how Daddy feels."

"'Daddy.'" Ethel's voice quavered with contempt.

Don't hate Daddy! Miriam wanted to beg. *We are all he has.*

The night before, Miriam hadn't been able to sleep. Misery through the night. She could feel her skin itching, burning. Her sensitive skin. Rehearsing what she would tell her father that would make him love her. That was all it was, trying to make Daddy love her. When she'd been a little girl, the baby of the family, it had been so easy, Daddy had loved her, and Mommy, and her big brothers, who'd adored her when they had time for her. Then something happened. Miriam had gotten older, Daddy wasn't so interested in her or in his family. Daddy was distracted, Daddy was in one of his moods. Drinking, Miriam knew. That was it. Part of it. He'd had disagreements with the roofing contractor for whom he worked. He'd tried working on his own but that brought problems, too. Ethel said, *Things change, people change. What's broke can't be whole again* but Miriam didn't want to believe this.

Driving to Ogdensburg that morning, Ethel had been unusually quiet. That week she'd worked at Tupper Lake for two days, two nights and so she'd had that drive and now the drive to Ogdensburg and she was tired. She was tired, and she was resentful. Not one of Miriam's brothers was coming this time, which meant Ethel had to drive both ways. Miriam was only thirteen, too young for a driver's permit. Ethel had her own life now. In Tupper Lake. At home, the phone rang for her and she took the portable out of the room, speaking guardedly. Miriam would hear her laugh at a distance. Behind a shut door.

She's seeing men. Les better not know. Miriam's brothers were uneasy, suspicious. Gideon hadn't yet confronted Ethel. Miriam was frightened, preferring not to know.

Her skin! Her face. Broken out in hives and pellet-hard little pimples on her forehead; her fingernails wanted to scratch, and scratch.

"Miriam, don't."

Ethel caught Miriam's hand and gripped it tight. What had Miriam been doing, picking at her face? She was stricken with embarrassment. "Do I look really bad, Mom? Will Daddy notice?" Ethel said quickly, "Honey, no. You look very pretty. Let me fluff your bangs down." Miriam pushed her mother's hands away. She was thirteen, not three. "I can't help it, my face itches. I could claw my ugly face off." Miriam spoke with such vehemence, Ethel looked at her in alarm.

"Yes. I know how you feel. But don't."

At last they were led into the visitors' room, where Inmate

Orlander was waiting. Ethel poked Miriam in the side. "Smile, now. Give it a try. Look at Momma, I'm smiling."

Miriam laughed, startled. Ethel laughed. Clutching at each other, suddenly excited and frightened.

"Go on, honey, Your daddy wants to see *you.*"

Ethel urged Miriam in front of her, like a human shield. The gesture was meant to be playful but Miriam knew better. Ethel would hold back while Miriam talked with Les; she wasn't so enthusiastic about seeing him as Miriam was. They had private matters to discuss. Their transactions were likely to be terse, tinged with irony and regret.

Miriam smiled and waved at her father, who was standing stiffly behind the Plexiglas partition waiting for his visitors. Les Orlander in olive gray prison clothes, one inmate among many.

Here was the shock: the visitors' room that was so large, and so noisy. You wanted the visit to be personal but it was like TV with everyone looking on.

And the plastic partition between. You had to speak through a grill, as to a bank teller.

Les was frowning. Seeing Miriam, he smiled, and waved. Miriam didn't want to see how he glanced behind her, looking for Miriam's brothers and not seeing them.

Third visit in a row, not one of Les's sons.

"Sweetie, hi. Lookin' good."

He would look at her, smile at her. He wouldn't ask about the boys, in Miriam's hearing.

". . . got something for me there?"

They brought Les things he couldn't get for himself: magazines, a large paperback book of maps, *Civil War Sites.* These Miriam was allowed to give to her father, with a guard looking on. Harmless items, printed material. Les seemed genuinely interested in the Civil War book, leafing through it. "We'll go to Gettysburg. When I get out."

It was unusual for Les to allude to getting out to Miriam. There was a kind of fiction between them, in this place, of timelessness; so much energy was concentrated on the present, cramming as much as you could into a brief visit, there wasn't time to think of a future.

"So—what's new, honey? Tell me about school."

School! Miriam couldn't think of a thing.

For visiting Daddy she'd cultivated a childish personality not her own. Like auditioning for a play, reading lines with a phony forced enthusiasm, and smiling with just your mouth. Bad acting and everyone knew but it had to be done for you could not read in your own flat, raw voice. To sound sincere you had to be insincere. Miriam told her father about school. Not the truth but other things. Not that, this past year, her teachers seemed to feel sorry for her or that she hadn't many friends now, in eighth grade; she'd lost her closest girlfriends, like Iris Petko she'd known since first grade, guessed their mothers didn't want them to be friendly with Miriam Orlander, whose father was incarcerated in a maximum-security prison. Miriam supposed that Les didn't know what grade she was in or how old she was exactly, for he had other things on his mind of more importance. Still he seemed to want to hear her news, leaning forward cupping his hand to his ear. In prison he'd become partially deaf in his right ear, the eardrum had burst when someone (guard? inmate?) had struck him on the side of the head shortly after he'd arrived at the prison. Les had not reported the injury as he hadn't reported other injuries and threats, saying if he did, next time it would be his head that was busted, like a melon.

Miriam's father was a stocky, compact man in his late forties. He'd had a hard-boned good-looking face now battered, uncertain. Scars in both his eyebrows like slivers of glass. His dark hair had been razor-cut military style, leaving his head exposed and vulnerable, the tendons in his neck prominent. He was prone to moods, unpredictable. His eyes were often suspicious, guarded and watchful. Miriam loved him but also feared him, as her brothers did. So much of her life had been waiting for Daddy to smile at her, to single her out from the others in his sudden, tender way; as if Daddy's feeling for Miriam overcame him, caught him by surprise.

Hey, sweetie: love ya!

He'd been wounded by life, Miriam knew. The hurt he'd done another man had rebounded to him, like shrapnel. Les had the look of a trapped creature. You never wanted to antagonize him; he had a way of striking out blindly.

At Ogdensburg, Les was assigned to the metal shop. Making license plates, dog tags. His pay was $1.75 an hour.

Again he was thanking Miriam for the Civil War book. The Civil War was one of Miriam's father's interests, or had been. Les had never been in the army but his father, Miriam's grandfather she'd never known, had been an army corporal who'd died in his second

191

tour of Vietnam, long ago in 1969. Les's feeling for his father was a confusion of pride and anger.

"We'll go, baby. I promise. When I get out. I'll be up for parole in . . ." Les tried to calculate when: how many months.

It was time for Ethel to talk to Les. Ethel's hand on Miriam's shoulder, to release her.

Miriam waved good-bye to her father, smiling hard to keep from crying. Les mouthed *Love ya, baby!* as Miriam backed away.

In the visitors' lounge there were vending machines, a scattering of vinyl chairs. Everyone who visited an inmate at Ogdensburg seemed to be hungry. Cheese sticks, potato chips, candy bars, doughnuts, soft drinks. Mothers were feeding children from the machines. Children sat hunched and eating like starving cats. Miriam was faint with hunger but couldn't eat, here.

She never wanted to hear what her parents talked about. Never wanted to hear that low quivering voice in which Ethel spoke of financial problems, mortgage payments, insurance, bills, work needing to be done on the house. *How can I do this without you. How could you leave us. Why!*

There was no answer to *why*. What Miriam's father had done, in a blind rage: use an ax (the blunt edge, not the sharp: he had not killed the other man, only beaten him unconscious) against a man, a home owner, who owed him money for a roof-repair job, and Les had been charged with attempted murder, which was dropped to aggravated assault, which was dropped to simple assault to which he'd pleaded guilty. If Les had been convicted of attempted murder he might have drawn a ten-to-fifteen-year sentence.

Everyone said, *Les is damn lucky, the bastard didn't die.*

"Hey: want some?"

A fattish boy of about seventeen surprised Miriam, thrusting out a bag of CheeseStix at her, which Miriam declined. Out of nowhere the boy seemed to have stepped. He had a blemished skin, a silver ring clamped in his left nostril. He wore a jungle fatigue jumpsuit with camouflage spots that looked painted on the fabric, crude as cartoon spots. He was a head taller than Miriam, looming close. "Hey: where're you from?" Miriam was too shy not to answer truthfully, "Star Lake." The boy whistled, as if Miriam had said something remarkable. "Star Lake? Oh man, where's it? Up by the moon? That's where I'm headed." Miriam laughed uneasily. She guessed this was meant to be funny. She hadn't ever quite known how girls her age met boys outside of school, what sorts of things they said.

Miriam knew from overhearing her brothers how cruel, crude, jeering, and dismissive boys could be about girls to whom they weren't attracted or didn't respect and she wasn't able to gauge others' feelings for her. ". . . your name?" the fattish boy asked, and Miriam pretended not to hear, turning away.

Wishing she'd asked Ethel for the car key so that she could wait for her outside. She needed to get out of this place, fast.

"We could go outside, have a smoke. I got plenty."

The fattish boy persisted, following Miriam. He seemed amused by her as if he could see through her pretense of shyness to an avid interest in him. Asking again if she wanted a smoke, tapping his thumb against a pack of cigarettes in his shirt pocket with a suggestive leer. Miriam shook her head no, she didn't smoke. She was aware of the boy's shiny eyes on her, a kind of exaggerated interest like something on TV. Was he flirting with her? Was this what flirting was? Miriam was only thirteen but already her body was warmly fleshy like her mother's, her face roundly solid, not beautiful but attractive, sometimes. When her skin wasn't broken out in hives. The boy was saying, "I saw you in there, hon. Talking to, who's it, your old man?" Miriam backed away, smiling nervously. She was becoming confused, wondering if somehow the boy knew Les, or knew of him. He was saying, mysteriously, "There's something nobody ever asks in here, who's an inmate," and Miriam said quickly, "I have to go now, I have to meet my mother." Again the boy spoke mysteriously, "Not what you think, hon. What nobody ever asks." Miriam was trying to avoid the boy, making her way along the wall of vending machines where people were dropping in coins, punching buttons, but the boy followed her, eating from his bag of CheeseStix. "We're up from Yonkers visiting my brother, he's gonna max out at six years. Know what that is? 'Max out'? Six years. What's your old man in for? 'Involuntary manslaughter'—that's my brother." The boy laughed, sputtering saliva. "Like, my brother didn't 'intend' what happened, that's the deal, only know what, hon?—that's bullshit. Bullshit he didn't. You max out, you don't get no fucking parole officer breathing down your neck." Miriam was walking more quickly away, not looking back, trying not to be frightened. They were back at the entrance to the lounge where another corridor led to restrooms. The boy loomed over her, panting into her face. "Hey, hon: nobody's gonna hurt you. Why you walking away? Think somebody's gonna rape you? Any guy tries to talk to you, think he's gonna rape you? That is so sick, hon. What'd you think,

Baby Tits? Your ass is so sweet, a guy is gonna jump you, the place crawling with guards?" The fattish boy spoke in a loud, mocking drawl. Miriam heard the anger beneath. She hadn't understood, something was wrong with this boy. Like the special ed. students at school, you tried to avoid because they could turn on you suddenly, like Lana Ochs. A female guard approached them. "Miss, is this guy bothering you?" Miriam said quickly, "No." She hurried to the women's restroom, to escape.

Igneous. Sedimentary. Metamorphic.

Miriam was underlining words in her earth science workbook. In green ink writing in the margin of the page. Beside her, driving, Ethel seemed upset. Wiping at her eyes, blowing her nose. Each time they visited Les at Ogdensburg, Ethel came away upset, distracted. But today seemed worse. Miriam pretended not to notice.

Miriam hadn't told Ethel about the fattish boy in the camouflage jumpsuit. She would recast the experience, in her imagination, as a kind of flirtation. He'd called her hon. He'd seemed to like her.

Ethel said suddenly, as if the thought had just surfaced, in the way of something submerged beneath the surface of the water that suddenly emerges, "I wanted to go to nursing school at Plattsburgh. You know this, I've told you. Except that didn't happen." Ethel spoke haltingly, with an embarrassed laugh. "Seems like my life just skidded past. I loved Les so much. And you, and the boys. Except I'm not *old.*"

Miriam could make no sense of her mother's words. She dreaded hearing more.

They were headed south on Route 58, nearing Black Lake. A windy November day, gray sky spitting snow. Ethel drove the old Cutlass at wavering speeds.

Miriam especially dreaded to hear why Ethel had dropped out of high school at seventeen, to marry twenty-year-old Les Orlander.

"Miriam, I told him."

Now Miriam glanced up from her textbook. "Told him—what?"

"That I've been seeing someone, and I'm going to keep seeing him. I have a friend now. Who respects me. In Tupper Lake."

Ethel began to cry. A kind of crying-laughing, terrible to hear. She reached out to touch Miriam, groping for Miriam's arm as she drove, but Miriam shrank away as if a snake had darted at her.

Ethel said, "Oh God. I can't believe that I told him . . . and he

194

knows now." Repeating, as if her own words astonished her, "He knows."

Miriam shrank into herself; she had nothing to say. She was stunned, disgusted, and frightened. Her brain was shutting off, she wasn't a party to this. Maybe she'd known. Known something. Her brothers knew. Everyone knew. Les Orlander, whose relatives visited him at Ogdensburg, had probably known.

". . . nothing to do with you, honey. Not with any of you. Only with him. Your father. What he did to us. 'I don't know what happened. What came over me.' My own life, I have to have my own life. I have to support us. I'm not going to lose the house. I'm not going down with him. I told him."

A heavy logging truck had pulled up behind the Cutlass and was swinging out now to pass, at sixty-five miles an hour on the two-lane country highway. Ethel's car began to shudder in the wake of the enormous truck. Miriam felt a sudden desire to grab the steering wheel, turn the car off the road.

I hate you. I love Daddy, and I hate you.

"Can't you say something, Miriam? Please."

"What's there to say, Mom? You've said it."

The rest of the drive to the house on Salt Isle Road passed in silence.

5.

. . . in silence for much of the drive to Gettysburg. And hiking in the hilly battlefield, and in the vast cemetery that was like no other cemetery Miriam had ever seen before. *All these dead,* Les marveled. *Makes you see what life is worth, don't it!* He hadn't seemed depressed or even angry, more bemused, shaking his head and smiling like it was a joke, the grassy earth at his feet was a joke, so many graves of long-ago soldiers in the Union Army, dead after three days of slaughter at Gettysburg: a "decisive" battle in the War Between the States.

They would question Miriam about that day. Afterward.

The long drive in the car with Les, what sorts of things he'd said to her. What was his mood, had he been drinking. Had he given any hint of how unhappy he was, of wanting to hurt himself. . . .

Wanting to hurt himself. The words they used. Investigating his death. *Hurt* not *kill.* Les's relatives, friends. Miriam's brothers could hardly speak of it, what he'd done to himself. At least not that

195

Miriam heard. And Ethel could not, there were no words for her.

Les had been paroled five months, when they'd made the trip to Gettysburg they'd been planning so long. Five months out of Ogdensburg and back in Star Lake picking up jobs where he could. The roofing contractor he'd worked for, for years, wasn't so friendly to him now. There was a coolness between Les and his brother-in-law Harvey Schuller. Les had served three years, seven months of his sentence for assault. In Ogdensburg he'd been a "model" prisoner, paroled for "good behavior" and this was good news, this was happy news, the family was happy for Les, the relatives. If they were angry with him for what he'd done, bringing shame to the family, still they were happy he'd been paroled, now his drinking was under control, his short temper. Though Ethel had her own life now, that was clear. Take it or leave it, she'd told Les, those are the terms he'd have to accept if he wanted to live with her and their daughter, I am not going to lie to you, I don't lie to any man, ever again. By this time Ethel had been disappointed with her man friend in Tupper Lake. More than one man friend had disappointed her, she'd acquired a philosophical attitude at age forty-seven: you're on your own, that's the bottom line. No man is going to bail you out. Ethel had gained weight, her fleshy body a kind of armor. Her face was a girl's face inside a fleshy mask through which Ethel's eyes, flirty, insolent, yearning, still shone. Miriam loved her, but was exasperated by her. Loved her, but didn't want to be anything like her. Though Ethel had a steady income now, comanaging a local catering service, no longer one of the uniformed employees. Ethel didn't need a husband's income, didn't need a husband. Yet she'd taken Les in, how could she not take Les in, the property was half his, he'd built most of the house himself, they'd been married almost thirty years, poor bastard, where's he going to live? Nowhere for Les to take his shame, his wife had been unfaithful to him and worse yet hadn't kept it a secret, his wife barely tolerated him, felt pity for him, contempt. Maybe she loved him, maybe that was so, Ethel wasn't sentimental any longer, all that was drained from her when Les lifted the ax to bring the blunt edge down on another man's skull, but what kind of love was it, the kind of love you feel for a cripple, Ethel didn't mince words. Take it or leave it, she'd told him, things are different in this house now. So far as the Ogdensburg parole board knew, Les Orlander was living at home with his family. P.O. Box 91, Salt Isle Road, Star Lake, NY. *Makes you see what life is worth,* Les said. *Dying for a good cause.*

It was early June. A few days after Memorial Day. Everywhere in Gettysburg Cemetery were small American flags, wind whipped. Miriam had never seen so many graves. And such uniformity in the grave markers, in the rows of graves. Row upon row of small identical grave markers, it made you dizzy to see. Miriam imagined a marching army. Ghost army of the doomed. She felt a shudder of physical revulsion. Why for so long had she and Les planned to come *here?*

For an hour, an hour and a half, they walked in the Civil War memorial. It was a cool bright windy day. Warmer in southern Pennsylvania than it would have been in Star Lake in the Adirondacks. Of course there were other visitors to the memorial. There were families, children. Les was offended by their loud voices. A four-year-old boy clambering over graves, snatching at miniature flags. Les said something to the child's father that Miriam didn't hear, and the young father pulled at his son's hand, rebuked. Miriam held her breath but there was nothing more.

Stocky and muscled, in a hooded pullover, jaws unshaven, and a baseball cap pulled down low over his forehead, Les wasn't a man another man would wish to antagonize unless that man was very like Les himself. Was your father angry about anything, did he seem distracted, what was his mood that day, Miriam would be asked.

As if, after her father's death, Miriam would betray him!

She did tell Ethel what was true: on the drive down, Les had been quiet. He'd brought tapes and cassettes and a few CDs of music he wanted to hear or thought he wanted to hear, rock bands with names new to Miriam, music of a long-ago time when Les had been a kid, a young guy in his twenties just growing up. Miriam was disappointed; some of the songs Les listened to for only a few seconds, then became impatient, disgusted. Telling Miriam to try something else.

It was awkward, in Les's company. Just Les alone, not Ethel or one of Miriam's brothers. She had to suppose it was the first time they'd ever been alone together in the car like this though she could not have supposed it would be the last time. Somehow, the trip to Gettysburg had come to mean too much. They'd planned it so long. It seemed to have something to do, Miriam thought, with her father's memory of his own father. Not that Les said much about this. Only a few times, in the way of a man thinking out loud. If Miriam asked Les what he'd said, he didn't seem to hear. She was sitting beside his right ear, that was his bad ear. You didn't dare to raise your voice to Les, he took offense if you did that, even Ethel knew better than to provoke him, for sometimes he seemed to hear normally, and other times he didn't, you could not predict. And so sometimes he talked without hearing, without listening. In the cemetery at Gettysburg, the wind blew words away. Miriam saw how Les walked stiffly, like a man fearing pain. Maybe one of his knees. Maybe his back. His shoulders were set in a posture of labor; he'd done manual labor most of his adult life. Roofers are particularly prone to neck and spine strain. Miriam watched her father walk ahead of her, along the rows of grave markers, hands jammed into the deep pockets of his jersey pullover. He seemed to her a figure of mystery, still a good-looking man though his face was beginning to look ravaged, his skin sallow from prison. After he shot himself to death with his deer rifle a few weeks later, in a desolate stretch of pine woods beyond the property on Salt Isle Road where he'd used to hunt white-tailed deer and wild turkey with Miriam's brothers, Miriam would be asked if he'd said much about the cemetery at Gettysburg, or about his father, or Gideon, who was stationed in Iraq, and Miriam said evasively she didn't remember.

Les hadn't said much about Gideon. He hadn't seen Gideon in nearly a year. He was bewildered and angry that Gideon had enlisted in the army without consulting him, Iraq was a dirty war, a sham war like they'd said of Vietnam. Like Gideon had wanted to put distance between himself and Star Lake, was that it? Between himself and his family.

Miriam was walking fast to keep pace with Les. She'd thought he was going to head back toward the parking lot but he seemed to be walking in the opposite direction, back into the cemetery. Overhead clouds were shifting in the sky, like soiled sailcloth. Miriam didn't want to think that the trip to the Gettysburg memorial had gone wrong somehow. Maybe it was too late. Les should have taken the family, all of them, years ago when Miriam's brothers were young, and Miriam was a little girl. Somehow, the trip had come to be too important to Les and Miriam, there was a strain to it like the strain of a balloon being blown bigger and bigger until it threatens to burst. And then it bursts.

There was a tall plaque beside the roadway. Miriam read aloud, in fragments: "'. . . Lincoln's Gettysburg Address, November 19, 1863, the greatest speech of the Civil War and one of the greatest speeches ever given by any American president. *Four score and seven years ago. All men are created equal. Brave men, living and dead, who struggled here. The world will little note, nor long remember,*

what we say here, but can never forget what they did here...'"
and Les interrupted, "Bullshit. Who remembers? Who's left? Just
Lincoln, people remember."

It was the afternoon of June 3, 2004. Miriam's father would disappear from her life on June 28.

6.

Months after the funeral, after Labor Day, when Star Lake emptied
out and the downstate homeowners were gone, they trashed one of
the new houses on East Shore Drive. Stoned on crystal meth like
lighter fluid inhaled through the nostrils and a match lit and
whup! whup! whup! it was like a video game, wild. A replica of an
old Adirondack lodge of the 1920s except the logs were weatherized
and insulated; there were sliding glass doors overlooking the deck,
and the lake. Maybe it was a house their father Les had worked on,
the brothers weren't sure. Not Gideon (after the funeral he'd flown
back to the Mideast, his duty had been extended) but Martin and
Stan and some of their friends. Forced a back door and no security
alarm went off that they could hear. Trashed the place looking for
liquor and found instead above the fireplace mantel a mounted
buck's head, sixteen-point antlers, shining their flashlights outraged
to see a Mets cap dangling from one of the points, a small American
flag on a wooden stick twined in the antlers, sunglasses over the
glass eyes so they pulled down the buck's head to take away with
them, stabbed and tore leather furniture with their fishing knives,
smashed a wall-screen TV, smashed a CD player, tossed dishes in a
frenzy of breakage, overturned the refrigerator, jammed forks into
the garbage disposal, took time to open cans of dog food to throw
against the walls, took time to stop up toilets (six toilets!) with
wadded towels; in the bedrooms (five bedrooms!) took time to urinate on as many beds as their bladders allowed, it had something to
do with Les Orlander though they could not have said what. Sure,
they'd remembered to wear gloves, these guys watched TV crime
shows. Martin wanted to torch the place but the others talked him
out of it. A fire would draw too much attention.

Miriam wasn't a witness to the trashing, had not been with her
brothers. Yet somehow, she knew.

199

7.

"My damn mother, I wish . . ."

This second time. The words came out sudden and furious. Whatever was in her bloodstream had got into her brain. And the music was hurting. It scared her, the way the blood arteries beat. ". . . wish somebody would put that woman out of her misery, she'd be better off." What was his name, he'd been Gideon's close friend in high school, Oz Newell was Miriam's friend here. Oz Newell was protecting her. Leaning his sweaty-haired head to Miriam, touching her forehead with his own in a gesture of clumsy intimacy asking what's she saying and Miriam says, "I want somebody to kill my mother, like she killed my father." So it was said. For months it had needed saying, building up in Miriam like bile and now it was said and the guys stared at her but maybe hadn't heard her, even Oz laughing so certainly he hadn't heard. Hay Brouwet was trying to tell him something. Nobody could talk in a normal voice, you had to shout so your throat became raw. Hay was cupping his big-knuckled hands to his mouth, so Miriam could see that Hay was shouting but the music was so loud, must've been she was so stoned, she couldn't hear a thing.

Whatever is done. Whatever you cause to be done. It will have happened always. It can never be changed.

In that other time, before her father had killed himself. On the drive home from Gettysburg. If Miriam had said: what words? If Miriam had said *I love you, you are my father. Don't leave me.* Of course, she'd said nothing. Underlining passages in her earth science workbook as her father drove north on the thruway, home.

It was later, then. They were somewhere else, the air smelled different. There was less noise. The vibrations had ceased. When they'd left the Star Lake Inn, Miriam didn't know. Possibly she'd passed out. An inky mist had come over her. She remembered laying her head down on her crossed arms, on a table to which her skin was sticking. Though she knew better there was the fear that her brothers would see her, drunk, disheveled, sluttish in the company of older guys, some of them bikers, stoned, excited, looking for a way to discharge their excitement, a dog pack sniffing for blood. In this pack, Oz Newell was her friend. Oz Newell swaying on his feet and oozing sweat would protect Miriam, she knew. There was an understanding between them. Miriam believed this. For Oz carried her to his beat-up Cherokee, lifting her in his arms, Miriam was limp, faint headed, her mouth slack and eyes half shut, she could feel his arm muscles

straining, the tendons in his neck. Oz's face was a strong face like
something hacked from stone. The skin was coarse, acne scarred.
The jaws were unshaven. It was late, it was past 2 a.m. Miriam had
to be carried, her feet were bare, very dirty, the soles scratched, bleeding. One of those dreams where you have lost your shoes, part of
your clothing, strangers' eyes move onto you, jeering. The stained
red T-shirt and cord skirt riding up her thighs, Miriam tried to tug
the skirt down, her fingers clutched, clawed. She'd been running in
the gravel parking lot. Hair in her face, panicked. "Don't! Don't
hurt—" but no one was listening to her. Kevin had left the inn, the
pack had followed him, Miriam clutching at Hay Brouwet's arm,
he'd thrown her off as you'd flick away a fly. Miriam had not remembered that Kevin was wearing a Yankees cap but this had to be Kevin,
big-jawed boy with sun-bleached hair straggling past his ears, Kevin
with the rich father, Kevin complaining of the sleek white sailboat,
he was headed for a Jeep, ignition key in hand he was headed for a
steel-colored Jeep parked partway in weeds at the far end of the lot
when Oz Newell and Hay Brouwet and Brandon McGraw and their
friends advanced upon him cursing—"Fuckface! Where ya goin'!"—
and Kevin turned to them with a look of utter astonishment so taken
by surprise he hardly had time to lift his arms to protect his head, the
men were whooping and rushing at him fierce as dogs in a pack.
Kevin tried to run but they caught him, cursing him, slamming him
against the Jeep, the Yankees cap went flying, Kevin's head was
struck repeatedly, Kevin fell to the ground as the men circled around
him punching and kicking with their steel-toe workboots. Miriam
clutched at their arms, pulled at them, begged them to stop but they
paid no attention to her, even Oz Newell shoved her from him, indifferent to her pleas. And a part of her was thinking, *Hurt him! So
he will know.*

There was justice in it, such a beating. You felt this. Though you
could not acknowledge it, not even to Oz Newell and his friends.

In the gravel, partway in the weeds at the end of the lot, the bleach-
haired boy lay writhing and vomiting. His clothes were torn, his
chest exposed. He had not been hurt. It hadn't been a serious beating.
They laughed in derision watching him crawl toward the Jeep.
Bleeding from a broken nose but a broken nose isn't serious. His
front teeth were maybe loosened. The pretty-boy face had been
roughed up, he'd had to be taught a lesson. Rich fucker. Rich guy's

fucking son. Stay away from the Star Lake Inn, fucker. Stay away from our girls. Next time it's your head that'll be broke. Your brains you'll be puking. The guys were feeling good about this. They were grateful to Miriam, who was their friend Gideon's young sister, for needing them. For turning to them. The adrenaline high is the best high, the purest high. Laughing so tears stung their faces like acid. Except they had to get the hell out, fast. What if somebody inside the inn had called 911. Two or three of the guys had come on their motorcycles, some in pickups. Oz Newell had his beat-up Cherokee that smelled like he'd been living in it. There was a plan to meet at another place a few miles up the road at the Benson Mines, open till 4 a.m. But Oz Newell said he'd better get Miriam the hell home.

On Salt Isle Road the wind was moving in the tops of the trees like a living thing. There was the moon sliding in the sky, about to disappear behind clouds. And the clouds so thin and ragged, like torn cloth, blowing across the face of the moon. "Look!" Miriam pointed. "Makes you think there's some reason to it." Oz glanced sidelong at Miriam, sprawled in the seat beside him. He'd had to toss soiled shirts, Styrofoam wrappers, beer cans into the back to make room for her. ". . . like the moon makes a center in the sky. So the sky isn't just . . ." Miriam was losing the thread of what she was saying. It was an important thing she meant to say, might've said to her father, maybe it would have made a difference. The Cherokee was lurching along the narrow lakeside road. Whatever had gotten into Miriam's brain was making her feel like she wasn't inside her skull but floating a few feet away.

Oz Newell said, surprising her, his voice was so deliberate: "Back there, Miriam, what'd you say, about your mother? I didn't maybe hear."

So Oz had heard. Heard something. Miriam thought, *He will do it. For me.* It could be an accident. There were so many accidents with guns. All the men owned guns. Boys owned guns. Even off-season you heard gunfire in the woods. Les Orlander had not been one of those who'd owned many guns, just two. The shotgun, the rifle. The rifle taken into custody by the county sheriff's department, then released to the family, and Stan had appropriated it, and the shotgun, to take back to Keene with him. Oz could use a rifle. Oz could fire through Ethel's bedroom window. Oz could hide outside, in the bushes. Oz could fire through the windshield of the Cutlass. When Miriam was driving into town. It could be a robbery. A stranger. This time of year there were many strangers in the Star Lake area. There were many strangers in the Adirondacks. There were break-ins, burglaries, vandalism. There were unexplained beatings, killings. It would happen swiftly and then it would be over and Miriam could live with Martin in Watertown where he was out of rehab now and working as a roofer and he'd seemed lonely, and Ethel had said, honey, come home, live with your sister and me, and Martin pushed her off, saying he'd sooner be in hell.

In childish bitterness Miriam said, "My mother. What she did to my father. She should be punished," and Oz said as if perplexed, "Punished how?" and Miriam said, wiping her mouth on the shoulder of her AU SABLE BOATHOUSE T-shirt, "Some way." Miriam's brain was becoming vague again. It was like clouds being blown across the face of the moon, you couldn't see what was behind the rapid flowing movement, if it was moving also. Oz, driving the Cherokee, braking at curves, said nothing. He was driving more deliberately now, as if he'd realized that he shouldn't be driving at all. Miriam could hear his panting breath. She said, "I'm not serious, Oz. I guess not."

Oz said, hunching his shoulders, "Shouldn't say a thing like that. About your mother. See, somebody might misunderstand."

Turning into Miriam's cinder driveway, Oz cut his headlights. Miriam saw with a pang of dread that the front rooms of the house were darkened but the outside light, at the carport, was on, and lights were burning at the rear of the house: kitchen, Ethel's bedroom. "Miriam, hey! Christ." Oz laughed, Miriam was clutching at him. She was kissing him, his stubbled jaws, the startled expression on his face. He pushed her away and she crossed a leg over his, jamming against the steering wheel. She was desperate, aroused. It felt like drowning, wanting so to be loved. Should be ashamed but it was happening so quickly. Her mouth against the man's was hot and hurtful, her hard, hungry teeth. She had no idea what a kiss is, the opening of mouths, tongues, the softness, groping. Oz laughed, uneasy. Pushing her away more forcibly. "Miriam, c'mon."

She was too young, Gideon's kid sister. She was a sister to him, or she was nothing. He was sure she'd never had sex with anyone and damned if he'd be the first.

"I love you. I want to be with *you.*"

"Sure, baby. Some other time."

Miriam jumped from the Cherokee, made her way wincing barefoot into the house. So ashamed! Her face pounded with heat.

The kitchen was two rooms, one a former washroom. Les had

knocked out the wall between. There was a long counter with a scarred white enamel sink. The beautiful cabinets of dark polished wood Les had built. On the linoleum floor were scattered rugs. Miriam saw that Ethel wasn't in the kitchen even as, in her bathrobe, a cigarette in hand, Ethel entered the kitchen, from the direction of her bedroom. Ethel's eyes brimming with emotion, fixed on Miriam in the way of one staring at a blazing light, blinding.

Miriam's heart gave a skid. She loved this woman so much, the two of them helpless together, like swimmers drowning in each other's arms.

Her voice was brattish, exasperated. "Why aren't you in bed, Mom? I told you not to wait up."

Now that Les was gone and would not be coming back, Ethel was in mourning. Her face was pale and puffy without makeup, raw. Yet strangely young looking, her mouth like a bruise, wounded. In the chenille robe her body was slack, ripe, beyond ripeness. The loose, heavy breasts were disgusting to Miriam, who wanted to rush at her mother and strike at her with childish, flailing fists. Miriam who was staggering with exhaustion, limping barefoot, hair in her face, and her ridiculous tight red T-shirt and white cord skirt stained with her own vomit. Wanting to hide her shamed face against Ethel's neck that was creased, smelling of talcum.

Somewhere distant, in the mountains beyond Star Lake, a melancholy cry, a sequence of cries. Loons, coyotes. Les had taken Miriam outside one summer night to listen to plaintive cries he identified as the cries of black bears.

Ethel smiled uncertainly. Knowing that, if she moved too suddenly, Miriam would push her away, run from the room. Barefoot, wincing in pain. The door to her room would be slammed shut, it would never open. "You look feverish, honey." Ethel must have smelled male sweat on Miriam. She smelled beer, vomit. Unmistakable, the smell of a daughter's vomit. But shrewdly deciding not to go there, in that direction. So grateful that the daughter is home. Coming to press a hand against the daughter's forehead. Miriam flinched, dreading this touch. For hours she'd been dreading it. Yet the hand was cool, consoling. Ethel said, her voice throaty, bemused, "Where've you been, are you going to tell me?"

For a moment Miriam couldn't remember. Where had she been? Her mouth was dry, parched as sand. As if she'd slept with her mouth open, helpless in sleep as a small child.

"Nowhere. Now I'm back."

Four Poems
Reginald Shepherd

DIRECTION OF FALL

And then this ruined sky again. Memory
came like migratory birds calling *reaper, reaper,*
reaper, hungry ghosts threshing distance

at the extremity of private sound: whatever wandering
makes sing. Memory came to fragments, then
composed itself, the endless sequence

of silver-dollar days came down
in April hail. Clouds are fools
in whiteface, gone gray with their heavy freight

of rain; Florida falls into mud, leaving
behind flood warnings, hurricanes, watch for
small tornadoes. Late landscape wears its past

as scars, suffering from too much weather,
the many weathers we've had. (This body
is almost mine, but sleep won't take me back.)

The sound of wind welcomed me, wind's indecisive,
noncommittal wing invited me, incited me
to part-recited theories of the half correct,

starting with the names of stars, lessons
we don't tell the music: myths
abound in me, I woke baroque and unafraid.

Reginald Shepherd

MY IMMORTAL

—For Brad Richard

A hero is a monster, isn't he?
The boy I know is a road through when
dressed up in mortality, incognito
under all that skin. He dissolves
the colors, dismantles glory,
and thrives on lack of light.
The gods feed on human death, especially

the ones who say *I am the only one;* men die
lying miraculously near each other.
He sits crushing pieces of world
between his palms: it's what gods
do, or so he's read in handbooks, manuals,
how-to guides. Thales says
the world is water, and he pours it

from open hands, not knowing
how deep is far enough. There are laws
concerning bodies colliding, the bias
of bent wings: he wants
to learn them, break them one by one.
He drifts half dressed through adolescence
like some courtyard Eros, grows up

to be a slaughterhouse. No god
could survive such hindered
devotions, warlike densities hacking a path
through him—his introspection
and wounded politics, his ache
and assignation of blame. (He stinks
of cumin, cloves, and ginger,

cinnamon, nutmeg, mace, and cardamom:
a cargo of rare commodities
to keep that meat from rotting.
They cost too much.)
The fall of Rome is never ending,

a desperate grandeur, all nothing
lent an air of what once was: the cracked

basilicas and toppled colonnades
quarried for next century's aqueducts,
retaining walls, an intricate wound
to be paved over.
He rains stature on late landscapes
made of marble, made of granite,
made of bronze; stands up to wind,

rain, snow, or any weathering.
A country wears its history
on its skin, strip-mine and clear-cut
scars, landfills, slag heaps, tailings.
The cure of birds, the animal rain,
sunset was singing *God is dead*
but wouldn't say which one.

PERSEPHONE'S CELESTIAL SPHERE
—For Catherine Imbriglio

Moonlight pools in her hollow bones,
quicksilver slowed to lead, liquid mercury's
indolent poison loitering in the marrow,
cooling, collecting there. It silts her blue blood
viscous, clotted, thickening
to immobility. "I think I was a daughter
once. Some flowers
stained my hands I can't recall." Night
tarnishes her breath to pewter, lead
alloyed: darkening, and flaking off in air.

*

She shades her eyes against glass morning's
tangled branches, wind plays drying leaves
with no sound, equivocating between shape
and shapelessness. "We speak in shadows here,"

207

but no one spoke. She knows his voice
by now, his hand pretending to be a cloud
passing between her sight and sun. Eclipse
becomes his proper name, but she won't call him that.

*

The yellowed light begins to fray, disintegrating
distance, discontent (the lower the observer, the higher
and more intimate her visible
horizon). A shift toward orange skims across,
then thoroughly bloodred (having the longer
wavelength, greater patience weighing on her):
his violent beauty of composition
producing form from vista,
or she remembers hers.

*

The apparent surface of the heavens, on which
the stars and other bodies (ghost moon attending
bleeding copper) look as if fixed.

*

If he were a hand he would open five petals, offer
these snapped-off starfish, iridescent beetle
carapaces, stippled eggshell tesserae (smashed
glass bits, lapis pieces), rusted sprays of
pine straw. "Here are some things
love might be." Becoming shadow hampers him,
keeps nowhere well in sight. The sky he alters
alters him to crows just now arriving
for the winter, from the north,
a fog over black mountains
she can't find. Her eyes
close to the repetitious days, blot out
the excess color.

*

She calls him smoking water, he calls her
flower face in no one's voice.

A SHOULDER TO THE WHEEL

Sun cycles through the sky
as always, can't be seen through
pewter, spilled tin-pot gray:
the morning darkens, gathering tarnish.

(one world horizoned with refusals,
trapped in its present tense)

It was raining and about to rain,
clouds showed the work
of puzzling out drowned days
assembled in the drip points
of live oak leaves, indeterminately deciduous.

(we've been busy making lists and
naming the names of things)

Revisions and collisions, a downpour of wings
and unleavened hair. We call them leaves
trees have sucked dry, discarded,
sweep the concrete day clean
after each day's hard rain; the gutters fill
with brown and beige.

(a body of work, a body
of words, never enough confusion
between body and soul)

Or raking the moon from a puddle
of stagnant storm water, it's just
a street lamp's yellow-orange globe
caught reflecting on the rural route nights
I can't get back to sleep again.

(my life a clutch of rust brown leaves
clinging to a wind-broken stick in the driveway,
purpose in search of something
to put to itself)

We lie down with natural history,
our dreams indelibly grass stained,
a craving for salt in our veins.

By the Waters of Babylon
Rosmarie Waldrop

1.

We take language for granted, as we do sitting and weeping. Unfamiliar speech we take for inarticulate gurgling. Filtered through sandbags.

A searchlight beam makes a statement.

The order of the world is so foreign to our subjective interests that we cannot imagine what it is like, says William James. We have to break it. Into histories, art, sciences, or just plain rubble. Then we feel at home.

I could list the parts of the body as in a blason. And how they can get hurt.

2.

Unless we recognize a language we do not recognize a man. We wrap entire villages in barbed wire.

My father used to close his eyes and remain as motionless as possible to let his body image dissolve.

I repeat myself often.

Time has no power over the id. But heat passes from a warm body to a cold body and not in the reverse direction.

3.

Language plays a great part in our life.

There is chaos and void. No man or beast. Not a fly or stalk of ragweed. We think "primal soup," and already there is a world. And fed.

Then somebody thinks "Operation Ivy Cyclone." "Operation Plymouth Rock." "Operation Iron Hammer."

In 2005, in Baghdad, ninety-two percent of the people did not have stable electricity, thirty-nine percent did not have safe drinking water, twenty-five percent of children under the age of five were suffering from malnutrition.

4.

Whereas the concept of spatial measurement does not conflict with that of spatial order, the concept of succession (bombings?) clashes with the concept of duration (U.S. presence?).

Tanks enter the discussion, and the case for absolute time collapses.

We speak our own language exclusively. It embodies the universal form of human thought and logic.

I toss in my sleep. As do many women.

5.

Four thousand to six thousand civilians have been killed in Fallujah.

It is impossible to describe the fact that corresponds to this sentence, without simply repeating the sentence.

A cat chases a yellow butterfly. My father sneezes.

Unlike the id, the ego—through which alone pleasure becomes real—is subject to time.

6.

There used to be harbor where downtown Providence is, a pond full of perch under the civic center, Roger Williams's body under an apple tree.

Where the Sumerian cities of Umma, Umm al-Akareb, Larsa, and Tello were there is now a landscape of craters.

The ultimate origin of the idea of time, it is said, lies in our perception of difference and resemblance.

When I look at the mirror in the morning I see a gray mist. Then it is hard to rescue distinctions.

7.

Trenches filled with trash. Sandbags filled with archaeological fragments. Men filled with fear.

Language is a network of easily accessed wrong turns.

At the dedication of the Abraham Lincoln Presidential Library and Museum, the president compared his War on Terror with Lincoln's war against slavery.

Sometimes the clouds race along Elmgrove Avenue. Sometimes they hover over city hall.

8.

In one version, reality is desperate attacks by a few desperate individuals. In another, we have been in a civil war for a long time.

We place mirrors in our bedrooms. We hope their virtual depth might reflect on our loves.

Greater accuracy in measurement can be obtained by means of atomic and molecular clocks. Implicit is the hypothesis that all atoms of a given element behave in exactly the same way, irrespective of place and epoch.

If I try to say the whole thing in one sentence I say the same thing over and over.

9.

My father, from his balcony, looks at astral spaces where the orbiting of a planet, a suicide bombing, and his breath condensing in cold air are equally part of the system.

He wonders whether he must fit his perceptions to the world—which world?—or the world to his perceptions.

Fifty thousand U.S. soldiers in Iraq had no body armor in 2005. The equipment manager had placed it at the same priority level as socks.

Some do not like blood outside the body. Others do not like body counts.

10.

In Swan Point Cemetery, there is a gravestone in the form of a little house. With the inscription GONE HOME.

"Assassinated: four clerics, two officials from the Ministry of Defense, the dean of a high school; killed by bombs: nine National Guards, thirteen civilians, two engineering students. In all, thirty-one dead, forty-two injured, and seventeen abducted. A fairly quiet day here in Baghdad."

The flux of time helps us to forget what was and what can be.

I would prefer to be able to explain the air. The sun. The Adam's apple.

11.

Corpses of small children, families lying in pools of blood in their homes. The president promises investigation. And sidesteps the problem.

Heine's curse: *Nicht gedacht soll seiner werden.*

One way of thinking links thoughts with one another in a series, another keeps coming back to always the same spot.

The flux of time is society's most natural ally in maintaining law, order, conformity. We learn that every pleasure is short and are resigned even before society forces us to be so.

12.

The spring rain splashes up cones of water from puddles formed by the broken asphalt.

The crimes of U.S. soldiers in Iraq are as inevitable as the crimes committed by soldiers of other imperial armies. It takes many years before it comes to light that they are official policy. Fifty years, in the case of No Gun Ri in South Korea.

The aspects of time that were significant for primitive man were repetition and simultaneity. Even in his first conscious awareness of time, man sought to transcend, or abolish it.

My writing is nothing but a stutter.

13.

Nothing new under the sun. Which comes and goes. When it stood still at the prayer of Joshua, did time nevertheless continue?

I would like to concentrate on the rotation of the earth and the winds it brings about.

Eight months before the invasion, the chief of MI6 reported to Tony Blair that the U.S. was going to "remove Saddam, through military action. . . ." But because "the case was thin, Saddam was not threatening his neighbors, and his WMD capability was less than that of Libya, North Korea, or Iran . . . the intelligence and facts were being fixed around the policy."

Our language seduces us into asking always the same questions. As long as there is a verb "to be" that seems to function in the same way as "to eat" and "to drink," we'll be asking questions of identity, possibility, falsehood, truth.

14.

"Well, I knelt down. I said a prayer, stood up, and gunned them all down."

As the physicist Steven Weinberg said, for good people to do bad things it takes religion.

I suddenly start to wonder at birth, death, sleep, madness, war. As if awakening.

Time helps us to forget, and to forget means to forgive. What should not be forgiven.

15.

My father cuts himself shaving. While he looks for a Band-Aid he thinks of his astral body and if it is bleeding, too.

Time is the form of our inner sense, said Kant. And Guyau, that a being who did not desire, did not want anything, would see time shut down in front of him.

Everywhere people wind clocks to prevent this from happening.

The battle of Agincourt was fought in hours, Waterloo in a day, Gettysburg lasted three days, the Battle of the Somme four and a half months, Verdun ten, Stalingrad six. There were the Seven- and the Thirty-Years' Wars. The president told the West Point cadets: "Iraq is only the beginning."

NOTE. This poem includes quotations from Eliot Weinberger, *What I Learned about Iraq in 2005*; G. J. Whitrow, *The Natural Philosophy of Time*; Herbert Marcuse, *Eros and Civilization*; John Keegan, *The Face of Battle*; and Ludwig Wittgenstein, *Culture and Value*.

From The Woman in White
Elizabeth Robinson

—*To the memory of my father, Bruce Robinson*

The scale necessitates its own balance,

beautiful field, bastardy

These many forms of seizure

Once

Sited again

Hushing

The blanket crocheted itself over the sloping plain, and all
was woolly and opaque   Not to be perturbed   Portent's
sharp consonant softened to omen

Muffled

Elizabeth Robinson

In the dim plane, the blade scrapes wax away from the wick

Nicked at   Gloss   Raw skin

Shimmying flake of wax:

this white dark, this flesh

Sheltering midroad

on the unlikeliest portion of night

We beseech you, she sighs, to say nothing of my name

which was unknown to all

Resolutely the night itself puts on its muslin
gown, loyal to a lost benefactress

Elizabeth Robinson

Since when does a place

    matchmake with its landscape

        (when a body is promised to an earthen spouse)

The stone, not the dress, should be virginally white

    as the one besmirches the other

        Something wanting, something wanting

            the sound wafts as resemblance

            the face is an open window

            she walks through

        cognizance

made from the snarled stuffs of correspondence

Elizabeth Robinson

So it appeared that the prey escaped

      and what was a hare

      leapt away

      Became lamb

                  Everywhere

             purity would sway

         intention,   scrambling

      so as to allay

      the ivory reversal

      of pursuit

     The pursuer's eloquent lie

Two Meditations
Peter Dale Scott

MAE SALONG

After the Thai government granted the KMT [Kuo-mintang] refugee status in the 1960s, efforts were made to incorporate the Yunnanese and their families into the Thai nation. Until the late 1980s they didn't have much success, as many ex-KMT were deeply involved in the Golden Triangle opium trade. . . . Because of the rough, mountainous terrain and lack of sealed roads, the outside world was rather cut off from the goings-on in Mae Salong. The KMT never denied its role in drug-trafficking, but justified it by claiming that the money was used to buy weapons to fight the communists.

—Lonely Planet, *Chiang Mai and Northern Thailand,* 247

the wrinkled woman
splashes tea over the table
rubs the cup with both hands

and savors the fragrant oolong
from bushes in tight neat rows
on the steep ocher hillside below us

a crop substitution program
not like the denuded
Myanmar crags to the west

sleeping in their mist
that not so long ago
were still dense with poppies

221

Peter Dale Scott

The booths across the street
of Akha women in cowries and coins
(their monkey chained to a pole)

line what was once an airstrip
below the monumental
tomb of General Tuan

who profited handsomely
from the opium trade
his son runs the resort   *Lonely Planet 248*

We read the damp-stained captions
about the hundreds who died
in the 1970s campaign

against local insurgents
and we stop for a moment
before the pagoda

in the middle of the courtyard
of this fortress settlement
(*almost an independent state*

until the road was sealed)
out of respect for the dead
Having written to attack

the KMT drug traffickers
and General Kriangsak who in gratitude
for their defense of Thailand

and personal payoffs
of *half a million per year*   *Mills 770*
gave them Thai nationality

and now startled by the photo
of General Tuan with two grateful
bhikkus in saffron robes I wonder   *monks*

Could I have been wrong?
the monks here survived
while those in Cambodia not far away

were killed by the thousands
(the bride's story of her aunt
whose throat was cut   publicly

for having eaten a raw potato
while working in the field)
by the hate-driven Khmers Rouges

who at one point both China
and the U.S. supported
in the days when I myself

from naive broad-mindedness
quoted from Chairman Mao
The mosque at the center of town

across from the Golden Dragon
reminds me of the grandiose
plans of General Chennault

to contain China from the west
by inciting the Yunnanese Muslims
descended from the armies of Kublai Khan

that lapsed into the lawlessness
of marauding Shan armies
Kachins Karens Was

and I think *not one of us is free*
from this karma of suffering
the cemetery too large

for a mountaintop village
is some miles away
near Mae Sai the city

Peter Dale Scott

evacuated just last year
because of cross-border shelling
And yet this nation

where five Buddhist schools
were bombed on Wednesday
disturbs and frightens me less

than the college-educated
planners of preemptive war
back home in the Bush White House

>   *the fighting here was local*
>   *the fears human*
>   *almost everything that happens here is human*

the sow studies the dead piglet
children squat in the once-crowded courtyard
I eat cashew chicken

in the tourist restaurant
that was once an army canteen
and ask our fifteen-year-old waitress

who brings us the bill *Were*
you born here in this village?
And she answers *No*

in China   China?
in this KMT village?
Does this have to do with Islam?

Or with the *tons of heroin*
still exported through Thailand
each year for the last four decades?

>   *By not knowing*
>   *we enter the way*   Ryokan

as the monkey gestures with its chain

Peter Dale Scott

WAT PA NANACHAT

Ajahn Chah . . . spent . . . a very brief but signifi-cant time with Venerable Ajahn Mun, the most outstanding meditation Master of the ascetic, for-est-dwelling tradition. Following his time with Venerable Ajahn Mun, he spent a number of years traveling around Thailand, spending his time in forests and charnel grounds, ideal places for de-veloping meditation practice.

At length he came within the vicinity of the vil-lage of his birth, and when word got around that he was in the area, he was invited to set up a monastery at the Pa-Pong forest, a place at this time reputed to be the habitat of wild animals and ghosts. . . .

In 1966 the first Westerner came to stay at Wat Pa Pong (Wat=temple), Venerable Sumedho Bhikkhu. From that time on, the number of foreign people who came to Ajahn Chah began steadily to in-crease, until in 1975, the first branch monas-tery for western and other non-Thai nationals, Wat Pa Nanachat, was set up with Venerable Ajahn Sumedho as abbot.

—Web: ksc15.th.com/petsei/biography.htm

leaf forms trembling
in the forest pool of marble

where monks at night
once listened for tiger's breath

we watch a long green snake   *a python*
loop itself through the ironwork

then belly-flop—phlat!!
into the dry teak leaves

behind the sun-spattered terra-cotta Buddha
impossible for some minutes

to keep eyes closed
to stop listening

225

Peter Dale Scott

for slither

insuperable biases of language
one side talking   *spirits* and *devas*
the other of *superstition*

I only know
that when I come back by *tuk-tuk*   *three-wheeled taxi*
and step through the forest gate

my pace slows
I stop looking

for the crimson sunbirds
as I feel breathed into me

something from beyond this
linguistic aporia   *difficulty, straits (Greek)*

around us on all sides
the slow creaking of the tall bamboos

big leaves you can almost hear
when they zigzag down through the butterflies

from the dipterocarpus and strangler figs
in the almost sunless gloom

the darkness of the forest
opening the darkness within us

the wat once walled
inside the forest
as Thailand in Buddhism

and now the forest
or what is left of the forest
walled inside the wat

The Thai student from Cornell
who interviewed elderly monks
about the *thudong* tradition   *ascetic practice*

wrote in her Ph.D. thesis
Between 1950 and 1975
the U.S. provided Thailand

with $650 billion in support
of economic development   *Tiyavanich 368*
dams golf courses and tourist resorts   *Tiyavanich 244*

In the 1960s, nearly 60%
of the country was forested
and now *17%*   *TIMEasia.com 8/21/02*

until *in November 1988*
rain falling on denuded hillsides
killed hundreds of people   *Tiyavanich 245*

logging since then illegal
meaning another source of graft
along with prostitution and drugs   *Pasuk 141-42*

eucalyptus planted
for export to the Japanese
in the midst of the peasants' rice   *Tiyavanich 247*

Her dissertation director
who had approved of this *high rate of growth*
as *a very considerable achievement*   *Wyatt 282-83*

and justified clearing forests
by the *major security crisis*   *Wyatt 290*
in the shadow of Vietnam   *Wyatt 285*

wrote a foreword to her book
everything I knew
had to be thrown away and rethought   *Tiyavanich xi*

227

he had already written
that Sarit after his coup
arrested *intellectuals and journalists*   *Wyatt 280*

but not how he put Phimontham
the leading meditation monk
into prison for five years

if everyone closed his eyes
how to *watch for communists?*   *Carr 10; Tiyavanich 231*

the wandering monks chastised   *thudong monks*
some of them maybe killed

every kuti was burnt down   *monk's cell*
all the fruit trees around the wat
mango longan lime coconut   *Tiyavanich 234*

while Ajahn Chah
gave up the wandering life
created his own *wat pa*   *forest monastery*

and later Wat Pa Nanachat   *International Forest Monastery*
Theravadan Buddhism
now in England California
Australia New Zealand Switzerland

insight   the power of caring
as we never knew it in America

the power of Luang Por Ophad   *Venerable Abbot Ophad*
to read our minds
in less than fifteen minutes

saying first to Ronna
after spitting his betel nut
into a bronze spittoon

words I had used that very day
about teaching in Thailand

you can't do one hundred percent
if you can do fifty
do fifty

and then scolding me
You have little bit samadhi   *enlightenment*
but your mind is sokopok   *dirty, defiled*

and too scattered
as if reading my own fears
so as to change my life

this power of insight
was once as widespread
as the transboreal forest

saints like Alcuin and Wang Wei
drawing on its images

to express the wilderness within   *Scott 525-30*
imprinting their holiness

which aged inevitably
into education and science
social development

at the expense of mental development   *bhavana*
I learned this as a medievalist

all the dhammas are one   *dharmas*
converging

under the glass case
containing the portrait and skeleton
of the young woman who killed herself
when her husband was unfaithful

Peter Dale Scott

I sit trying to breathe *chi*
into the spaces of my spine

thinking *what have we done to Thailand?*
good roads electricity
no beggars here at the gate

like the children carrying babies
crowding around us in Tachilek
across the border in Myanmar

or the two Cambodian girls at the border
searching each other for lice

or those banging their pans in Varanesi
their legs crushed or amputated
for the sake of charity

if you spend a night
at Tha Ton Riverview Resort
you can hear shots over the border
or wake to a corpse
floating down the Mae Kok River

as down the Mekong in Laos
arms battened to a frame of bamboo

part of me thinks
            no question about it
            Thailand has escaped
            the bitter colonial legacies
            of Britain and France
            still leaving their imprint
            of poverty and hatred

but Thailand independent
since the eighteenth century
when Ayudhya was larger than London

remained a forested country
until the 1960s
and the American billions
for *counterinsurgency* and *development*

with villagers displaced
from the new growth eucalyptus
to *become migrant workers*
or *prostitutes in Bangkok*   *Tiyavanich 245*

even after the insurgency
Phra Prachak discovered
when he ordained the oldest trees
by wrapping them in saffron robes   *River 12*

that what was left of the forest in Dong Yai
remained a battleground   *Tiyavanich 246*

illegal loggers
in league with the military
grenades thrown at his monastery
the roof of his hut
splattered with M16 shots   *Pasanno*

officials petitioning to have him defrocked
till he was finally arrested

now nothing left
but a saffron robe in a kuti   *monk's cell*
books strewn on the floor
small statues of Buddha in disarray   *Bangkok Post 1/4/98*

villagers forced out at gunpoint
some of their *crops plowed under*
in other places orderly rows
of another crop planted
in the middle of their rice   *Tiyavanich 247*

Peter Dale Scott

Ajahn Wan: *in today's society*
those who know how to extort
oppress and control others
are regarded as geniuses   *Tiyavanich 243*

and Ajahn Chah: *if you try to live simply*
practicing the Dhamma
they say you're obstructing progress   *Tiyavanich 241*

but part of me thinks

> it was happening anyway
> even some Buddhists
> engaged in the crackdown
> Ajahn Uan the sangha head
> looked down on meditation monks
> and *tried to force them out*
> *forbidding villagers to give them alms*   *Tiyavanich 173-75*

> until he *became so sick*
> *he had to take food intravenously*
> and *meditation practice*
> *helped him gradually recover*   *Tiyavanich 194-95*

> even then *the Sangha Council*
> *in 1987*
> *ordered all ascetics to leave the forests*   *Tiyavanich 249*

I try to look on it
as an exercise
in letting go
that gladness or sadness
is not the mind
only a mood
coming to deceive us   *Chah 1*

caring   *teach us*
to care and not to care

great fame in the end
for Luang Por Chah

232

people came by busloads
they say they're looking for merit
but they don't give up vice   Tiyavanich 289

Ajahn Chah *often said*
he felt like a monkey on a string
when I get tired
maybe they throw me a banana   Tiyavanich 292

the cuckoo-like bird
sings gaily *Moha*
Moha   the death of the dharma

in the withered sun-loud glade

BIBLIOGRAPHY.

Carr, Stephen. "An Ambassador of Buddhism to the West." In *Buddhism in Europe*, edited by Aad Verboom. Bangkok: Crem. Vol. Somdet Phra Phuttajan, Wat Mahathat, 1990.

Chah, Venerable Ajahn. *A Taste of Freedom.* Bangkok: Liberty Press, 1994.

Mills, James. *Underground Empire: Where Crime and Governments Embrace.* New York: Dell, 1987.

Pasanno, Ajahn. "Saving Forests So There Can Be Forest Monks." *Forest Sangha Newsletter*, January 1996. On the Web at www.abm.ndirect.co.uk/fsn/35/.

Pasuk Phongpaichit, Sungsidh Piriyarangsan, and Nualnoi Treerat. *Guns, Girls, Gambling, Ganja: Thailand's Illegal Economy and Public Policy.* Chiang Mai: Silkworm Books, 1998.

River, Jess. "We must learn to be leaves." *Earth Island Journal*, Fall 1993, 12. On the Web at sinosv3.sino.uni-heidelberg.de/ FULLTEXT/JR-ADM/river.htm.

Scott, P. D. "Alcuin's *Versus de Cuculo:* the Vision of Pastoral Friendship." *Studies in Philology*, LXII, 4 (July 1965), 510–30.

Tiyavanich, Kamala. *Forest Recollections: Wandering Monks in Twentieth-century Thailand.* Chiang Mai: Silkworm Books, 1997.

Wyatt, David K. *Thailand: A Short History.* Chiang Mai: Silkworm Books, 1993.

A Little History of Modern Music
William H. *Gass*

THE SPRING SEMESTER IS almost over, Professor Skizzen said as he slowly paced, almost drifted, from one side of the classroom to another, a manner he had just recently adopted; only a week, a week and a half remain, and most of you will leave the campus, leave this community, for your summer vacation and your menial job in a fast food restaurant. Then after a few months—to play the alternatives— those of you who haven't failed this class or some lesser subject; those of you who haven't transferred to one of the cheaper Ivies, graduated to the job market, or run away to Europe or the circus; those who remain will return. That means most of you will be back, for who fails at Wittlebauer? we are so built upon success. Of course, in order to come to college you had to fly from your nest, bid bye-bye to your yard, your toaster, your elm tree with its tired swing—too many loved things for me in this shaved hour to touch on or to name—and from that vantage point . . . hold on . . . you may have brought your toaster with you to school—true—bags of clothes, toaster—yes, certainly—indispensable—anyway, from that perspective what you shall do next is fly back to your old neighborhood. Take your toaster if that pleases. Note this—you shall go home even if the elm is dying. Even if an aunt is. Even if you don't want to. This cycle—of departure and return—evaporation and rain—yo and yoyo—will be repeated in one form or another your entire lives.

I beg your pardons, all. . . . I used a misleading migratory metaphor—branch, nest, yard, garden—not wise, because the migratory bird has two homes, its cool summer cottage and its warm winter cabana. Hands if you see the difference. When you achieve physicianhood you may be able to afford it. But let me turn this inadequate image to account. Twin homesteads are not unknown to sociological research. Our earth has two poles. Such divided loyalties are regularly demonstrated by those in the dough, though one habitation is usually the castle while the other is a cabin. If you have too many homes, however, as the jet-setter presumably does, we are compelled to say you are homeless as only the very rich can be. Such people are on permanent vacation—not to and fro, but fro and fro. A woeful situation.

Miss Rudolph, if you have a cough that bad you should go to the infirmary.

The dorm room, here, is your local habitation from which every morning, if you can manage it, you rise from your bed and wobble off to crunch some sugar-laden processed wheat or corn before it sogs in the bowl. You proceed through a habitual schedule throughout the day and return at the end to that same rubble of a room to study, perhaps to play, to chat with a friend, before sleep once again takes you into its chamber of dreams and its crude simulation of death. Perhaps you will drive a tin lizzie back to your home, or your family car will come for you—father and Aunt Louise—or you will ride a bus with a bunch of strangers from another world. . . .

What?

Ah, I see. . . . We don't say that anymore. . . . Too bad. Lizzie makes an appropriate sound. Anyway, while you are traveling, you will leave the car to fuel, leave it for relief, leave it to snack, to stretch your legs—candy, restroom, gasoline, coffee—get out, lock, and return. The vehicle will seem in such moments to be your special place, your familiar surroundings where your guard can roll down like one of its windows, where your can of pop, wad of highway maps, or sweet roll waits. Small cycles turn inside of wider ones. Wheels within wheel. Like Ezekiel's wheels, wheels with eyes, eh? Show of hands. . . . Ah, yes, no surprise, ignorance is epidemic.

In my home my desk is yet another haven—for my pencils and the seat of my pants—and when my mother calls from her garden her sound will be one I go to as if it were a beacon. Meanwhile, noises on the street I shall ignore. They are not a part of the composition. They revolve about other suns, have other eyes and other axles. Yet you know that when you arrive home, leave and arrive, yin to yang, come to go, this familiar cycle and its center won't roll on forever, because you expect to have a job one day, a car and dog and garage of your own, an office to go to, a kitchen to cook in, main and subsidiary bases like a diamond to traverse—ball diamond don't you play on? bases to stand safely at, stages on any journey, on life's way don't you say?—and so you expect the future will be full of places to return to. You expect homes to be here and there all over the place all the time. To spring up like spring does every year, and fresh blooms crack open, birds sing, new leaves hatch. Imagine. Homes to come home to, homes to leave. Everywhere. Imagine.

Who is imagining as you were instructed? Hands. Hands up.

Home is not just the last square on the Parcheesi board—oh I beg your pardon once again—occult reference—shame makes my cheeks show red—it is not just the tape you break at the end of the race or the plate you run to put your foot on—score—that's clearer for you?—but it is a set of things, habits of using them, patterns of behavior, met expectations, repeated experiences.

Now, then, take notice, pay a quarter, will you? for my voice and your attention: these homey spaces—so many—familiar voices, scents, satisfactions—comfort food, don't you say?—will be more important to you than other things, they can even dominate your thinking, monopoly your feeling, they will be in the major keys, but there will be minor keys, too, lesser variations, hierarchies will appear like old royalty arriving at a Viennese café where there will be requests from the customers, preferences in tables, order in the kitchen, ranks throughout the staff, competition in the silver, even among the pots and pans, bowls fit for barons shall sit on peasant plates, an ordinance will promulgate, a subordinance will sound like a summoning to church.

How many of you knew I was speaking of music all along? its inherent hierarchies? show of hands, please. Hah. . . . You are such good students. Why do I complain?

Because many of you have not turned in to me your analysis of that little tune I gave you. Such a simpleton task. A simpleton could do.

Where there is alter there is subalter. Where there is genus please expect species. Order among the tones. Order among the instruments. There is no note born that doesn't have a lineage, a rank, a position in the system. The force of past performances. Imitations of the masters. Traditions of teaching. Centers of learning. Habits of listening. Among them who will rule? for someone must rule. The horns? surely not the winds. This theory, not that, shall be abided. Therefore the French style will be enforced, the German manner obeyed, the Russian soul (it is always the Russian soul) obliged.

Where music is, Vienna is. The maestro is. You think music takes place in isolation, in some hermetic solitude? Cakes, coffee, gossip, and the Gypsy violin—loopy swoons and much mealy schmaltz surround the violinist's form and dismal dress. Huge, too, the opera *haus*. High the hats. Gaiety. Flirtations. The hunt. The waltz. Vienna tuned out the terrifying world to listen to Strauss. To *Fledermaus*. A social round of balls. Yet there must be a leader or there will be chaos, all those instruments braying at once. There must be a home to come home to, didn't the Austrians at one time suppose, while longing for the Reich to envelop them like a mother's milky white warm arms? There is a home for you. The bosom of the family. The leader raises his baton, Stukas scream from the skies.

Did not Odysseus strive to reach his wife kid dog and palace—you remember him? ah many of your hands need washing I can see—too few pink palms . . . through countless trials and tribulations, too, re-member the delays, the teases—one two three ten twelve thirty troubles, trials, tribulations, did I say?—lures of ladies, comforts of creatures—in wait like rocks—to bring the wayfarer down, to sink his soul to his sandals. So, too, we depart from the tonic, we journey farther and farther afield until it seems we've broken all ties with the known world, we are farther away than anyone has ever been, we are at the edge of the earth, we can forehear the Wagnerian downfall, the brink, that splashes into silence . . . when . . . lo, behold, magically, the captain, the composer sees a way, steers us through the storm, and we modulate do we not? sail ride walk to the warm and wel-coming hearth again, the hiking path winds but takes us to our hotel in safety just as the signs said they would: what relief at what a climax . . . the sight of a spire, familiar stones at one's feet, the smell of a pot on the stove. Nice walk, good hike, healthy return.

Poor Miss Rudolph. Glad you're back. Nice of you to cough in the hall. No music there.

Or shall we let a cough be music? With our new instruments of bedevilment might we not record all sorts of sounds out there in the world that calls itself—that call themselves—real; where squeaks and squeals and screams are on the menu, where dins assail us by the dozens—the crinkle of cellophane, whishiss of small talk, the fan-ning of five hundred programs—where we fill our ears with one noise in order not to hear another . . . yes record, preserve not only the roil of the sea but the oink of pigs and moos of cattle, the wind rattling the cornstalks like the hand of an enemy on the knob, and put them in . . . in the realm of majesty, of beauty, of purity, in . . . in music, let them in—poor Miss Rudolph's cough included—why?—why would we come to such a detrimental thought? or why should we learn to sigh at silence as if it were a sweet in the mouth, as if it were a pillow soft as a sofa, why should we order our instruments off! as if silence were an end? Only to invite ruck to rumpus us, to ruin our holy space?

*

Just then we had a silence, did you hear? a rest. Broken like a pane of glass by . . . explanations.

Because music has its holies, has its saints, has sounds all its own that no one else, no else like thing, no motion that the muck of matter makes, nowhere is one like them. These tones. Pure tones, resolute tones, resonant tones, redolent, refulgent, confident tones. We have artisans whose ancient art is to fashion instruments so different from the heartless machines that now chop idle raucouses into eekie parts and blast them at our ears like earclaps, earboxes, boomdoomers, save us save us save us from those ruffians, yes . . . give us smooth wooded bodies instead that glow in anticipation of being played, shining trumpets proud of their purpose, soothing tubes from which much love emerges, and virtuosos who have devoted their lives to learning how, from these wily and noble objects, to elicit the speech of the spirit. Consider: a quartet of them: four men or women. Centuries of preparation will go into their simplest tuning—a single scrape of a bow—nor will they be togged like Topsy or some ugly ragamuffin, but garbed and gowned for these rites, these magical motions that make truly unearthly sensations. This is where we should worship if we had the wit. Today Köchel Five Fifteen will pray for us. Play on our behalf. Be our best belief. Besides, this C major quintet is assigned. You will note how the apparently harmless theme sinks into C minor only to startle us with a chromatic passage meant to be stunning and achieving a vibrant numbness. That's the way to talk to God.

Now, children of our century, inheritors of what is left of the earth, calculate the consequences. Of a cough.

The musicians begin. After sufficient silence is imposed on the audience—for the slate is being wiped, a space cleared of all competition (note that, but return all notes before you leave, we dare not lose any)—then, and only then, they play. There are vibrating strings. Vibrating air in vibrating spaces. Vibrating ears. Vibrating brains. Do the notes fall out of them like spilled beans? out of these instruments as if they were funnels?

By the way, did you know that "spill the beans" means to throw up? Hands please. You others may sit upon yours and be uncomfortable.

No, the notes do not confess. They emerge like children into an ordered universe; they immediately know their place; they immediately find it, for the order you hear was born with them. Did I not just say so? Hands? Every one of them, as each arrives in its reality, immediately flings out a sea of stars, glowing constellating places. As a dot does upon a map or grid. As a developer on an empty field sees himself standing on a corner in a city that's yet to be. For these notes are not born orphans, not maroons surrounded by worse than ocean, but they have relatives, they have an assignment in a system. Did I not just say so? do you suppose that this will be on an exam?

Relations. . . . As you have in your family. Aunts, uncles, haven't you? oh I dare say, and addresses, underclothes, honor codes, cribs. The whole equipment of the gang. Yes, for even gangs have their organization, their nasty-nosed bullyboy boss and the boss's chamberlain—first violin.

But now . . . now remember the honest reality of that home—so sweet—a home . . . there's no place like it just as the song says. Let us have a second thought about that collection of clichés. . . . Those relatives—remember them?—arrived like ruinous news: they broke the peace; they ate the candy; they spoiled naps; they brought their own rules. Their kids cried. And you were punished for it. Sweet home? Dad is seeing his secretary on the sly, Mom is drinking long lunches with her female friends or shopping as if a new slip or a knickknack would make her happy. Sweet home is where heartfelts go to die. Sweet home is where the shards of broken promises lie, where the furniture sits around on a pumpkin-colored rug like dead flies on a pie. Home is haunted by all the old arguments, disappointments, miseries, injustices, and misunderstandings that one has suffered there: the spankings, the groundings, the arguments, the fights, the bullying, the dressings-down, the shames. Yes, it is a harbor for humiliations. A storehouse for grudges. A slaughterhouse for self-esteem.

Families are founts of ignorance, the source of feuds, the fuel for fanatical ideas. Families take over your soul and sell it to their dreams.

Somewhere during the slow course of the nineteenth century, the children of the middle class woke up to the fact that they were children of the middle class—well, some of them did. They woke one morning from an uneasy sleep and found they were bourgeois from toe to nose; that is to say, they cherished the attitudes that were the chief symptoms of that spiritually deadly disease: the comforts of home and hearth, of careers in the colonies, of money in the bank where God's name was on the cash, of parlor tea and cake, of servants of so many sorts the servants needed servants, of heavy drapes and heavy furniture and dark woodwalled rooms, of majestic paintings of historic moments, costly amusements, private clubs, a prized share in imperialist Europe's determined perfection of the steam engine and the sanitary drain. Daughters who could demand dowries were in finishing school where they were taught to tat, paint, play, and oversee kitchens; sons were sent to military academies, or colleges that mimicked them, where they would learn to love floggings, reach something called manhood, stand steady in the buff, and be no further bother to their parents. And in these blessed ancient institutions both sexes would learn to worship God and sovereign, obey their husbands, serve and love their noble nation, and dream of being rich.

It was inevitable. It was foregone—the drift of the young to Paris. Where the precocious began to paint prostitutes; they began to write about coal miners; and they began to push the diatonic scale, and all its pleasant promises, like the vacuum-cleaner salesman, out the door. They took liberties as if they had been offered second helpings; they painted pears or dead fish instead of crowned heads; they invented the saxophone. They shook Reality in its boots. Fictional characters could no longer be trusted but grew equivocal. First there was Julian Sorel, then Madame Bovary. Novels that undermined the story and poems that had no rhymes appeared. Painters tested the acceptability of previously tabooed subjects, the range of the palette, the limits of the frame. With respect to the proscenium, dramatists did the same, invading, shocking, insulting their audiences. Musicians started to pay attention to the color of tones. They pitched pitch, if you can believe it, from its first-base position on the mound. They fashioned long Berliozian spews of notes, composed for marching bands as well as cabarets, rejected traditional instrumentation, the very composition of the orchestra, and finally the grammar of music itself. . . . Notes had traditional relations? they untied them. Words had ordinary uses? they abused them. Colors had customary companions? they denied them. Arts that had been about this or that, *became* this and that. The more penetrating thinkers were convinced that to change society you had to do more than oust its bureaucrats, you had to alter its basic structure, since every bureaucrat's replacement would soon resemble the former boss in everything including name. Such is the power of position when the position is called "the podium."

Who shall build from these ruins a new obedience?

They . . . who are they, you ask? they are the chosen few, chosen by God, by *Geist*, by the muse of music: they are Arnold Schoenberg,

Alban Berg, and Anton von Webern. They chose, in their turn, the twelve tones of the chromatic scale, and thought of them as Christ's disciples. Then they sat them in a row the way da Vinci painted the loyals. I don't want to convey the impression that this disposition was easy, no more than for da Vinci. Suppose out of all the rows available, the following was the order of the group—ding dong bang bong cling clang ring rang chit chat toot hoot—and that we found the finest instruments to produce each one, the finest musicians to bring them forth, and sent them—the musicians, I mean, but why not the notes?—to Oxford to Harvard to Yale to Whittlebauer, to Augsburg even—thank you for the titters—to receive the spit of polish.

Yes, it is true, this music will be keyless, but there will be no lock that might miss it. Atonal music (as it got named despite Arnold Schoenberg's objection) is not made of chaos like John Cage pretended his was; no art is more opposed to the laws of chance. That is why some seek to introduce accidents or happenstance into *its* rituals like schoolboys playing pranks. Such as hiccups. Miss Rudolph's cough. No, this music is more orderly than anybody's. It is more military than a militia. It is music that must pass through the mind before it reaches the ear. But you cannot be a true-blue American and value the mind that much. Americans have no traditions to steep themselves in like tea. They are born in the Los Angeles of Southern California, or in Cody, Wyoming, not Berlin or Vienna. They learn piano from burned-out old men or women who compose birdsongs. Americans love drums. The drum is an intentionally stupid instrument. Americans play everything percussively on intentionally stupid instruments, and strum their guitars like they were shooting guns. But I have allowed myself to be carried away into digression. Digressions are as pleasant as vacations but one must return from them before tan turns to burn.

Imagine, then, that we have our row: ding dong bang bong cling clang ring rang chit chat toot hoot. Now we turn it round: hoot toot chat chit rang ring clang cling bong bang dong ding. Next we invert it so that the line looks like the other side of the spoon. Hills sag to form valleys, rills become as bumpy as bad roads: hat tat chot chut rong rung clong clyng bang bing dang dyng. We are in position, now, to turn this row around as we did our original. Or we can commence the whole business, as Schoenberg himself does at the beginning of *Die Jakobsleiter* by dividing the twelve tones into a pair of sixes. Thus the twelve tones are freed from one regimen to enter another. What has been disrupted is an entire tradition of sonic suitability,

241

century-old habits of the ear.

Then come the refinements, for all new things need refinements, raw into the world as they are, wrinkled and wet and cranky. The rule, for instance, that no member of the twelve gets a second helping until all are fed. They have a union, these sounds, and may not work overtime. Compositions, too, will tend to be short. Audiences will admire that. For instance, Webern begins his Goethe song, "Gleich und Gleich," with a G-sharp. Then follows it (please hear it with your heads): A, D-sharp, G, in a nice line before slipping in a chord E C B-flat D, and concluding F-sharp, B, F, C-sharp. You see, or rather, you intuit: 4 in a line, 4 in a chord, 4 in a line. Neat as whiskey.

What a change of life, though, is implied by the new music.

I hear a distant bell. It might have come from any bracelet in this room, from a bell flower that my mother's grown, a garden row, or from some prankster in the audience. Shall we include it in our composition, or tell it to shush?

Because this rustic buzz is as regular, dare we say, as clockwork, it is only half an accident, like a typewriter's clacking, the tiptaps of Morse code, a few wails from police sirens, and the hoot of a railroad train that Cocteau wanted to include in his conception of *Parade*—you know this ballet, hands?—suggestions that Diaghilev killed—hands for him? who you say? so, no applause. Sweet sweet deity, why have you put such ignorance in this world?

With this question I conclude my little history of modern music.

From Draining the Sea
Micheline Aharonian Marcom

MARTA, THIS IS MY INQUIRY, an inquisition of the air: you say that you cannot be undone, and you say (with your looking) that I am a beast of clean proportions; you say nothing with your words, in fact you have no words in my language (and I none in yours) and you insist in your dark cold chambers, in the capital of darkness, you bring me there, into the pit with you, with the other handless corpses, the half-deads, the unclosed eyes of the dying: you, the rats and diptera girls, and faceless cockless boys, and black-bowed beetles, and intrepid moths on your skin eyelids—that I stay with you in that place, that I take up your hands (beautiful veins of indifference) and bundle the unringéd, unpainted fingers fingernails to your mother in the Highlands, to your dead mother, the dead brothers and father, the crucified brother, who beat each other in the winters and for whom hunger is like an iron feast: send them these artifacts of the body, you say; rescue me from this hole, this hollow they've made for the half-deads; and I am crying uncontrollably now and I can't see you amidst the piles and it is you and then it is my mother giving me her five phrases of the dead Armenian grandmother when I am a boy, and the long distances between home and here, and then it is me, alone in my car, driving along the streets of Los Angeles. Never so alone and not-alone either: a dog corpse making a fiesta from the trunk of my car.

I have wondered if the dogs make spirit; I have wondered about the soldier in the mountains who carried the mongrel on his back (an order from his superiors) and who with the other recruits slaughtered without an implement, his hands, drank the blood and ate the entrails of the bitch he had carried for miles on the path up into the mountains; his bitch-friend for days on the trek into the Highlands; how he told her of his dead father and the mother who beat him like a dumb beast and that he would love her and that they would live together as family and killers in these mountains in this . . . This the

243

shame, the mark of wood, and once assumed not removable like broken glass or cracked asphalt or a broken tympanum on the descent into steep valleys: I am making an essay into the man; he is American; he is fatter and he looks like something I could hate; he is a man who collects corpses. A purveyor of the dead. He is stained and dirty; the blood the violence of the last breath has mutated his form; he thinks that a dog ought to be buried in a marble mausoleum; he thinks that the dogs ought to have their place in politics, in the movies, in love. There is money; plastic cards symbolize credit, providence, hope, and things he can buy (cars, shows, clothes, and girls); there are dogs and drivers of dog corpses, and all the while his dear and lovely Marta lies in a pit at the army technical school, which is no pit for a drama of love, or for the sentimental movie watchers and makers (there is no profit from it, or to be entertained by it, and happy endings are not happy): this is a pit in the capital of her country, in the Antigua Escuela Politécnica de Guatemala, Avenida La Reforma, 1-45, Zona 10, Ciudad Guatemala: she and the hundreds of half-deads await their next rendezvous with the ununiformed men, the boys who arrive in the garden with their garden-variety black ski masks, hellos, black-tinted windows, and 9mm pistols: these are the G-2 men; and he drives while she waits, and he waits with her as he can; this "with" a small and untruthful word in his English; in his city the Washingtonias rise high and bright above his head.

Here is the church the Spanish fathers built in 1678 when they came to the ancient village of Acul, and the soldiers made us come here to the plaza to save the nation today. Where would you like to go, they say in their small and decided screams, to heaven or to hell? You (the boy with the black hood on his head has pointed out your uncle the neighbor's boy the catechist from houses away); you. And we are sitting standing waiting (a boy's blood runs out a few houses away and his mother has pleaded with the soldiers so that she may return to her boy, staunch the blood's dispersal onto the dirt floor of her home and killing her son in this way with its unabated flood; and she is quiet now with her own split face and hands) and the small children would like something to eat (the soldiers arrived before dawn and it is midmorning now and they are hungry, tired) or to sit down quietly or to please return our sons to us (the now-departed boys, they are taken to hell, which is inside the church building); girls are crying loudly in the distance—you hear them?—this wail, relentless, it takes up residence in the middle ear, the tympanum—traitor to the race—turns the wails into wails, and from that moment it does not cease: terror once begun and entered into the body with sound and these blindly seeing eyes that day in the plaza on a Tuesday in April 1982—is like any of the tightly wound string-catchers, without sur-cease, unstoppable until it itself stops, only to begin again in the mind, in dreams, at any moment on the street corners in the capital, walking toward the river, by the corner of the Polytechnic, on the Pan American Highway, behind the cypress in the plaza: to become, then, this inheritance for the terrified, the embittered, the fucked-ones who remain so unwillingly. Fear awakens inside sound like a good and obedient dog awakens at dawn.

Communist bitches; they are screaming now at the girls and huddled women (like bees) and the one mother begins to plead again for the bleeding boy she abandoned in the hut (the soldier'd entered, the machete in the gullet of the thirteen-year-old boy who is looking when they arrive, for the pigs, they say, and they say it in Spanish, which is not your language, and you understand the word —puerco— because); she now dispatched, like a memorandum from the capital; like the New National Security Program Initiative papers; Operation Ixil; and our respective presidents are having drinks shaking hands and smiling into the camera lenses from a hotel in Honduras say-ing that *Everything is good in Guatemala;* like a small wind that lifts your plaits in this infinitesimal way, only you notice its breath on your nape, only you know now seeing the arrival of the soldiers that this, for you and yours, will not end today, did not end yester-day, and the time of the clock, like history, little consoles you in this lifetime.

Acul is a small village in the Western Highlands of Guatemala. It is located in the Ixil Area, some three thousand meters above sea level, a two-and-a-half-hour walk from the town of Santa María de Nebaj. The Ixil call this the Tierra Fría; a gray mist hangs above the village on most days; the Cuchumatán mountain range rises tall and green and black-gray above the hamlets and the town. At dawn you can see the smoke rise from the dispersed huts to the low-hanging clouds; see the girls carrying the bowls of maize, jugs of water, on their heads; see them make tortillas like good girls and cook them over the wood fire; the costumes of the girls are red and green and beautiful, and the lovely Indian ladies in their hand-woven skirts, shirts, and they smile at you when you see them on the dirt path and they will step to one side gracefully; bow to the bosses like dignified gazelle; hear the constant crowing of the cocks throughout the morning and afternoons; the dogs' endless gray barkings into the night; bend under the leña because it is a heavy load that the boys and men carry homeward down from the mountains, the wood stacked like ladders down their backs, like the master they once carried on their backs in a wooden chair tied to the waist; and in Guatemala, as in Mexico, a *carga* is still used as a measurement of weights: equal to two hundred pounds—the amount an Indian can carry on his back thirty to forty miles in a day.

*

It is these structures I am trying to essay: the roads, the effect of roads and motorcars on the mind, on this urge, on the sky and data and words and the clouds that sit on the mountains today like girls, do not rise or fall, on me, Marta, on you? Tell me what it is, why I write you day after day and seek you here in the fleshless place even as my semen smells up from my hands feet, and the stench of my body its fluid is irredeemably warm and I am repulsed by it and it is me and all that I have of you here amidst the English of my phrases sadnesses and distances and made in another place but I make it here also: this *made*; and the syllable is uninterruptible and its sounds make men and roads, made the tar and stones that covered my soul and sealed in a black loneliness, the reams of time, and the words I seek here to find you, Ixil girl, to understand why it is and it is the inquiring that this man makes, he is a driver, a corpse-collector, smells the semen on his feet, the stench has risen to his nose and he would eat his seed and he thinks it could make children it could make pleasure, it could be a father's ecstasy and not this shame at night, late, as he eats hamburgers, candies, he is repulsed by it—the American man without glory, with nothing but false ideas of a place with a modern man's failure to know failure because love cannot be contained because I can love all of the women and why should this love be contained by morality's compass by roads and the time of the clock, which is: whose? who made it? profits by it?: a death for the living, a half-life that is not a life but a time among the cannibals, but instead of flesh we allowed to eat, we eat roads; we tarmac the world; we eat our neighbors' complaints and the News and Politics and Shows; we hate our neighbors, ourselves, and the outside inside urges—you—a foreign girl in a foreign place (you do not exist in the News in Politics in Shows), and here I am foreign to myself to you; you make hills and trees and blouses are woven with hummingbirds: make me, Marta, make me back into the me I have not been, but could be; inside; could have been; unashamed alive, mouth agape, the gate opened, your agapet here among the dead pages.

The dead are here among the electric lights. I see you in the corners of things, behind the sofa beneath the dust motes and inside the detritus of the living, the uncleaned corners, which I am cleaning now and taking out and disinfecting the surfaces of and I am sitting in the dark inside my closet and the electric lights are outside with you and you are with me every day and closer than my own pupil my image in the mirror is foreign to me and this Marta I carry next to my blackness returns inside and I am seeking the byways outside of time and reason to remake your house, to find you in Los Angeles, which could be as if I were walking the paths of Acul (the tarmac has not arrived to your hamlet; the road built in 1983 by the hands of the survivors; a dirt road; the army rationed the builders nine tortillas each day while the soldier held the Galil above their bent backs, supervised their good work as free men, as the Galil made the free men make the dirt road), and I see your hut in the distance, it is the house from before the holocaust, and there are dozens of houses in Acul and each separated by this plot of land and the maize makes wind in the fields between houses and the beans grow at the base of the maize plants in their curled and verdant maze, a green animal, and I see smoke emerge from the chimney pipes at dawn, find your home and I enter the door, this lintel that crosses time, it is blue, the centuries undone as I walk down the paths of your village and into your home and you make the tortilla by hand with hands of grace and each time I see you making them, the pounded maize and your hands like gods from the repetition of the gods, I am hungry and you offer me sustenance and I would like a drink (I am thirsty) and you give me water you have fetched from the river and we sit in the dark interior of your belly in the darkness of the house your grandfather made from cypress and the sun does not enter (there are no windows) and the embers are hot and you will give me some atol to drink when you are finished preparing it, and it is warm sweet corn milk, and reminds me of my childhood in Los Angeles when I drank black teas, hot milks, and I would like to undo time, Marta—undo all of its useless strange mendacious and then the norm of the terrible the man who must drive to work to fill his car with petrol phone strangers (this is business) for business and pay bills watch games kill cut the barbarian into small pieces and feed him to the dogs; use the fat of the vanquished Indian to assuage the Spanish soldier's wound. He is a soldier and he is made to carry a dog on his back from the metropolis up into the mountains of your nation and mine and into pity and the places without roads or pity carries the dog on his back like a good soldier and the young bitch, he loves her, and the dog does not cry, she is a bitch who understands that the nation is not a whim or simply a man's desire to make but, rather, it is the tooth we live by like the god's eye that is printed on the dollar and all-seeing (*I am coming as I write this, Marta—my semen spills onto the page; this my American history of the dead half-deads the half-lived you and me*). I am this soldier boy as he walks up the mountain paths; he is an Indian in a book I am reading and in another book his name is   . His mother discards him at six and his father discards him after his semen ejaculates into the mother's cunt. His father's ecstasy cannot, however, be denied and perhaps it is the best thing about the boy; it is, darling, what I love about him, what I refuse to deny for any newspaperman or politician's academic's moral pleasures. He climbs the miles into the mountains from the capital with his bitch on his shoulders; she is young, no more than a year perhaps, pied and four legged; at the tip of each ear there is a patch of white as if a sign from God he thinks: God, he thinks, has given him this trial. He has joined the Kaibiles to save the patria: (*from?*): from the communists the atheists the dogs unbelievers and killers; those who would destroy the beautiful fatherland; because he is hungry; shoeless and cold in the streets of the capital; and because: the Army takes him by force from the streets on a cold morning in January 1979. He walks and he is beaten with sticks and clubs as he walks up these mountain paths—Move it mother-fuckers pussy-fuckers faggot-fuckers Indian-dogs and fuckers: move! (and yes, darling, he is your killer coming up the mountainside—your brother's killer, he'll rape the young girls and her friends, he'll unlive what you love, your childhood will burn in him, by him, the village desecrated and decimated in fire—and is his story blinded then? should we sacrifice him to the gods of the Army? to a moral or an immoral character? *continue:*) he is walking and they are not allowed to drink water and the dog begins her moaning, she cries to him and her bound legs and she is suffering and he shoves his fingers inside her mouth, her sex, and he thinks that she will be his domestic pet, his companion in the mountains, and so he whispers to her as they make their way up the mountains—that he will love her, that he can care for her, that his mother did not love him, that his father's ecstasy was not enough for the boy who did not own shoes until taken into the Army at sixteen, and that now his boots pinch his feet but that he is proud of the pinching, the blistered heels, and crippled toes—he loves them like he could have loved a mother and an ecstatic father—and he walks higher and higher into the mountains, up to the Tierra Fría, and into the Ixil Area—your killer comes to you, Marta; he approaches your village, although he is years from you still, still untrained, not-blooded, he would like to love the dog on his back and tells her more and more of his history and he is a hungry man and he is angry that he has been hungry for this lifetime and a filled belly is not familiar to him, like shod feet (and his toes are stones in these boots) and warmth and sugary sweets during the day and at nights and without payment of any kind he walks, climbs, and he is sweating, pays in exertion for this heat and the bitch is quieter now, she mourns moans, she knows what awaits them at the apogee, but he insists that he will love her always and she tells him that he is blind, that a soldier must earn his keep, and he does not listen to her as they walk, he climbs and she holds to his back, pisses down his spine and into time and into his trousers, down his legs, and the boots are pissed and he imagines that all good soldiers have their dogs for comfort like a shepherd will have his (and he has no flock this soldier boy: unshod, unfilled in his belly, and a mother who sold him for two pounds of maize when he was six years old to the plantation owners on the coast in Oriente) and your killer is a lonely man, Marta; he could be lonelier than I—his hunger is like fear. And it is not for forgiveness or atonement or a confession, but simply that we can say: Yes, I know it— my killer was a lonely man; a boy whose belly was never filled to; a boy who thought that despair was a shirt for everyday use, his only wardrobe inside a black polyethylene bag. And when the lieutenant tells them how they must do it, they arrive at the camp in the mountains and they are tired and hungry and happy to have arrived! and each recruit takes the dog from his shoulder and rubs his aching shoulders and the sweat and dog piss have wetted his shirt through and each recruit has not had anything to drink for many hours and the cold winds in the mountains come down the mountain and the hot sweat is fast cold and they want: "Now you must do it, boys: do it quickly," the lieutenant says to them, barks it out, like a dog. And each boy, who is becoming the good soldier, lifts the dog from the ground and each boy who is a recruit for the fatherland and each boy must prove must make himself into this defender of faith of god of roads of time's required acts; the nation; now, the lieutenant says to them, you must do it (or, as usual, the boy's fate will be the dog's). And the lieutenant raises his pistol and knife, this Army man who has been a man for many years and (who remembers when his friends from school punched his face and he vomited and how his mother threw her shoes across the room at him and he cried, and the hands of the father holding the black rod above his head, and he will laugh when these boys twist the necks of the bitches) he orders them: with your bare hands!, and their girls look into their eyes, thanking them, offering them this blood and meat and all of the girls' blood and viscera is placed in a bowl, as if in a church ceremony, and the boys line up like penitents and (do it or we'll kill you, he says) they drink the blood the body of their girls; they drink the vomit of the boy in front of them also. They are in line and the boy whose vomit has mixed in with the blood and viscera is ordered to rejoin the line and in the queue he waits; he drinks again; blood is soup today, they say, and love is like soup in the mountains. The new recruits are made to drink and eat their girls, each other's bile, until they manage to keep it inside their new bodies.

And when the recruit drank the blood and ate the meat of his dearest companion, and the blood and flesh surged back up through his throat (uninvited to leave), he ate and drank and ate again until she no longer returned—when he did it he did it because he wanted to live more and "We'll kill you fuckers; do it or we'll kill you" and blood could be wine and the body is love.

The semen dries on my feet now and you wash my feet in this essay; I eat a meat sandwich—meat salt sugar and wheat, and it is good, and I am happy that my belly is filled.

*

250

Your Guatemala has changed me and then it cannot be yours because can a dog be a citizen of the nation?—this invention, this *Goatemala,* as foreign to you as the men in the capital who have taken you down and then further down the recesses of pain. Not made by you, has not been yours; the invention of an idea, of men who write books as I write this book to you, which is no letter but a set of treaties, treatises, manuals, and fables about why: I long to lick your back; the *naturales* are dogs; the dogs are rickety boned and tail tucked, you turn your eyes down in shame and when the soldier who is from another region, his broken Spanish slams into your face as he slams his cock blades into your cunt, *puto,* he says, when you know that the sun is masculine and burns into eyes that don't close, because, you decide, you will look at the man who has been made into a blade, a rickety-boned blade, an awkward Castilian metal, a boy (and you could have loved a boy) who is older than your brother, and younger than your brothers, whose eyes have become suns (we laugh together at this harsh lying poetry): whose eyes are brown, then black, and opaque gods do not reside there while he fucks you bloody, dirty, dead then—but you don't die, it is not the only death, and there are more and there are the mountains and there is the neighbor girl you carried on your back and the boy you carried on your belly and the child whose hand you held dragging her running up into the mountains with the other fleeing villagers after the massacre, and there are more and there is more (a palm that kills your own son nine months later), and I couldn't see it, Marta, and I was watching the television and I was saddened by the girls who would not fuck me at the cocktail parties, who turned from me in disgust—fat ugly undignified and dirty—who, when I walked into the shop, gave me their eyes as if their eyes could make looks like steel and a chemical look, a look that made the body detestable, made this boy lonelier and then more lonely: have I said it enough? that I am an ugly man, a fat man, a whorish man and I have been monstrous—and I only have the women I can pay for; the girls I pay to speak with on the telephone; my skin pock marked, my teeth matted and gray, and I am fatter and my cock is smaller and this is the man who does not bring the girls at the fiesta, and this the man who is shy to return such a look of loathing (Why this loathing look from them, these vile and beautiful girls: what have I done for such a look? Why this look of hate from the beautiful? When what I want and have always wanted . . .)

Micheline Aharonian Marcom

I do not wish to see: this you beside the administration building, his eyes are brown and the opaque pieces of his iris spill onto the whites, his black fingernails, his look of rage (like the epic hero's rage), he is a hero for the nation; he doesn't look into your eyes, won't look, while he fucks you. Let me say how beautiful you are (I am a man who admires the beautiful its horror and its music and the cunt is beautiful; the fat sticking thighs, an ass haired and unhaired (by the girls in my city) and the half-shaven cunt hairs: all of it I can love), your clothing and the plastic sandals, they are not broken yet, and the colors woven into your hair, your *huipil* looks like something beautiful and happy: the hummingbirds tell the old myth of jealousy of love on your blouse; the barbarians are happy in paradise, a savage couture. Why does the blood enter into my reveries of paradise, beautiful and bare-nippled girls, a soldier who kindly takes her hand, kisses her fingers like stars and moons—all of his words said correctly and true with the victor's tongue, which has become common to the place—Guatemala and our Americas have become places—like the eucalyptus on the hillsides near my home become commonplace, and in the canyons of dust and distant memories I am searching then for love's intersection and locale: for you. Are you here in my Americas? They are mine, I have been made here and I have been schooled and I have posited questions, Marta, to all of the learned men in university, and the late-night p.m. store clerks, and the men holding their hands over the cash register's gleam and guns can be wider and I continue apace: why are we, then, these miasmic tale tellers? Because fictions are the bones of these Americas? Mine own fictions? America is built like a tall limestone monument, like tarmac roads and highways, like the dirt plaza where your brother your uncles and (Where is your father? He is alongside the pit by the new cemetery, he will die in two days' time of this *susto*) America is no more real than those places, than these places of worship—we do not exist, no, but killers can wrong can be fictional tales, and still the machinated machining up of the world does not abate; progress of the fabled Progress, monuments to the new gods.

Marta: this is true and this is real—I am an ugly man: I am sick and my kidneys pain me; a horror; and I sit here in a padded and green armchair and I am eating ice cream and good and white flour and white sugar sweetened and my belly has never been empty or fatigued from eating mountain grasses and leaves and falls over my

belt and hides my penis and not-shitting from the grasses and roots
we ate today in the mountain if lucky and without luck the child on
your back has died and then the girl in your hand has gone and then
not even the watery roots today or the UH-1H helicopters can be
heard or you can build a small fire if the clouds hang low enough
to conceal the smoke; there are bombs; there is a girl in the pit of
the capital, sees the christ's penis removed, and lungs like bells in the
tree towers, and none of it, Marta, changed any one thing in your
mountain, on my chair. The mountain, you whispered, saved us. Did
your geography save you? make you? did your Tierra Fría do that?
Does topography save a girl who runs high and the rains come down
for months and the plastic sandals are now broken and the toenails
blacken, then fall out, and the forehead swells with the animals who
are small and live beneath the skin, making mountains in your flesh,
make hunger for absent gods, hunger for which the gods were killed,
they came like the torrential rains, then bombs, then flesh torn apart
and you are running higher and higher, and like an animal, you say,
we lived in the mountains for fifteen months: without food, shelter
for the babes, fire, and when the babes were birthed in the mountain
the mothers cut the umbilical cord with their teeth and they did
not tie the ends off: a baby dies quickly this way, you tell me, you
whisper it in my ears in Los Angeles and I cannot hear you I have not
been able to hear these bone-words because it is late, it is the middle
of the night—it is effortless to kill a child like this, you say (How
many children died in those mountains, Marta? by their mothers'
hands, the Cessna A37-B bombs, the hunger and thirst and no med-
icines: dysentery is a killer also.) Do we take these whores for killers
then? Should we string them up in town squares, run the gasoline
into a discarded black tire, hang the tire around the whores' bent
necks and burn the savage dirty blood from our eyes (like suns)
which can't see, will not make light? Not me, darling. I am sitting in
my green armchair and I am eating ice cream and watching the
shows and I am happy and if the bombs fall onto your skin, as if this
were possible—show me the proof of it? who would do such a
thing?—and if the roots you dig up are desiccated today and so today
you are denied the teaspoonful of root water that the mountain gives
selfishly as if obsessed (by demons, by the light not-shines, by your
dead) and if—then no; and no; I may switch the channels, watch a
comedy, it blares loudest inside my middle ear like black flies, like
the small animals that have burrowed beneath your skin, made their
shelters there on your forehead, made carnal mountains, a new and

bodied topos—you the deformed god when you come down the mountain naked and absented shoes that plastic and broken lie up in the mountains with the bones of the children then fathers then neighbors and old men (the old men die quickly in the cold). The dogs arrive! they say, as you walk through the central square in Nebaj, and your shame is like Eve's, yes Marta, give this rib back to me for a penance. Give me your flesh, this man, this ugly and fat and small-cocked man would like you, seeks you, writes you up in his America while his history lessons continue apace on the television (of liberty and the freedom of freedoms and a democratic cunt wish) will devour it, will return to your cunty paradise in America, beneath the humus of your flesh—the mountain's gift of root waters.

An Affectionate Companion's Jottings
Can Xue

—Translated from Chinese by Karen Gernant and Chen Zeping

IT'S THE 28TH TODAY, and my owner has run out of patience. Ever since breakfast, he's been looking out the window. I can hear all his pores growling, and his eyes are flashing a fluorescent green. He's a cultured man, a bachelor with time on his hands. A person like this doesn't usually show his brutality unless he's really provoked. At breakfast, he had kicked me on the forehead and I had fainted at once. What led to this? Milk. That's right—milk. Naturally, he knows how much I love milk: previously, he had always split a bottle of milk with me. But this morning, because of the black person, everything went wrong. Without paying any attention to me, my owner had poured the whole bottle of milk into his bowl. I'd lost no time in tugging at his pant leg, and had also called him softly, but he had ignored me. It seemed he was going to drink it all, so in my anxiety, I nipped his leg—not a real bite, just a reminder. Who'd have guessed that he would explode? Later, I figured this had given him an excuse to do what he'd been wanting to do anyway. Definitely! If a person was nursing grudges, then he'd stop at nothing. When I came to not long afterward, I realized that I'd better reassess my relationship with him. Delving into it more deeply, I concluded there was nothing superficial about it. Maybe the word "ownership" not only connoted dependency and obedience but also, at some point, conflict and manipulation. After all, I knew the secret relationship between him and the black man, didn't I?

In fact, my owner had no reason to lose his patience, for I knew that sooner or later, the black man would pay another visit to this small high-rise apartment. It was three o'clock in the morning a year ago when my owner got out of bed and went to the kitchen in search of something to eat. I noticed he was barefoot, not even wearing slippers. When he walked, he held his arms out in front of him, and his face was blank. I knew he was walking in his sleep. Since he'd done this several times without ever having a problem, I didn't tag along. He opened the refrigerator, took out a beer and some cold cuts,

255

and sat at the tea table to enjoy them. Smacking his lips, he ate with great relish, but I knew he wasn't awake. Perhaps food tasted even better in dreams than in reality. I was itching to go over and mooch some. But I didn't. I couldn't wake him up at such a time, for that would be harmful to his health.

Just then, someone rapped on the door three times. Who could it be in the dead of night? My sleepwalking owner heard it at once, and got up and opened the door. I thought, if it's a thief, he's a goner for sure: with one blow, a thief would make sure he'd never wake up again. Luckily, it wasn't a thief, but a man with lacquer black skin. Around his neck he was wearing a shiny gold chaplet, and on his hands were two skull-shaped silver rings. My owner nodded at him and said, "It's you." The fellow answered laconically, "Yes." I could see that my owner wasn't awake yet, for he was moving stiffly. After the fellow sat down, my owner brought him some food from the refrigerator, and soon the tea table was loaded down with all kinds of cold cuts, sausages, and thousand-year-old eggs. The black man sat erectly and clenched his teeth, unwilling to loosen up at all. He didn't touch the snacks, but denounced my owner with his eyes. My owner didn't notice; perhaps he was "seeing without seeing"—as sleepwalkers generally do.

"Won't you have a little beer?" my owner asked.

"My chest hurts." As he talked, the black man tore his shirt open with a single motion. "I was burned in the forest fire. . . ."

There wasn't a hair on his bare black chest. You could see the distinct throbbing in the lower left side of his chest: was there something seriously wrong with his heart?

My owner didn't look up at him. He was muttering to himself, "Why won't he even drink beer?"

The black man was grinding his teeth—to me, this sounded like a duck quacking—and rubbing his feet surreptitiously on the floor. In order to relieve the tension, I sprang to his lap and deployed some feminine charms. The black man petted me with his beringed hand, but it wasn't ordinary petting, for his fingers were gripping my throat harder and harder. I began struggling, clawing the air helplessly. When I was just on the edge of losing consciousness, he pushed me down to the floor. I was afraid he would hurt me again, so I played dead. At the time, my owner seemed unaware of what was going on. I saw him pacing restlessly back and forth in the room, maybe waiting for the black man to start something. As for me, since I'd already been the target of the black man's malice, I was afraid he would do something even worse.

As the black man stood up to leave, my owner humbly begged him to stay a while longer.

"My chest hurts. Your room is suffocating," he said as he flung the door open.

He left. My owner—his sleepwalker's arms held out in front of him—seemed about to follow him, but instead, he just walked absently around the room, repeating over and over again, "Why couldn't I get him to stay? Why couldn't I get . . ."

My owner was a serious stuffed shirt of a man. He had a job at a newspaper office, but as a rule he worked at home. I had settled down here quite by accident. At the time, my former owner had taken his anger out on me and thrown me out. With nowhere to go, I'd been loafing around on the stairs when, all of a sudden, I saw a door open a crack, and a thread of light came out. In the wee hours of the pitch black night, the thread of light stared at me and cheerily beckoned me inside. The room was clean, with everything in its place. My present owner was sitting on the sofa, deep in thought, one hairy arm propped up on the armrest, his huge head in his hands. He saw me at once, and jumped up and said, "Ha! An old cat!" From then on, my name was "Old Cat."

I quickly realized I was more comfortable here than with my former owner. My starchy new owner was not the least bit stiff with me: trusting me to discipline myself, he never set limits for me. After thoroughly inspecting his domicile, I, a cat of some breeding, chose the rug beneath the tea table for my bedroom.

Every day, I dined with my owner. Since he believed in equal rights, we each had our own bowls and saucers. I ate whatever he ate, except that I didn't drink beer, nor did I like fruit.

My owner was efficient in his work. As a rule, he worked for two hours in the middle of the night, and then sat around the whole day, as if afflicted by a certain kind of depression. I sympathized with him: I supposed he was unhappy with his life or frustrated in his work. I also thought that he was essentially a strong person, and that after getting over the present difficulty, he'd be fine. But I'd been here a long time now, and not only had he not improved, but his depression was even worse than before. Had he been unhappy all along in both life and work? After some consideration, I rejected this view. One day, a wretched-looking person came over. He meekly called my owner "editor in chief," thus making it clear that he was a colleague from the newspaper office: from this I concluded that everything was going well at work. I also discovered that, for no reason, my owner looked for trouble. Except for the two hours that he shut himself up in his bedroom and worked—I had no way of knowing what he was like then—most of the rest of the time he was an unhappy man.

One day, he asked someone to hang an iron pothook from the living-room ceiling, and from it he hung a hemp rope. When I came back from a stroll, the door was open, and as soon as I went in, I saw him dangling, unmoving, from that hemp rope. I screamed in terror, and with that, he began swaying. He stood on tiptoe on the table, loosened the noose, and jumped down. The rope left two purple marks on his neck. After freeing himself from the noose, he looked much more relaxed and was actually in high spirits as he went to the kitchen and fried an ocean fish for me. But it was hard for him to get into such a good mood. As I ate, I was watching him in terror and thought to myself, is this a valedictory dinner? Of course it wasn't, because after a bath, he strode briskly into his bedroom to work. The next day, his old trouble recurred: now, besides being depressed, he was also in agony. His intermittent roaring was oppressive.

In order to help him, I jumped up and nipped his hand. This little trick worked: he calmed down as if just waking from a dream, and urged me to bite him a little harder, until I drew blood. My owner must have been possessed by a demon, making it impossible for him to focus his energy on anything at all the whole day long. He couldn't find any way, either, to vent his unhappiness. Or perhaps he had too high an opinion of himself to try any of the ordinary ways of venting. Sometimes, self-abuse could temporarily postpone the ultimate destruction, but it couldn't solve the root problem. Each time, it took more intense stimulation. Just when all of his remedies were almost exhausted, the weird black man had appeared, thus instantly changing his entire attitude toward life.

That night, after the black man left, my owner slept for a long time. He didn't wake up until the third morning, forgetting even his work responsibilities. After he woke up, he pulled out of his depression and rushed to the balcony, where he lifted weights dozens of times. Then he began sweeping the apartment. He cleaned the place until it was spotless, and even went so far as to buy a flower to brighten the living room. He washed the heavy drapes, and let the sunshine

258

splash the living room: the whole room overflowed with the atmosphere of spring. I really didn't like his turning everything upside down in the apartment: the dust he stirred up made it impossible for me to breathe, and the rose made me sneeze uncontrollably. My owner wasn't young. How could he be so hyperactive? He was acting almost like a teenager. The only thing I could do to get away from his cleaning was to go out and stand on the stairs.

He kept this up for a long time. His face reddened and his eyes flashed. But every morning and again at dusk, he looked bewildered, expectant. At such times, he strolled to the balcony and fixed his eyes on the distant sky. I knew whom he was waiting for, but I couldn't help him. Despite my anxiety, I was unable to do anything.

The black man was savage and cruel. I'd already experienced his strong grip, and I didn't know why he had eventually left me with my life. My owner was good to me, but as soon as this black man arrived, he simply didn't give me another thought. He was indifferent to the black man's brutal treatment of me. I felt vaguely hurt. My owner thought constantly about the one rogue whom he'd encountered while dreaming, even to the point of making him the center of his life. This made me quite angry. Wasn't I the one who kept him company day and night? Wasn't I his only companion during his lonely days? When he was in the depths of despair, when he had lost all the fun in life, who was it that jumped on his lap and comforted him? But then, thinking about it more dispassionately, perhaps my affection had always been unrequited. My owner was an extraordinary man—unfathomable and mulling everything over at length. Even a cat like me who was particularly sensitive couldn't catch anything but the surface of his ideas. Now, since he was looking forward to the black man coming, he must have had his own reasons. I'd better not impose my views on him. In a few minutes that night, my sleepwalking owner must have communicated at the speed of lightning with the black man. This kind of communication was far beyond my comprehension.

With a charcoal pencil, my owner drew a pair of eyes and hung them on the living room wall. At a glance, I knew whose eyes they were. That man's penetrating stare had left a deep impression on me. When my owner finished his work in the middle of the night and emerged from his inner sanctum, his face showed his exhaustion and he would sometimes stand and mumble something for a while beneath that drawing. I thought my owner was waiting for his idol: all he could do was console himself with false hopes and meet with him

259

that way. The black man's mysterious comings and goings were hard on him. Judging from his behavior that night, the black man also felt unbearable agony. It made him sort of unearthly. What I mean is: his suffering had gone beyond this world. This was different from my owner's suffering. I felt that, although my owner was unconventional, his anguish stemmed from everything he did. Although I was a cat, able to observe dispassionately, I really didn't know whether this black man had anything to do with this world. When he gripped my throat with both hands, he did so unconsciously. That's to say, he didn't know that it was my throat he had gripped. Why did my owner feel so attracted to this sort of fellow?

After the first rush passed, my owner was no longer so overstimulated: he entered into a period of calm. Every day, he hid out in his inner sanctum and worked for two hours. Then he frittered away the rest of the time. Aside from making purchases and occasionally going to the newspaper office, he didn't go out. During this period, a clerk from the office came by once. He was an old man with a thin, sallow face, who had come to bring drafts. He left a bad impression on me, probably because of the thumbtack in the sole of his shoe. After he came in, he scuffed the gleaming floor, leaving a lot of metallic marks on it. This man wasn't clean, either; he smelled sour, and he spat wherever he pleased. My ever-starchy owner, however, didn't seem to mind any of this: he led the clerk warmly over to the sofa, seated him, and poured a beer for him. They evidently had a special relationship.

"Has he been to the newspaper office?" My owner seemed fearful as he asked this.

"I asked the receptionist. I was told that he just stood in the lobby three minutes, and then left." The old man sipped his beer calmly, his eyes flashing malicious light: he was obviously taking pleasure in my owner's misfortune.

"Are you sure he said three minutes?"

"That's exactly right."

My owner slumped onto the sofa: a load had been lifted from his shoulders.

The old clerk had left some time ago, but my owner was still agitated by the news he had brought. I couldn't figure out whether my owner was happy that the black man had gone to his workplace or whether he was fearful. My owner was so jumpy that he couldn't sit still, couldn't eat much, and couldn't sleep. I noticed that he was dazed as he sat on the sofa. He sat there for two hours, often simpering, as if he'd picked up something valuable. While he was in this trance, disaster befell me: he completely overlooked my existence. Sometimes I was hungry and thirsty, and jumped onto his lap and kept meowing, but my entreaties didn't move him at all! In desperation, I tried to open the refrigerator myself, but I couldn't. Finally, thank God, he thought of food. My stomach was grumbling, and my paws kept quivering. I snagged a sausage from his hand and ate it, but I wanted another and there weren't any more. He was preoccupied with eating, and didn't even hear my cries. My owner's behavior infuriated me: after all, I was a living thing, not an ornament. I had to eat, drink, shit, and piss every day, just as he did. In his care, I had long since become a cat aware of equal rights. I had to make him notice this! I decided to start championing my rights. When my owner opened the refrigerator, I scurried in: I wanted to eat to my heart's content!

He didn't see me, and closed the refrigerator door on me. I found the fried ocean fish that he'd been saving, and wolfed it down right away. While I was eating, I felt more and more that something was wrong. The frightening chill not only coursed through my hair, but also pierced my guts. It quickly became difficult for me to take even a tiny step. Crouching on the refrigerator shelf, I soon lost consciousness. I had a long, troubling dream, in which the sky was filled with frost-shaped butterflies. Two of them fluttered and landed on the tip of my nose. After moistening my hot breath, they melted into two streams running down my face: I couldn't stop sneezing.

This nap came close to killing me. When I woke up, I was lying on the rug in my owner's bedroom. It was the first time I'd been to his bedroom, for I had always considered it his inner sanctum. The furnishings were so simple that they lent the room an air of poverty: a hard wooden bed, wooden chairs, a rough desk, and a bookshelf heaped with documents. This room used to have windows, but my owner had hammered them shut with plywood: not a thread of light could enter. On the right-hand wall was a weak fluorescent light—the only source of light in the room. I wanted to cry out, but my frozen mouth and throat hadn't recovered yet. I couldn't move, either.

"Why do you have to learn my ways? A few days ago, I hanged myself at home: this was psychologically necessary. It's only because I'm a person that I have these peculiar needs. You're a cat: even if you understood me better, you couldn't become a human. So you can't possibly have the kind of psychological needs that I have. Isn't that right? Now look at the state you're in. I feel terribly guilty. You shouldn't have gone into the refrigerator. You don't belong there. If you're so hungry, you can always take a bite out of my leg. Why didn't you do that? You're too soft, and that isn't good for either of us. It will just make me become even more treacherous by the day. Even more cold-blooded. Can you hear me? If you can, move your eyeballs, please!"

I had never thought of my owner as an ugly person, but after he finished talking to himself, I thought he was extremely ugly. Yet he talked so reasonably! He'd been at his desk, with his back to me, when he said these things. He wouldn't see me move my eyeballs, even if I did. I made an effort to open my eyes, but he had slumped into deep thought. I heard someone going up and down the stairs. Was it he?!

After the refrigerator incident, I had a bum leg and now I limped inelegantly. Overcome by remorse, my owner raised my standard of living. I had fresh fish and milk at almost every meal. And because I ate too much and exercised too little, I frequently had diarrhea. My injury left a big impression on my owner. He was worrying about me more and more, so he had to change his ways. Every morning, he had to go to the market and buy food—and not just for himself. His main concern now was giving me three meals a day. Now and then, he also added some delicacies to my diet—things like seaweed and dried fish. He was gradually beginning to live like an ordinary person. Inwardly, I had conflicting reactions to this. Although I was secretly happy, I also felt guilty and a little uneasy. I felt that my owner was making sacrifices for me, and that this could lead to unfortunate consequences. For sure, he wasn't an ordinary person, but one with special requirements. Now, he was reining in his very nature: could this lead to an outbreak of its dark side? You have to know that, before I came into his life, he had lived for decades without caring about anything, and he had never compromised himself for anything, either.

But, gradually, it seemed I was worrying too much. My injury hadn't made my owner any more abnormal. Quite the opposite: he perked up a little. He had a lot more to do, and was no longer as idle as he used to be. If people were a little particular about their daily lives, fixing three meals a day and cleaning the apartment could take up a lot of time. When I was first hurt, my owner was still not enamored of doing these things, because he'd long been accustomed to a simple life. At that time, everything in the refrigerator was prepared food, but now he had to buy fresh food and he had to cook especially for me. So sometimes he was almost scurrying about. Since he was very capable, he quickly had the housework under control. Recently, he even seems quite enthusiastic about doing the housework, for he whistles as he works! As it is now, he doesn't have much time for woolgathering—except after he gets up in the morning when he can't help but sink into daydreams for a short time. Then, as if he's heard an alarm, he springs up and "plunges into the flood of daily work" (this is the sentence I use to describe him).

Something occurred that surprised me a lot. One day, when I came back from a stroll, I saw the black man standing at our door. He seemed irresolute, but then he went in. Five seconds later, he came out again. He looked the same—teeth clenched, eyes menacing. Like a thick black shadow, he dodged into the elevator and quietly descended. When I went inside, my owner was wearing an apron and busying himself with cooking fish soup. What had transpired in those five seconds? Had they had a brief talk, or had my owner not even seen this uninvited guest for whom he lived day and night? After looking into it, I decided the latter was most likely. Could it be that the idol in his heart was collapsing?

The next day, I looked at him even more carefully. Early in the morning, when he was daydreaming on the balcony, I stared at him. My observation told me that what he hoped for from the bottom of his heart hadn't faded at all, but was even more intense because of the telescoped time. Gripping the railing convulsively, he was looking at the horizon: I was afraid he would jump from this high building. After a while, tears of regret filled his eyes. What did he regret? Had he been unaware of the black man's presence, and then learned of it later from traces left behind? Then why had he grown so numb that he even missed the arrival of the person whom he yearned for day and night? As I saw it, although the black man moved as if floating on water, he couldn't be completely soundless. I could only conclude that everyday life had numbed my owner's senses. By the time I thought of this, he had already calmed down. He rinsed his feverish face with cold water. Then, without looking back, he picked up his shopping basket and went to the market. He had a lot more control over himself now.

He must have been working much more efficiently. Sometimes I saw him go into his inner sanctum and reemerge within the hour.

And in his work he seemed even more flushed with success. He still wasn't close to anyone: he was sticking to his lonely bachelor's existence. It was from the old clerk's mouth that I learned of my owner's promotion: I heard the old man call him "big boss." He also reproached him for living so simply, and said he should try to have some fun. At the time, I had a sudden thought—if the black man told him to give up everything and go with him to the ends of the earth, would he do it? What followed proved me absolutely wrong.

As a rule, my owner went to the office only once every two weeks, because another big boss was in charge of the day-to-day work. My owner discussed work frequently with him on the phone. Sometimes someone from the office also telephoned, but not very often. Recently, all of this had changed a lot: our phone now rang all the time. From my observations, in general, these people weren't calling him about work, but were complaining about some old scores that hadn't been evened up. These people evidently belonged to all kinds of opposing factions. They were all attacking each other. My owner's responses seemed very odd—he showered compliments on everyone who phoned and parroted what they said, so on the phone everyone was happy. As a spectator, I heard a lot of conflicting language coming out of his mouth. Today he said this, the next day he said that: he was glib on the phone, but after hanging up, he kept sighing and was endlessly remorseful, absolutely fed up. Still, the next time the phone rang, he rushed to answer it again. Sometimes this meant he had to put off doing the housework. I was very much repulsed by those "gossips" from the newspaper office. I thought they were all vermin. At the same time, I was captivated: how could an aloof, idiosyncratic character like my owner care about his despicable underlings, even going so far as not hesitating to mingle with them in the cesspool? To show my revulsion, I jumped on the tea table several times and pretended it was an accident when I jumped on the telephone and took the phone off the hook so that there couldn't be any incoming calls. But my owner had recently become especially watchful. Every once in a while, he checked to see whether the phone was back on the hook. It was as if he had eyes in the back of his head, so my little plot failed.

Things grew more and more serious. Phone calls weren't enough for those people: I heard them pressuring my owner to deal with their disputes. It seemed that everyone who phoned asked my owner to "give evidence" on his behalf. I secretly felt things were going from bad to worse. I grumbled to myself that my owner was too un-principled: he shouldn't mingle with those people and intervene in their filthy mess. After each phone call, he was terribly distressed, and didn't get over it for a long time. After a few more days, these people began to press their demands even more forcefully, and there were even a few menacing implications. One of them mentioned the black man: he said the black man had presented himself at the newspaper office's lobby and was waiting for my owner to meet him there. After my owner took this phone call, he paled and was weak in the knees. In a daze, he tidied up a little and then rushed to the newspaper office. The rest of the day, I felt as if I had dropped into hell. I believed that his going there this time boded ill—that a col-lective plot to murder him was going to be actualized.

It was late at night before he returned. Not only had he not lost his life, but he was in such high spirits that he was singing in the bath-room. After a bath, he was full of energy as he went into his inner sanctum to work.

The next day, the phone was ringing off the hook again: my owner kept using vulgar language on the phone and telling dirty jokes. He seemed a changed man, but except for the phone calls, he was still treating me well. He found time for housework, and seemed in good spirits. I thought I'd better get used to his new ways. I should make an effort to observe his train of thought, and catch up with it. In the afternoon, the black man asked someone to phone and tell him to go to the office (I figured this out from my owner's expression). When he heard this, he took off immediately, beside himself with agitation. After these two times, I finally got it: it was the black man's idea that my owner should mingle with the others in the cesspool!

That evening, he brought two ugly guys back with him. Each one sat on the sofa, crossed his legs, chain-smoked, and spat on the floor. Before they'd been here even a minute, they began talking about the old clerk, hinting that he was a sycophant. I knew that my owner and the clerk were on very good terms, and that in their work they agreed about everything. I couldn't understand why he was letting these people slander him. He sat there listening gravely and nod-ding his head slightly, indicating that he sided with them. Thus encouraged, the older one was emboldened to suggest that my owner tell the old clerk "to get another line of work" and give this position to someone else. As the old guy was talking, the door creaked and opened: the black man was standing there. In the light from the corridor, his face looked ashen and was etched with deep grief. Pea-sized beads of perspiration rolled down from his forehead. He was shaking badly. The old guy stopped talking, and everyone stared at the black man outside the door. Suddenly, it was as if the black man had been shot in the neck: all at once, his head drooped. An invisible force was dragging him back, all the way to the elevator door. As soon as the door opened, he tumbled into the elevator, and it slid swiftly down.

"He's a guy who really means well and always has to be in the thick of things, even if they're none of his business." The ugly old guy sighed. "If he knew that someone as dishonest as the old clerk was mixed up with us, he'd want you to get rid of him, too. What do you say?"

"I guess you're right. I guess so."

My owner was agreeing absentmindedly, but he was still staring at the elevator, as though the black man would suddenly step out of it. I was not pleased with my owner's behavior. It had never crossed my mind that he could change so much. Sometimes he looked almost like a scoundrel. But why on earth was the black man grieving so deeply? It also occurred to me that since my owner was able to get along with people now, perhaps he no longer needed me. I had always thought he did. When I was alone with him, it was the two of us against the world. I reveled in this. Now that this defiance was gone, would he kick me out? After all, he'd agreed to get rid of the old clerk, hadn't he? The more I thought about this, the more I despaired. If he kicked me out, all I could do was hang out on the stairs, because I couldn't be so heartless as to abandon him. Someday, he would need me.

I was most repelled by the younger visitor. He didn't talk, but he was constantly drumming his feet on the rug under the tea table, thus jiggling the table so much that the soft drinks fell to the floor and made a mess of the rug. You have to remember that this rug was my bed. I really wanted to bite his leg, but this guy was as agile as an acrobat. And so I not only didn't succeed in biting him, but I also landed on the floor, unable to move, when he kicked me in the back.

My owner said, "My cat always has to get the best of others."

This infuriated me.

My owner was probably afraid the guy would hurt me again, so he carried me to his bedroom, put me on the wooden bed, and then closed the door. I fell asleep and didn't even know when those people left.

I woke up at midnight, and saw my owner scribbling excitedly at the table, his inspiration gushing like a spring. From behind, he looked like a lunatic. I didn't understand the things he wrote, for newspapers were out of my element, but I did know that this time my owner had climbed to a very high plane and was more exhilarated than other people could ever be. I was happy for him. You have to remember that only a few hours earlier, I was worried that he had become a scoundrel. His rapid change was beyond my comprehension.

Seeing that I was awake, he walked over and sat next to me, sighing as he talked. "Old Cat, why did you have to offend my colleagues? You really should stop being so self-righteous. See, you learned a painful lesson this time. I also know that you purposely took the phone off the hook so that my colleagues couldn't get through. Why did you bother? You must realize that even if they can't get through on the phone, they can think of other ways to get in touch with me. No one can keep them away. You'd better understand that even though you're one smart cat, my thoughts are a lot more profound than yours. For example, these colleagues of mine: you think they're too vulgar for words, and so you scorn them. I don't see it that way. They truly care about me; otherwise, they wouldn't come so far to see me. You mustn't be hostile toward them; you should think of them as friends. That would be a big help to me. Old Cat, you have to believe me. If even you don't believe me, what meaning would my life have?"

By the end, he was talking quite tearfully. Although I didn't appreciate his words one bit, his affection moved me. So I also shed tears. Both of us wept.

After I had cried for a while, my back also felt much better. I had no reason not to believe my owner. No matter what kind of person he was, I had to believe him, come hell or high water. I made up my mind: even if he sometimes got fed up with being a person of integrity and wanted to be a scoundrel, I would still be loyal to him. As he said, he was much more profound than I was, so I'd better not judge his behavior on the basis of superficial things.

After I had thought this through, my back pain vanished. I stood up, climbed onto his lap, and snuggled at his chest. The two of us wept silently again. I wasn't too sure why I was crying. Was I touched? Was it a mix of sadness and happiness? Or was it a certain regret? Or a certain sympathy? My owner's tears must have meant something even more complex. Since I couldn't figure it out, I would just muddle along and stick with him. My owner, who had been so excited in the daytime, was now shedding so many tears that my hair was all wet. He kept repeating in a hoarse voice, "Ai, Old Cat— ai, Old Cat . . ."

After this, we went to the kitchen for a great meal of sausage, smoked fish, and milk. While we were eating this wonderful midnight repast, I suddenly felt much closer to my owner. As he had in the past, he raised a glass of beer, and then his hand stopped for a couple of seconds in midair before he finally brought the glass slowly to his lips. He didn't drink the beer in one gulp, but sipped a mouthful and held it in his mouth, shilly-shallying for a long time before swallowing it. I had long been used to this habit of his, and hadn't paid much attention to it, but tonight I felt there was something new about it. As I stared at him, I realized that he needed me to understand him thoroughly.

My owner grew uneasy under my gaze. Setting his glass down, he asked, "Does anyone in this world feel an affection that's deeper than our affection for each other?"

Even so, when all is said and done, I didn't completely understand him. Perhaps the only thing I could do was to wait patiently, wait until everything cleared up of its own accord, wait until the black man who came and went without a trace met up with him again, and divulged even more about the mystery of life.

Tribute to H.D.
Martine Bellen

IN CORFU WITH FREUD

I sit in a hotel room, await my father's return. He is with his lover. I, who sit,
Awaiting Freud

Tear jars
      Tense
            Unable to specify the time I mean, the meaning of time

He tells me to stop checking my watch, to trust
My old Janus, guardian of doorways and roads, beloved lighthouse keeper,
                          Keeper of the journeying sun

With him I anoint my father's anger, my father's tenderness

Sometimes the twins are sisters

A constellation, circumstance to fit

The garden that corresponds to sky:

Vase of cut stars placed at the temple bough

Like transparencies set before candles in a darkened room

Batlike thought-wings / winds

Confined space of a wicker cage   flickering wicks

Adoring souls, wicked

News of war broke in me   He said, *trust I will not let you break*

269

Martine Bellen

He would take me to a world geographically to my dreams

Greece!

Where I saw the writing on the wall   *(Now Gnostic) Know*

                                                                                       Thyself

He believed I roamed through dangerous walled cities

Events out of time

What's it like outside   ???   , he asked.   Chalked swastikas down Berggasse

          Fortunes that divine "Hitler Gives Bread"

                    To greet the return of the gods

                                        We roam through dangerous times

Dolls of predynastic Egypt

Thought-winds carry me /   Searchlight Search

          A dim shape forming on the wall. Foaming swells. Finding

Orange trees in full fruit and flower outside the window.

          Osage orange. The walls were ocher.

The house in early shadow. Light on shadow not the other way around.

Object projected

          From my brain, basin, buried mind

          Washstand / saucepan or tripod

          Of prophecy. Our thoughts translated into

          Secreted language. Entombed.

Monument wall / will

Between ink, space flies, flanked by butterfly and dying

      Psyche

Death: You can't always get more than your due.
Apollo: We weep when the goods are destroyed.

And how do we know when he has died   ???   When we walk down Wall
Street and see no Centaurs—Centaurs who once felt everything. . . .

[The following scene takes place in a room on the other side of the wall.]

This is said by me and a voice I'm overhearing that would say what I'd say, if
I were in the next room on the other side of the wall:
                  I am disturbed he has no idea death won't kill him
                  He will shed his locust-husk
                  The sun-conscious world of sleep
                  That final healing when he sloughs off his skin.

                *

If a woman plants herself by a river,
Gods of trees, air, water
Grace her as a poplar, mulberry, laurel

Globes of gold
Apples, flecked with russet
A skeleton leaf

Her daughter bears the weight of the lost
Child—never grows beyond eight pounds,
Even after she's agéd, wizened—Mother
Carries her in the fifth pocket.   Mother is a poem.

    Outline in shadow a lone symptom or inspiration

Martine Bellen

SAPPHO

Shaft of scarlet lilies, crushed hyacinth, sea-grass gold,
Leaf melody of unfinished rhymes, of rocky rhythms, rocks
Polished by water
                    Water beating ragged edges; they are never finished,
Flowers blow through flowing water, not a streaming song
But water's wayfaring spirit, its crystal crash myrtle-berry.

The daughter of God
Chariot pulled by sparrows blur aquiver across high steep air
And none alive remembers you gray among ghosts

Niké, the winded runner, the wingless runner, the girlish black-eyed girl.

Desire has shaken her skeleton
Leaf of the osage orange flutters in charmed air
From inside out she shakes to escape
The ache of dancing flame pillages her walls of flesh and downy hair.

CHATS TO CATS

The Old Man of the Sea, Sigmund Freud, stood before me
He stands before me now seventy-two years later,
A little lionlike creature paddles in my direction.
Everyone carries an animal in them.

War is not over.

Our deep place where we hate—where Thoth and Apollo reside
Riding a gap-toothed goat.

Last night Freud heard the familiar siren shrieks, then the soul-shattering
"all clear."

Danger is out there—the Professor's eternal preoccupation, occupation.

Nemean lion clearing birds from the mind's rafters, fate.

Planting his steadfast foot in the stream of consciousness
Each line in a poem can't avoid acting as a series of questions
That stands half hidden in the river reeds watching over
A life that's being born. This is life—see!

His is a frail bridge, strong enough for the gods, who weigh little.
His is a bridge only few can cross. The building construction
Of phantasms across the bridge are lines of poetry. We reach deep
Inside ourselves and become Gods, light enough to pass, to cross
The rickety bridge over to a housing project
Made of poems.—Mid-income.

He is comfortable leaving this set of phenomena

Guardian of all beginnings

Isle of the Signatories
Marjorie Welish

1.

The following lines were omitted:

Even in Arcady I exist
e-signature in whose writings
lies the body
or its facsimile
Et in arcadia, I also, Pierre
Saw "Pierre" there also.

2.

The following lines were omitted:

I, too, have known Arcady
Name, signature
Here lie
Ego's avatars also
I, Jacques Rivière,
The lie:
Fabrication requires a thinker, he said.
Whereas, he went on, attempting to think
Any thought, yet

Attempting to think henceforth
As a text though ex temporare
All were reprinted
With the lyric effect
His and "there is"
By adverting to the effect.

3.

The following lines were omitted, probably deliberately:

I, Marni Nixon, unpaginated
—spacing.
And the corrected typescript
At table, as a text
Attempting to think henceforth
To think as the corrected typescript would think
through the lyric effect
incited to rhetoric where structure had been.

Followed by an additional line:

I, writing.

4.

Followed by an additional line:

I also dwell in Arcady,
The best signature on the subject
Lightly written yet penetrating signature
Sprightly, fair-minded, and comprehensive signature
None has the intellectual and personal authority of this signature:

I also Pierre saw "Pierre"
beneath this stone.

The writing said:

Tempting thought.
Primarily any "irrepressible"
Irrepressibly meant
Spontaneity.
For "poetry" read "lyric"
His and "this" and "Here lies"

Ivy, underappreciated.

5.

Don't/ Do not. In all printings prior to CEP.
Unnumber
Do not paginate: leave
istoeria where structure had been.

I, Jacques Rivière,

Writing.

In an itinerary of identity, I, too,
Ego's avatars also, I, Jacques Rivière,
Am signing my name, relentlessly.

6.

here interred
is "Pierre"
of the picture plane

it them   it and them
if then   if them
not to mention

someone else
nonempty pagination
it is said here

7.

It is said here lie these peoples:

Uncorrected proof
Underpaginated

It them   it and them
Not to mention the counterfactual

Were it the case that
Were it so

Following a different ambidextrous line
That is to say the three broad responses

The three broad responsive
~~The following lines were omitted~~

Probably deleted
Themnpting thought

8.

Forgetting
To anticipate, he advocated,
Enables listening to her

Less damning to
Hearing her

Followed by an additional line:

The lyric effect creases the self-evident

Reference
She sang

Followed by an additional line:

I, too, am in Arcady
(signed) Marni Nixon
the unpaginated voice

incited to narrative.
What is narrative?
What is science?

9.

(signed)
Marni Nixon, the unpaginated

Voice incited to narrative

His anticipating the identity
Of poetry

What is poetry?

10.

Even in Arcady, I (Death) am here
A disputa

And decipherment
She sang

Through other texts
A palette

Or irritability
Constitutive of

A signature—
Her singular voiceprint

Which is to say "I am here"
The competent reader

11.

Albeit

ventriloquism
I death even exist here in Arcady

A New York Encounter
Stephen Crane in 1895
Edmund White

NOW HE AWAKENED and for a moment he was still in the bright environs of his dream—New York on a busy, sunny day, a building going up on every corner, the clangor of cast-iron beams being hammered into place, the greased roar of the El pivoting overhead, the hollow staccato of horses' hooves dragging big-wheeled wood carts dangerously close to each other. A yellow cable car was sliding past, the sun dazzling off its windows. Women were rushing by, the breeze fingering the feathers in their hats, their practiced hands lifting their skirts to negotiate the muddy curb. Everyone was talking at once, or crying out their wares, selling things from pushcarts. It was an unexpectedly hot day in his dream and the men and women appeared to be steaming in their wool clothes and many layers. In the dream there were no children. That was odd: no children. And then, beside him, smiling up at him, was Elliott, a distinct person in his own right but somehow part of him as well, as if they shared something crucial—a spine or a lung, say.

After he'd met Elliott on that cold day in front of the Everett House, they'd sat at the table so long that eventually the joint was wheeled past in its silver cart: the roast beef, the lamb with its mint sauce, the goose with its apple sauce, the boiled corned beef and cabbage, and the boiled leg of mutton.

It sickened Elliott even to look at it, Stephen remembered, but I ordered him a plate of white meat of chicken, no skin and no sauce, as well as a dish of mashed potatoes, no butter. He was so weak I had to feed him myself.

"Are you ill, Elliott?" I asked him.

"Yes, sir."

"You don't need to 'sir' me. I'm Stevie."

Elliott's eyes swam up through milky seas of incomprehension—

279

this man with the jaunty hat and scuffed shoes and big brown over-coat wanted to be called Stevie! Elliott whispered the name as if try-ing out a blasphemy.

"Tell me, Elliott—what's wrong with you? Do you think you have consumption?"

Elliott blinked. "Pardon?"

"Phthisis? Tuberculosis?"

More blinking.

Huneker butted in and said, "Good God, boy, bad lungs? Are you a lunger?"

Elliott (in a small voice): I don't think so, sir.

Me: Fever in the afternoon? Persistent cough? Sudden weight loss? Blood in the sputum?

I laughed. "You can see I know all the symptoms. If you are in the incipient stage, you must live mostly outdoors, no matter what the season, eat at least five times a day, drink milk but not from tuber-cular cows—"

Huneker: Are you mad? The boy is a beggar so of course he lives outdoors—not in nature but in this filthy metropolis! And he'd be lucky to eat a single meal a day.

Tell me, boy—

Me: His name is Elliott.

Huneker: Far too grand a name for a street arab, I'd say. Tell me, Elliott, when did you eat last?

Elliott: Yesterday I had a cup of coffee and a biscuit.

Huneker (scorning him): That a nice, generous man gave you, upon arising?

Elliott (simply): Yes.

After Huneker rushed off babbling about his usual cultural schedule, all Huysmans and Wagner, a silence settled over the boy and me. We were between shifts of waiters and diners and the windows were already dark though it was only 5:15 on a cold, rainy Thursday night in November. We breathed deep. The warmth of the hotel's luxuri-ous heating had finally reached Elliott. He relaxed and let his coat fall open. He was wearing a girl's silk shirt, dirty pink ruffles under his blue-hued whiskerless chin.

He smiled and closed his coat again and told me he hadn't spoken in his normal boy's voice for weeks and weeks. "Usually we're all shrieking and hissing like whores."

Me: And saying what?

He: If you want to say someone is like that, you say, at least we say, "she"—and of course we really mean he—"she's un peu Marjorie."

I laughed so hard he didn't know whether to be pleased or offended since laughing at someone's joke turned him into a performer, a figure of fun, and Elliott didn't see himself that way.

He said the perverse youngsters he knew called themselves Nancy Boys or Mary Anns. Automatically I pulled out my little black reporter's notebook and moved the elastic to one side and began to take notes. The boys would accost men at a big rowdy saloon on the Bowery they called Paresis Hall and ask, in shrill feminine voices, "Would you like a nice man, my love? I can be rough or I can be bitch. Want a rollatino up your bottom? Is that what you are, a brownie queen? Want me to brown you? Or do you want to be the man? Ooh la la, she thinks she's a man—well, she could die with the secret!"

As for his health I divined from all the symptoms he was describing that he had syphilis and the next day I arranged for him to see a specialist and follow a cure (I had to borrow the money—fifty dollars, a minor fortune). I had to convince him that he needed to take care or he'd be dead by thirty. Though that threat frightened him no more than it did me. I expected to be dead by thirty or thirty-two—maybe that was why I was so fearless in battle. He seemed as weary of life as I was; we both imagined we'd been alive for a century already and we laughed over it.

I said, "Isn't it strange? How grownups are always talking about how life speeds by but it doesn't? In fact it just lumbers along so slowly." I realized that by referring to grownups I was turning myself into a big kid for his benefit.

He said, "Maybe time seems so slow to you because you look so young and people go on and on treating you in the same way."

I was astounded by this curiously mature observation—and chagrined by the first hint of flirtation. He was flirting with me.

I told him that I'd lost five brothers and sisters before I'd been born, which left me just eight. That made Elliott laugh, which he did behind his hand, as if he were ashamed of his smile.

"I'm the youngest of four, all brothers," he said. "My mama died when I was three—she and the baby both. We lived on a farm fifty miles beyond Utica. When I was just a little thing my Daddy started using me like I was a girl."

"He did?" I asked. I didn't want my startled question to scare him off his story. "Tell me more."

"And then my brothers—well, two of the three—joined in, especially when they'd all been drinking, jumping me not in front of each other but secretly in the barn after their chores or in the room I shared with my next older brother, the one who let me be. My Daddy had been the county amateur boxing champion thirty years ago and he was still real rough. Almost anything could make him mad."

"Give me an example," I said.

"Well, if the breadbox warn't closed proper and the outer slice had turned hard—don't you know, he'd start kicking furniture around. We didn't have two sticks stuck together because the two oldest boys took after him, and they would flash out and swear something powerful and start kicking and throwing things. The only dishes we kept after Mama died were the tin ones and they were badly dented. Things sorta held together when Mama was around and we sat down to meals, at least to dinner at noon, and she made us boys go to church with her though Daddy would never go. Then when she died, we stopped seeing other folks except at school but us kids missed two days out of three. Daddy could write enough to sign his name and saw he said no rhyme nor reason in book-larning for a field hand. I liked school and if I coulda went more regular I might've made a scholar, but Daddy liked us home, close to him, specially me since I fed the chickens and milked all four cows and tried to keep the house straight and a soup on the boil but Daddy always found fault with me, in particklar late at night when he'd been drinking and then he'd strap my bottom and use me like a girl and some days my ass, begging your pardon, hurt so much I couldn't sit still at school without crying. The teacher, Miss Stephens, thought something might be wrong, 'cause I had a black eye, sometime, or a split lip, and once she pushed my sleeve back and saw the burns where Daddy had played with me."

By this point we were walking up Broadway toward Thirtieth Street, where I lived with five other male friends in a chaotic but amusing bear's den of bohemian camaraderie. I hoped none of them would see me with the painted boy. The rain was beginning to freeze and the pavement was treacherous. I steered Elliott into a hat shop and bought him a newspaper boy's cap, which he held in his hands and looked at so long that I had to order him to put it on.

The more Elliott talked the sadder I felt. His voice, which had at first been either embarrassed or hushed or suddenly strident with a whore's hard shriek, now had wandered back into something as flat as a farmer's fields. He was eager to tell me everything, and that I was taking notes, far from making him self-conscious, pleased him. He counted for something and his story as well. I sensed that he'd guessed his young life might make a good story but he hadn't told it yet. There was nothing rehearsed about his tale, but if he hesitated now he didn't pause from fear of shocking me but only because till now he'd never turned so many details into a plot. He had to convert all those separate instances and events into habits ("My Daddy would get drunk and beat me"). He had to supply motives ("He never had no way of holding his anger in") and paradoxes ("I guess I loved him and still do but I don't rightly know why").

He slipped on the ice at one point and he grabbed my arm but after another block I realized he was still clinging to me and walking as a woman would beside her man and I shook him off. As I did it I made a point of saying something especially friendly to him; I wanted him to recognize I was his friend but not his man. I felt he was a wonderful new source of information about the city and its lower depths, but I drew back with a powerful instinct toward health away from his frail, diseased frame. I couldn't rid myself of the idea that he wasn't just another boy but somehow a she-male, a member of the third sex, and that he'd never pitch a ball in the open field or with a lazy wave hail a friend fishing on the other shore. The whole sweet insouciance of a natural boy's mindless summer was irrevocably lost to him.

Of course I'd had a difficult childhood, too. I'd not had an easy time of it.

Nor had my mother. I was her fourteenth child and she was forty-five years old when I came along. The four babies born right before me all died just after birth. As I told Elliott, my father, the Reverend Jonathan Townley Crane, was dead by the time I was seven or eight and my mother when I was twenty; the poor woman was worn out by childbirth and the struggle to stop other people from drinking. She was a good mother—she'd arranged for me to do my first bit of journalism at Asbury Park.

But if we were poor and I was passed from one older sister to another, nevertheless no one beat me and I had strong but loving women to feed me and shelter me. I was sent to a private school and later, in college, first at Lafayette and then at Syracuse, I was such a good baseball player (catcher then briefly shortstop, then catcher again) that after school people said I could get a job on a

283

professional team, even though I was just five foot six and weighed only 125 pounds. Now I weigh even less—in fact I've made no headway at all since I was twelve.

I invented words, I read Flaubert and Tolstoy, I fell in love with brainy virgins, I satirized middle-class beach life at Asbury Park and at every step I was surrounded by bemused and tolerant relatives and friends. I could afford to smoke my pipe, let my hair grow long, sweep about in a borrowed ulster and lose the buttons on my shirt, which never had a clean collar, all because my brother Edward was impeccable and my father had been irreproachable. I was the bohemian exception.

My hunger was real enough and often in New York I could only afford to breakfast on potato salad, the cheapest item at the nearest delicatessen, or I had to dine on chestnuts, which I roasted in a candle flame. But I could always get a good meal if I went to Port Jervis and the house of my brother the judge. My childhood was just the opposite of Elliott's, whose father buggered him thrice a week from age six on, who was supposed to cook and clean and work as the family squaw-man. No sports, no friends—and the worst of it was that he had to keep a big secret. He had to tell no one about the bruises and lash traces, about his brothers and father taking turns. All his psychic energy went into a dull, repetitive prayer: I mustn't tell, I mustn't tell, I mustn't tell. In a musical score, Huneker told me, if one measure is repeated several times without a change the shorthand mark is a slant with a dot on either side. Elliott's thoughts could be scored that way.

At a corner I said goodnight to Elliott and told him to meet me the next day at three beside the statue of Washington in Union Square. I promised I'd make a doctor's appointment for him (he had a chancre) and go with him; what I didn't tell him was that I wouldn't trust him with money since he might spend it frivolously (no more than I'd trust myself or Cora with it). I had no idea where he went that night or slept but at least he'd eaten a hot meal, which I'd been able to pay for only because I'd just sold a story on street life to the *New York Press.*

That night I tried out a mention of my new encounter on one of my friends, Corwin Linson, but he who always laughed at my adventures (the bearded lady, the Siberian twins, the Negress of Hoyt Avenue) grew strangely silent when I revealed I'd met a painted boy. He was an artist who'd studied in Paris with Gérôme and whom I thought of as terribly worldly (he was seven years older than I). He'd done that portrait of me in profile in which I'm all cheekbones and pasted-down Napoleonic spit curls; the first time we'd met he told me I resembled Napoleon "but less hard," to which I murmured, "I would hope so." We called him "CK," maybe because "Corwin Knapp Linson" was a mouthful.

He'd laughed and laughed when I'd advised Armistead Borland to stick to black women if "they're yellow and young" though I meant it perfectly seriously. But now he wasn't laughing. He squirmed out of his chair and added a red dot to the canvas on the easel. I'd brought up a subject that would embarrass any man, no matter how wild and anarchic he might be. Which made me feel alone and understand how lonely and defiant Elliott must be (I refused to call him "Ellen," as he wanted me to).

Why could I tolerate him? Or rather why did he appeal to me, to my innermost being? Why was I the only normal man who could see how wounded he was? My Cuban battle pieces will be called "Wounds in the Rain," and that could serve as the name of Elliott's portrait in words, something fluid and vague and painful. Maybe I responded to him because we were both ill. I had a hacking cough even then and a kid's face; he and I both looked like sick waifs. And then maybe he appealed to me because he was a whore—after all, I always felt good around prostitutes and they bring out something gallant in me. Christ, my own wife is a whore and a whoremonger. That's one way to escape the curse of a Methodist upbringing.

But there was also something hard-eyed and disabused about Elliott that touched me. I suppose there's nothing more appealing than a small person who is in obvious pain but unreachable. Whose child's heart is still alive, still beating inside a block of ice. I had the strong impression that I could look through the ice to see it, trailing its veins and arteries, pulsing not with contractions but with light.

Two Stories

Rikki Ducornet

PANNA COTTA

HE IS COOKING FOR LUCINDA and their friends; their laughter rises and falls above the sound of good Danish butter sizzling in the pan. He serves the trout with toasted almonds and a julienne of caramelized citrus. Ablaze in the candlelight, the dish might be of hammered gold. The moment he sets it down, his friends burst into applause.

"Don't," Lucinda admonishes, or pretends to. "Flattery goes to his head." Will he ever grow accustomed to her teasing? "Fathead!" From across the table she blows him a kiss. Everyone laughs when he offers up a toast to his "dulcet-tongued Lucinda."

*

He had left his first wife when he realized that she would always be chronically enigmatic. Lucinda isn't enigmatic, she's impalpable. A gadfly, she flits from this to that. As slender-waisted as a child, she has elbows and knees as small and round as ping-pong balls. And she is flagrantly blonde, her skin and hair the color of cream.

Lucinda is a healer. Like a pale hummingbird suspended in the ether, she hovers over her clients who, adrift on grass mats, listen to the soothing ping of wind chimes and hushed platitudes. They learn to trust their intuitions, to discover the healing power of their hands, to share Lucinda's gift, her heightened capacity to know and to name unfathomed humiliations. Summers she teaches female masturbation at the Omega Institute, and this fact never ceases to astonish and inspire them. Week after week they return so that they can live in the world without succumbing to despair. Sometimes their faith in her terrifies him.

If Lucinda is a healer and a telepath, he is not. Granted, he is a good cook, perhaps a great one, but, as she eagerly points out, he does not *get people.* A master in the kitchen, he will always be a babe in the

286

woods when it comes to understanding others. He tells her that one cannot cook without understanding others! Bah! says Lucinda. Of course one can! Well, then, why won't she teach him? But no. She is unwilling. Because of the nature of their relationship. Its intimacy.

He wonders: what *is* the nature of their intimacy? And *is* it intimacy, exactly? If it is, why is he so lonely? Then, again, it is likely that loneliness is part and parcel of the human condition. Hadn't Lucinda told him that when she carols to her class:

You are lonely!

they gasp and grunt in agreement, and always someone weeps. Yet his own loneliness dissolves as soon as he enters the kitchen. When he approaches his raw materials, an irresistible music claims him and his staff. The work proceeds seamlessly in a state of grace. When he sets a pan of quail on fire, he embodies the spirit of transformation—something of a monster, eccentric, extravagant, irresistible, incapable of error. Dishes surge forth into the night like stars. Meanness and banality are banished from the dining room. His diners are joyous, celebratory, smarter, kinder. Perfect strangers toast one another, suggesting what it is they must try: "The tagine! The hen with apricots! The saffroned risotto! The brandied pears!"

This explosive euphoria gives way to a sagacious quietude. An hour into their meal and his diners grow thoughtful. Like those lucky children who have not yet been smacked, they believe in the goodness of things. His is the sort of food that in a better age would have inspired chamber music.

And Lucinda, too, is swept up and away by what can only be called an intoxication. Her cream in repose, she eats his risotto and takes on a gravitas he finds reassuring. This is how they meet: she at one of his tables silenced and deepened by his risotto.

But this cannot last. One day Lucinda rebels. An esteemed motivator, she cannot stomach being held in thrall by another for long. Without warning she tells him his cooking reeks of death, his kitchen is a morgue in which cadavers by the dozens are stacked—"Cadavers?" he gasps. "My fresh racks of Oregon lamb?"

His kitchen is a charnel house. Fire, alcohol, spices—all this is not *natural!* His kitchen stinks of war. "Of *war?*" He cannot believe his ears. His feasts are funerals! She will deign to eat his salads, but only if his beets are raw.

"And if I bake you a pie of peacock hearts, my beloved . . . even that would not tempt your sharp tongue? Will you, my dearest, never again *eat me?*"

287

"Horrible!" she calls him. "Horrible man! *Mortician!*" she sputters and seethes. "How dare you tease me! How dare you question my personal life choices?"

He proposes an encyclopedic platter of cheese. She professes a horror of *grease*—she who had so recently loved her bechamels and brown butters. *She fears death*, he supposes. *The body's corruption.* When on those rare occasions she enters the restaurant to graze on celery and salt, she glowers at the other diners with visible repugnance. *Virtual cadavers eating cadavers!*

He begins to dislike her.

*

In her company, he is now hangdogged. Poor soul! He begins to entertain something like paranoia. And this because he can no longer share with his beloved a passion for pig trotters, braised rabbit, and soft-shelled crabs. Instead he must listen to her endless chatter about her own career; she speaks of it and of her clients with a certain fevered animation. Her clients desire her; well, of course they do. Doesn't she stoke their fires? Dizzy with fear he asks if she returns their heat.

"Well," she replies, with a new haughtiness, "one can't rebuff what one has inspired. Not when healing is involved."

"Ah. Yes. But . . . ," he insists. "Surely. Having been, ah. Warmed by your, uh, *ministrations.*" He hates the word, archaic and clumsy—yet finds no other. "Couldn't they, can't they, I mean. Well. You've liberated them after all to go elsewhere, to live, passionately *elsewhere.* Are you. Must you. Must you be *all* things to them? The medium," he strokes her cheek, "and the prize?" (How he struggles for his words!)

He has broken into a sweat and his hands are perceptibly shaking. Seeing how distraught all this has made him, she reaches into his shirt and caresses a nipple.

"I only let them hold me, and only sometimes. Just a hug, darling. As is acceptable among friends. And then I send them on their way, reassured! Empowered! So that yes—that's it, exactly. Off they go to get *it on!* With somebody else." She sings these last three words in a voice he recognizes as Madonna's. "I'm a facilitator! Not a dominatrix!"

If this is true, why is it that whenever he is in the house alone, he finds himself stalking the clothes in her closet for clues? He stares at her silk saris, the Indonesian scarves and gilded sandals and cannot help but imagine her embracing a client on the floor after hours like a Tantric temple whore providing at once something sacred and profane. He pokes through scraps of paper in her desk drawers and although he feels a fool still his heart pounds because of the terrible danger he is in—desiring, disliking, and distrusting a woman simultaneously. Instead of attending to the myriad things his life demands, he finds himself dialing a phone number scribbled on the back of a small square paper napkin.

Drained of blood, he listens to a message in an unfamiliar male voice that seems smug, somehow, and also suggestive. Putting down the receiver, he finds himself thinking: *Well. All people are impossible. It just depends on how long one knows them and how much one can bear.* He considers the possibility that what he has always thought of as her openness, her boundless enthusiasm, is all due to a lack of self-awareness and an unusually thick skin. And if she is a narcissist? Enamored of her own powers to liberate and enslave? That night as she sleeps, he dials the number on the napkin. This time the man answers. "Peggy?" he says. "Peg? Aw! Sweetheart! Don't hang up!"

Sometimes, she tells him, she waives her fees. Doesn't that imply the relationship has tumbled into lubricity? Considering what he fears—fears! It keeps him up nights!—the waived fee is proof of his cuckoldry—an outdated word, a foolish word—but one that satisfies his mood. When he attempts to discuss this, she loses her temper and tells him with real anger that he has no business at all, none whatsoever, prying into her professional life.

"Do I ask you," she shouts, "what goes on in the kitchen? How do I know you're not buggering your cheflings in the larder?"

He becomes unraveled. His mind wanders. He pierces his thumb with a fish knife. He is a powerfully built man who suffers a helpless sensation in his knees. Briefly he considers suicide, a dramatic seppuku in the middle of his kitchen on a busy Saturday night. If only he knew how to, he would break down and sob. Their impending breakup is now common knowledge.

When he walks into his own glass-fronted door and chips a tooth, he knows he must pull himself together.

Exhausted at ten in the morning, he throws himself on his office floor and falls asleep. He dreams of a fantastic panna cotta—a savory panna cotta of outstanding flavor and size. His dream is a revelation, and his sleep refreshing.

He invites their friends to a feast to celebrate the inevitable separation. He throws himself into an event that will transform his longing and his rage into something like beatitude; a profound satisfaction, sweetly vertiginous. He cooks his way out of the end of the affair, and feeling joyous puts on a tuxedo.

When everyone arrives the table is rife with candles. In the center, a panna cotta Lucinda crouches sphinxed, cuffed, and socked in sashimis and lobster quenelles. If the panna cotta is one-third life size, still it is wonderfully impressive, the way a suckling pig or entire roasted lamb is impressive. The panna cotta is served on a platter of old faience—a thing a museum curator would die for.

*

Lucinda is seated at the head of the table, and at once suffers a stunning realization. Her months of extreme asceticism are founded in guilt; she has, after all, been sleeping with a client. She acknowledges the toast in her honor: from her end of the table, she gazes at him with renewed affection.

"I feel," she says, "like the lead in a film by what's his name." She accepts a plate of sashimi, cannot resist the quenelles nor the panna cotta, studded as it is with bronzed scallops.

His imagination is unleashed; he feels happier than he has in months, and dashing. With unaccustomed ferocity of humor, he tells a story of one Metrocles, a student of Aristotelian philosophy, who, having devoured a deep dish of spiced lima beans, farts publicly in the midst of an oration. Profoundly ashamed, Metrocles tumbles into a melancholy so extreme he can no longer sleep or eat. As he approaches death, his friends convince him to return to class one last time. There his teacher, Crates, farts so eloquently in his pupil's favor, his life is saved. Metrocles goes on to become a philosopher of consequence—and a gourmet of delicate tastes.

His friends' laughter unleashes him further. He proposes that a stomach is like a brain; it has a mind of its own, it suffers fevers, tantrums, sleepless nights, fits of longing and self-loathing. In other words, the stomach "has a soul!" He says something strange:

"The stomach is an intermittent sarcophagus." But before anyone can ask him what that means, he leaps ahead: "I mean a *factory!* Turning raw materials into bricks more or less cooked!"

"Speaking of *cooked!*" Lucinda calls out from her end of the table. "Grill me a cutlet, sweetheart, or two? A rack! Of that organic

290

Oregon lamb!

But no. He tells her: tonight the menu is *fixe. She* is all there is to eat. However, he agrees with her; she makes for a fine hors d'oeuvre, but not for a satisfactory meal. At this remark the handsome wife of a mutual friend, an aspiring vintner, abroad, laughs aloud. With a pang of real unhappiness, Lucinda knows she has just been eclipsed. And he? He continues to suggest the oddest things. He says:

"The moment one swallows a live oyster, one might as well be a boa constrictor."

"A boa constrictor," Lucinda's sudden rival breathes, "or a wolf in a fairy tale. Swallowing lambs and babes entire!" The rival is radiant, brown as toast spread over with honey. "Your riddle," she continues, "the one that goes: 'Why is a stomach like an intermittent sarcophagus?' I know the answer."

"Why?" he asks, gazing at her with intensifying interest.

"Because it is only the first step on a protracted right of passage."

The table explodes with laughter. Everybody laughs except Lucinda, that is, whose cream has begun to visibly turn. And to recede.

THE DOORMAN'S SWELLAGE

—For L. H.

Good day, sir! Looking out upon the street, I could not help but notice your interest in the Perlmutter Building. The noon is hot above and the air a plague of flies. Seeing you so well turned out, I take the liberty—one of the real pleasures of my profession—to call out to you. Please step in! Note that I do not open the Perlmutter's portals for all and Sunday.

Well, then! Allow me to introduce you to the Perlmutter. Note the generous use of morganite in the lobby and the luminous lamp dish overhead. She is the only building of her type and class in the city, and she has just been revived and refit. But if you hope to move in, I regret to say there is nothing on hand, although a current occupant— the wondrous Mrs. Gastroform—is very, very old. Should the Perlmutter quicken your interest, I would be pleased to appease you of her departure and give you a tinkle—care for a mint?—although the waiting list is long. However, between us, sir, I'll do my part to put you *right on top!* Make no bones about it, sir. My pleasure, sir! I know a gentleman when I see one. No small thing these days when all and Sunday are out and about in their birthday suits engaging in who knows what low type of nonfeasance! *O Tempura! O s'mores!* Please let me relieve you of your muffler and your hat. No? As you wish, sir!

Aha! A rotogravure has caught your eye! It is—you've guessed it— the Perlmutter in her heyday, taken by Rotifer Nubbin in 1892. *All* the rotogravures in the lobby are Nubbinses. Look at them and see the Perlmutter inside and out: everything *and* her kitchen sinks! All sixty-six of them. Now then, sir: follow me.

Here in the hallway: more Rotifer Nubbinses. This series is of the Hum Tollog suite, named for Perlmutter's mother, who lived here until she died of an overlapsed pessary. (She was said to hide out in the funk hole on less than happy days.) This rotogravure shows the Rookery, no longer extant, with its forty-four roods and perches; this is the Mew. Don't ask me what Perlmutter kept there; he kept dames in droves—but not at the same time. Here's your parlor and here's your pokery; the Ambuscade and Chummery are long since gone. That brass head is "Old Camel Dung"—Perlmutter's mother. (In this house the weaker sex was not always honorably regarded.)

After you, sir. This room's called the Mummery. Note how each object—rotogravure, paperweight, *millefolle,* and statuette—possesses the magic power to awaken dormant sensations; they stimulate curiosity and so: *conversation.* Before you responded to my invitation, the Perlmutter was asleep, her splendors submerged in shadows and the gloom of absolute silence. My mood, too, was melancholy. Conversation has this ideal property: it alters our moods. One is gravity bound and then a conversation begins and provides buoyancy! But I simplify! I abbreviate! Life is full of apprehensions. You, sir, I can tell, are of a sturdy humor. A mint? I order them from Rhodes. Muscatel? A sugar drink? No? Well, then: follow me. Notice the gay Turkey carpet in the hall. We're walking on dragons. See: those squiggles there.

After you, sir: take a left. And prepare to be surprised! *This,* sir, *is the Swellage*—splendid, eh? The only one in the metropolis. It was conceived and executed by Mathew Mutterer, including the mortar boards and the table ends—all *du jus!* Note the bindings—I'll bet you are a bibliolater! I always know a bibliolater! Check out the compulsory moleskin. Stroke it, sir! Go on: *cheer yourself!* All stamped with gold *floor de leech!* And the leathers: sofa, elbowchair, grampus, *footoil,* the tripod, and squab—all designed by Mutterer for Perlmutter's mother, and all *de le pope!* (If you wish, sir, remove that muffler and your hat and try out the *footoil.* Rest those oars! No? As you wish, sir! A munchie? Neither.) Moving along!

That big potted plant—*watch your head!*—is a *vagus hippopotamic* and as old as the Perlmutter herself. Don't touch it, sir! Harsh desert forage; its thorns are full of brine. It was shipped all the way from the high cliffs of Akhmar by Perlmutter's maiden mother-in-law, the philanthropod and ethnogaff Lucy Strumpeter, whose book on nose mutilations—feel *that!*—is also bound in mole. That sappy greenness on the mantel is hers, as is the crystal dromedary, the crimp, and the barometer. She was a tepid traveler.

Sometimes there's teas held here. I've seen the finger foods! Celery and coconut cake and stuffed olives and crab wontons—the whole suppository! Wholesome smack, mouthwatering—although Mrs. Gastroform's small pug, smelling the meat, rejected it.

I can see that you are wondering about that spot on the carpet. *That*, sir, is the very place Mr. Perlmutter bled to death, stabbed many times over by his murderer: Mathew Mutterer. Those bookends, *du jus*, are the Apollo Belvedere cut in two. But, hey! I fear I've buttonholed you! I'll tell you, sir: you are one hot conversation piece! How you've got me hammering on! Yet, one cannot, should not, underestimate the connection between conversation and happiness. The mind shudders to imagine itself isolated from others, doomed to silence, the tongue rotting between the teeth from inactivity. Those? Bronze leg horns.

To tell the truth, I find solace here in the Swellage. And, sometimes, tears. See . . . sometimes just looking in on all the excitement, a sudden happiness surges through my heart and clutches at my throat and I have to repress the urge to shout and jump and sing. For, yes: I wear a skeleton on my sleeve. My service to the Perlmutter is the remedy to—what? A *wife!* You've guessed it! A wife less than a help meat, more a bitter worm in the pie.

Sir. Sometimes the Mystery of Sex is not enough to keep a couple going. Or maybe the mystery and the sex were *always* one-sided. Maybe I was always the only one mystified. Women were made to attract and fascinate men, but I wonder: does it work the other way 'round? (That ashtray is totally legitimate! Ditto the cracker tin.) But back to my marriage. I guess you could say I've exchanged one old lady for another. That's my life's paradox: home I'm shut out, and here: I've got all the keys! I'll tell you something, though. When I married the wife, *I was an enthusiast.* I'd greet the night with real excitement. In no time flat excitement gave way to dejection. You see: we didn't dally much; we didn't fool around—although I'd hoped we would. *Hurry up, husband!* she'd bellow: *I've got other fish to fry.*

Here at the Perlmutter, I've had plenty of time to think things over. I've come to the conclusion that my marriage was propelled by a delusion, and dampened by my wife's cunning management of my moods. That door? That door leads to the Hot Air Baths. They are heated from below. Perlmutter believed in promoting perspiration. He had a point. Unlike mine, his life was short and merry. It ended violently; a thing we might all aspire to. After fifty years my marriage hums like an engine that has no need of grease, no need of me. Should I complain the wife says: *Tell it to the Marines.* Marriage has taught me this: how to eat an entire meal without spilling crumbs on the floor.

There are more prestigious things I could do, perhaps. But I love the Perlmutter. She's a grande dame in a world of trollops and furthermore, she affords me—as she has today—verbal intercourse with strangers.

I think of myself as something of a gourmet: I accept only the best *popos.* Right now as we speak together, the air around us is disturbed. The sounds we make are elastic; like acrobats they bound about! Shadows stir, dust lifts, inertia is subverted by vibrations. Even before we have the time to appreciate what is happening, our ears have averted us to the *fact* of conversation. The vibrations, dear sir, are accompanied by . . . an emotion. You will agree with me: nothing is more marvelous than the faculty of speech. The greetings that open the door to friendship. Tell me, sir: does not the harmony of life depend upon the success or failure to converse amiably?

Sir. I can see that you are ready to be on your way. Perhaps another time I can show you the crypt. Yes—all the Perlmutters are there, except, of course, the ones who are living.

Well, then! A good day to *you,* sir! May I give you a squeeze? No? Thank you just the same. It was nice to *parsley.* Although we kept to shallow waters, I was pleased to ferry you about. May I give you a tinkle should Mrs. Gastroform call it a day?

From The Ghost in Love
Jonathan Carroll

THE GHOST WAS IN LOVE with a woman named German Landis. Just hearing that arresting, peculiar name would have made its heart flutter if it had still had one. She was coming over in less than an hour, so it was hurrying now to make everything ready. The ghost was a very good cook, sometimes a great one. If it'd spent more time at it, or had more interest in the subject, it would have been exceptional.

From his large bed in a corner of the kitchen a mixed breed, black-and-oatmeal-colored dog watched with great interest as the ghost prepared the meal. This mutt was the only reason German Landis was coming here today. His name was Pilot, after a poem the woman loved about a Seeing Eye dog.

Suddenly sensing something, the ghost stopped what it was doing and glared at the dog. Peevishly, it demanded, *"What?"*

Pilot shook his head. "Nothing. I was only watching you work."

"Liar. That is not the only thing. I know what you were thinking: that I'm an idiot to be doing this."

Embarrassed, the dog turned away and began furiously biting one of his rear paws.

"Don't do that—look at me. You think I'm nuts, don't you?"

Pilot said nothing and kept biting his foot.

"Don't you?"

"Yes, I think you're nuts, but I also think it's very sweet. I only wish she could see what you're doing for her."

Resigned, the ghost shrugged and took a slow, deep breath. "It helps when I cook. When my mind is focused, then I don't get so frustrated."

"I understand."

"No, you don't. How could you? You're only a dog."

The dog rolled its eyes. "Idiot."

"Quadruped."

They had a cordial relationship. Like Icelandic or Finnish, Dog is spoken by very few. Only dogs and dead people understand the language. When Pilot wanted to talk, he either had to get in a quick chat

295

with whatever canine he met on the street when he was taken out for a walk three times a day or he spoke with this ghost, who knew more about Pilot now than any dog had ever known. There are surprisingly few human ghosts in the land of the living, so this one was equally happy for Pilot's company.

Pilot said, "I keep meaning to ask—where did you get your name?"

The cook purposely ignored the dog's question and continued preparing the meal. When it needed an ingredient, it closed its eyes and held out an open hand. A moment later the thing materialized in the middle of its palm—a jungle green lime, a small pile of red cayenne pepper, or particularly rare saffron from Sri Lanka. Pilot watched, absorbed, never having tired of this amazing feat.

"What if you imagined an elephant? Would it appear in your hand, too?"

Dicing onions now almost faster than the eye could see, the ghost grinned. "If I had a big enough hand, yes."

"And all you'd have to do to make that elephant happen is imagine it?"

"Oh no, it's much more complicated than that. When people die, they're taught the real structure of things. Not only how they look or feel, but the essence of what they really *are*. Once you have that understanding, it's easy to make things."

Pilot considered this and said, "Then why don't you just recreate *her*? That way, you wouldn't have to fret about her so much anymore. You'd have your own version of her right here."

The ghost looked at the dog as if he had just burped loudly. "You'll understand how dumb that suggestion is after you die."

Fifteen blocks away, a woman was walking down the street carrying a large letter D. Had you seen this image in a magazine or television advertisement, you would have smiled and thought it was a catchy picture. The woman was pleasant looking but not memorable. She had even features that fit well together, although her nose was a little small for her face. She was aware of that and often self-consciously touched her nose when she knew she was being observed. What people remembered most about her was not the nose but how very tall she was. An almost six-foot-tall woman carrying a big blue letter D.

She wore brand-new jeans, a gray sweatshirt with ST. OLAF COLLEGE written in yellow letters across the chest, and scuffed brown hiking boots. These boots made her taller. Funnily enough, her height never bothered her: the nose, yes, and sometimes her name. The name and the nose, but never the height, because everyone on both sides of her family was tall. She had grown up in the midst of a bunch of blond human trees. Midwesterners, Minnesotans, they ate huge meals three times a day. The men wore size thirteen or fourteen shoes and the women's feet weren't a whole lot smaller. All the children in the family had unusual names. Her parents loved to read, especially the Bible, classic German literature, and Swedish folktales, which was where they harvested the names for their children. Her brother was Enos, she was German, and her sister was named Pernilla. As soon as it was legally possible, Enos had changed his name to Guy and would answer to nothing else. He joined a punk band called YouthinAsia, all of which left his parents speechless and disheartened.

German Landis was a schoolteacher who taught art to twelve- and thirteen-year-olds. The D she carried now was part of an upcoming assignment for them. Because she was both good natured and enthusiastic, she was a first-rate teacher. Kids liked Ms. Landis because she clearly liked them. They felt that affection the moment they entered her classroom every day. Her enthusiasm for their creations was genuine. On one wall of her apartment was a large bulletin board covered with Polaroid photographs that she'd taken over the years of her students' work. She often spent evenings looking through art books. The next day she would plop one or more of these books down on the desk in front of a student and point to specific illustrations she thought he or she should see.

She fell in love easily but walked away just as easily from a relationship when it went bad. Some men thought this showed she was coldhearted but they were wrong. German Landis simply didn't understand people who moped. Life was too interesting to choose suffering. Although she got a big kick out of him, she thought her brother, Guy, was goofy for spending his life writing songs only about things that either stunk or sucked. In response, he drew a picture of what her gravestone would look like if he designed it: a big yellow smiley face on it and the words "I like being dead!"

Little did either of them know that she *would* like it when her time came to die, years later. German Landis would move into death as she had moved into new schools, jobs, or phases in her life—full speed ahead, hopes high, heart filled like a sail with reasonable optimism and a belief that the gods were fundamentally benevolent, no matter where she was.

Shifting the heavy metal letter from one hand to the other, she grimaced, anticipating what she was about to do. Whenever she went to Ben's place these days to pick up Pilot there was almost always trouble between them of one sort or another. They would argue about big things and small. Sometimes there were valid reasons for these disagreements; usually they occurred only because these two people were in the same room together. Early in their relationship they had seen the Cary Grant film *The Awful Truth* about a couple who split up but, by sharing custody of a dog afterward, end up back together because of their abiding love. Neither of them liked the movie but it stuck on the walls of both their heads like a pink Post-it note reminder because some of the story had come to pass for them.

They had been in love once—equally and passionately. Like a spiderweb you walk into, it is not so easy to get all the tendrils of real love off after you have passed through it.

They only had contact now because of the dog. Both regarded Pilot as their adopted child and friend. Ben had given the dog to her on their third date. He had gone to the town animal shelter and asked to see whatever dog had been there the longest. He had to repeat that request three times before the attendants believed him. The whole thing was German's idea and it was the first of many of her ideas that effortlessly touched Benjamin Gould in the middle of his heart. Several days before, she had said she was going to buy a dog that no one wanted. She planned to go to the dog pound soon and, sight unseen, buy whichever dog had lived there longer than any of the others.

"But what if it's a skeez?" he asked half seriously. "What if it's got a terrible personality and weird diseases?"

She smiled and lifted one shoulder. "I'll take it to a veterinarian. Skeez and disease are OK. I just want to give it some kind of nice life before it dies."

"And if it's ferocious? What if you get a biter?" Ben asked these questions but didn't mean them. He was already a convert.

At the pound they took him to see a dog they'd named Methuselah because he had lived there so long. Methuselah did not lift his head from the floor when the stranger stopped in front of his cage and peered in. Ben saw nothing but entry-level dog. If the dog had any extras, Ben sure didn't see them. There was not one thing special about this animal. No soulful, sensitive eyes. No puppy's adorable, rollicking enthusiasm. The dog did no tricks. If he had a shtick, *cute* wasn't part of it. All the attendants could say about this mixed breed was that he was housebroken, quiet, and never caused trouble. No wonder all prospective customers had rejected him. Every single sign indicated this nondescript mutt was nothing but a dud.

Although he had little money, Ben Gould bought Methuselah the dud. The dog had to be coaxed from his cage and out on the street again for literally the first time in months. He did not look at all happy. Ben had no way of knowing that he'd bought a skeptic and a fatalist who did not believe anything good came of anything good. At the time of his adoption, Methuselah was close to middle-aged. He had lived a difficult life but not a bad one. He had had three previous owners, all of them forgettable. On occasion he had been kicked and beaten. Once he was struck a glancing blow by a passing truck. He'd survived, limping for weeks afterward, but he survived. When picked up by the dogcatcher, he was relieved more than anything else. At the time he had been living on the street for three months. From past experience, he did not really trust human beings, but he was hungry and cold and knew they were able to remedy that. What the dog did not know was that if he was taken to the wrong kind of animal shelter, he would be killed after a short time.

But he was lucky. In fact this dog's great turn of life luck began the day he entered this particular shelter. The place was funded entirely by a rich childless couple who loved animals above everything else in the world and visited the shelter frequently. As a result, none of the stray animals brought there was ever put to sleep. The cages were always spotlessly clean and warm. There was ample food and even rawhide chew bones, which Methuselah found disgusting and ignored.

He ate and slept and watched for the next three months—a great career move because he was missing a miserably cold and snowy winter outside. He did not knew what this place was, but so long as he was fed and left in peace, then this was an acceptable home for now. One of the joys of being a dog is not having a concept of the word "future." Everything is right now, and if right now happens to be a warm floor and a full stomach, then life is good.

Who was this man pulling on his leash now? Where were they going? They had walked many blocks through blinding, blowing snow. Methuselah was old enough so that the bitter cold pierced his bones and joints. Back home in the warmth of the animal shelter, the dog could go outside whenever he wanted but rarely did in weather like this.

"We're almost there," the man said sympathetically. But dogs do not understand human language, so this meant nothing to the now miserable animal. All he knew was that he was cold, he was lost, and life had just turned hard again after that pleasant respite in the shelter.

They were two blocks from German Landis's building when it happened. After looking both ways, Ben stepped off the sidewalk down into the street. But, slipping on the snow, he lost his balance. Arms flailing, he began to fall backward. Frightened by this sudden wild movement, Methuselah leapt away and jerked hard on the leash. The man tried to stop his fall and, at the same time, keep the dog from bolting into the street and being hit by a car. As a result of his body going in so many directions at once, Ben had fallen much harder than he might have if he'd just gone down. The back of his head hit the stone curb hard with a loud, thick thud, then bounced and hit it again just as hard.

He must have blacked out because the next thing he knew, he was on his back looking up into the concerned faces of four people, including a policeman who held the dog's leash.

"He opened his eyes!"

"He's OK."

"Don't touch him, though. Don't move him till the ambulance gets here."

Across the street the ghost stood in the snow watching this, utterly confounded. A moment later it fizzled and flickered like a sick television set and disappeared. Methuselah was the only one who saw it, but ghosts are nothing new to dogs, so the animal didn't react. He only hunkered down into himself and shivered some more.

The Angel of Death looked at the ghost of Benjamin Gould and sighed. "What more can I tell you? They've gotten very clever."

They were at a table in a crummy turnpike restaurant near Wallingford, Connecticut. The Angel of Death was nothing special to look at: it had manifested itself today as a plate of someone's finished meal of bacon and eggs. Egg yolk was smeared across the white plate. Inside this smear were scattered bread crumbs.

It was midnight and the restaurant was almost empty. The waitress stood outside, having a cigarette and talking to the cook. She was in no hurry to clear the table. Having found the Angel of Death here, the ghost of Benjamin Gould had manifested itself as a fat black fly now sitting in the egg yolk.

The plate said, "When Gould hit his head on the curb he was *supposed* to die. You know the routine—cracked skull, intercranial bleeding, and death. But it didn't happen. To oversimplify, think of it as a massive virus that had infected our computer system. Afterward, a whole bunch of similar glitches popped up all over the grid and we knew we were under attack. Our tech guys are working on it. They'll figure it out."

Unsatisfied by this explanation, the ghost/fly paced back and forth across the drying egg yolk, its little black spindly legs getting yellow and gooey. "How can *heaven* get a virus in its computer system? I thought you were omniscient."

"So did we until this happened. Those guys in hell are getting cleverer all the time. There's no doubt about that. Don't worry—we'll work it out. For now, though, the problem is you, my friend."

Hearing this, the fly stopped pacing and looked down at the plate. "Say again?"

"There's nothing we can do about you until we fix this glitch. You've got to stay here till then."

"And do *what?*" the fly dared to ask indignantly.

"Well, doing what you're doing, for one. You can continue being a fly for a while, and then maybe change into a person or a tree.... Changing identities can be lots of fun. And there's other pleasant things to do on earth: learn to smoke, try on different kinds of cologne, watch Carole Lombard films—"

"Who's Carole Lombard?"

"Never mind," the plate said and then mumbled, "She's reason enough for you to stay here."

The fly remained silent and unmoved.

The plate tried to change the subject. "Did you know that Ben Gould went to school in this town? That's why I'm here now—to do some checking up on his history."

But the fly wouldn't be sidetracked. "How long will this take? Just how long will I have to stay here?"

"In all honesty? I don't know. It could be a while. Because once we find the computer virus, then we're going to have to run a check of the whole system." The plate said this gently, knowing full well that it was on spongy ground here.

"'A while' meaning how long—a year? a century?"

"I cannot answer that—until they rid the system of this virus and then clean up the damage it's done. But if you don't mind some advice, I would suggest that while waiting, you go and live with Gould. With the right kind of help, he could skip having to live a few lifetimes and move several steps up the ladder."

"I am not a teacher—I'm a ghost, *his* ghost. That's my job. Read the job description."

The Angel of Death considered this and decided it was time to get to the point. "All right then, here's the deal. They've decided—"

"*Who's* decided?"

If the plate could have made a face it would have rolled its eyes in exasperation. "You know very well who I'm talking about—don't play dumb. *They've* decided that because it might take a while to sort out this virus problem and you're stuck here through no fault of your own, they'll offer you a chance to try something untested, just to see if such a thing works: if you can somehow get through to Benjamin Gould and make him a better person while he's alive, then you won't have to come back to earth after he dies and haunt things. We know how much you hate fieldwork, so if you succeed here, you can stay in the office and work from there in the future.

"We don't know how much longer he'll live now because he was scheduled to die from the fall that day. Now the matter of his fate is anyone's guess. That means there's no telling whether you have a lot of time to work on him or only a little."

The ghost was genuinely surprised by this offer and paused to let the intriguing proposal sink in. It was just about to ask, "If I don't come back here to haunt, what will I do instead in the office?" But the waitress came to the table, saw the fly in the egg yolk, and whacked it dead with an old newspaper.

Somewhere in everyone's inner city is a cemetery of old loves. For the lucky contented few who like where they are in their lives and who they're with, it is a mostly forgotten place. The tombstones there are faded and overturned, the grass is uncut, and brambles and wildflowers grow everywhere.

For other people, their place is as stately and ordered as a military graveyard. Its many flowers are well watered and tended; the white gravel walks have been carefully raked. All signs indicate that this spot is visited often.

For most of us, though, the cemetery is a hodgepodge. Some

sections are neglected or completely ignored. Who cares about these stones or the old loves buried beneath them? Even their names are hard to remember. But other gravestones there *are* important, whether we like to admit it or not. We visit them often, sometimes too often, truth be told. And one can never tell how we will feel when these visits are over—sometimes lighter, sometimes heavier. It is entirely unpredictable how we'll feel going back home to today.

Ben Gould rarely visited his cemetery. Not because he was happy or content with his life, but because the past had never held much importance for him. If he was unhappy today, what difference did it make if he was happy yesterday? Every moment of life was different. How did looking or living in the past genuinely help him to live in this minute, beyond a few basic survival tricks he'd learned along the way?

In one of the first long discussions they ever had, Ben and German Landis disagreed completely about the significance of the past. She loved it. Loved to look at it from all angles, loved to feel it cross her right now like a thick midday shadow. She loved the past's weight and stature.

Stature. What stature? Ben had asked skeptically, thinking she was joking. The memory of the delicious sandwich you ate for lunch is not going to take away your hunger four hours later. On the contrary—it will only make the hunger worse. As far as he was concerned, the past is not our friend.

They argued and argued, neither convincing the other. It became a joke and eventually a stumbling block in their relationship. Much later, when they were breaking up, German tearfully said, "In six months you'll probably think of me and our relationship about as often as you think of your third-grade teacher."

But on that subject she was one hundred percent wrong.

The great irony that held both Ben Gould's life and apartment captive these days was that he lived with not one but two ghosts, because German Landis haunted him, too. He went to bed thinking about her, and minutes after he awoke every morning he started thinking about her again. He couldn't stop himself, damn it. It wasn't fair. He had no control over it. Their failed relationship was an insistent mosquito buzzing close around his head. No matter how much waving away he did, it never left or stopped irritating him.

He was at his desk staring at his hands when the doorbell rang that morning. He was wearing only underpants and nothing else. He knew it was she. He'd known she was coming but had purposely

303

chosen not to get dressed. In recent meetings with her, Ben had grown increasingly remote and sullen, which only made the air between them thick and uncomfortable. Sometimes it got so bad that German thought, "Oh just let him keep the damned dog and forget it. At least that way I won't ever have to see him again." But Pilot was hers; Ben had given him to her as a present. She loved the dog as much as Ben did. Why surrender only because her idiotic ex-boyfriend made her uneasy for five minutes every few days when she came to get Pilot?

The ghost heard the doorbell ring and immediately tensed up. Pilot looked at it and then toward Ben's bedroom. The kitchen table had been carefully set with beautiful food and objects. In the middle of this setting was a blooming Star Gazer lily placed inside an impossibly delicate lavender glass vase from Murano, Italy.

Nothing happened. No sound emanated from inside the bedroom. A minute later the doorbell rang a second time.

"Isn't he going to answer the door?"

The dog shrugged.

The ghost crossed its arms then immediately uncrossed them. It made three different faces in the course of eight seconds and finally, unable to stand it anymore, walked out of the kitchen and over to the front door. Ben Gould eventually emerged from his bedroom looking both sleepy and confrontational.

The ghost looked at the man in his underpants and glowered. Again? He was going to pull this sort of immature, retard-o stunt with her again?

Gould rubbed his eyes with the heels of his hands, took a deep breath, and opened the front door. The ghost stood two feet behind him, holding a metal spatula in its right hand. It was so nervous about seeing German that it madly wiggled the utensil upanddown-andupanddown . . . at an impossibly fast speed. Thank God neither person could see this.

"Hello."

"Hey."

Both said their single words in voices as devoid of emotion as they could muster.

"Is Pilot ready to go?" she asked in a friendly fashion.

"Sure. Come on in." He turned toward the kitchen and she followed. She looked at his nice butt in the wrinkled underpants and closed her eyes in despair. Why was he doing this? Was she supposed to be shocked or embarrassed to see him in his underwear? Had he forgotten that she had seen him naked, oh, several hundred times in their past? She knew what he smelled like clean and what he smelled like sweaty. She knew how he liked to be touched and the most intimate sounds that he made. She knew how he wept and what made him laugh loudly. How he liked his tea and how he absolutely sparkled when, walking down a street together, she put her arm over his shoulder to show the world she was his pal *and* his tall lover.

Seeing where the two of them were going now, the ghost disappeared from its place by the front door and reappeared a second later in the kitchen. When they entered, its arms were crossed tightly over its chest in anticipation. Everything one could imagine wanting for breakfast was on that table. Warm freshly baked scones, strawberry preserves from England, honey from Hawaii, Segafredo coffee (German's favorite brand), a plate laid with long pink strips of northern Scottish salmon, another heaped with perfectly prepared eggs Benedict (another love of hers). There were two other egg dishes as well. Mouthwatering fare covered and graced every part of the small round table. It looked like a *Gourmet* magazine cover. Whenever Ben Gould watched a cooking show on television, the ghost watched, too, and often took notes. Any time German came by to get the dog, the ghost made one of these TV recipes or something else scrumptious from one of Ben's many cookbooks and had it waiting on the table for her when she arrived.

Of course German couldn't see any of it. What she saw now was only a bare wooden table with a single spoon off to one side, exactly where Ben had left it the night before after using the spoon to stir sugar into a cup of weak herbal tea. She looked at the spoon a long time before speaking. It broke her heart. For those glorious few silent moments, the ghost pretended German Landis was staring in silence because she actually *could* see everything that it had prepared for her because it knew how much she enjoyed breakfast.

Her favorite meal of the day. She loved to buy it, prepare it, and eat it. She loved to shop for fresh croissants and *petit pain au chocolat* at the bakery two doors down. Every time she went to the local Italian market, she happily closed her eyes so as to concentrate better on the heavenly smell of bitter fresh coffee while the owner ground the beans. She loved grapefruit juice, ripe figs, bacon and eggs, hash brown potatoes with ketchup. She had grown up eating monumental Minnesota breakfasts that buoyed everyone over the ten-degrees-below-zero temperatures and car-high snowdrifts outside. Like her mother, German Landis was a lousy cook but an enthusiastic one, especially when it came to breakfast. She was thrilled when people ate as much as she did.

The ghost knew all this because it had sat in this very kitchen many times watching with pleasure and longing while she assembled the morning feast. It was one of the traditions German and Ben had established early in their relationship: she made breakfast while he prepared all the other meals.

"Have you been eating?"

"What?" Ben wasn't sure he had heard her right.

"Have you been *eating?*" she repeated more emphatically.

He was thrown off guard by her question. She hadn't said anything so intimate in a long time.

"Yes, I'm fine."

"What?"

"What do you mean, *what?*"

German picked up the spoon and turned to Ben. While reaching for it, she put her hand right through the middle of the perfect seven-egg soufflé the ghost had baked for her. It was a masterpiece. But she didn't see or feel it because ghosts make ghost food that exists only in the ghost world. Although the living sometimes sense that world, they can't occupy that dimension.

"What have you been eating?"

Ben looked at her and shrugged like a guilty ten-year-old boy. "Stuff. Good stuff. Healthy things, you know." His voice dribbled off. She knew he was lying. He never cooked anything for himself when he was alone. He ate junk food from circus-colored bags and drank tea.

Pilot got up from his bed and walked slowly over to the woman. He liked the feel of her big hand on his hand. Her hands were always warm and loving.

"Hello, Mr. Dog. Are you ready to go?"

Suddenly and with almost a feeling of horror, Ben realized what it would be like in the apartment in a few minutes when the two were gone and he was there alone with nothing to do. German probably had planned a nice long walk with the dog. When it was over, she would take Pilot to her place, where they'd eat lunch together.

Ben had never been to her new apartment but could imagine what it was like. Full of bright colors and found objects, and her collection of Japanese toy action figures would be arranged on all the window-sills. The wickedly comfortable blue couch she'd bought when they were together and taken when she moved out would be the center of her living room. In all likelihood that couch would be covered with large art books both opened and closed. That image alone made Ben hurt because it was so lovingly familiar to him. The dog had his place on the couch next to her. He would not budge from there unless she did. Her new apartment would have to be light and airy because she insisted on both. German always needed a lot of natural light wherever she lived.

She also liked to open windows even on the coldest days of the year to fill any room she occupied with fresh air. It drove Ben crazy when they were living together but now he missed that quirk and all her others. The other day while sitting morosely over another cup of tea at this table and thinking about her, he had written her a note on a paper napkin from a take-out restaurant. Knowing she would never read it, he wrote what he honestly felt. "I miss you every day of my life and for that alone I will never forgive myself."

"Well! I guess Pilot and I'd better be going."

"All right."

"I'll be back with him tomorrow. Is two o'clock OK?"

"Yes, that'll be fine." He started to speak but, catching himself, stopped abruptly and walked instead to the other side of the kitchen to retrieve the dog leash hanging on a hook there.

German wanted to say something more, too. Seeing the expression on his face, however, stopped her.

Unexpectedly, a moment came when, exchanging the leash, both people let their guards down. They looked at each other with a frank mixture of love, resentment, and yearning that was immense. Both turned quickly away.

Sitting at the table, the ghost observed all this. When it sat down it had pulled the exploded soufflé toward its chest with both hands, as if trying to protect the ruined beauty from any further damage.

Now seeing that look rocket back and forth between them, the ghost slowly lowered its face into the middle of the soufflé right up to its ears and remained like that while good-byes were said and German left. It was still face-deep in the eggy mess when it heard the front door close.

Ben walked back into the kitchen, sat down across from the ghost, and stared directly at it. The ghost eventually lifted its head from the soufflé and saw that it was being stared at. Although it knew it was invisible, the intensity of the man's gaze was distressing.

Lifting the teaspoon off the table, Ben appeared to weigh it in his hand. In truth what he was doing was testing to see if any of German's warmth remained in the metal.

Suddenly he flung the spoon with all his might against the far wall. It ricocheted loudly off several places before landing and scudding across the floor.

The ghost lowered its face back into the soufflé.

From The Skylark
Peter Straub

ON SATURDAY NIGHT, KEITH HAYWARD and Brent Milstrap, absent from the lower room at La Bella Capri, greeted the arrival of the little group upstairs at Gorham Street in the manner the little group had come to expect of them. Milstrap sighed and looked away, and Hayward sniggered as he summoned a halfhearted wave of welcome. Propped on the floor between them and evidently salvaged from a nearby sidewalk, a tall, upright mirror with a foxed silvery surface offered a partial reflection of a dingy section of wall against which Spenser Mallon leaned, his rough blond hair glowing above a light turtleneck as he whispered to Meredith Bright. Her white sleeveless top made her look like his acolyte. Keith Hayward's eyes remained locked upon Meredith's chest as Dilly-O led Eel and Boats into the apartment. Apparently it was Hayward's and Milstrap's. That at least explained why Mallon had taken such conspicuous notice of their earlier absence: like Dilly-O, they had been present anyhow. Cigarette smoke and the buzz of intermittent low conversation hung in the room, where eight or nine other students had gathered. Entering, the Eel recognized a good number of these students from La Bella Luna, though Alexandra was not among them. Meredith had vanquished her only rival.

Mallon straightened up and said, "Thank you all for coming. I believe we should get down to business before this turns into a party. We can always party afterward." Several people laughed, and with his hand on the back of the one chair with armrests, Mallon gestured to the long table in the center of the room. Evidently he had delayed the beginning of business until the arrival of the high school students.

Under Mallon's gaze, people slid into place around the table with varying degrees of hesitation and assurance. As if by prior arrangement, the little group followed a nod from Mallon and took the first four places opposite him. Meredith Bright moved immediately to Mallon's left and smiled at the Eel. Keith Hayward appeared on Eel's left and claimed the chair directly across from Meredith's. Jeremy took the last chair on their side, and Josh and Seth, the other two bearded New Yorkers, settled at the end of the table. So they had not fled after all. Brent Milstrap sat at the table's head. It was his table, Eel thought, and, taking in the furniture and the pictures on the walls, which had apparently come from the house of an indulgent, well-off grandmother, supposed also that the apartment was really his, too. The same house, not a sidewalk, had supplied the mirror, probably an antique. Keith Hayward was from a city, Eel was certain, because he was no country boy, but none of his relatives had any money. Linoleum and lace curtains. He and Eel were alike that way, though in no other.

Everybody sat down. Keith Hayward kept staring at Meredith Bright as though he wanted to devour her on the spot. Giving him a wordless glance intended to awaken him from his obsession, Eel for the first time saw the unusually large pores on Hayward's face. They were like black holes randomly punched into his cheeks and the sides of his nose. Under the table, his hands were clenched, and his rigid posture advertised suppressed emotion. For the first time, Eel saw Hayward not as a clumsy buffoon, but an unknown, potentially frightening force. The Eel did not enjoy being frightened, and brought a foot into sharp contact with Hayward's left shin. Simultaneously, Mallon said, "*Keith.*"

For a second only, Hayward jerked his head toward the Eel. His eyes had become as dark and hole-like as his pores, and anger had tightened his mouth into a flat line. He looked much scarier than he had before. It was as though he had opened a window onto real monstrosity. Then his head swiveled back. "What?"

"Stop looking at Meredith that way, man."

The monster trembled once, violently. "What way?" Both he and Brent Milstrap, Eel noticed, wore beautiful sweaters a little heavy for the weather. Hayward's was a pastel blue, his roommate's a misty green. The way the fabric of the sweaters absorbed the light softly into its folds made Eel think it was cashmere.

"I don't sit and stare at people, for Christ's sake. I was thinking."

"Hey, a lot of people stare at Meredith."

"Only I wasn't."

"Then tell me what you were thinking about."

The monster jammed his feet under his chair and the pores on his cheeks tilted all to one side, like birch trees in a strong wind. He had forced his face into a smile so muscular that his eyes clamped down into slits.

310

"My thoughts. My dreams."

"It's always a good idea to think about your own thoughts. Do you also listen to what you say?"

"I don't know what you mean," Hayward said. His smile relaxed, and his eyes became visible again. Without quite knowing if Hayward understood what he had revealed, the Eel wanted to get away from him, and glanced from side to side. All the places at the table had been filled. A number of people were leaning against the walls and seated on the floor in whispering groups of two and three. Half the people in the room were paying no attention to the dialogue going on across the table.

"Try it some time. You'll learn a lot. These dreams, what are they like? Active?"

"Pretty active, yeah." Hayward had still not quite relaxed.

"I'm glad to hear that," Mallon said. "Active dreaming, that's what we want. *Visionary* dreaming. Great dreams do not necessarily exclude an element of violence, do they, Keith? In fact, I think you like it when I mention violence."

The Eel watched the monster's hands fold together on the table.

"Relax, Keith. You have extraordinary potential, more than I think you comprehend. Over the next couple of weeks, you'll play an important role in whatever happens."

Like everyone else at the table, the Eel's gaze turned to him, not without an element of appalled envy.

Mallon said, "Things are taking place all about us, great currents flow past us, around us, through us, and our poor instruments are barely enough to register the most powerful of these currents. We live in a time of profound transforming change. *Change,* guys. One kind of life is dying, and another is struggling to be born. That's why we are here, that's why we're together at this moment."

Apparently overwhelmed by the urgency of what he had to say, Mallon propped his elbows on the table and pushed his forehead into the cup of his hands. At that moment, his display of helplessness made him seem intensely charismatic, utterly worthy of the loyalty of everyone in his audience. A mild but potent electricity thrilled along the surface of Eel's scalp, shoulders, and arms. *This man is suffering for us.*

"Things are coming together all around us, all over the world, but particularly around us. There's Vietnam, there's crisis in the family, the whole idea of race in this country is being taken apart and put together again—we're questioning affluence, we're rejecting

311

materialism, we're in the process of curing the long neurosis of our own history. Capitalism gets everything wrong because it's built on the wrong premises, neurotic premises. Capitalism denies the erotic, and we must reclaim the free, loving expression of our bodies."

Over the next hour, he went on to say a great many more things. *Freedom is violence,* that was one of the sentences that penetrated the loose, foggy blanket of desire and anxiety that had begun to swaddle the Eel in its folds. Mallon's ideas had been inspired by a professor he had at U.C. Santa Cruz, Norman O. Brown. Brown was a genius, he had understood that when money appears in our culture's dreams, *"it appears as shit,"* but Norman O. Brown was a creature of the library and the lecture hall; he had never put himself to the test of experience. A mind could only do so much in a book-lined vacuum, even a great mind like Brown's. As he had discovered with his second master, a German named Urdang he had met in California and with whom he had traveled to the Far East, the test of experience was found only in the streets of villages and cities all over the world, on mountains and in the depths of valleys. Had Professor Brown ever seen a man's hand amputated in a Nepalese bar, had he seen the blood course, lively as a brook, down the bar?

Mallon wanted them to hear certain stories. After they had listened to his stories, they could decide whether or not they wanted to go to the next level, take the next step. It was up to them to decide if they were in or out.

The Eel was in, that had been decided some time ago, apparently without benefit of a conscious decision. Within an increasingly slumberous erotic fog, the Eel attended to Mallon's stories.

STORY #1

In India, which he had visited with Urdang, an odd, unsettling series of events began happening almost as soon as they reached the outskirts of a village named Sankwal. A great holy man lived in Sankwal, and they had been granted an audience with him. When Mallon drew near the village, a carrion crow dropped out of the skies. Villagers began to stream toward him, whether because of the carrion crow or because he and Urdang were fair-skinned strangers, he did not know. When they passed a hut on a barren scrap of land, a man pulled Mallon's sleeve and implored him, with many flapping gestures, to go into his hut and see something—the man jabbed a black fingernail at his right eye. Within the dim, hot enclosure, Mallon found that he had been invited to gaze at a small child with huge, impassive eyes and limbs like twigs. Looking at Mallon, the villager raised one of his hands and rested it gently on the boy's enormous forehead. "He wants you to touch the boy," Urdang said.

Reluctantly, Mallon had extended one hand and brushed the boy's head with his fingertips. Immediately, the father bowed and began crooning in gratitude.

"What did I do?" he asked.

"What does he think you did?" Urdang said.

Proceeding down a narrow lane in the village proper, Mallon carelessly extended two fingers and ran them along a foot or two of the mud-plastered wall at his side. The villagers set up an ecstatic babble: on the wall, two blue lines glowed like heated bars.

Mallon said he felt an electrical buzz filling all the spaces within his body, as if he could shoot sparks from his fingers. *I should touch that little boy now*, he thought.

The cheerful crowd pushed him forward. Eventually he reached a long wall with an iron gate that opened into a garden backed by a long, graceful terra-cotta building with a row of windows on both sides of an elaborately tiled front door. The dark heads of young women appeared in these windows. Giggling, the women retreated backward.

The villagers thrust Mallon and Urdang forward and clanged the gates behind them. Far away, an oxcart creaked. Cattle lowed from behind the long building.

"Come nearer," said a voice.

Mallon saw a small man in a long dhoti of dazzling white seated before a fountain in the middle of the garden. A moment before, he had noticed neither the man nor the fountain.

"You are Urdang," the man said. "Who is your follower, Urdang?"

"His name is Mallon," Urdang said. "He's my partner, not my follower."

"Perhaps he is your leader," said the little man. "Please sit down."

They sat before him in the lotus position. The great holy man had a shaven head and a hard, nutlike face. He did not appear to be pleased by their visit, but he ordered sweet tea and honey cakes to be served to his guests. They were delivered by two of the dark-haired girls, who wore beautiful, highly colored saris and sandals with little bells on the straps.

"When you came into our village, a crow fell from the sky," said

313

the holy man.

Urdang and Mallon nodded.

"The crow was a sign. Your friend both courts and opposes death."

There was more of this kind of thing. Mallon had touched a dying child, yet had he restored it to health? Even if he had, was the healing truly his work? Belief could heal as successfully as other forces. Was Mallon well schooled in the Sutras? How great was his knowledge of Buddhist teachings?

Urdang replied that Mallon was not a Buddhist.

"Then why have you come?"

"I come for your blessing," Mallon said.

"You cannot have it. Give me yours instead." The holy man spoke without humor. "Render it unto me as you did the child."

Reluctantly, Mallon scooted forward and extended a hand. The holy man leaned forward and permitted his brow to be brushed. His face contracted, no mean trick, and he ordered the two men to leave his village.

Urdang asked why.

"This man must leave now." He would say no more.

When they opened the gates, the villagers had fled back to their homes, and the lanes were empty. The air darkened. Rain began to fall. Before they reached open ground, the earth had been churned to mud. A loud cry came from the hut of the poor man with the sick child, whether of joy or pain they could not say.

STORY #2

Years later, in Austin, Texas, Mallon was spending a couple of weeks moving between fraternity houses and student flophouses near the university. One morning he walked out onto the hot, stony sidewalks on East Fifteenth Street about half a mile from Red River Street, and started to walk to his favorite coffee shop, the Skylark Diner. Soon he became aware that a man in a suit and a necktie was tagging after him on the other side of Fifteenth Street. For some reason, perhaps the formality of his wardrobe, the man made him feel unsettled, almost threatened. Mallon ducked into a side street and moved quickly to the next intersection, where he found the man waiting for him, still on the other side of the street.

The intermittent haze through which this information reached the Eel suggested that a lovely young woman, a young woman much like Meredith Bright, but in blue jeans and cowboy boots, had accompanied Mallon, and that his evasiveness had been primarily on her behalf.

Mallon thought he had no choice: he marched across the street to confront his pursuer. The man in the gray suit retreated, frowning. By the time Mallon (and his hidden companion, the Austin girlfriend) had crossed the street, the FBI agent, or whatever he was, had somehow managed to disappear. Mallon had not seen the man disappear into a shop or behind a parked car, he had not seen him do anything at all. One second, the government agent (he thought) had been walking backward with a look of displeasure on his face; the next, he had vanished, absorbed into the slightly hazy air or the pale brick of the building that had been behind him.

If only for a second, had Mallon glanced away?

Around he turned, and on toward the coffee shop he continued. After he had rounded the corner and returned to Fifteenth Street, he sensed a commotion of some kind taking place behind him, and, nerves already prickling, looked over his shoulder. Half a block away, the agent in the gray suit came to an abrupt halt and stared straight ahead, as if a wayward thought had captured his attention.

"Why are you following me?" Mallon asked.

The man in the suit pushed his hands into his pockets and shrugged. "Am I following you?"

"You know you are. What's going on?"

"Take care," the agent said. "I mean that in all sincerity, sir."

Mallon whirled around and strode, though he did not jog, to the diner. All the while, he had the feeling that the man was following along, although whenever he looked back, the sidewalk was nearly empty and his pursuer nowhere to be seen.

Inside the diner, he moved straight down the length of the counter past the booths, ignoring the empty seats. Marge, the waitress, asked him what was up.

"I'm trying to shake somebody," he told her. "Can I go through the kitchen?"

"Spenser," she said, "you can walk through my kitchen anytime."

This, at least, was what the Eel supposed Marge the waitress had said to Spenser Mallon as he sped through her domain. The slamming of the back door rattled the pots on their shelves.

Mallon came out into a wide alleyway where a few hand-painted signs indicated the entrances to little clubs that had taken over back rooms, basements, and storage lofts. A cluster of garbage cans stood against the wall to his right, and one of them, silvery where the others were dark, looked as though it had been purchased that morning. An unlined yellow index card bearing a few written words had been taped to its shiny lid.

He knew that the card had been left for him. Although a toxic fog seemed to hover about it, he could not force himself to walk away without reading the words. He peeled the card away from the gleaming lid and raised it to his eyes. In blue-black ink that still looked wet, the words on the card read, QUIT WHILE YOU'RE BEHIND.

STORY #3

In New York, a city he disliked and seldom visited, Mallon found himself with little money and less to do. The Columbia University students whose promise had seemed so great when he had begun working with them had proved to be incurious dilettantes. His gatherings in a room at the back of the West End had deteriorated into gabfests centered on grades and career advancement, thereby validating Mallon's private conviction that New Yorkers were essentially superficial. Privilege and an overheated sense of entitlement had stunted these insular people.

In frustration, Mallon had disbanded his circle to concentrate on research. A helpful acolyte had provided him with a forged student card, and while the last of his money ran out, he spent his days roaming through the literature of the arcane and occult: Giordano Bruno, Lully, the Order of the Golden Dawn, Madame Blavatsky, Gurdjieff, Elifas Levi. When in his research he came across a particularly helpful volume, he looked to see if it had been consulted in the past decade; if it had not, he withdrew it from the library, informally. This was not theft, he assured drowsy Eel and the rest of his audience on Gorham Street, but liberation. Through him, the book would move into a free and expansive circulation.

It was time for him to work his way west again, he thought, in search of the combination of people and events capable of producing the revelation he felt somewhere just out of reach but always before him.

Prowling through the stacks one day, he seemed to catch an odd light filtering into the long shelves of books. The light appeared to come from somewhere near the library's central core. At first he paid it no attention, since it was faint and intermittent, no more than an occasional half-seen rosy pulse. Odd things often happened at Columbia University. (Mallon had once seen the ghost, the literal ghost, of a nineteenth-century Danish clergyman, a prim, ascetic-looking gentleman in his midthirties with black clothing, a worn leather case at his feet, and a pince-nez on his nose, reading a little breviary on a bench near the university's gated entrance at 116th Street. When looked at closely, the Danish clergyman appeared to be no less corporeal than the students moving back and forth through the gates, though, unlike them, he could not be touched. Mallon's hand would have passed straight through the man's black-clad shoulder until his fingers met the iron bench.)

When the pulse became brighter and more distracting, Mallon began to move through the stacks, looking for its source. It is important to note here, especially in light of what was to happen later, that none of the graduate students roaming the stacks appeared to notice the pulsing, orange-pink glow. (The students in the vicinity of the 116th Street gates had not noticed the ghostly Dane, either. For Mallon, that summed up Columbia University in a nutshell.) The glow led him across the stacks in the direction of the elevators, growing more vibrant as he went, and finally brought him to the closed metal door of a carrel. There could be no doubt that the little carrel was the source of the glowing color, for it streamed out over the top, around the sides, and beneath the bottom of the metal door. For once in his life, Mallon was uncertain of his mission. It seemed to him that he had drawn near to the defining mystery of his life—the great transformation that alone could give to his existence the meaning he knew it must possess—and the sheer importance of what he had come upon paralyzed him. Two students coming down the narrow passage outside the carrel looked at him oddly and asked if anything was wrong.

"You maybe see a trace of color in the air around that door?" he asked them, referring to the pulsing, wavering waterfall of radiant orange-pink light that streamed toward them.

"Why, do you?" asked one of the students.

"I thought I did, for a minute."

"Wave particle diffusion," the young man said, and the two of them left.

Mallon summoned his courage and gave the door a feeble rap. No response came. He rapped again, more forcefully. This time, an irritated voice called, "What is it?"

"I have to talk to you," Mallon said.

"Who is that?"

"You don't know me," Mallon said. "But unlike everyone else in this building, I can see the light that's pouring out of your carrel."

"You see light coming from my carrel?"

"Yes."

"Are you a student here?"

"No."

Pause.

"Are you on the faculty, God help us?"

"No, I'm not."

"How did you get in this library? Are you on the staff?"

"Someone gave me a fake student card."

He heard the man in the carrel scrape his chair back from the desk. Footsteps approached the door.

"OK, what color is the light you see?"

"Kind of like the color of pink lemonade mixed with orange juice," Mallon said.

"I guess you better get in here," the man said.

Mallon heard the clicking of the lock, and the door swung open.

That's it! The story ended when the guy opened the door!

The story had to end there. You'll see. Everything stops when you open the door.

On his way out of the room Spenser Mallon touched Boats's shoulder, leaned over, and quietly asked him to "pick up" some items for him: a quart of white paint, two small paintbrushes, and some sturdy ropes. Boats asked him for the money, and Mallon said, "You don't need money, Boats. Get my stuff the same way you got the sweaters for the frat boys, all right? I think it's time to start using your talents seriously."

Three Poems
John Ashbery

SO, YES

Kids probably don't know what they're saying,
and we, we're one shy of all the stepchildren
it took to get here. In odder moments we'd contemplate
the swathe of water leading to the horizon
and pretend it was the grass had come full circle,
even to this sidewalk of cream and ocher brick. Those
who trespass against us slipped into rephotographed woods,
verifiable, at least for the time being.

He who stumbles at the brink of some great discovery,
perplexed, will endorse for many years
the fox and its entourage, part of some map
of life, he thinks. Emerging
from the shadow of his later career, he slides
into the contiguous states of America, all cherry trees
and floral tributes. It was right to behave as we have done,
he asserts, sending the children on their way
to school, past the graveyard. Evening's loftiest seminars
can't dim the force of that apostasy. So, yes,
others had to precede us, meaning we're lost in a swamp with coevals
who like us because we like to do things with them.
The forced march makes perfect sense under such conditions.
Let's celebrate then, let there be some refreshing change
overtaking all we were meant to achieve and didn't.
On the practical side it looks as though their team lost
and ours failed to languish, absent a compelling reason to do so.

John Ashbery

YES, "SEÑOR" FLUFFY

And the clouds fretted and flew, as though
there was a reason for their acting distraught.
There may have been, of course, but at this distance,
better to act dumb and accept the inevitable
as a long-anticipated surprise. Then if what lands
on your plate stares angrily at you and the other guests
"can't wait" to hear your reaction, why, it's checkout time
at the gazebo and no one will forget you too heartily
as the next-to-last spectator always glimpsed on the premises,
feigning the concern for the victim that marks you as the killer,
for sure. As for being in touch with you guys
another time, we'll take it under advisement.

So this moment's tremors mingle with others
on the departure platform. Who knew it would be this silly,
and so dense? Nevertheless, we have a right to know,
to have our impulses regulated and calibrated in the
interests of farther and fainter reaction shots. Sure,
you'll get your rights read to you and sooner
than you may have counted on. Let the monotonous
group of listeners pump you for details, we'll provide
backup and terminal ecstasy at the way stations.
It couldn't have been any other way. You knew that.

What's your name down there?
Despite misgivings, the story clicks to a halt,
as always. The credits surge. People rush to leave.
The shiny cars of another era are coming
to take us where we wish to be taken, lest we
outstay our welcome and sink in the embrace
of another mood.

John Ashbery

THE LONELINESS

"Bound and determined" one writes a letter
to the street, in demotic, hoping a friend
will find, keep it, and analyze it.
This much the future
is prepared to vouchsafe, with conditions:
You could design something at home.
Another's peace of mind isn't your concern
until the day it backfires,
and consequences wash over you, leaving you brackish,
untried.

OK, I'll try again:
peaceful, this time. Of course everyone likes light
lapping at the boathouse door, dredging
stones with sugar. It's as though a message
remained to be harvested, paperwork from me to you.

And we thought we were lost.
How many times haven't we given up in despair,
only to be reminded by time
of the firmness of its commitment
to our well-being, or lack thereof?

Shelley in the Navy-Colored Chair
Barbara Guest

—For Suzanna

I sit so close to him, our minds entwine.
I assume his stewardship through the cold and mist.

There is no other beauty with which he is equipped.
The pain, the exclamation!

Early morning when the tide lowers
and we manipulate our choices.
To see, to feel, to engender memory
of this place where Shelley walked.

He is near.
He breathes into the alphabet I found upon my chair.

A dissertation they brought me, exclaiming why
he failed to ride the unswept sea, and like
a nautilus drowned in heavy seas, windswept
like the alphabet he enriched.
Each day a chambered nautilus near my chair.

To add more stanzas to this alphabet
is the view Shelley takes.
More haste and less worry in the words gathered around him.
A light gleaming over their shoulder,
Before the ecclesiastic wonder breaks out
into praise for words he gathered,
pearls surround the armchair.

Three or Four Poems
Keith Waldrop

three or four
sights, but something you cannot
always
see

thicket of candles, "universe"
at "rest"

to the right of the
circle, all those
things which were

put aside

in the future

*

what have I
stolen

fish
plants
animals

historians, poets
philosophers, musical
instruments
jokes

drinking cups
the wealth of kings, the size
of ships

Keith Waldrop

crabs their characteristic
cross-amble

eagle or
horse

atmosphere
built of bricks, only one
course
physical

*

as the ice

appears
remembers surprises a

thousand years

*

this *is*
[happens]
no line between animate and

old, some

shapeless thing, a
ghost in first
flush as though
body never in

never

*

the porch goes first, rotten
from wear and weather, now the
calendar

324

slips and seasons shift, January
falls from winter, how

beautiful, as the proverb has it, to do
nothing, and then
rest

porch first and then
basement

*

caught: two bodies in bright
haze, only

thought

*

before to-
morrow's
sun no

sunlit

composition
of dust, dream

daybreak, a
shiver
fixed on

faster, on *tumult,* on
never

*

melodic line articulate, hands
cross

Keith Waldrop

construction
of a mark, minimum

ark

watch, now, here I build
my ruin, my ordinary
gripsack—*I lose*

track. . . .

house
child
temple, ways

weeds, trees, the green
clichés

corresponding
space, from man and

*

blood by a
thread, the natural

attitude, object
of desire, no matter

what is said

*

variegated
surfaces

an uphill walk

unfoldment, all
things to thy remembrance, right
hand and left

night

unimportant
enemy
amusement

*

exit

tired of sleep

steep
entranceways

*

each family kindles
family fire, serious

illness, old
resentments of the gods

blood

civil war, terrible as
nature

unfinished

and blood

*

same light from star and
antistar

random inter-
sections tell
great spaces, lines

Keith Waldrop

pushed
jumped, fell, or
echo

*

focus there, fine
particles in air
everybody betrays

betrayed
imaginary sea lines, imagined
rules

clenched hand, covering
sigh then let fall, inside

outside

wall

*

cycle or
city destroyer

blur of
blood cells, visible
in a vise of light

body
clothed
armed
besieged

amazed

aged

*

likeness, singing *To
Anacreon in Heaven*

to the tune of the
Star-Spangled Banner

*

ladder

where appetite
climbs

nothing

rhymes

nothing

*

pass, leaving behind
another

nothing

*

three or four

substitutes for
person, effigy

offspring
lover

light in every
direction, shadow
inside, nothing

to hide

*

soul moves, eye
lingers

straying among
details, twilight at evening and fine
morning, no longer

any straight line

*

light from star and
antistar, precisely above my
head

random inter-
section, space shrunk
to line

to read angles, two or three

ruts in the road pre-
cise black
smoke, shadow

on a wall, dangles
free

*

uphill
walk

windward, ancient air

falling
flickers, fresh, opposite

as if the world

opposite

*

leftovers from a former
world, stones left over from
rotten fruit, moves
in a game forgotten

semicircle of sky, weak
spin of a compass

present
state, action out action
in

absurd
body
leftover skate

*

and

what can I
prove

gusts and eddies, mantle
of snow

beauty by
moment of white

fleck

coven in flight, corporeality
of sign, pale
rind of night

Keith Waldrop

then
aurora, flesh tones

thigh

*

arc of the forest, love
of old houses

dark

*

the text (same
name) should all

run thus:

fall

*

three or four white
stones in a

dark yard

random

without food, without
drink rarely a
handshake
another part felt to move

the zero set to
zero

Studio Visit

Maureen Howard

Does one ever get over drawing, is one ever done mourning it?

—Jacques Derrida, *Memoirs of the Blind*

EVERYTHING MUST BE ARRANGED. She has placed the last postcard, posted it, you might say, with a Lucite thumbtack that pins it to the canvas. A murky photo of the Chicago Stock Yards, in color no less, before color was invented for film. The haunches of the cattle glisten, a uniform dark brown. They are being led to slaughter by a fellow with a prod in his hand, his face bright orange under a dun-colored cap. The sky, washed-out blue. A dreary scene, but the postcard is one of many. The Poussin, for instance (*Earthly Paradise*), though reduced to an absurdity, is all dense edenic growth with a sunlit distance, a small shimmering lake and above a celestial figure (God?) riding a cloud, looking down on our first parents, naked as the day they came to mind. Eve, center stage, points at the apple tree, urging the reluctant Adam on. You know the story, so did Louis XIV, to whom the painting belonged.

On an easel, Louise Moffett seems to have been copying the Poussin, or at least the apparatus of her craft—paint, turpentine, brushes—are displayed on a table nearby. They may be for real or props. Perhaps the copy will always remain half done, those two figures arguing, stuck in their best moment, deleted. Mealy or tart, what were apples like back then, or for that matter in 1662? Also pinned to the canvas, *The Ruins of San Francisco City Hall* (1906), the gilt dome intact as well as the classical columns at its base. Only the center did not hold. The bare ribs of the tower still stand. The stretched canvas seems black. A big bulletin board, that's all it appears to be.

Louise wears a painter's smock, a thrift-shop treasure. You recall the floppy garments worn so as not to soil the artists' clothes in the atelier photos of Matisse, Mary Cassatt, et al. She places a wooden palette with dabs of color—some right from the tube, some mixed—on the table, runs her hand over soft sable brushes. The smell of oil paint, a thrill. Deep-breathe it. She is a good-looker heading toward middle years, her gray hair dusted with leftover gold. Winsome? That may be the word, as though something she once cared for has gone and she wonders . . . A sweet wince of a smile as she pins *St. Catherine of Sienna Dictating her Dialogues* (Giovanni de Paolo, 1457) to the canvas. One more postcard may be the answer for this particular day.

The studio is an outbuilding, a quarter mile down a path from the white clapboard house where she lives with her family. Her husband is home today, caring for Maisy, down with her third cold of the season. Cyril has gone off on the school bus, no sweater, a ripped T-shirt proving he's cool. Everything now arranged. North light filters through maples no longer flaming. Her studio with a sliding-glass door may have been a small barn, poultry perhaps. Canvases are properly stacked in a loft above, temperature control softly humming, sixty-eight, kettle on the boil, tidy kitchenette in a cubby. Once a stall? Louise, raised on a farm, thinks too narrow for horses. Exactly eleven o'clock when the curator arrives. He has been told to follow the path back, a bit bumpy in this early October freeze. Louise has not expected the driver. Will he come in with Blodgette, who is to look over her new work for a show? She's been expecting a tête-à-tête. Blodge, still in the black BMW with New York T plates, looks to the driver, taps his watch as if to say he'll not be long. Through the shingle sides of the studio she hears the blast of music—salsa, Afro-Cuban? Can't be Blodgette's choice, no way.

Now bussing her, one cheek, then the other.

Isn't this swell. Legendary. Moffett's retreat.

The world he brings with him is of this moment, apparent in his haircut, slightly gelled, his two-day beard. His torn jeans sport their patch like a price tag. The leather jacket, silk soft, seems almost live as she takes his arm, faces him toward the postcards on display. It's been some years since she's seen Blodge at openings in the city, or at the museum, suited for the trustees. To be fair, they are both costumed. They now stand side by side, Louise in that artist's smock over black turtleneck and L.L.Bean cords, wool socks, leather sandals. Her glasses, thick lenses, hang round her neck from a chain mended with Twistems, at the ready in case, just in case she does not see clearly the aerial view (six by four inches) to be Wells Cathedral, or that the bombed church (Moselle, France) with the big clock face standing in rubble (Paul Strand, 1950) reads 9:35. Time of the blast?

Blodge will have tea. No milk, no sugar.

Lapsang souchong?
Beautiful.

But when steeped, poured into their mugs, the smoky fragrance mingles with the oils, the turp—faintly nauseating. The music finds its way in from the car. Like street music, do what you will, no way to silence the din, as if in the city on Lower Broadway where Louise Moffett worked in her loft, mid- to late nineties. Blodge takes in the current scene. In this barn she has set up a diorama, his term, calling it that with arms spread in an expansive gesture—her postcards on canvas, tools of the painter's trade abandoned, half-executed copies, the Poussin without its tiny human figures, *St. Catherine* delivers her dialogues to an inkpot. No scribe. Louise has reproduced each of the black-and-white photos as a photocopy, the uncertain blur of that medium freeing the camera's frozen moment: *Cotton Picker* (Dorothea Lang, 1940). Moffett's men: Baryshnikov as Giselle; Duchamp at the chessboard; John James Audubon in his demented old age, eyes scummed with cataracts.

Christopher Blodgette leans in, examines the background, the canvas itself (four by six feet), size of a throw rug.

Louise on the defensive, laughing. *It's not black-black, not a shroud, don't you see? More organic, soil composted with manure.* Now why talk country to this creature of the city?

The bulletin board, as you said, is painterly.

Did I say?

Notices in the school hall, Louise.

She bridles at his instruction, or more likely at his deep misreading of her work past and present. He goes on about her continuing vitality as though she must be propped up to carry on beyond her time. Music now pulsing, Pearl Jam or maybe Nirvana. Once she could have called it: *Teen Spirit.* Louise claps her hands over her ears.

Blodge raps on the glass door. Keep it down. They watch in the blessed silence as his driver jogs round the car pursuing his puffs of cold breath, then stretches against the hood.

Bing needs his workouts, sitting all day in the car.

Bing?

Back to Blodgette's curatorial business. *Truly amazing, the random collection. The works diminished. Then rescued with the investment of your documentation.*

Documentation?

Your reenactments, Lou, bringing it all back home.

He takes up a small drawing, size of a postcard, *Washington Crossing the Delaware.* In Moffett's rendering only the prow and founding father are sketched in. The rest of the crew still awash in the cold river?

Perfect draftsmanship.

She takes that as a cut. Since when did dusty old draftsmanship figure in his vocabulary? Since he learned to please old ladies with money, partner them at benefits, Park Avenue dinners. Louise remembers Blodgette fresh from Cambridge with the proper degrees, a lanky boy scarfing down the hors d'oeuvres, gobbling art world in one sitting. Fond of him, she had so looked forward to this day. They'd been friends on the rise, not close but of an age. Once they'd stayed up all night in her loft drinking jug wine, last of the tokers, that's how she remembers it, Coltrane on a summer night, pressing PLAY again and again, the big windows thrown open to the noise of revelry below. They had no interest in each other, not really. Discrete fondling, sex consumed by their dreaminess, or was it ambition? She was ahead of the game, her first postcards so carefully observed and painted, photographic in detail. Small sightings of where she came from—dairy farm in Wisconsin, the landscape of memory mocked, distorted as memory will have it. Now the sky performs one of its tricks, quick clouds moving in. Louise gets a glimpse of herself in the glass door, sees the weight she's put on, the uncontrollable blink of her tired eyes while Blodge drinks the dregs of his tea as though sipping from the fountain of youth, a rather crusty cosmeticized youth, still . . . And the show he proposes is a group show in the planning stages. Louise has missed a beat in his e-mail request for a studio visit. Retro: had he not made that clear? Artists of the nineties, eighties if we can look back that far. He runs through a list of possible survivors. Moffett's pulled through?

He speaks of the return to her strong suit, narrative; then pops *Spiral Staircase, Statue of Liberty* off the canvas for a closer look. Two boys and a man who might be their father are trapped in the belly of this cast-iron symbol of our liberty, climbing toward the torch as Blodge reads it. The visit dwindles to gossip, past the demise of pomo to talk of the market.

Christopher? Her voice hushed, barely audible. *I have lunch back at the house.*

Lou-Lou, I must take a pass. He's going on to New Haven, to chat up folks at the Mellon . . . but they are distracted by the driver, who stands at the glass door huffing and puffing. He is large, a big untidy boy, his sad moon face begging his release.

When they are gone—Bing and Blodge, really!—she replaces the spiral staircase—unlovely industrial green, the great weight propping Miss L, that's all she meant if she meant anything at all. She wraps a shawl round her smock, begins the walk back up to the house.

Artie will ask, *How'd it go?*

Her husband has never got the hang of these visits. In his world of mathematics things mostly work. If they don't, go figure. He understands her anxiety, that Lou no longer courts exposure. It's not unlike . . . but there his comparison ends. Math is most often content with its equal signs, unlike art with uncertain proof of the pudding. Today she will tell Artie that the visit was something like a courtesy call.

So he looked?

That's all. Nothing on the dotted line.

Best keep it to herself, the group show with golden oldies and that Blodgette's response to the piece, which she will call *Last Mailing*, was inattentive, rambling at best. He had not opened the book right there on the table, a ledger with a worn marbleized cover. On its pages lined for debit or credit, she had written messages for each postcard mounted, and for those stacked next to it, which he did not shuffle through. On the path home Louise experienced not anger, just the melancholy of solo flight often felt when she is working. Her ledger has no narrative at all; jottings, no story. At this point she kicked a stone aside as though it were Bing huffing and puffing, or his friend the curator who had not been curious about her new work, just dropped by, pumping her studio full of hot air. She thought bitterly, *He must call his exhibit Old Masters*, which is not her way of thinking at all, but it lightened her way to the house where a child is sick and needs her attention.

Then, too, red-winged blackbirds flitted across her path, birds now seen too often in the marsh encroaching on their land. Birds that should be out of season. For a moment she longed for Central Park with its spectacular migration, the city all round that rectangular plot less than her father's megadairy. Or, last lap of her journey, did she long for a girl with a neat ponytail who flagged down a bus early, before the milking? It stopped by the side of the road where there was no bus stop at all, picked her up with one suitcase and a portfolio of drawings to show the world. The defiance of that girl long abandoned, only her looming shadow in which she might see herself, sharp as a silhouette with all the forgiving details gone.

I should have said, Open the book.
Should she have said? The old chestnut of regret.

Open the book. You see, it's people I'll never meet, greetings from where I've been, not really, but where I might like to go. To Marienbad (1923), pink clouds over the Grand Hotel. *Allegory of the Planets and Continents,* Tiepolo (1770–1776). *Open the book, Blodge: 0 through 9,* Jasper Johns (1960), *the artist's numbers consuming each other in a magician's scribble. That's for Artie, my math husband, who will love my Cobb salad,* the bib lettuce scooping still-life goodies presented on an Italian platter (Deruta, 2003). You might say an inspired show curated for Christopher Blodgette with a bottle of Beaujolais nouveau in season.

Cyril comes in the kitchen door. It's past noon, Friday, half day of school. He hears his parents at a distance, finds them in the dining room.

What's this? Tablecloth, weird gourds in a basket. He slings down his backpack.

Salad?

No thank you. Pepperoni pizza at school, its being Zig's birthday. Cyril is ten, a scrawny kid, red hair courtesy of a grandmother he never knew, owl glasses, wry smile as though he knows what's up. Maybe he does. Shivering in the T-shirt though he will never admit it. Good boy, he asks after his sister. Maisy is watching, is allowed to watch a DVD. Odd about his parents drinking wine middle of the day, like they were practicing for some holiday when the whole dairy-land crew comes from Wisconsin. General talk of the weekend, soccer match at the high school where his father teaches. His mother offers cumulus clouds on a soupy pudding.

Floating island?

No thank you.

It is awfully quiet. Only Maisy's cough, now persistent, finds its way to where they sit at the round table with the unlit candles and bread crumbs. Louise runs for the stairs, turns back to her boy.

Run down to the barn. Not calling it the studio. *Latch the door.* Pleading as though it's urgent, *Please put on your sweater.* She never does lock up. There have been no incidents in the neighborhood. Moffett's barn is safe as houses. True, there has been an intrusion. And who knows? In the bluster of this fall day perhaps her postcards will scatter.

338

*

Maisy is watching a rabbit fool a fox, a fairly brutal episode—pops to the head with one hell of a carrot. Her mother's hand on her forehead is cool, cooler than the sweat that breaks her fever. They sit together on her little low bed, watching a cartoon they have seen many times, Lou not following the blow-by-blow script. On the path back to the house she admitted she had looked forward to the curatorial eye with just enough of the old desire to show work in progress. Everything arranged, then she had not welcomed the visit. Going through the paces with Christopher Blodgette she'd been at best inhospitable. Should she have defended her reverence for the tools of her trade? See, I've not abandoned my craft, only give it half-hearted attention, might as well collect postcards, not a random stack, my people great and small. Tour my chosen places—most never seen. As for diorama—taxidermy art, Blodge knew it. Well, she is not yet stuffed, posed behind glass. She can post her many views, change scenes. So why tears, just a few as she trotted the path home? Brisk wind, not sorrow? The fox has a net—aha!—stretched over the farmer's garden. He watches his unwitting prey chew a whole row of leafy lettuce, then makes his move. We knew the net would entangle him, still Maisy laughs and so does her mother as the rabbit digs his way out of this fix.

The studio door is latched, a flimsy arrangement. It will be easy for Cyril to break into his mother's sacred place. He thinks about it, then tests the bolt, which springs back against the shingles. Before he enters, he looks at the setup framed just like a picture behind glass, her big dark canvas, a painting half done on an easel and all her stuff on a table. He slides the door open. Warm inside, cozy. Who's to hear the tread of his sneakers, see him rub the sleeve of his sweater across the snot dribbling from his nose? Catching his sister's cold? Or the chill of this day? He sits Indian style facing the postcards his mother's stuck on the night sky of her painting. Funny and fun, two words, he thinks, that go together. There's the little green one, he gets it—Adam and Eve, and the fuzzy picture of a bearded old man looking dead eyed at the camera. He is Audubon, responsible for his parents' bird watching, for the most boring hours he's ever lived, trailing them in silence for the flap of a feather, a flicker, a tweet. Fair is fair. Cyril has his lepidoptera pinned in glass cases. Slews not yet

339

collected. Even now the pupae dig in, wintering over. He flips the postcards: that guy at the chess table should sacrifice his rook, save the queen. The saint doesn't look like she's talking, but that monk, a spook if ever, is writing. What's awesome is the wall above them dissolving and who's there? Christ, that's who, coaching, cheering them on.

He opens the book full of his mother's swirling cursive, the way she writes even the list of eggs, milk, soup she needs at the market. He reads, but only pieces that go with the pictures he likes.

The cotton picker screens his face from the camera, covers his mouth with that big worn hand. What would he say, or dare say, that isn't in his eyes or the concealing shadows?

Washington standing up in the boat. Father of our country surely knew with the ice floe and waters raging what any boy on a camping trip knows. Rock the boat. Aim for the heroic.

St. Catherine is not speaking, so what is the scribe taking down with his pen and ink at the ready? Tempera and gold on wood: the medium was the message.

Cyril skips, but stops where his mother draws a little nest of numbers. He's good at numbers, even at this early age can deal with minus zero. His mother has written: *Artie likes teaching his students to see the beauty of shapes and numbers. At night he is often content with his mathematical journals, or so I must believe. Must believe he has survived his youthful promise. I do know I will never balance this book of my magpie collecting and spending. No final answer.*

Well, that's his mother, loopy. He closes the book, suddenly shy as any child should be, embarrassed by the note about his father. He shuffles the stack of postcards, comes up with a smiling lady. Her plump body takes up most of the foreground. It's hard to see the sheep, cows, and men working. *Mrs. Heelis on Her Farm* (Beatrix Potter, watercolor, D. Banner). It's sunny, so why the shawl and umbrella? She holds a quill pen in her hand. Cyril remembers once liking her stories. He takes a thumbtack, pins Mrs. Heelis right up on the canvas, between paradise and earthly destruction.

Playing Hurt

Lynne Tillman

ABIGAIL PLANNED ON RETIRING at forty and kidded around with her friends about how she'd better lay her golden eggs fast. But all bearers of wishes and jokes are also serious. In the future, she would be her own benevolent despot, spend what she had accumulated, and indulge herself. Maybe study Chinese or Arabic, certainly Latin, shave her head, if she wanted, because, literally, she would have earned it.

From her desk, Abigail reveled in the Chrysler Building's beautiful austerity, the sun dropping away in its own time. She admired nature's independence. Her Harvard Law School friends wondered why she worked in an investment bank, no adventure, no social meaning, they teased her, but she believed everyone had a right to happiness, and that took money. Mostly her friends came from privileged families and didn't have her special fervor, so, in a crucial way, they didn't get her. But as a scholarship student, Abigail grew up observing them and learned to recognize the secret operations of class and power.

Nathaniel Murphy walked past her glassed-in office. He still had most of his hair, his good looks, he was almost too handsome, though his nose had thickened since she'd first seen his picture when he was twenty-eight. The Internet golden boy had grown fleshier, even as his world had shrunk, but there he was in his Armani suit. She could smell his aftershave lotion, Vervain probably.

The numbers on the accounts blurred, Abigail pushed her glasses to the bridge of her nose, thrust her face closer to the papers, and self-consciously tugged on her short skirt. He was headed to the vault, distracted or worried, she thought, and he should be. He would soon open a security box, which probably held birth certificates, his parents' wills, some gold, jewelry, certificates. Abigail had helped the elder Mr. Murphy draw up his will; he had left most of his fortune to charitable foundations, but his son's fortune had vanished, along with other dot-commers.

Nathaniel Murphy stayed in her imagination. His fall had been dramatic, public, and she wondered at his profligacy and hubris.

While the sun sank at its own speed, Abigail imagined the younger Murphy's hand hitting the sides of the metal security box. He was in a dark hole, yet everything surrounding him gleamed. He was like a character from a Patricia Highsmith novel, not Ripley, but others whose guilt registered on a human stock market. Abigail felt she had suffered too much to be guilty about anything, but Nathaniel had cost people millions, he'd wasted everything he had from birth and more. Being poor again terrified her, the thought made her sick, but he had no idea what it was like, and, rather than provoking resentment, it added allure to his mystery, even innocence.

The elder Mr. Murphy once revealed that Nate's wife had asked for a divorce right after the crash. He couldn't help him, Nate made terrible choices; he gambled, not invested; he's a playboy, his father confided, with time to kill. He's drinking too much, and the girls sail in and out of his life. She liked Mr. Murphy, who was a gentleman, but she would have protected his son better, guided him. Abigail kept close watch on her own money, talked to her broker daily, and flushed with warmth when, each month, she saw her accounts swell.

A guard closed the vault's massive doors behind Nate. He turned a corner and walked down a hall, where Abigail encountered him. Abigail hadn't planned it, she'd gone to the women's room, and their paths crossed. They had several times before, when they would nod indifferently, but Abigail was never indifferent, she'd admit later. This time she stopped, and he did also.

—I'm sorry about your father, I liked him, Abigail said.

—Thank you, he said. He liked you, too.

She had never noticed how green his brown eyes were, almost olive, then she realized they were just standing, not talking, and she must have been staring into his eyes. She tugged at her short skirt, meaning to return to her office, when he smiled familiarly at her.

—You like it here?

—Sure, I'm here, yes, I do.

—They let you wear short skirts.

—I wear what I want.

Five weeks later, the younger Mr. Murphy moved in.

That first night in a corner of the bar at the Hotel Pierre, Nathaniel kissed her with restrained ardor, and Abigail knew much more inhabited him. He told her about his insecurity because of his father's reputation, she told him her mother cleaned houses, her father couldn't keep a job. But what mattered was being close to him. The next night, he whispered words that infuriated her, yet her breath stopped anyway. He'd been in love with her since he first saw her, his father told him she was the one, and with him her life would be happy—I am happy, she said—he could make her happier, babies, if she wanted, millions of orgasms. I've heard that in hundreds of movies, Abigail said, maybe not the bit about orgasms. After he kissed her without restraint, Abigail lost the sense of where she was. I'm not a movie, Nathaniel muttered into her ear, I'm just a soft touch for you. Curiously, she saw old Mr. Murphy in him.

You're the soft touch, her friends insisted, you're nuts, he'll screw you. They'd never seen Abigail like this, she had never felt like this. You'll wash his stocks at night, her best friend quipped, but nothing swayed Abigail. Against her exasperated friends' advice, Nate moved in.

They were happy. What her friends hadn't realized was that Nate was crazy about Abigail, devoted. He lived up to his promises, she told them, he quit drinking completely, and every week he took meetings with smart entrepreneurs like himself. She knew both his desire and his drive, they both loved the game of business, and she adored him, he made her swoon. With her, she knew he'd succeed, and Nate told her he'd thrown away his little black book. But Nate had seen that in too many corny movies, so actually it went into the security box, a document of his bachelorhood, Abigail wouldn't mind.

They married in a mauve room in the Hotel Pierre, where her friends and his celebrated, his dotty mother in attendance, Abigail's family discreetly absent. A few days before, almost as a joke, they had signed a prenuptial agreement. It didn't mean anything; she was a lawyer, that was all. The newlyweds were delirious. She felt sexy and content with him, he felt like a man again.

Abigail's clients loved her, she helped them, a few lost big, there was some ruin, some bankruptcies, but, bottom line, she made money for the firm. A partnership came next. There was hardly time for sex, though Nate persisted in wanting to add to Abigail's orgasm account, as they called it. She turned him away once, saying, I'd prefer you made money, like, Make money not love. He was shocked and angry, and she took it back, but he was hurt, even wounded. You're soft, his father used to say, toughen up. Abigail tried to soothe him, but really she wanted him working, back on his feet, emotional support was one thing, financial another. She saw him retreat a little, but he'd come back, he'd understand. She didn't notice his drinking, he hid it, doing it only when she was at work or asleep. Now, less and less, he wanted to have sex, and she was too tired anyway.

Nate's best friend at Princeton called with a brilliant idea, and since Nate owned the sharpest biz head he knew, he wanted him as a partner, if Nate liked what he heard, and he did—an environmentally important and scientifically significant venture to develop microbes that absorb waste in the ocean. Nate needed a couple of million to invest, not much really, but he didn't have it. He would borrow it from Abigail, he told his friend, he'd pay her back when the business saw its first profits. She trusts me, Nate told him.

Later, Abigail unlocked the door to Nate's embrace. He repeated the conversation, every word, with embellishment more bubbly than the champagne he'd opened. She looked into his olive eyes, at his too-handsome face, and her friends' and his father's admonitions returned, as if written upon that face. He would use her, leave her, he'd take her money, he was a playboy. She fought her fear, an instinct maybe, after all she must love Nate, her husband, she should help him to succeed. Even so, she told him she needed time to think, because that kind of money was serious. Nate was stunned. Abigail saw disbelief in his eyes or weakness, like in her father's eyes, a beaten dog's eyes. In bed, far from Nate, Abigail dreamed someone was trying to kill her. Nate couldn't sleep.

Some days later, Nate said there's gold in the security box, grandmother's jewelry, take it as collateral. She hated his pleading, his putting her in an impossible position, he knew she had to protect her future. What if, she thought, what if . . . and she wasn't being selfish, life was unpredictable. She wondered why she'd ever fallen in love with him, he didn't know her at all. A hardness insinuated itself inside her, and a space opened between them that was palpable to Nate. He appeared to wither before her eyes, too insecure, she realized, he's nothing like his father. She couldn't name what he was doing to her, but it was wrong, everything about him and her felt wrong. Meanwhile, Nate's potential partner waited, an intrepid humiliation returned, and Nate even drank in front of Abigail.

Still, Abigail suppressed her nameless protests and went with him to open the security box. It was strange walking down the hall where they'd first talked and fallen in love, but more terrible she felt it was her death march. The guard opened the door, and Nate and she entered the vault, where two straight-backed chairs were brought to them and then the gray steel box. There was some jewelry, she could have it appraised, some certificates, gold, and bonds. Nate lifted one up to show her, and beneath it lay his little black book. When Abigail reached for it, Nate put his hand on her arm.

—It doesn't mean anything, I kept it like a scrapbook.

She shook his hand off.

—You lied to me.

She rose, his address book in her hand, evidence of everything she'd been thinking, no one could blame her, she wasn't responsible, leaving him wasn't selfish. But it meant nothing, he repeated the next day. It means everything, she repeated, she could never trust him again. He claimed she already didn't, she wouldn't lend him money, she insisted that he wouldn't have asked for it if he really loved her. She wanted a divorce.

—You never loved me, he said.

—That isn't true, I can't ever trust you again.

To Nate, her abandonment confirmed his father's bad opinion of him, and also that his past had caught up to him, it always would. Abigail had to protect herself, no matter what, he didn't understand.

Their prenuptial agreement made divorce relatively easy, and she was so calm, her friends believed she was in shock, but his betrayal had been awful, they all agreed. When Abigail heard he'd returned to all his old ways, proving her right, that he would've just dragged her down, she felt sad but also secure in herself. And she was herself again, her friends thought, especially because Abigail volunteered at an animal shelter on weekends and fed strays on the street as she had during law school. When people at the office asked why, she'd explain she trusted cats and dogs, humans domesticated them, so they're defenseless without us. But people, she occasionally added, people usually deserve what they get.

Story with Advice*
Rick Moody

Q: DEAR STORY WITH ADVICE, even though it's the furthest thing from my wishes, my wife seems to be in love with a waiter at the restaurant up the block. Can you help me?
Signed, Halfhearted and Disappointed to be Alive

A: Dear HH, what kind of wife are we talking about exactly? Are we talking about a Valkyrie wife who rides ahead of the armies dressed in chain mail and who is merciless with her unlucky foes? Does she practice a recondite martial arts technique featuring the *nunchaku?* Or are we talking about a wife whose nail polish matches the faded leatherette interior of her Mustang convertible as she crawls provocatively down the streets of the shuttered local shopping district? Are we talking about a wife who once laughed and joked freely, but who now greets her morning cup of half-decaf with a joyless resolve? What would it mean to give up all hope, HH? And why is coffee so important? Is your wife the sort who crushes suspension bridges between her teeth and then uses the remains to pick out bits of spinach or broccoli that are trapped between her crooked incisors? And have you evaluated *your* commitment to *her* commitment to *your* misery?

Q: Dear Story with Advice, I used to feel that my job—copy editor at a small golf-themed magazine—was exciting and fulfilling. There was the potential for upward mobility. I believed I was contributing to a good-natured dialogue within the golf community. But now I just want to garrote the editor and hide his body behind the HVAC ducts in the subbasement. It's the same soul-destroying task, month after month, year after year. Does no one know the difference between restrictive and nonrestrictive clauses?
Signed, Despondent and Detail-Oriented

---

*All questions genuinely submitted.

A: D&DO, are you the same guy who wrote the letter about the wife who was in love with the waiter? I'm afraid I can't be responding to some malcontent twice in one week. It wouldn't be fair to the legions of respondents who have urgent questions. Hammertoes! Gender dysphoria! Tuna casserole! I have work to do! Nevertheless, I recognize that I did forget to ask what kind of restaurant that waiter worked at. What variety of cuisine exactly? The cuisine is germane to my reply. For example, I personally can't eat Italian food. Allow me to explain. As a young, innocent Story with Advice, a cocksure stripling who dreamed only of a successful owner-operated business involving compassionate advice giving, I lived under the auspices of a patient and generous single mother who almost certainly had issues with chronic depression. She'd walked out on the autocratic paterfamilias because of his insistence on *whole milk*, and for her this was an empowering gesture in the heady days of "first wave" feminism. In the years following, my siblings and I were not allowed to eat any kind of sugary cereal. Nor were we permitted colas or other corn-syrup-enhanced soft drinks. Despite my feelings, then, of imprisonment, I think this nutritional approach is sound for any and all children. No sugar cereal! Cereal should help build sound dietary habits. Raw fish for breakfast!

The point is that my generous and loving mother, who, as I say, almost certainly had an affective disorder, served the Story with Advice pasta rather often. In those days "pasta" was more frequently known as "spaghetti." And in those days the sauce for "spaghetti" came out of a jar that did not, I'm afraid, have Paul Newman's face on it. This entrée, this so-called "pasta," was served regularly enough that on the days when it was *not* served, the omission was noteworthy. The result of dietary monotony is well documented in the professional literature. The Story with Advice can no longer eat Italian food of any kind, not *gnocchi*, not *parmigiana*, not tomato and fresh mozzarella cheese. So, my detail-oriented correspondent, if the restaurant employing the aforementioned waiter-Casanova happens to be an Italian restaurant, then my feeling is that you are in deep shit. Indian food, OK, as long as it's not one of those bargain-basement Indian restaurants where the lamb is probably feline. Mexican food is always satisfying, and in this case your wife's Lothario is liable to be a foreign national or at the very least a recent immigrant, which suggests that this waiter may be able to repair your grouting.

Rick Moody

Q: Dear Story that Gives Advice, I keep writing questions for you, but they all seem to involve sex or loose stools. I become embarrassed and erase them. I guess my real problem is that I am embarrassed about who I *am*. I second-guess myself in every situation, always feeling there is some other better way to be, think, or talk. It takes all the fun out of life. Can you help me?
Signed, Woman who Asks Stories for Advice

A: Dear Woman who Asks . . . *loose stools?* Well, this certainly is a topic I can sink my teeth into. Not like *that,* but you know what I mean. Let me hasten to point out that loose stool is not a subject that people often write about. In fact, yours may be the first mention of loose stool in the entire history of the Story with Advice. People might be reticent about any kind of *stool,* or *scat,* as it is sometimes called, and this despite the fact that they have likely seen episodes of animal-related television programs in which *scat, droppings, wastes, feces, dung,* or *stool* are useful as tracking residues. As you know, in these episodes, there is usually discussion of whether the scat is warm or cool. In these broadcasts, indigenous populations are presumed to have less abject relations to scat temperature assessment. Yet I imagine this amounts to a crypto-imperialist representation of indigenous persons. When these aboriginal guides crouch down on their hams and attempt to warm their palms over the steaming piles of feces, I imagine that some kind of Orientalist nonsense is taking place. Still, I assume, Woman who Asks, that you are not inquiring about steaming heaps of elephant dung, but about your own stool. You are wondering if loose stool would be acceptable, if, for example, you were being tracked in some kind of reality program. What if a group of indigenous persons were attempting to locate you in, say, the greater Los Angeles area in order to fire blow darts into you, the type of blow dart that would make you keel over and dream? Would you prefer in this instance that your *scat* or *stool* were warm and of a firm consistency? For the cameras?

I say there is no normative standard for stool consistency! Any kind of stool is acceptable, as long as you have a balanced diet! As long as you are eating liberal daily helpings of roughage! Indigenous persons should not stoop to the prejudices of stool profiling, based on criteria of consistency or temperature, not in polite society! I support legislation along these lines! Indigenous persons, according to carefully negotiated contractual arrangements, should, during any broadcast, think of you as a worthy and noble antagonist, despite the quality or quantity of your droppings. Meanwhile, you, Woman who Asks, need to accept yourself as someone with loose or unfirm stool, and if that means gentle affirmations prior to waste production, so be it. If you can't feel good about waste production, you certainly aren't going to feel good about anything else in your life. I have composed a text for the affirmations I'm suggesting, and can make them available to you for a modest price. Please contact my interns at the e-mail address shown below.*

Q: Dear Story with Advice, the normal clothing size for American women is size 14. But can you advise me on what is the normal size, on average, for the labia? One measuring standard could be when a woman is standing with her legs slightly spread. How much of the labia can be seen—for instance, is it an inch that hangs below the outer lips? Please advise.
Signed, Anatomically Curious

A: Anatomically Curious, you can tell me. Are you the gal who asked the earlier question above about loose stool? What is this? Some kind of conspiracy to get me to address only questions that will redden the face of the Story with Advice? Next you'll be wanting to tackle *smegma*, which as you know is the cheesy, sebaceous matter that collects around the glans penis and in a similar spot in the female of the species. Let's just get it out of the way, shall we? I know very little about *smegma*, but I have an excellent research team. I can point you in the direction of self-help groups that aid and counsel those with a self-hating problem as a result of their smegma production. There are myriad Web sites on the subject.** But wait! Anatomically Curious, you didn't even ask about smegma. No! You asked, in fact, a question that clearly reveals you to be a worshipper at the Temple of Bodily Dysmorphia. You have any number of dysmorphic tendencies, I suspect, such as a belief that one of your breasts points in the wrong direction, or that your nose is too large, or that your earlobes do not hang free far enough, and this constellation of dysmorphic tendencies, which affects one in fifty, here in this country of obese persons and Diabetes Type II, has become common enough that it is now possible to offer cut-rate elective treatments to persons with your complaint, procedures such as labia minora

---

*info@livesofdignity.com.
**For example, www.circumcisionquotes.com/index4.html.

reduction, labia majora remodeling, pubic liposuction and lift, reconstruction of the vagina and external genitalia, vaginal rejuvenation, and clitoral reduction. I will require only a nominal finder's fee for pointing you in the direction of board-certified professionals. Personally, I like the idea of *vaginal rejuvenation,* and if you are a person of reasonable means and have already exhausted the more obvious parts of your physique, I think you may as well undertake *all* these aforementioned procedures as well as pledging yourself to the Temple of Bodily Dysmorphia. There's an urn in the church that serves as a repository for severed toes! And need I say? These toes were *electively* eliminated.

Q: Dear Story with Advice, I require a narrative that delivers a transcendental epiphany and that affirms certain basic human truths, such as the need for compassion among the wretched peoples of the earth. Can you deliver?
Signed, Young Media Worker

A: Dear Young Media Worker, were I to ignore your question, or to fail to give it the earnest reply it solicits, I would run the risk of seeming as though I, the Story with Advice, do not provide advice on *all* subjects and am somehow unable to manage your larger philosophical problem. However, I have a reputation to protect. I am a first-class life counselor, easily as good as any of those rank amateurs at Promise Keepers. Werner Erhard shudders at my name, as does what's his name, the guy with the teeth. I have a program that I am getting on its legs at present, so that I may retire more securely than I might do as a mere piece of literary fiction, and that program is entitled *Lives of Dignity.* I don't want to belabor Lives of Dignity just now, because I don't want to distract from the rollout of its product line, which you can anticipate in the coming months, perhaps as soon as winter 2007.* This journey of discovery may be the very thing for you. Allow me, if you will, some backstory. Your humble Story with Advice has lived through adversity, through dark nights, including decades of alcoholism and periods of major depression. Yes, notwithstanding my pharmacologically enhanced breezy attitude, I am an Advisor with a Dark Past. Just recently, on the way

---

*For those with busy lives, Lives with Dignity announces the new 900 number. Available anywhere anytime for just pennies, the Lives with Dignity 900 number promises results for vexing problems in under five minutes or your money back on all future calls! Just dial 1-900-R-E-S-U-L-T-S today! Operators standing by!

home from a weekly tennis outing, I was lamenting how, in middle age, a Story with Advice will inevitably come to feel that he was once a person of more passionate feeling for whom everything was *not* a joke or a confirmation of the hopelessness of what people used to call the human condition. Certain songs associated with those I once loved leave me misty eyed and remorseful. Now, in lieu of ambition and diligence, what I try to do is *keep the money rolling in*—this is, in fact, one of my professional motivational slogans—so that my dependents can live the life to which they are accustomed. I see myself as failing, basically, one day at a time, failing better, failing in ever more glorious ways, failing at length, failing from sunup to sunset, failing with people, failing with institutions, failing with ideas, failing for the sake of history, and I see my body as collapsing, my hair falling out, my skin getting more patchy and mottled, and my virility beginning to be compromised, *but* . . . hang on a second, there's someone at the door . . . hang on—

Who should enter into the scene, occasioned by energetic battery at the door? None other than **American Literature,** *here dressed in a rather casual workout outfit, one made entirely of synthetics. There is a mesh top. His pectoral muscles, swollen with human growth hormone or other banned training enhancements, are easily visible beneath his weave of petrochemical crosshatching. So baggy is the bottom half of this outfit that a jumpy or excitable person would imagine that* **American Literature** *is carrying a concealed weapon, a shiv, or perhaps a semiautomatic handgun, fully loaded.* **American Literature,** *despite his reputation for gentle, meaningful depictions of everyday dramas, despite his concern for the little guy, turns out to have a fair amount in common with a regular street thug or gangbanger. Thus, before the Story with Advice can continue with the train of thought sketched out above,* **American Literature** *interrupts, claiming a mandate from what he calls* rank-and-file members *of a shadowy academic organization or book group about the condition of the pages you have just read, including sentence-by-sentence criticism, suggestions for cuts, and a reminder that the story would be improved with the presence of lovelorn women of Canada. There is also a passing remark on the differences between classical and modern architecture. Why? Who knows?* **American Literature,** *who is unable to pronounce the big words in the rhetorical argument that follows, nonetheless attempts to deliver this missive from the so-called* rank-and-file members *in a stentorian but halting reading style. He occasionally stops to scratch his groin:*

"Dear Story with Advice, a k a R_____ L_____ of Middletown, CT, age forty-two, balding, ten pounds overweight, with anchor tattoo on right buttock, delinquent frequently on car payments. The following is intended as a discussion of the housing structure built and owned by the Story with Advice and his common-law wife of fourteen years—also occasionally inhabiting at this domicile, when not delinquent, the son known as Junior. We, the undersigned, respectfully request to know if it is true that the Story with Advice has engaged the services of an architect who specializes in a certain subgenre of modernist architecture relying heavily, for interior design, on the domestically manufactured product called *duct tape.* Do you, Story with Advice, we respectfully request to know, believe that duct tape amounts to up-to-code construction material, such that you would allow duct tape in all the rooms of your house, even in the presence of water or mold spores? Would you use duct tape to resolve your water damage, would you use it to patch old mortar? What about in the presence of peeling paint? Would you use duct tape at all times and in all places? Why are you so fervent in the matter of duct tape? We, the undersigned, have elected to engage the services of **American Literature** in order to express our belief that standards of decency militate against a house built entirely out of duct tape or duct-tape-reinforced building supplies. Moreover, we prefer, as **American Literature** will reiterate to you in the presentation of these arguments, that all domestic structures have gables, mirrors, his-and-hers bathrooms, a two-car garage, trees known as cypresses, little lines on the door jamb that indicate how tall Junior was at various stages of his life, a doggy door, a backyard with poison ivy and certain kinds of herbs, an obstreperous neighbor with body odor who complains about the noise you have made in the past and will continue to make, and coyotes.

Did we mention a proper chimney? A chimney is required for the national winter holiday shopping spree, which is the engine of the American economy. By opposing the use of a chimney, you are opposing the national winter holiday shopping spree, and unfortunately this is the time of year during which **American Literature** is most effectively marketed. We urge you not to antagonize **American Literature. American Literature** has been to anger management classes on several occasions, and he has points on his driver's license

for aggressive tailgating. He once took a baseball bat to the windshield of a neighbor's Chevrolet Suburban. **American Literature** is part of the recovery movement, it's true, but he may also have had relapses, and he may even have tried new drugs we know nothing about, such as *crank*. It would be better for you if you had a chimney or a television aerial. **American Literature** can do things you will never be able to do. **American Literature** can bench-press three hundred pounds, and can do two hundred sit-ups. **American Literature** has taken classes in business administration. **American Literature** protects his younger sister, and when **American Literature** needs to fix leaks in the pipes under the sink, or when **American Literature** needs to move a sofa out onto the street, he doesn't call some Middle Eastern mook on the telephone, he simply undertakes the relevant task. **American Literature** believes in rugged individualism, not in medication. **American Literature** once beat up a homosexual who offended his honor, and that homosexual died of his wounds. **American Literature** contains no foreign words, few adjectives, and it prefers quotation marks for dialogue. **American Literature** likes open space, and he likes filling up the open space with computer-designed subdivisions. **American Literature** believes in personal responsibility. If you care at all, take up your sword and fight.
Signed, Raymond Funster, PhD, Morris Stewart, Shelley R. Kuhn, et al*

At some point in the recitation of this argument, the Story with Advice, who has taken note of the fact that **American Literature** *is unable to read effectively and to monitor his surroundings at the same time, has crept up from behind with a blunt force instrument, namely a common fire iron, and has administered repeated blows upon the cranial structure of* **American Literature.** *The back brain, which houses autonomous function, is particularly affected by these blows, and yet none of the furious assaults constitutes the sought-for* coup de gras. *Tenderer readers may be unprepared for the bloodletting that thus begins. You know how head injuries are. The first blow falls right above the right ear of* **American Literature,** *and actually threatens to excise that ear from its body, and* **American Literature** *groans dully as the blood begins to fountain forth from the crevice above his ear. He is still gaping at the gouts of blood, as these spatter his white synthetic*

---

*More than twenty-five names were appended below those shown.

353

basketball outfit, when the second blow strikes him fully in the temple. Who would have known that the Story with Advice would be such a coward as to attack an unarmed literary allegory, when that personage has done nothing but read aloud a letter about duct tape? The blow administered to the temple seems to have no other purpose than to erase **American Literature** *from history, here on a calm, genteel suburban street. The Story with Advice cries out with unbridled abandon, "You thought you could mess with the Story with Advice, motherfucker? You thought that because I am slight of build and am a pacifist on most international conflicts that I am a pushover? Fuck you, buddy, I'll see you in hell!" He then attempts anew to puncture-wound* **American Literature** *with the fire iron. However, whereas it seemed in the early rounds of this confrontation that* **American Literature** *couldn't possibly come back from such a strategic disadvantage, the fact is that the Story with Advice has few decent punches in his arsenal—well, maybe an irritating right jab.* **American Literature,** *on the other hand, was trained in the boxing rings of the inner city. He has good footwork. He specializes in the heavy bag, and in moving around an opponent. His trainer is an old one-eyed Chinese man with cerebral palsy who is skilled in the ways of the ancient ones. Thus, within moments,* **American Literature** *has bloodied the Story with Advice's right eye, and the blood is now occluding the fighter's vision. The Story with Advice attempts to wipe away the blood but this costs valuable time. He stumbles. Despite* **American Literature's** *speed and agility, a moment arrives when the opponents sit at opposite ends of the couch in the living room, catching their breath, bleeding profusely. When recovered, they redouble their efforts. Immediately, the Story with Advice finds himself pinned down against a coatrack, where his kidney is being bludgeoned repeatedly, savagely. Is this not enough? Does not a legend like* **American Literature** *avail himself of mercy when the time is at hand? Is this not what we have learned from the great books? Hardly. Now* **American Literature** *removes from his basketball trousers a .357 Magnum, and he levels this deadly weapon at his foe, who is, after all, a middle-aged academic who drinks too much, wears old tweed jackets, attempts to seduce the wives of friends, and who was never good at any sport.* **American Literature** *remarks thus,* "Any last words you wanna say? Something for your fan club?"

The Story with Advice, again huffing and puffing, awaits.

Certainly, he must know that his time is short. There is the matter of his legacy, as writer and critic. What was it all for? A few scraps of the good old times call to the Story with Advice now, as the weapon is leveled at him, summer days with perfect breezes, as when he first tried to explain to Junior the basics of Texas Hold 'Em while they were canoeing on the Colorado. Still, the Story with Advice determines that he will not dignify his annihilation by sentimentalizing the past. He will die upstanding, unrepentant, which is exactly what he does, as gunshots ring out in Middletown, CT.

The gore is astounding. An enormous hole is blown at short range into the midsection of the Story with Advice, the exit wound being even more viscous than the entry, and because he is standing near the sofa, his entrails are scattered wide upon sofa and coffee table, likewise upon books piled everywhere. The intestines of the Story with Advice look like sausages, one length of which is cradled in a fresh bowl of potpourri. His liver, largely intact, resembles a manta ray drifting in the bottom of his son's fifty-gallon fish tank. And the chandelier in the nearby dining room shimmers with pinkish highlights, the patchy bits of his muscular tissue. In this tableau of savagery, what remains of the Story with Advice crumples to the floor.

American Literature *looks at what he has done, at the slaughter he has committed, and it dawns on him that he is now a* **wanted man.** *From one hand drifts the letter you read above, from the other his illegal and unregistered handgun. In an instant, everything has changed. There's no time for regret.* **American Literature,** *the murderer, begins to run. The front door of the house belonging to the Story with Advice hangs open on its hinges. There is the smell of saltpeter and emptied bowels. A woman across the street, in the act of watering hydrangeas, commences to scream.*

In the week that follows, the tragedy of the Story with Advice lingers in human consciousness. Not only in the headlines, but in the following way. Advice questions that had been disregarded or cast aside, in a cheerier, friendlier time, a time of leisure and confidence, begin to appear through publishing channels analog and digital. These letters seem to have an uncanny, elegiac quality. We now present these posthumous writings for the first time.

355

Rick Moody

Q: Dear Story with Advice, I'm obsessed with my fear of head lice. I cannot sleep, thinking that there is something crawling on my scalp. It's affecting my work, and my husband won't discuss it with me anymore. I feel shunned by my friends, and I've even turned to my young son for scalp inspections. What should I do?
Signed, Lousy with Fear

A: Dear Lousy, have we not all felt adrift on floodwaters of fear? Have we not trembled at the possibilities in store for us? Have we all not found that we are scratching unreasonably at parts of us that are not socially acceptable? I'll be honest with you. A day has not passed that the Story with Advice has not searched out shelter that afforded him the luxury of digging into his trousers, front and rear, in order to remediate an itch. Sometimes my eye sockets bother me enormously. On one occasion, I was given a powerful medication to help me relieve myself of this itching. This medication left me sleeping the sleep of the blessed and naive, and I emerged from this itchy time a better adviser to those who would put their questions to me. Who are we, finally? Are we identical with our bodies? If bits of our bodies were to be chewed off and carried away by pygmies, would we think of this as a reflection of our moral standing? Would our identities, our *selves* be any the less? Peace of mind is a worthy goal, serenity is fleeting, but what is that noise behind the wall, that sudden report? Are you familiar with that fragment of early romantic poetry that goes, "The louse is good, the louse is fair, and when he's gone, none visits there. So brush thy locks, take up thy comb, the louse would have thy raven hair."

Q: Dear Story with Advice, where can I find a nicely designed two-sided clock?
Signed, Equal Opportunity Shrink

A: Dear Shrink, I have done some research, or at least my team of assistants has done some research, and we have found a number of high-end stores that offer two-sided clocks, many of these designed for the elite market of PhDs, CSWs, MDs, and others who hunger for these timepieces during the fifty-minute hour. Apparently, two-sided clocks are not such a niche technology among discerning retailers of the two coasts. What these retailers do not realize, what *you* do not realize, is that with a two-sided clock, Shrink, one side of the clock will always run *backward*. Perhaps, Shrink, this is in fact what you are looking for? Perhaps subliminal in your request is a desire to undo the time you have given over to the myriad neurotics of your lengthy practice. Think of those many hours, Shrink, that you might thus repeal! How many years of sexual compulsion, marital tension, drug addiction, and bulimia. I'm guessing that you feel, like I do, that there are many days that have escaped. You are now counting these days, watching suns tumble into the end zone of the horizon, knowing that destitution and physical decline await you. And you are wondering, with all the miracles that science brings us: can it really be so hard to design a clock that will repeal these wasted years? I feel your pain, Shrink. The Story with Advice knows, too, that his time is limited, he knows that the good days are now mostly recollected. He knows that recollection is sweet, but is not nutritional enough to fortify. Has not the Story with Advice also wept at the fleetingness of all this, at the many things from which he must soon take his leave? He has felt like weeping. And yet, Shrink, he is unwilling to long for what he cannot have, and thus he looks forward, even welcomes the time when someone else can be answering letters as desperate as this one, when someone else can succor the needy and destitute. This is the way of mankind. One day I hold you up, and tomorrow it is I whom you carry. When we are gone it will be another's turn. Make do with the digital clock and quit complaining.

Addendum, by Sheriff Gates McCoy, Luna County, NM

I was informed about the fugitive in this case by law enforcement officials from the Northeast. The wanted man, according to bulletins issued, was considered armed and dangerous, and this despite his reputation for having been of service to the township. Persons remarked, over the course of years, that the fugitive was a model of the community, that he kept largely to himself. Never bothered anybody. Was always kind to pets. For perhaps fifteen years, he has been a sexton at a nearby church, letting in prayer groups, locking up after, saying hello to the elderly, helping pregnant parishioners to and from their automobiles. While he was never considered effusive, never offered more than the minimum, while people occasionally found his piercing stare disturbing, the fugitive was a trusted fellow in this small-town landscape of his youth. How to square this with the violence of his crimes? In one six-month spree, according to the files perused by this writer, he put several cancer patients out of their misery at local hospitals, smothering them with whatever was at hand; he used unlicensed handguns to kill at least three security personnel at convenience stores and other cash businesses; he savagely attacked a number of homeless persons, remarking, according to one survivor, that their "lives were less than worthless"; prostitutes came in for grisly dispatch, involving hours of cat-and-mouse torture. In almost every case, at least from what can be inferred in reports, the fugitive's victims were the left-behinds, the people without hope, without means, without resources. Children from foster homes, orphans, the disabled, illegal immigrants, the elderly.

When I was told that the fugitive had come to my part of the country, I was naturally a bit concerned. It's not part of the job of sheriff, in my view, that I should be unduly preoccupied with the life stories of crime victims. Everyone has a heart, and what a heart means—besides the pointless hankering for things that you're never liable to get, anxious worry about the people you love, and the recognition that your life is short and will never amount to a hill of beans—is that you know what a crime victim feels. So you don't need to go too far out of your way to understand why it's important to apprehend a criminal this unprincipled. Law and order is what it says. It's about order. Stuff gets out of whack, you put it back where it belongs. Luna County doesn't have that much violent crime, just smuggling and border shenanigans. People swimming across the Big Muddy with possessions floating behind.

Still, when I got to the part of the file about the murder of the advice columnist, I have to say I came up short. I guess I'm the kind of fellow who occasionally reads advice columns in the papers. I like to watch television programs where advice is meted out for the regular folks. In general, I suppose I admire a willingness to help out another guy.* I just can't see what cause there is for a massacre like this, an advice columnist in his house, and you leave behind a bloody mess for the wife of the advice columnist to find? And what about his son? His son finds that body? The son stands up in the memorial service, a week or so later, and tries to

---

*I like the comical letters, too! For example, I admired the exchange that went: "Dear Story with Advice, I feel profoundly bored with my life. What can I do? Sincerely, Olive Hedgehog. Dear Olive, this letter has been impounded by the federal government because of the likelihood that with it you are signaling to foreign nationals in dormant terrorist cells."

make sense of all of it? He tries to find words to memorialize his dad, his dad who did nothing but try to help a few folks, and who had a few weaknesses, like anybody? The fugitive pried out his eyes. *Wasn't content to take his life, to silence his voice, paint his house in blood. He had to* pry out his eyes, *so that the columnist would never again see the cardinal fluttering up the street, or the lemonade stand by the post office and the earnest entrepreneurs gathered there.*

If the guy was in Luna County, I was going to find him, and I was going to lock this guy in a cell, no matter what it took. I put out the word to the boys across the county, and then we waited. Just as law enforcement was waiting elsewhere. I didn't wait like nothing was happening, of course, I didn't sit passively for the fugitive to appear drenched in blood. I went in search. But the problem that preoccupied me was that I just didn't understand why the fugitive—with his intellectual pedigree, with his understanding of arcane things—wanted to come to the desert of New Mexico. New Mexico is big, which is good when you're on the lam, but there just aren't that many places here to hide.

I looked in all the spots where a sheriff might look, here in the expanses of Luna County. I looked in the empty lands, where no bird and no livestock would pass the days of summer, I looked in the caves of distant mountains, where the mountain lions huddled by day, I looked in the river valleys, where the antelopes gamboled, I strode through the highlands, between stands of piñon, soundlessly, with weapon drawn, I snuck around the back entrances of the honky-tonks, where out-of-work cowboys loitered, where heartbroken barmaids with varicose veins served up last call, I wandered into empty storefront churches, where the preachers had run off the faithful and kept the donations, I visited the late-night supermarkets, where sleepwalkers dropped six-packs into their bottomless shopping carts, I hid behind the crumbling pillars of minor-league ballparks, where jugglers kept the shills happy during the seventh-inning stretch, I went to rodeos and scanned the faces of the red-faced desperadoes who awaited their chances to tame the wild animals, I unlocked the back doors of the municipal offices and county courts, I put listening devices in the telephones of high-school students who wore black overcoats, I went undercover into the nightclubs where the public address systems were long since exploded. I didn't care if it took months, I didn't care if it took years. I had let go of the people of

*my life, I had let go of the cashier at the dollar store, who I used
to take out for pie when her shift ended. I let go of the men working at the meat-packing plant, who drank at the saloon I fre-
quented, I let go of the bird-watching club, whose adherents
rousted me on the weekends.*

*It was in October that we believed we had him cornered. A
filling station at the edge of the ghost town known as T_____
had suddenly, ominously closed. The proprietor, a man of gre-
garious reputation, had not been seen in weeks. The looted
pumps had run dry. People who attempted to stop for gas believed they were being observed. And there were strange rustling
sounds in the shed out back. As though someone, or something,
was attempting to scratch out a Morse Code testament to his
confederates.*

*What a place of loneliness! Vultures just out of reach, circling,
waiting for the kill. Wind whipped over the prairie, itself bent on
getting out of this part of the state. When I came upon the scene,
I knew that I had never tasted love, I knew that I had done nothing but give up on the things I'd been good at. In pursuing the fugitive, the murderer, I had become* like *him, had become homely
and mean. Did I try to enter the building myself, or did I call for
backup? Did other men need to give up what I had, just to apprehend the killer? Did I ask them to make such sacrifices?*

*Again, I drew my weapon. It was cocked and ready. My revolver
had served me well over the years. It was cool in my hand. I circled around the side of the service station. The corrugated tin
roof, the broken-down neon, the empty shelves, the overhead
console where the cigarettes were normally stored. It was a filling
station, all right. There were any number of spots where a man
might hide. Then, behind the building, over by the shed, I heard
that inscrutable rustling. The heartbeat of the criminal? The latest victim, attempting with his final breath to make known his
whereabouts?*

*When at last I stood behind the filling station, I looked down
across a sweeping plain, toward Mexico, and it was then I saw
what was making the ominous sound, disturbing the grim silence
of that place—the leaves of an ordinary hardcover book, blowing
in the breeze.*

Her Monkey
Julia Elliott

AT THE DOORSTEP OF MY beautiful, disturbingly aromatic young girlfriend I paused to study the way the sunlight brought out the spots on my arms. I had spots aplenty. I felt gray and yellow, malodorous and pissy. To me, the cicadas sounded like a thousand snakes, rattling away in the desert. Poisonous oleander seethed around me, blooms the color of cartoon blood.

I wasn't ready to meet Chloe's monkey. Leave it to a girl like Chloe to have a monkey, and a story to go along with it: two months in the Amazon tracking a tree frog on the verge of extinction (a tiny purple creature that nested in the throats of flowers); partying with the Yanomami (they made her an honorary man and let her snort the sacred bark); sabotaging the traps of poachers who ransacked the jungle for bright pelts (that was how she'd found Kibi, eyes rolling in skull, fur clotted with diarrhea, ankle bone crushed). She'd blown her drinking money on a veterinarian. She'd spent the rainy season in a malarial tent, feeding the animal morphine and butterfly guts. Kibi was her spirit animal, she said—*a damaged phantasm of the trees.*

Yes, Chloe was a poetry slammer. She worked in a used bookstore owned by a man so old he claimed he'd done opium with William Blake. Because his shelves overflowed with paperback volumes of crusty verse that dropped a yellow dandruff when you opened them, and because the old bastard fancied himself her mentor, my Chloe's poetry was bloated with Chaucerisms. But she was lovely, with her frizzy mess of mad-princess hair, her velvet bodices, pomegranate lipstick, outmoded medical dictionaries, peacock feathers, amulets, fake nervous tics, nineteenth-century vibrators, and antique lace.

We'd been dating for three months and I'd not yet met her monkey. According to Chloe, monkeys are extremists—they either love you or hate you. The feelings of Kibi, Chloe assured me, did not always match her own. Kibi hated Dr. Dingo, her boss, which would, in Chloe's opinion, be like hating Santa Claus (I hate Santa Claus, and I'm pretty sure that doctorate is a scam). And Kibi'd loved her ex-boyfriend (a nervous glam nerd who worked at the library), whom Chloe hated.

I wanted the monkey to adore me. I wanted it to frolic on my shoulders when hyper and curl in my lap to nap. I wanted to feed the creature berries while stroking its delicate spine. If the animal loved me I'd dote like mad, but if it hated me?

Chloe's cheap plywood door, with its scabs of old varnish, was like the hideous rind of a desert fruit. But she opened it and led me into her pink interior. The Victorian revival wallpaper, once crimson, had faded to a mildewed mauve. She had a wine velvet sofa and red lampshades made of polyester gauze that gave the room a cheap glow. The purple shag was stained, and, according to Chloe, mushrooms grew in a certain corner. Scattered about were gilded frames, broken dolls, paper plates sprinkled with Pop-Tart crumbs, eye shadow kits, balding taxidermied animals, Mountain Dew bottles, spray-painted bones, paperbacks, CDs, and crumpled Camel packs. Her laptop sat on the medical cabinet she used as a coffee table. This was my first visit to her apartment, due mostly to the nervous state of her nine-inch monkey.

As far as I could tell, no monkey prowled the room. Chloe had not answered the door with the beast perched on her shoulder. I couldn't hear the patter of tiny paws because window fans roared hot air through the room. It was one o'clock. Chloe was already fucked up. She sipped red wine and scratched her flea-bitten calves with her long toenails. She stuck her tongue in my ear and said, "Kibi's being coy," then collapsed on the couch with a small eruption of her short crinoline. She sported a fake mink corset and upper-arm rubber-snake bracelets. On her bottom lip was a cold sore I wanted to suck. She flopped and sighed and flashed bewitching crannies of pink flesh. Her mood ring glowed like a toad's third eye.

"Where is it?" I said.

"Where's what?"

"That monkey of yours."

"What monkey?"

Chloe burst into giggles. She sat on the other end of the couch. Was there or was there not a musky primate lurking around, weird thoughts crackling through its meatball-sized brain? I felt like an idiot for believing in the monkey, though I thought I smelled monkey in the room: the warm, fresh smell of kitten laced with a wilder, darker funk.

My soul screamed for a cigarette, but I didn't appease it. If the

362

monkey existed, it might be disgusted by my cigarette breath. But then again, Chloe smoked, so the beast was probably addicted to secondhand smoke, which meant that breath untainted by cigarettes might actually smell alien, even frightening, to the monkey.

"When you were tracking the tree frogs in the Amazon," I asked, my voice ugly with sarcasm, "what kind of device did you use?"

"Device?" Chloe's huge eyes widened. "Oh, a microchip, of course."

I think she was smirking at me.

"What kind of microchip?"

"I don't know. To me it just looked like a speck of glitter. Each chip had a microscopic barb that penetrated the silky wet skin of the frog."

She grinned triumphantly.

I would have to Google tree-frog-tracking techniques.

"Kibi's probably under my bed," Chloe said.

We peered under her bed: hatboxes, battered shoes, piles of bald Barbies.

No monkey.

"Let's just forget about the monkey for a while," Chloe said. "She'll creep out eventually."

We drank wine and watched music videos, and when I tried to slip my hand into her corset, Chloe mock-slapped me. "I'm not that kind of girl," she said, imitating some fifties heroine, then she let loose a shriek of laughter, had a coughing fit, ran to the bathroom, slammed the door, stayed shut up for forty minutes, and then emerged, finally, in velvet shorts and a feather bra.

"It's time for Dr. Dingo's party," she said.

Dr. Dingo collected antique clocks, and when he had parties he thought it funny to set them ticking all at once. In the loft above his bookstore, clocks droned like insects and my girl flung her body around in the humid air. She laughed with her head thrown back, flaunting her throbbing throat. She charmed and coddled them, all the old liars on the geriatric art scene. In the stale church-smelling air, she scattered her fairy dust, ate the weird fish dip, drank the pink wine, danced to the tribal electronica, and flattered the bag whose paintings filled the room (they looked like children's Bible illustrations). I inched toward our host. He was talking about alchemical imagery in metaphysical poetry and the torments of his sinuses.

He'd cornered a humorless hippie who seemed relieved when I butted in with my lame theories on Martin Luther's diabolically possessed gastrointestinal system.

"In short," I concluded, "we can blame the religious right on a bad case of colitis."

The hippie stared at me and walked off. I suggested that the learned doctor convert his sinus ordeal into a religious philosophy. The learned doctor did not laugh. The learned doctor's small red eyes quivered behind lenses as he studied me.

Then he snickered and slapped my back.

"What do you think of Chloe's monkey?" I ventured.

"Monkey?" he said, becoming thoughtful again. A grin opened like a lesion on his face. "Her monkey." He elbowed me. "I'm very familiar with the silky little thing."

"Oh," I said, "well, does it like you?"

"Like me?" He frowned. "When I can catch the rascal!" The doctor chuckled, then strolled away to dazzle some bohemian bat. I was looking around for Chloe. Where was my magical sylph? Acid was gushing up from my esophagus. I swallowed the filth, clenched my fists, and moved toward the balcony.

The free wine that flows at art openings is like the sugar water in hummingbird feeders. Put it out and the iridescent birds will come. In the sweet night air the beautiful people were getting wasted— hoodlum poets and fake vampires, angelic guitarists and satanic busboys, waitresses who looked like ruined princesses, prep-school Yankees dressed like fifties rednecks, androgynous anarchists, SUV hippies, bois, grrrls, iridologists, and DJs, potters, putterers, hicksters, hams. A fat moon hung over the black spine of the Appalachians. Below on the empty street, a purple-haired urchin pedaled by on a retro bike. Exhaust floated over from the murmuring interstate.

Laughing, snorting, Chloe ignored me. I didn't want her to think of me as her jailor. But I couldn't stay banished in the loft with the sixty-plus frumps. So I inched around the edge of the young crowd, hunched, scowling, my seventies nylon dress shirt no longer cool, my jeans the wrong color, my gums receding, hair thinning, ass drooping, face crumpling, bones eroding, brain juice drying, cells mutinying. I sat down to sulk on a plastic chair. I think it was my liver that hurt. I said, Fuck it all to hell, and lit a cigarette. Let me kick myself tomorrow, I said, probably aloud, in a voice croaking with repressed tears.

And then one of the cashiers from the food co-op flitted over to ask me how my dissertation on the commodification of prison art was going. We shot the shit. I chain-smoked and drank the sick wine, eyeing Chloe like an anxious biddy. I said that all art, after a certain point in history, was prison art. The girl thought this was profound. An acupuncture student joined our conversation, changed the subject to the *Kama Sutra*, and spit drink upon my sleeve. We talked about Van Halen and genetic engineering. I faked expert knowledge on both, and the young folk blinked like wobbly fawns. The acupuncturist's horoscope had said she'd meet a wise teacher. The moon floated. Car doors slammed. I shook my cigarette at her, said, Watch out for filthy old frauds like me.

Then I noticed that Chloe had drifted away to a dark corner, and she was whispering with someone. Someone small and young and quiet. A librarian with skin the color of ripe figs, strawberry-chocolate milk, doves, dusky mushroom gills, etc. All this imagery came from Chloe's poems. Naturally I was haunted by Chloe's poetry, but not in the way that she wished. I stood up. I clutched wrought-iron railing. We'd forgotten to eat supper again. And lunch, what had I had for lunch?

I staggered over to Chloe. She and the librarian hushed up. I said something really stupid and pretentious, something along the lines of:

If the moon were a piñata and I bashed it with a stick, what terrible gifts would rain down from the sky?

Then I grinned like a chimp with termites in its teeth. I introduced myself to the librarian and shook his incredibly soft hand. I chatted him up about bands and films. And finally, I looked him in the eye and said, Have you met Kibi?

"Kibi?" he said. His long eyelashes fluttered as he stared down at his shoes (some kind of pointed leather sneakers I'd never seen the likes of before).

"My monkey," Chloe barked.

"Well, the thing is, well, just once," the librarian rasped. "And it was dark, so, you know."

"Did the monkey like you?" I gazed into the librarian's eyes. The librarian studied his plastic cup. "And so? Did the monkey? Or didn't the monkey? Like you?"

"I don't know," he said. "Um, you know; I'm not really sure."

"The monkey adored you," Chloe whispered, then she made a run for the bathroom. Seconds later her ex's new girl crept up, took his hand, tugged him away. She was much less flashy than Chloe—

Bermuda shorts, boyish hair—but very pretty. And I recalled another poem about the librarian, a little number called "Tightrope," in which the librarian hid in the shadows as Chloe, dressed in an orange ball gown and balancing ten monkeys on her head, rode a unicycle on a giant spiderweb excreted by a three-hundred-pound black widow. *I'm a one-woman circus,* the poem kept repeating. That and: *My moth, you sip from cryptic flowers.*

We were down by the ditch and frogs were singing their fat black songs. Every time Chloe retched, the frogs would shock the night with silence, then pitch into song again. On the way home from the party Chloe had kept up a giddy stream of gibberish, but when we pulled into her gravel drive, she'd burst into tears and run from the car, down toward the ditch where fetid water trickled and Queen Anne's lace glowed under the moon.

I held her hair while she puked. I stroked her spine. Chloe referred to herself in the third person and said that she wanted to die. Her ex'd said she'd never be a real poet. He'd published a story in some zine. He'd called her a drama queen. He'd never touched her breasts. He had a nipple phobia. He was allergic to perfume, sickened by bright colors, thought animals were too dirty to keep in one's house.

"Do you think he's gay?" she asked me.

"Let's discuss his sexual orientation inside," I said. "Come on, the mosquitoes are killing me."

"Kibi loved him, but he thought she was dirty," Chloe said. "He was reading some book on parasites and was really freaked about fleas. The whole time we were dating he was reading that book. He carried it around in his backpack."

"Come on, Chloe. Don't you need to check on your monkey?"

Chloe grabbed my hand and squeezed it.

"He couldn't stand my cigarette breath, but he hated the taste of gum."

"Fascinating fellow."

"I mean, I think he was, um, kind of allergic to me. I gave him hives. That's it. I made him break out into big fat hives." She laughed, then gazed at the moon to deliver her next bit: "I was poison to his tender young skin."

She let go of my hand and jogged toward her rotten back porch. I (fool) literally ran after her. Her keys had fallen out of her beaded bag; I had them in my pocket; I was waiting for her to need them, need me. For my usefulness, I was rewarded with a kiss on the cheek. And Chloe said: "Please don't leave; please stay with me. I've got to write a poem, but I don't want to be by myself."

Chloe brewed a pot of coffee. Chloe brushed her teeth. Chloe put on a loose ruffled gown that looked like something the Empress Josephine would've worn when on the rag. This gown matched the bleeding wallpaper. And Chloe paced and paced, massaged her temples, chain-smoked, flung herself down on the couch to tap at her laptop. She was writing a poem about a boy who was allergic to a girl. As I ghost-drifted around her apartment, she was giving her ex-boyfriend a rainbow of color-coded skin conditions, from jaundice to purpura. I felt monstrously bored. I tingled with animal feelings. I knocked a week from my lifespan with a smoking binge. Every time I tried to leave, Chloe'd stick her tongue in my mouth. Or stroke my ears. Or smooth my wild eyebrows with her thumbs. Of course I was looking for glimmers of her monkey the whole time: a tail flicking like a hairy tentacle, a paw reaching out to grab something shiny, a set of huge yellow eyes glowing in a dark corner. I listened for the mischievous crackle of monkey chatter. I sniffed the carpet for the spice of its piss. Sometimes I thought I smelled monkey. Sometimes I thought I heard monkey. I saw a dustball shoot up from a chair ruffle as though batted by a playful beast. Under this chair I found a rotary telephone and a green mermaid wig, which infuriated me.

"Where do you keep the monkey food?" I said, after searching Chloe's kitchen cabinets.

"Monkey food?"

"Yes, monkey food."

"Monkeys don't eat monkey food."

"What do they eat?"

"Kibi likes the same stuff I do."

Chloe rolled her eyes and went back to her poem. She was busy punishing her ex-boyfriend with a long list of archaic intestinal diseases. The poor fellow was pretty much defecating his own bowels, which my darling compared to purple ribbons and black Medusan serpents. I became so starved and depraved that I ate a whole box of Pop-Tarts, crouching on the back porch and smoking cigarettes between sugar rushes to give myself something to look forward to. I drank coffee, then beer, then tea, then bourbon. I threw up. I sat out in the moonlight and the clouds hurt me. I smoked half cigarettes, butted them out, then lit them back up again. I could think of nothing but Chloe and her monkey, which, for some reason, had started to appear in my mind's eye with green fur and twinkling silver teeth.

I dreamed of the monkey and the dream monkey woke me with its shriek. I lay in dewy grass, hungover in the cool dark, but soon, soon the fury of the sun would beat down on my flaky scalp. I'd drive home to my efficiency cube. I'd pick through my catalogs of prison art, sigh, drag myself to the shower with its black mildew. My mouth was full of glue. I felt green and bloated, sick with shame, enraged, filthy, hideous, stupid, damned, spastically boweled, vomit-breathed, crooked of spine, starving, nauseated, robbed of nasal moisture. I could imagine eating a spitting-hot sausage smeared with mustard and that's it. I sat up, shook off the spins, and staggered across the lawn, my left foot bare, my right foot wearing a drenched canvas tennis shoe. Near the concrete stoop I fell to my knees, hawked a sepulchral goober into brown azaleas, and had a cigarette. I found a half bottle of wine on the porch and sucked it down. I smoked another cigarette, went inside, fixed myself a cup of tea, and sat down in the living room where Chloe lay sprawled, her lips parted, the window fans blowing soft damp streams of night across her adorable body. A poem snaked down her computer screen. Her skin, yes, glowed, white under the strumpet red lamp. She did not twitch, cry out, murmur, or moan in her sleep, like my last girlfriend had, a short woman who'd taught emotionally handicapped children and abused Xanax.

I got semidrunk all over again. I thought I heard the monkey, crepitating what sounded like cigarette cellophane in the bathroom. There I found no monkey, but I did find a mess of female hygiene products wreathing the bathroom trash. And then something, some kind of musky animal electricity brushed near me as I stumbled down the dark hallway, but when I found the light switch it was too late to catch the creature in the flesh.

I would find the monkey. I vowed to find the monkey. I brewed a pot of coffee for this task.

I would methodically search each room, closing doors so the monkey couldn't slip from one room to another, beginning with the living room. There I discovered what looked like a purple turd, dried and seedy, under Chloe's dusty guitar. It smelled like tea; it might have been a piece of her insane jewelry.

My girl slept on, rolling over, smacking her lips, as my claws sifted through her stuff. I fingered the damp cups of the bra she'd shed earlier. I sniffed lipstick stains on dirty glasses. I smirked through her vinyl and kicked at her paperbacks and squeezed the lumpy bellies of her antique dolls. I avoided her laptop as I would have a glowing X-ray machine. I moved to the kitchen and closed the door behind me. I rifled through her weird blend of packaged organic super-foods and filth from Food Lion, finding, behind Jell-O boxes, a dried roach and a pack of flea collars. I found a syringe in a drawer that rattled with broken knives. I discovered a nest of newspaper under the sink, down among bleach bottles and ant spray, the kind of nest a monkey would probably make, the newspaper crumpled and chewed and flecked with short dark hairs. I examined the hair in the light—coarser than a cat's but softer than a dog's—and sucked one into my nostril when sniffing it.

Window fans blew night air through the house, blurring the love calls of crickets, infecting my old skin with longing, blood deep in my pores. I closed the kitchen door behind me. I stepped on the damp hallway shag, and when I pulled the string that set the lightbulb aglow, I went dizzy. Gnats crowded around my head to drink.

The hallway smelled musky again. Tufts of carpet had been scratched up and fuzzballs floated. I recalled that certain nocturnal monkeys had inch-long claws that enabled them to slice the bellies of lizards and feed on their dainty guts, skewering jewels of organs and hunks of haunch and crispy snips of tail. And of course, all monkeys had teeth. I imagined teeth so sharp that victims of monkey bites would feel no penetration, only the tug of the strong, small jaw as the angry little thing tore.

I stepped into the wet perfumed air of the bathroom and whisked the psychedelic shower curtain aside: shampoo bottles, gritty soap, a dank loofah. The wicker hamper contained no animal curled and dozing among sour clothes. But in the medicine cabinet I found a prescription salve, dated from a year ago: *For Kibi. Rub into inflamed area twice a day.* The crust around the mouth of the tube was brown. It smelled coppery. The beast, whatever it was, had to be in the bedroom. I shut the bathroom door.

When I turned on her bedroom light, flecks and wisps of debris floated over the bed as though something had been jumping on it. The air pulsed, and I knew that a kind of animal burned in the dead room, stinking and thinking and breathing the same air I breathed. I did not stick my head under the bed to peer. I did not want my eye barbed by a fingernail that'd evolved to probe bark for larvae. I squatted and lifted the frill of Chloe's ironic dollhouse bedspread. No monkey prowled among the hat boxes. There was a dresser the beast might've lurked behind. The monkey could've been cowering under one of the ruffled frocks Chloe'd left on the floor, or playing dead in her toy box, sprawling among mangy velveteen animals. But I sensed the monkey, tucked deep in her closet, back among her ugliest clothes.

The animal's nose probably quivered as it took in whiffs of my personal odor, processing information on my testosterone and adrenaline levels, the bacterial colonies in my mouth, the sad industrial processes that tainted the soap scum on my skin. Could the monkey, I wonder, sniff out the booze in my sweat and the dandruff on my scrotum? Could it detect despair in the pheromones my body spurted hopefully into the world? Did it notice the enzymatic havoc in my digestive tract and the acid that collected in a bitter glob at the base of my tongue? Did my liver smell rusty? Did my immune system stink, a brown and foggy emanation?

I felt hideously self-conscious as I eased open my girlfriend's closet door. The moldy odor of her vintage clothes floated out. The heart-pine walls of her closet had never been painted, and I could smell sap in the dead wood. The closet lacked a light and Chloe had stuck a stainless desk lamp up on a shelf that overflowed with sweaters and scraps of fur. I plugged in the ratty extension cord she'd hooked to the lamp. I stared into her closet. The right side of the closet was shallow, but the left side cut deep into the wall. And up in the far corner of the beadboard ceiling, above a stack of shoe boxes, was a big jagged hole. Familiar attic smells drifted down from the hole. And if Chloe's monkey existed, I knew that it would be up there, in the weird attic dark, in dusty air compressed by some outmoded and toxic form of insulation.

One by one I removed Chloe's costumes from her closet and draped them over her bed, until the pile of clothes toppled over, spilling silks and brocades and Technicolor wools onto the floor. I took a shot of bourbon. I grabbed the two fat dictionaries Chloe kept by her bed and stepped into the closet. The humming in my ears grew as I inched my way deeper in. I made myself a stool with the dictionaries, but it wasn't high enough. I went back to the room, grabbed two medical encyclopedias from Chloe's bookshelf, entered the closet, added them to the pile, climbed my shifty stool. Squatting, I lifted my face toward the hole. I did not thrust my sweaty head into the hole. I grabbed the lamp first and stuck that in, waved it around, spattering the red naked rafters with light. I listened for the sound of a shocked monkey hopping. I heard nothing and felt almost positive that there was no monkey (how could there be a monkey living in this apartment? what did it eat? where did it crap?). So I said, Fuck it, set the lamp down on a mushy section of attic floor, raised my arms into a dive pose, burrowed armpit deep into the warm dry attic air, and sputtered, sarcastically, the word surprise, my voice echoing, nerdy and reedy.

A white insulation that looked like fake snow filled the rafters. A tart smell blended with the stale cigar scent of ancient attic, an exotic yet familiar smell I could not at first place, but then recognized, with a spinal jolt, as the arrogant tang of animal pee. I thought I felt breath on my nape. And when I turned around to look the beast in the eye, it did not retreat. Nor did it come closer.

The monkey perched on a rafter a yard from my head, regarding me coolly with huge amber pop eyes, designed for nocturnal vision in a jungle where the moon is cut to pieces by thick canopies of trees. Its ears—fleshy, brown, semitransparent—shifted like high-tech satellite equipment. Its spiny, cartilaginous nose twitched. The nose was both slimy and hairy, the nostrils flaring like trumpet flowers. Its mouth was prim, pinched. The monkey held a nut-sized thing in its left paw, rotating the object with the blobby tips of its tree-frog fingers. The monkey crouched on thick haunches, ready to hop into oblivion again. Its tail, covered in gleaming blue scales and bristly near the tip, whipped in the dim air behind it.

Deep in the womb of the Amazon, where the soil is black and sweet as licorice, where trees never stop dripping and buzzard-sized butterflies flap in slow motion, mammals sometimes develop iridescent fur. Looking at this monkey, I understood the greed of poachers. I wanted to stroke the creature, relishing the contours of its skull, the way the fur changed where it grew from a thin layer of fat over bone, the way it thickened around the thighs and thinned near the belly, where silky pink skin showed through. I wanted to examine the shell-like chambers of its ears with a penlight, peer into its nostrils, and test the tips of its fangs with my fingertips. I wanted to tease its claws from their furry sheaths and stroke the long bones of its feet.

As a child I had squatted in bushes and spent intricate hours calling cats to me, in a language I fancied was feline. I had words for things cats loved—fish and sand and sleep—and I made promises to the cats, pulled them from their safe patches of shade, out into the sunlight where their fur sparkled. And in this old language my tongue curled and hissed once again, and I felt the same dry throat, the same fat heart.

The monkey had ears that closed flat and airtight to its skull during rainstorms, and these ears twitched to catch my music. The animal's pupils swelled. Its whiskers stirred. And the monkey leaned forward.

I rasped and hummed and clucked my tongue, and the monkey inched along the wooden beam until it was two feet from me. Its lips parted. A fang glimmered. I lifted my sweating hand into the air and presented my fingers, six inches from the animal's nose. It studied my hand and spent long minutes sniffing it, eyes unreadable. The monkey couldn't blink. It had some kind of nictitating membrane, fat wet corneas, irises with a lacy musculature. I kept crowing, kept murmuring, as my hand crept toward the monkey's soft neck ruff. I felt the tickle of fur against my fingertips. I stroked the airy outer layer. Moaning, crooning, I moved my fingers deeper into its silky coat, where the warm skin tingled with pleasure. I pinched each sharp knob of the primate's backbone, moving upward toward the spot where spine plugged into brain. My mouth clucked and whistled. I pressed my thumb into the throbbing place between the monkey's neck tendons. The beast jerked as I snatched it into the air, switchblade claws shooting from fingertips, but then it hung limp and swinging, light as a boot, arms splayed. Its eyes looked cloudy. Its pupils shrank to nothing. The animal might have been dead but I knew that it was not dead, that I could, with a special wriggle of my thumb, send volts of life rippling through its mysterious system.

Four Poems
Rae Armantrout

WORTH WHILE

A rod: a list,

a mop-top palm
cut out
against sunset,

chocolate
pastries in the shape
of pyramids,

an elderly, bent figure
beneath a feathered Stetson.

*

Terri fears
she may be risking her job
as an afterlife consultant.

Melinda is comforted by Jed
when she twists her ankle trying
to evade an angry ghost.

Unanswered questions
change things
beween Booth and Bone.

*

Rae Armantrout

A string of raindrops
dangling
from an iron bar reveals
opportunities for
clarity.

At the breakfast table,
Mary's dead parents
become impatient
when she counts the wad
of small-denomination bills
they presented her with
on her birthday.

FETCH

1.

Was it a flaming mouse
that burned Mares's house down
or was it just the wind?

On Tuesday Mares and his nephew
stood by the original version.

Is this plausible?

Fire Chief Chavez said Tuesday
that he thought so.

2.

Let's see

your itty-
bitten specificity
fetish,

your mom's phantasmic
what's-it

held conspicuously
under threat.

Day hoists its mesh
of near
approximations

(its bright
skein of pores).

Eyes fetch thrown
shadows

AMPLIFICATION

Some think
in the first days

Hunger and Lust
arose separately
and then paired up by chance

having only
self-love in common—

and what is that?

Still, what a pair they've been!

*

Some think we can
achieve escape velocity

if only we can make
our thoughts bounce

Rae Armantrout

harder and harder off
the near walls—

the limits—
of what is known,

what is trite
about these characters.

*

We have it
on good authority

that we're dying
to express this

one thousand times more
or less precisely,

dying to practice

LATER

1.
To be beautiful
and powerful enough
for someone
to want to break me
                                    up

into syndicated ripples.

Later I'll try
to rise from these dead.

2.

How much would this body
have had to be otherwise in order
not to be mine,

for this world
not to exist?

When would that difference
have had to begin?

3.

The old lady invited me to her soiree. Maybe I was even older
than she was. I was mysterious, at any rate, a rarity, until the room
filled up. Then not. When she handed out chocolates, she forgot
me. I gesticulated as if it were funny and she gave me two pink
creams. Me! As if I would have ever wanted these!

4.

They drive me
out to sea.

Secretly, I am still
_____, the mysterious.

I speak in splashes.

Later
I have the lonely dream

Four Poems
Lyn Hejinian

BETWEEN DAYS

The twin enemies of spontaneity are forgetfulness and doubt
As to the intention of the pigeons who are watching me
Watering the potted nasturtiums and the snapdragons
Between my fingers
Open their overlapping jaws and scream
Like paper silently
Pink, yellow, and green
Overhead
The clouds open to receive
Exhalations
Which the pigeons pass on—but I am nothing
After all
To them
But to you—the strange woman
And eleven girls—
Things would if they could be
Something—
"No addition, no subtraction—
Therefore perfect?"
Good!
The challenges set (or, as now's the case, sent) by the woman
Are only half met (as half meant) in music
As the afternoon light strikes
Strings, Venetian
And quivering, near twins
This night of all nights as an arrow flies
Between owls
When thought turns to distinctions we make
Between days
Mixing their realities with dreams and nights
Mixing their dreams with realities

Which are over and over the same
Again
Mockeries
Crow mocking cow, duck mocking truck, trowel mocking soil
And soil's worm
Mocking mockery
While we watch the clock clocking
Mockery's interval
Closing
The gap between pursuer and pursued
Which grows endlessly
More minute
And is never entirely lost
To memory
In which we accumulate history
Whose events are no more merely transitional
Than a bombing of Baghdad
Produces just a shift
Of possibility
Or of probability renowned and rising
Hands extended toward a black stone set at a safe distance
From a woman
Scrupulously harnessing fiction in its highest documentary form
Knowledge
Which is only a very fast sun but naturally
We want to be sure of this: the difference
Between that
And this between ice whispering and symbolists
And inks in horrible acts
Spreading
In exaggeration something protracting, radiating, prolonging,
    communicating, plunging
Like a free and wild body
Knowledge
Which only exists as *embodied* knowledge
And that's only very briefly ours

Lyn Hejinian

A DREAM OF A MACHINE

A dream, still clinging like light to the dark, rounding
The gap left by things which have already happened
Leaving nothing in their place, may have nothing to do
But that. Dreams are like ghosts achieving ghosts' perennial goal
Of revoking the sensation of repose. It's terrible
To think we write these things for them, to tell them
Of our life—that is, our whole life. Along comes a dream
Of a machine (why? what is being sold there? how is the product emitted?).
It must have been sparked by a noise, the way the very word "spark"
Emits a brief picture. Is it original? Inevitable?
We seem to sleep so as to draw the picture
Of events that have already happened so we can picture
Them. A dream, for example, of a procession to an execution site.
How many strangers could circle the space speaking of nostalgia
And of wolves in the hills? We find them
Thinking of nothing instead—there's no one to impersonate, nothing
To foresee. It's logical that prophesies would be emitted
Through the gaps left by previous things, or by the dead
Refusing conversation and contemplating beauty instead.
But isn't that the problem with beauty—that it's apt in retrospect
To seem preordained? The dawn birds are trilling
A new day—it has the psychical quality of "pastness" and they are trailing
It. The day breaks in an imperfectly continuous course
Of life. Sleep is immediate and memory nothing.

FOUR FABLES

Once there was a village surrounded by mountains and no one
in the village could stand up for longer than one hour without
laughing and falling down

Once there was a tiny black ant that scurried, paused, turned,
scurried, turned, and paused again, and twice there was one and
a third time, too, once, there was a tiny ant

Once there was a wayside weed that pleased those who saw it as
it bent in the wind and bounded back again in the sunlight and

380

died and came back as a frog whose singing lulled children to sleep
until it was swallowed by a heron and came back as a strong and
gentle horse that once hauled a wagon full of tired travelers over a
mountain and later lived in a field without much grass where it
died of starvation and came back as a musician who was very wise
and very knowledgeable and could remember everything that had
happened to him, including having been a wayside weed

Once there was a prince who liked to eat cherries and roll their pits
around and around in his mouth, past his teeth and under his
tongue and up again against his lips and sometimes from between
them the pit would pop out and drop

A SMALL SAGA

In the certainty of seeing something looking
Thinks across
Sudden switches linked to leaving
Timed to the arrivals and departures of trains
Of messages
Bound to each other by a subject heading becoming less and less
Relevant to the contents of the chain of events around which the
    messages clink
And clank in horror
Or shame at seeing
Maggots on meat
Or a mutilated boy
Objectively, as if anything could be viewed as uncharged
In a milieu free of charges and with no one
In charge
As tugs labor from the harbor
Pushing barges bound for bargain
Basement warehouses
Home to contests without context—mere spectacles
Interfering at eye
Level with reality—my favorite thing
And all there is however
Sad
It's said to be

Lyn Hejinian

So here it is, so near and far
From acrid smoke and smitten dogs
And girls with basketballs and bugs
So small or swift they can't be seen in my myriad
Dreams of other things—jackpots and a woman whining
That she doesn't understand this proposition
Or "that is why they cannot be composite"
Because "objects make up the substance of the world"
At noon, which will be along
Soon shucking corn
Past the orange house in which, fingers curled, the pumpkin people
     live long past the prime of life
But last
Like whales sipping plankton
From the Mediterranean Sea with rock fury
And rolling poetry that buoys a dinghy full of fisher folk pulling
In bass as the lighthouse beam passes like a hand
Of a clock
Rounding the bend that's a beacon for Evelyn—Evelyn—
Evelyn, have you legal experience—till she can't stand it
Anymore
And she races out the door to the Bering Strait
Legs crossing like scissors cutting an hour
From the journey and making it less
Gratifying than a bumpy ride in a wicker basket under a blue balloon
With three companions in search of the northern route
To the nutritious sun
As full of milk as the jug on my desk
From which my lamb whom I call To-the-Sky
Laps like the tide from sand or a child
From a cone
And beside it is my duck's egg and my rooster's comb
And turd almost immobilized under the sofa
On which I set sail under a thousand eyes
From inside
A rectangle no bigger than a grave
But it's a bed and its sheets are white and its blankets are red

Two Ligatures

Forrest Gander

LIGATURE

—For Valerie Mejer

It's not an insult to refuse to drain the glass, she tells me
And a fly crawls from the bowl of sauza picante.

Would you choose to bury the organs with the child?
And he retreats to his room and closes the door.

Here, birds in the zócalo whiz and tweet like children's toys
And there, a charred corpse hanging from the bridge.

From the seat behind, he pokes her head with a plastic fork
And getting no response, tests it on his own head.

Would you turn the damn wipers off, the attendant asks
And the odor of manure and wet hay hits us.

A kind of mystery gloms to those who have suffered deeply
And thank you Mr. and Mrs. Radiance.

It sounded like the chimmuck of a rock dropped into a stream
And the piston-driven breathing of sex.

The couple at the bus station—when had we kissed like that?
And *Nice evening—Yes it is—A bit skunky—That's for sure.*

Terrorist and victim circling the last chair as the music stops
And the valves of their mouths snapping open and shut.

When I rise out of myself into occasion, I said
And when do you rise out of yourself into occasion, she asked.

Late enough to count maple loopers and geometrids at the window
And our boy will be coming up the porch steps when he comes.

The long row of treadmills choiring
And above them, televisions replay the disaster.

LIGATURE

The name of my beloved is Irrecuperable. Liar.
The way to listen, announced Albert Ayler,

is to stop focusing on the notes. Listen
to everything together. I brushed on nipple rouge

in the morning. In the evening
I scrubbed it off. Devour me.

You said, *Two men are inside me. Remember
the other one. The one who did not do this to you.*

Eternally en route.
Like a dog is ripping my heart out.

This music I cannot listen to, it makes me dizzy.
While the pendulum swings stably in space,

the floor is carried around by the earth's rotation.
Yesterday the snow came, bearing no message.

The wooden chair on which you sat at your desk.
How you wrapped your shins behind the front legs.

From The Perfume of Meat
Jessica Hagedorn

I STOOD A FEW FEET AWAY, watching him Dumpster-dive in that alley by Heaven, foraging for food, God knows what else. *Heavenly! Girls! Girls! Girls!* The blinking neon of Heaven's marquee illuminated his intense scowl, the tight clench of jaw as he sifted through trash and debris with his bare hands. Neon blinking on exposed, sallow flesh. He was young enough to be my son, gaunt body a garish museum of mysterious names, mundane phrases, and sacred images. All he wore—in spite of the winter chill—were tattered pants, plucked at random from some Goodwill bin and much too big for him. His feet—caked with dirt, covered with open sores—were stuffed into rotting Adidas. His longish hair was matted, no doubt crawling with lice. I wrapped my arms around myself, dreamt of lice crawling through the veins beneath my skin.

I'd seen others like him, of course. Prowling the greasy twilight streets of the Tenderloin, death's silver aura shimmering above their heads. Would it make any difference if I told you that I'd been watching him for days from my little window that overlooks this alley? That he'd been climbing in and out of that overflowing Dumpster, finding nothing but always coming back? Tonight, he scraped something off one of those Styrofoam takeout containers and shoved it in his mouth. Tonight, with a swiftness and fury that were startling, he jumped down from the Dumpster to confront me. Such a face, chiseled and worn by anger and grief.

What the fuck you want, lady?

Nothing.

Fuck that. You get off lookin' at me?

There's a church around the corner. They'll feed you. Give you clothes and things.

Fuck that.

Don't ask me why, but in my bag was one large, ripe tomato. A very expensive, organic tomato—my one extravagance for the day—that I bought at some hippie gourmet food boutique in the Embarcadero. Take it, I said. He snatched the fruit. Bit into it, the juice and pulp running down his hand.

Not so fast, I said. You'll get sick.

He devoured the tomato in seconds. When he was done chewing, he licked his hand. Got any money?

No.

Why not?

What's your name?

Want me to fuck you?

What's your name?

If you pay me I'll fuck you.

What's your name? I'm Nena.

Mickey. Who is not the fucking son of fucking God or the fucking Holy Ghost as you might have fucking guessed, so leave me the fuck alone!

I stifled a laugh and didn't move away. Neither did he. Briny piss, dried shit, stale sweat, musky sex. His stench was overpowering. I pointed to the vertical Aztec serpent tattooed on his sternum and said: When I was a child, only convicts and sailors did this. *Fertility? Good luck?*

Power.

I pointed to *Zulma,* the name tattooed in gothic script on one side of his pelvis. And this? Wife? Long-lost love?

Mother, he answered.

I touched the tattoos on his right chest lightly with my finger. He kept his eyes fixed on mine. Flaming heart, I said. Crown of thorns, dagger, roses, teardrops . . . Mexican?

His voice was flat and calm when he spoke: pain of the world.

A lizard peered out from the hollow eye of a grinning skull tattooed on his right upper arm. Gothic, clichéd, yet gorgeous. I said: This one's easy. Death.

Then I touched him, pulled my hand back, couldn't bring myself to touch him again.

You got more food? he asked. I wouldn't mind more food.

At home. Not far from here.

You invitin' me?

I took the shawl from Kashmir off my shoulders. It's cold. Put this on.

He hesitated, sniffing the cloth before wrapping it around himself. I started walking away from the alley, gesturing for him to follow. Am I walking too fast? I asked at one point, not really expecting an answer.

Where I lived was one of those forlorn, five-story tenement walk-ups from another era. Soon to be razed and resurrected as a parking garage or five-star hotel, so the rent was cheap. My apartment was on the top floor, a railroady sort of thing with more rooms than I actually needed. The neighbors pretty much ignored me—stoic refugees and post-op trannie tenants who had more than enough troubles of their own. The manager, Mr. Tranh, lived on the first floor with several mangy cats in a tiny studio jam-packed with ancient toasters, broken-down radios, and obsolete printers and computers salvaged from the streets. Things that he had every intention of repairing and reselling, but never did. Mostly he smoked crack, indifferent to the tenants' comings and goings as long as we were on time with the rent. Which suited me fine. He once rang my doorbell at four in the morning, stoned out of his mind. When I opened the door, he shoved a portable thirteen-inch TV in my arms.

Comment ça va, professeur?

This isn't mine, Mr. Tranh. I tried giving the TV back to him.

Found in alley, the old man said, what was left of his voice a hoarse whisper. Black and white, superb condition! For you, *ma chérie,* only twenty dollars.

That's really nice of you, but I don't watch—

TV excellent for people alone! TV excellent for people who don't sleep! Like me . . . like you! Mr. Tranh cackled. You have twenty dollars?

Didn't you hear me? I don't—I tried giving the TV back to him a second time.

The old man wouldn't have it. Fifteen. Anything? I'll hook up your cable, Madame. No extra charge. No problem.

I shook my head. Tranh stared at me, dazed and disappointed, then left without saying another word.

So there it was. A dinky TV that hissed to glorious life when I finally turned it on. My addiction was immediate. I began watching *Law & Order* reruns when I didn't want to write, when I was bored and too lazy to go outside and take one of my walks. *Law & Order* is perfection in black and white. I was enthralled by the formulaic episodes: banal conversation followed by the discovery of a corpse or two, the subsequent investigation, arrest, and trial, the nervy and blunt-edged "tung, tung" theme song, the corny banter between detectives, the authentic New York locations. Tranh was right. TV made soothing company. I slipped a twenty-dollar bill under his door a couple of weeks later, along with a note of thanks.

I hurried past Tranh's door and climbed up the stairs to my apartment, Mickey close behind me. Tranh stayed hidden in his dark cave, from which wafted the toxic perfume of cat piss and burning incense. We heard the old man's hacking cough, what sounded like an exasperated woman's complaint. Harry, she was saying. Jesus Fucking H. Christ, Harry.

I unlocked the door and turned on the dusty overhead light. Large moving boxes were stacked against the wall, full of books and papers, shoes and clothes I didn't miss. Outside of one box, I never bothered unpacking when I moved here four years ago.

You movin' in or out? Mickey asked.

I've been here a while, I said.

Yeah?

Long enough, I said. Funny how little one needs in order to live.

No shit, Mickey said. There was a moment of silence, then: You're not afraid of me?

Should I be?

You a freak, he said.

Then maybe it's you who should be afraid of me.

Yeah, he agreed. There's always *that*.

I was almost sorry I'd said it. He suddenly resembled an old man, thin lips set in a grim sneer, ready for life's battery of disappointments. I took his grimy hand and led him past the kitchen to the bathroom. You can wash up, I said. I'm going out to buy lice shampoo. Flicker of a bemused grin on Mickey's face. I handed him a fresh towel and washcloth. Have fun, I said, closing the door quietly behind me.

I hurried over to the nearest Walgreens on Geary Street, wondering if he'd still be there when I came back. Would he steal from me? Slash open the moving boxes with a knife, hoping to find something, anything of value? I imagined he would be relieved at finding himself alone again, as he slipped off those tattered pants and putrefying sneakers. The cold tiles of the bathroom floor would feel good beneath those raw, bare feet. The tub was one of those deep, old-fashioned, claw-footed things with a shower. I imagined the sudden gush of warm water making him wince with pleasure; imagined how scrubbing himself with my harsh, pine-scented soap would make the lesions on his body sting.

A girl wrapped in a silver coat stood transfixed before the display of Christmas ornaments. She was achingly young, achingly beautiful despite the ravage. There any more trees? she turned to ask me. The white disco kind. Gotta have that. Artificial . . . white on white . . . y'know? That's what I want.

Sorry, but I don't work here.

My answer didn't compute. The thing is, the girl continued, growing more desperate, it's gotta be white! Just branches. No leaves or shit, nothin' to interfere. White! White on white!

Elegant, I said, attempting to soothe her.

She looked pleased, Yeah! *Elegant.*

I hated Christmas so much I hadn't noticed it was all around me. The treacly carols, the tinsel and frenzy. I thought of the boy back in my apartment, how he'd empty his bladder with a groan, watch the blood orange piss dissolve in water down the drain. When was the last time he'd felt so purged and clean?

I'm sorry I can't help you, I said to the girl who couldn't keep still.

She wrapped the silver coat tighter around herself. Tha's OK, lady. Happy fuckin' holidays to you anyway.

The shower was still running. I knocked softly on the bathroom door before opening it and depositing the Walgreens bag inside. I'd thought of everything. Toothbrush, a set of Hanes jockey shorts and T-shirts, a pair of gray sweatpants, a pair of flip-flops, a bottle of A-200 shampoo. There, I thought. Clean generic clothes to go with his now clean, nongeneric body. I retreated to the kitchen, busying myself at the stove. There were leftovers to reheat, rice to prepare

389

from scratch. He was starving and would want food next, surely. I didn't want to think about what I had done by bringing him home. Mad impulse. Same mad impulse that caused me to flee Manhattan. I didn't want to think too deeply about *that*, either. Cooking kept me occupied, while Mickey stayed in the shower for another half hour. The water had to be cold by now, unbearable.

Where my shoes?

Threw them away.

Need my shoes!

You need new ones. Just sit, why don't you.

Mickey sat down and glowered at the food on his plate. White rice on a white plate. Chicken adobo with collard greens. He began eating. The sauce would taste vinegary strange and delicious. What kind of food is this? he asked me with a look. He ate too fast. Slow down or you'll throw up, I said to him. He ignored what I said and helped himself to more rice and chicken, wolfing it down. I grew bored with watching him, moved to the adjacent living room, and turned on the TV. It didn't matter that I'd probably seen every *Law & Order* show ever made; and over and over, at that. Ah, bliss. Jerry Orbach's horsey, lived-in face appears on the tiny screen. It's a scene from one of my favorite episodes: the one where everyone is destroyed by guilt. Sam Waterston drinks too much, Jill Hennessy dies in a car crash. And it's poor Jerry Orbach as Detective Lennie Briscoe, ex-Broadway-Hoofer-Man-with-Too-Many-Demons Jerry Orbach, who ends up having to witness pretty Jill's abrupt, violent death. Love that Jerry. Those lame jokes he makes, those drowsy, heavy-lidded eyes. A notebook lies open on my lap. *Once upon a time . . .*

In the kitchen, Mickey finishes eating. He remains at the table with the oddest of expressions, staring at nothing in particular. I wonder if he'll demand money again. Or rape and kill me. Or kill, then rape me. My decomposing corpse and the crime, like a typical *Law & Order* drama, will go undiscovered for weeks. Until some neighbor complains about the mysterious aroma wafting out of my apartment, until Mr. Tranh snaps out of his crack haze just long enough to trudge up the stairs, pissed off that I haven't paid the rent. The stink of decay will sober Tranh up in a flash. Not bothering with a key, the old man somehow summons the strength to kick down my flimsy door. I imagine him crying out in that sweet, hoarse whisper of his: *Ou vous êtes, Professeur Nena? Ou vous êtes, ma chérie?*

From The Abolition Journal
Brenda Coultas

EMANCIPATION PROCLAMATION

If I said "Emancipation" or said "Manumitted" in this county
If I said "Reparations" (some might say those are fighting words)

Or if I said "Lyles Station," the first black town in Gibson County,
or I could say "Stevenson Station," a black settlement within
shouting distance of the South
In Vanderburgh County, I could say Lincoln Gardens (a historic
housing project in Evansville)

The palmist heard many voices, a mournful ocean coming from
my right hand
And felt a deep sadness.
She heard,
"I went to the underworld and this is what I found"
She heard,
"I have her body."

Then I heard the word and the word was "Autonomy"

Born 93 years after,
My mother born in Indiana 62 years after
Her mother born in Kentucky 1896
Her mother born in the Carolinas, and during her lifetime
The first grandchild born 121 years after the news of emancipation

BLOOMFIELD

My town was called Tippecanoe although we are far from that
river or battleground. My town was once called Yearbyville, after
my mother's family because a plethora of Yearbys lived there.

A post office but every store was.
When we tear it down, what will be found?
Hidden love letters?
Lost buttons or wedding bands?
Square-head nails or wooden spikes?
Silver dollars, with the Liberty walking in full stride?

Under the Rockport bluff, a plaque noting the cave of first white
family in the county, of Tecumseh Lankford who begat Bloomfield
once called Tippecanoe once called Yearbyville

Daniel Grass first white property owner in this township. His family killed by arrows

Spier Spencer died at Tippecanoe and so they gave this county his
name. In 1812, everywhiteman said Tippecanoe too.

A PLACE OF BREAD AND MILK

Green walls, candy case, cash register embossed with curliques,
all the cent and dollar amounts pop up in the window: the wooden
change drawer, the adding machine's black body with ivory and red
keys. The soda cooler where the drinks stood in water. An upright
woodburner not a potbellied stove. Spittoons, brass and fancy, or an
empty tin can will do.

In 1976
I went to the store to pick up
milk
bread
grape juice
saltines
milk of magnesia
jelly

Walk in posey pike gibson dubois daviess knox vanderburgh
counties and watch the tornadoes

Brenda Coultas

Bloomfield, Midway, Sandridge, Enterprise, Fulda, Jonesboro,
Eureka, New Boston, Rockport, Hatfield, Evanston, Buffaloville,
Santa Claus, Pueblo, Pyesttsville, French Island, Lincoln City,
St. Meinrad, Mariah Hill

                                        No, I have not been everywhere

I've been around
even to Bullocktown (Warrick County)
although the post office closed in 1895
I mail a letter

NOTE. *The Abolition Journal* is an investigative poem about the historic border I
grew up on: namely the north-south border between Daviess County, Kentucky,
where Josiah Henson was enslaved, and Spencer County, Indiana, where Abe Lincoln
spent his boyhood. When I think of Indiana, I think of the Klan, so I thought to know
what is better. Did any underground railroad activities take place there? Who aided
fugitives from the South? How were freed men and women treated in my county?
This section explores what remains of the past: for example, the nineteenth-century
origins of the names of villages and townships.

The Vice Admiral's Elements
Scott Geiger

NOW THEY'RE PUTTING ON their helmets while the ground crew checks the tethers. Then one by one each member of the formation turns to me for the send-off speech. Their enamel white helmets flash in the morning's sunshine. All but one of the sixteen balloonists wear the white insulated suits and tightly wound blue scarves, the recommended apparel. It's a teenager or disadvantaged person far down the line from me who's the exception. He's wearing a Montgolfier purple kit with the large, pointed collar and that black helmet ergonomically curved to fit the neck. From across the hill the crew chief signals an all go. I put the megaphone to my mouth only to lower it for the dramatic pause. It's not even on yet. Jeanine knows by now that this is my favorite part of the job. She folds her hands below her waist in a prayerful way. No one could guess how she is with me in private. How could someone so still and pleasant looking be the way she is? I know she sees the Montgolfier suit. I'm not eager to hear what she's bound to say. I turn my head upward, and I can tell that everyone in the formation does, too. The sky overhead looks a hard and brittle blue, something to be cracked with a spoon. Only a slight westerly wind spoils the complete hush while all sixteen members of the Sandusky branch steel themselves for the journey.

I click on the megaphone and return it to my mouth.

"A journey across fantastic distances at tremendous heights awaits all of you this morning," I tell them. "The Addison Balloon is for voyages, for extraordinary, life-altering, meaning-making voyages. Today's life does not abound with voyages. Karl Addison knew that and you know it, too. So it's with great pride that Jeanine and I, on behalf of the entire Addison Enterprise Institute, wave you off this morning on your first weekend *Wanderjahr*. I remember leaving home on the first voyage of my life, two decades ago, long before anyone ever thought about what a twenty-foot bag and a couple hundred cubic feet of gas could do for them. I was on the *Ticonderoga*." I recount the part of the story about Tierra del Fuego and how our ship came round Cape Horn at sunrise and I saw the penguins. When Jeanine coughs I know it's time to swerve back on message. "Karl Addison," I say imperatively, "Karl Addison, on his trip out of this world, likely felt much of what you all feel right here and now. Think of him as the world dwindles below you, as the winds spin you, and you give yourself over for a day to the skies." I say some more about the vastness, the skies, the touching the face of God bit. It all comes out of my mouth and everyone applauds.

"How blue is it?" I ask them.

"Deeply blue!" they say back.

Enthusiasts invented the cheer years ago.

There's more clapping as I doff my vice admiral's bicorne and start shaking hands. Jeanine follows behind me and we both say our bon voyages. This crowd is the typical sort. Here's the bachelor living alone in a small old house at the foot of a hill. Here's the retired librarian with a cat and a weather journal. The all grown-up quiet suburban boy teeming like a kettle with sentiment. People entirely unlike me, people with books, people who, unable to find their way into the world, hear or read about Karl Addison and think to themselves, Yes, I would like to do that myself. But what prompts them to say that, what inspires their leave-taking, is a wholly personal matter.

I go down the formation line congratulating and well-wishing until at last I come to the balloonist in the Montgolfier suit. I can't believe that it's a girl, a teenager even. Most balloonists are men. Our studies have shown the people least interested in Addison Balloons are females aged eight to eighteen. She's chewing gum and has a look on her face like she doesn't know what's good for her, a look that reminds me of a girl I used to make time with in the ivy patch long ago on the other side of my life.

I take the pocket square from my coat and unfold it for her.

"You don't want to choke on that."

She shrugs and tongues it out of her mouth onto the handkerchief.

"So you're his brother, right?" she asks.

I tell her I am, even though my name is different now.

"But," she says, "you don't really look like him either."

"How's that?" I ask, wadding the cloth and her gum into my coat.

"You don't look right. You look abstracted."

Jeanine elbows me along to the next balloonist. Her prod sharply insists.

The girl in the Montgolfier suit limply shakes my hand.

"Abstracted?"

"Or something," she says.

When we finish with our farewells, Jeanine and I walk back to the hill above the formation. The balloonists put on their goggles and before I have time to wave my official hat in final farewell, the first one pulls his rip cord. The car-sized balloon lurches up just a little at first. It seems to hesitate. They move like jellyfish near the ground, fluttering and gelatinous; only at altitude do they bloom fully sphere-wise as shown in our marketing kits. Then it's like the balloon has just discovered that it's off the moorings and leaps up into the wind. The tethers go taut and then there's the incredible sound of an adult body raptured right up into the air. Sometimes they grunt things like "Rock 'n' roll" or shout, "I love you, Beatrice" as they go. But this group is pretty quiet and we hear each of them whistle off. The Montgolfier girl goes third from the last. She runs upwind with the balloon until it pulls her off the earth. Her legs keep cycling even after the takeoff and that makes her sway under the balloon like a hypnotist's watch. Jeanine, the crew, and I watch the balloonists borne off into the achingly bright sky. We no longer hear them. They don't curve over the horizon; there is no arc to their vanishing. Instead they get bluer and thinner, bluer and thinner until the sky eclipses first the person and then, at last, the balloon to which they're tethered.

Those westerlies pick up, moving vestiges of the winter just passed.

This is the first time for everybody in the Sandusky branch, even the crew, and it's gone well. The group liftoff is a growing trend. That's what Jeanine says. First-timers find it easier because they're not alone and that's reassuring for them. We're invited all the time to events like this, but Jeanine says we can only afford key markets. I get to make a speech, we shake hands, and everything goes according to plan. We've had only one bad group of first-timers. There was a woman in Spartanburg who changed her mind after pulling her rip cord. The balloon was already aloft, so nothing could be done. The way she screamed spooked some of the others and they decided not to go.

The crew thanks us for making it out and then starts digging up the moorings.

Jeanine wants to drive but I have the keys. We hang up our vice admiral jackets from the hooks in the back and toss our bicornes on the backseat. We drive east. She cracks the window and lights a menthol cigarette.

"You lost it a little," she says. "That extemporaneous sea yarn."

"Sincerely felt ad lib running parallel to the message isn't losing it."

"Poor recovery, too. You were a hairsbreadth from saying, 'Well, don't think about how he disappeared. That won't happen to you. Your balloons are especially calibrated. You won't die, promise.'"

"He's not dead."

"Stick to the approved goods."

"Not everything in life can be shtick."

"This isn't life, Buddy, this is business. I'm the fifteen-year veteran, and you're a *boat-swain*."

"*Bosun*," I correct her.

Jeanine scoffs. She refuses to look at me until she finishes her smoke. She flicks the butt into a ditch full of cattails between the road and some railroad tracks.

"That girl was completely outside our traditional demographic," Jeanine says, putting on her tortoiseshell sunglasses. "Your 'Only the Lonely' model is void, Buddy. That check is cashed."

"One girl isn't a trend," I say.

We argue. She criticizes me for my lack of vision. She says the Montgolfiers are on to something with their merchandising. She thinks an analysis would show how much more lucrative they are than the institute.

"Everybody still needs a balloon," I remind her. "And Addison is still the center of attention, not backpacks, not T-shirts, not silly colors and logos. You heard that little girl ask me about him. Just wait till the statue's finished. You'll see."

"We need a newer product," she says. "It'll have to be exhilarating yet strangely familiar."

I say, "Yeah. We're sticking with Karl Addison."

"Something bigger and more serious," she says. "It'll need permanence and maybe even luxury."

"Don't lose sight of the public's affection for his story."

"A house in the sky or maybe a kind of air yacht."

"Addison is still their personal Columbus, and that won't change any time soon."

Jeanine says it's like I'm not even listening to her anymore. She takes off her sunglasses and cups her hand over her eyes. She says she doesn't want to fight with me.

*

Completion nears on our statue of Karl Addison, the contemporary aeronaut. It will stand one and three-quarters times larger than life beside the rose garden at the edge of Wake, Ohio's town plaza. The body will be Mexican porphyry polished to a lustrous imperial violet. Above and behind him the balloon will rise like a metal moon. Gustavo Jimènez de Cisneros, the sculptor, has found someone to fabricate it from paper-thin titanium scale. The town council didn't care for that at first. They thought titanium looked gaudy and urban. *Blingy,* one of them said. But I eased them into it by explaining how the light will shine off the balloon and we'll be able to see our faces in it. Everyone likes to see themselves elsewhere, in items and in other people, but especially in art. The statue will show Addison at the last moment of his leave-taking, just before he is fully airborne. No pedestal or plinth will be used. It will all balance precariously, almost impossibly, on his porphyry heels. That's how I imagine it, my brother being taken up violently and backward. The right hand will grip one of three steel rods meant to be the tether cables leading up from his waist to the balloon. The left hand will trail below, though not voluptuously. We're not about the voluptuous. No hint of muscle, blood vessel, or tissue in his arms and fingers will be evident. His famous obesity will, in our statue, become an attractive, aerodynamic fuselage. And his face will be expressionless, his nose more of a fin, his lips a vent.

When Jeanine and I get back to the office from Sandusky, I eat my lunch alone on the bench across from the tent. We've built a dark blue tent over the site on the town plaza, where the Mexican sculptors and their engineers are at work. People on the sidewalk stop and listen to the whistles and bangs. Diesel exhaust belches occasionally through a special flap. There's work under way here. An earthmover is there one day and gone the next. Trucks arrive, trucks depart. I hear shouts of Spanish unintelligible over the distance.

I manage the project myself because Jeanine's so busy. She's always on the phone with the warehouses and the factories and the banks. Jeanine works late often and even brings her work home. She talks a lot about robust development and strategy and what we'll do going forward. It was her money that made the institute, after all. She has a vested interest, but the statue has been on the table since the very first day we met at a commemorative merchandising conference in Knoxville.

I want a famous dedication for the statue on July 16, an extravaganza everyone can get behind and feel good about. That's Addison Day and the eighth anniversary of his flight. People from cities and towns, kingdoms and countries, states and empires—especially Japan, where every other household includes at least one Addison balloonist—will come to Wake, Ohio. That's how I sold it first to Jeanine, then to the council. We'll release one hundred birds of various species. Jeanine will probably want a mass liftoff, too. I will wear a blue chambray shirt with the sleeves rolled and a red tie, in the fashion of our local politicians. From the podium in the rose garden, with city council and the institute staff behind me, I'll be allowed a lengthy and detailed speech act, at the end of which I'll call him up to the stage and award all credit to him. We will have for him a white admiral's jacket and bicorne.

Whether my estranged brother will attend the dedication of his statue, I cannot say.

If not, my monument will survive him. It will at least be his public afterlife. Picnics will surround it and kites will fly over it for all the summers to come. Winter snow will pile on the shoulders while our children roll snowmen and erect forts along the elms. What I most look forward to are my solitary visits with the statue, late on warm nights when my arthritis eases up. The monument will give me someplace to go when Jeanine has started to snore. We live now on a cul-de-sac in a mansion like you wouldn't believe. But with all those rooms, I sometimes feel like I have nowhere to go. A man needs at least one place he can go.

These days I get a lot of letters with questions.

"Who is Karl Addison?"

Or: "Why did he tether himself to such-and-such balloon?"

And: "What did he find in the sky?"

There's a formal reply we've developed here at the institute, a suitable biography that goes in pamphlets and literature and my mouth whenever I'm interviewed by journalists or field questions at trade shows. The statue will embody it nicely, I think, even better than the commemorative coin. The coin was my idea. I remembered that in high school Karl was the president and sole member of the numismatics club. I thought it might get his attention. Our coin is stamped out of zinc, about the size of a quarter, though a little thicker, so it's useless in pay phones. One side shows him carried aloft by an enormous balloon over tree-lined streets and telephone wires, rooftops and a water tower. The obverse is the side with Karl's face in profile exhibiting the thin lips and pillowy double chin I wish we could redact. Arcing over his profile, where a quarter might say, "Liberty," read the words *"Ars Volandi."* That's our motto here. The Art of Flying, the Flying Art. The coins sold better than anticipated. Only a limited quantity remains. They're in the box under Jeanine's secretary's desk. I keep a few in my right pocket for the hell of it. To have something there to jingle.

But what I want to say when posed questions like this—what's clamoring to be said as I answer for the hundredth time such questions is that I, too, have been on voyages. I shipped out at age eighteen on the *Ticonderoga*, went four times around the world, and that at Brazzaville once—but no. My life is neither here nor there. I have given myself over to the promotion of my big brother's triumph and made myself rich merchandising his reinvention. OK, if once more I find myself in his shadow, if once more his life takes precedence, at least this time it's a shadow of my own design: we have reinvented him for the world to gawk at and to fondle, to take home, to devour.

Years ago, however, upon my survival and return, I sought Karl Addison. I met with figures native to our distant past, traveling a bee's pattern from one to the next, finding by sips and drams what little news I could of his adult life. His popularity was already gathering in those days, turning out misinformation spun by pretenders of every sort.

There was Lyle Ogive, called "the Crocodile" for how he says what he says to women about his parents' deaths, who claimed to have been an adjustor with my brother at Cusco. He answered my ad. What channels are available to find the long lost? Once I saw a late-night infomercial where people sought out their high school flames, distant cousins, even a border collie named Charlene. But I thought I could do it myself; my independence is fierce. I used newspaper, radio, but not television. I couldn't afford that. Government agencies let me down. Was it easier to find people in times past, a century ago, maybe, when there were fewer places to go?

Ogive—once paid—told me that Karl Addison took a vacation by himself to Lake Chautauqua and stayed alone in some cracker shack rental for seven days. He knew Addison lived with his father and that after the flight, his father moved to Florida with the money he got letting the network use his house as the set for the made-for-TV movie based loosely on Karl Addison's later years. Father also appeared on a number of late-night talk shows with Taylor Zachary, the Wake real estate broker who caught Addison's takeoff on video. On one show, Father said that he was recovering from prostate surgery. The host said, "First, your only son, Karl, and then cancer . . ."

"That's how it is," Father said on national television. "One thing after another." Father told the audience he was doing OK. There was no news of Karl. The weeks-long search at last had been canceled. "All I can do is go on," he said. "Go forward."

"Good for you," said Taylor Zachary in the adjacent chair. His hand touched Father's knee. "Good for you." Zachary is a well-meaning opportunist; you can tell from his commentary on the Addison documentary that runs round on loop in the institute's lobby.

Karl Addison was once a real boy. We called him Curly at home.

He was born two years before me in our elm-shaded Ohio town. He was plump at birth, and never in his thirty-three years did his body achieve what could be called healthy proportions. Mother and Father loved Curly with an animal affection so overwhelming that just the sight of their toddler doltishly staggering down the hallway triggered an onslaught of kisses and hugs. They spent all of it at once. Their feelings for me were a cooler kind of affection. Alexandra, who came last, had it even worse. By then our parents had careers, which thinned and flattened them in my mind. They became like the Old Testament God, consequential only in times of trial and crime. They punished, dispensed monies, and delivered us here and there. Almost nothing was asked of me except that I be calm, quiet, and progress through life with modest vigor and nominal success. My side of the covenant: be always a son on autopilot.

We were distant from the start, he and I. Addison was but the clumsy pink stranger who could walk and utter, who spent his afternoons in the region of the living room where a bright trapezoid of light fell from the window to spread warmly across the red carpet. Every day he'd wait for the light to move across the floor to him. It was his brother, not I. I crawled over him, learned to walk to him, learned to utter like him, made him gifts of chocolates and leaves and marbles. He would lie there like a stranded whale's carcass or a pagan idol, deaf to my sounds, blind to my gestures.

I beat him once with what memory has made a fire poker. How much more alive the past is than the present. Ever on the metamorphosis, memory sprouts new and unasked-for branches. This fire poker was in reality, maybe, a wooden spoon.

"You, Karl!" I said.

He whimpered and cowered as they hauled me off to my room.

Vague atmospheres of our prehistory together linger with me even when the details have subsided. I recall summers as a blue-and-green world of swimming lessons, visits to strawberry patches, mysterious clambakes steaming our twilit yard with pungent salt air. After the greens and golds of Christmastime's indoor trees tricked out in lights and sentimental glass ornaments, we learned to anticipate the billowing whiteness at cold windowpanes and the silvery fangs that grew on gutters. Through it all, Curly was no more than a guest in our house, appearing at mealtimes, when he sat with us like a foreign emissary or outside observer or indeed like the insurance inspector he grew up to be. He was only watching our lives.

Yet our parents doted on Curly without reward: their love went into him like starlight into a black hole. He was an awkward child prone to falls and accidents with corners. They encouraged him to play quietly in the living room or outside in the grass near the ivy where they could watch him from the kitchen windows. Curly later came to dislike the noisy and athletic effort of the sports that other children enjoyed so much. The messy activities of finger painting and cobbling together Play-Doh shapes were equally dissatisfying. His clumsy hands were inexpressive. His body in motion tended to stay in motion only long enough for him to trip over a tree root. So, at an early age, he found that what he loved most in life was to loaf drowsily about on the lawn while gawking at the world around him, particularly at colorful objects and moving things. Because it is colorful and animated and silent, he was inevitably drawn to the sky.

No one will ever know that our statue of Karl Addison is anchored to the earth's crust. That much will be its invisible feat. Elena, the engineer from Chihuahua, and I climb down the ladder into the wide parabolic pit dug for our statue's counterweight. It's seventy-nine inches wide and ninety-six inches deep, say the Prussian blue construction documents. A flashlight turns on in Elena's hands and she takes a step back from me. Wire mesh forms cover the walls to contain the soil and loose shale, flecks of which sparkle in the flashlight's beam. Here and there, anonymous roots thick as my fingers have been amputated. The assistants have all gone home for the night, and we are alone under the tent in a grave for two, simply because I am the client and I have scheduled a ten o'clock meeting.

Elena says that when she cannot sleep, she solves questions from a trigonometry workbook until she feels drowsy.

They've had to dig a foot and some inches deeper than expected to hit bedrock.

"He isn't really your brother?" she asks me at last. "Is he?"

"My long-lost brother."

"Were you lost? Or was he?"

I want to tell her I went four times around the world in the merchant marine, about Arctic sunsets and Pacific storms, about the island of Eldey, where great auks massed until they were killed off. But Elena preempts me to say she has long-lost brothers, too. Nine of them, all welders and machinists. They paid for her college education. I ask her if she sees them ever, and she says no, not really. I ask her if she misses them.

"I've gotten used to it," she says.

I still have things to say about the afternoon I spent on Eldey as she runs the flashlight along the floor to show a stainless-steel frame fused to the bedrock with eighteen enormous screws. Elena squats around one of the screws and explains how it was implanted with a water-cooled drill. She wraps her right hand around one of the screws. She wears her black hair short and parted above her right temple. The collar of her white shirt is brown. The day's perspiration shines on her skin like glaze on ceramic.

Elena laughs. "From here it looks like we're building a bridge," she says, taking the drawings out from under her arm.

We go over where the epoxied rebar will be installed when the concrete is poured over the screws. The compression from eighteen iron ingots riding on the carriage frame and eleven-foot pins, one running up into each of the thighs, will permit an illusion of liftoff. She says an authoritative French word I don't know, her lips shaping as if to pinch a maraschino cherry.

"Do you like our statue?" I ask Elena.

"It's Karl Addison," she says. "He's very popular these days."

She scrolls up the drawings.

"Our balloons are on back order. The factories can't make them fast enough."

I ask her has she ever used the balloon, and Elena says she has thought of it. She says she's due some vacation soon. I tell her I'll bring a kit by later in the week.

"I'd like that," she says.

"People say it changes their lives forever."

I offer to let her climb up the ladder first but she says she'd rather follow me up. As I climb, I think of her bare feet leaving the ground.

"I could help you assemble and prep, too."

She says perhaps.

We were still little when my brother said he saw the sky staring back at him. To my mother and father, of course, not to me.

It was a humid morning in the middle of May. Karl Addison laid himself down on the warm lawn of our backyard between the ivy and the big tulip beds. I was in the ivy holding Marvin the Frog. All morning he lay there on his back looking up into the air. The sky was gauzy with slow-moving cirrus clouds. Birds went up and down, beetles trekked across him. Over his belly, a dragonfly hovered. Mr. Coffee, the neighbor's greyhound, dashed through the yard and hurdled him. What a portly hurdle he was, even then. Nothing stirred Addison. Was he watching the progress of the clouds? Was he waiting for the blue in the sky to flicker like a television set tuned to blank cable? I crept from my hiding place in the ivy to figure him out. I remember being close enough to kiss him, kneeling over my brother like a squire over his fallen knight. His chest rose and fell, his lungs filled and emptied. His breath smelled like Cheerios and milk. Snot had crusted in the corner of his left nostril. The mole on his chin told time like a blunt sundial.

I tapped him. I poked him in the ribs with a twig. I dropped stones on his belly.

Karl Addison had gone somewhere else.

Had something broken in him? I listened to his chest, unsure if his heart had stopped without the lungs somehow. The air funneling into his nostrils and coming out over his lips made a dry ripping sound.

I got Miss Broom, our sitter, who was watching the spiders from her lawn chair in the garage because she was a witch.

"Something's popped loose in him," I said. "I can hear it rattling. Come quick."

Miss Broom leaned over him and I saw where her brown nylon stockings ended.

"Curly," she shouted. "Curly. Wake up!"

She turned around and looked at me with her witch eyes. "You do this?" she asked. "You hit him with a shovel or a hammer?"

A sucking sound like a full sink draining came out of my brother.

"Oh this is bad," said Miss Broom. "This is it, Norma. This is it."

Then Karl Addison sat up panting and gasping, like a diver breaking the ocean's surface after a deep dive.

"I was flying, Miss Broom," he said. "Just a little bit, floating, you know, right above the grass." He must've felt his weight subtracted, his body lightened in nearly imperceptible increments. He must've thought to himself, *I am flying,* though he felt no higher than the tips of grass.

"Oh thank goodness," Miss Broom said. "Are you hurt? He didn't hurt you, that little villain?"

Karl looked at me and then back at Miss Broom. His head shook a negative.

He told Miss Broom later that summer that he had conducted himself like a flying carpet around the yard, brushing up against the maple trees and scattering their propellers across the ivy patch. I had been in my ivy hole holding Marvin the Frog all that time and no, no he had not flown and scattered the propeller seeds on me. But Miss Broom believed him. She found a propeller seed in my hair when she was cleaning me up before Mother got home. "Here's one of Karl's propellers," she said.

Those August mornings, she'd even send me out into the yard to smear sunblock on him. "You're brother's flying in the sun again," she'd say. "Go put this on him." I smeared it on his arms and cheeks, between his fingers and along the crest of his ears. I put it on his nose and around the clock mole. He never knew and never thanked me. For that matter, neither did Miss Broom.

We sat eating lunch on the patio once. I asked him, "How do you fly, Curly?"

He blinked at me and said, "Stare up at the sky until it stares at you back."

"Oh," I said. "That's not too hard."

"But don't try to follow me," he said.

Marvin the Frog and I tried on the front lawn of the house every day for a week. The sky I saw was a busy, trafficked place. Clouds interdicted. They reminded me of buildings and cars and sailing ships, sometimes all of those at once. There were clouds shaped like Marvin and clouds shaped like countries in my atlas. For everything on earth, there is now or was once or will be a cloud. Even a cloud Karl and a cloud Bud. Distant planes and helicopters and swooping birds were in the way, too. And there was rain. Whole floods smuggled across the sky in broad, dark plates. If I couldn't get a good look at the sky, how could I tell when it was staring back? The police came on my last attempt because a concerned neighbor had called. When it was all cleared up, Miss Broom sent me to my room without a sandwich for lunch.

Marvin's leg fell off toward the end of that summer. To keep him safe I left him on my dresser each morning, his taped-on leg leaned against his froggy belly. When I learned to play baseball that September, I began to miss him less.

Jeanine is staying up tonight at her desk in the study, a new and more elaborate balloon growing stroke by stroke under her Flair pen.

A talk readies in me. I badly want to land it, like a circling jetliner's pilot.

"Shh," she says.

Your typical Addison Balloon is a mild gray nylon-cotton bladder with a nipple to take lighter-than-air gas at inflation. Helium is always the recommended gas, though the original Karl Addison used eight years ago had in it hydrogen, a much cheaper, more dangerous gas. A unique one-size-fits-all harness depends some fifteen feet below the balloon by four elastic PVC cables. Nothing to the design is particularly innovative or compelling. The balloon goes up, sails for approximately twenty-four hours, and then comes gradually down as the bladder begins to seep gas after having stretched at altitude. There are no comforts, no frills. Those come in the add-on upgrades Jeanine devised. Fins, racing stripes, personalized colors, and specially printed bladders are available at additional cost. A kind of sock that keeps the balloonist warm and snuggly for his voyage remains our best seller; the AddChute lands consistently in second. A balloon kit has only one life, so customers must make the most of it.

Some customers are purists. They prefer a balloon that is as close as possible to the aerostatic weather balloon my brother modified for his voyage. They tell me they want to feel the wind, the cold, etc., on their skin the way Karl Addison did. Really orthodox users fly only once a year, on Addison Day. Jeanine feels that's not enough. Different balloons will be needed to grow the business, she argues.

Funny how we've never used the Addison Balloon ourselves. No, I don't think it has ever held any appeal for me. When balloonists hear that, they ask me why I do what I do, and I tell them about my vertigo as a way to bring up my ordeal in Zaire. The vertigo paired with my experience as a hostage, I've found, makes for convincing and powerful narrative. But these opportunities are fleeting. Talk often returns to my brother and the various goings-on at the institute. The next season's merchandise, always next season's merchandise. If they press me, I eventually mention a desire to own a family business and collaborate with my brother, even if only in spirit. Jeanine insists that it's good marketing and I don't mind saying it myself. It's nice to hear the words in my voice and pretend that they're the truth.

I tell Jeanine I can't sleep again, and she says I should make some warm milk. She goes on at her drafting table, scheming, finding new flourishes, new angles to exploit. It might help me to have a cup of green tea and hold hands on the sofa. But instead I tell her that I'm going for a walk at midnight, and she says, OK, honey, like I wasn't once held hostage in Brazzaville for twenty-nine days in a newspaper-lined cage.

We have a situation now, Jeanine and I, but the crash is coming.

I walk out of the development and up through the lamplit patches of inorganic white light to the town plaza. I sit on a bench under the scrutiny of stars and sable space. My mouth begins the mutter-mutter. Jeanine says I just need to talk to somebody, to get what happened off my chest. You should be able to do it yourself, but it isn't the same without a listener. I sit on my hands and my mouth runs its course.

"So," I say. This is how I always start. "So—"

I start at the beginning and work forward until I've hoodwinked myself into a doze. That's when I'm weakest, when the Flying Dream is likeliest to come on. And so it does: he leads me quivering and terrified through the capes of clouds and the bright blue arcades. I hang from his shoulders like a scarf. Up and up he pulls me until the colors and clouds fall away, for there would be neither colors nor clouds anymore. We outsoar the wind and it falls away, for there would be no wind. Past the moon and the sun, which fall away behind us, too, for there would be no moon and no sun. The stars rain past us, becoming one great wash of white light. Even the names Karl and Buddy expire, for there would be no such thing as a Karl or a Buddy. The glossy white white.

When I get home, the house is marbled with dark and silence, my elements. She lies stored there in bed, Jeanine, my wife, my employer. On my pillow is a yellow sticky note and a piece of tracing paper. I take them into the extraordinarily capacious bathroom and switch on the light. The note reads: "B: New milestone in the history of inflation." The tracing shows her new balloon in colored pen.

Four Stories
Diane Williams

WEIGHT, HAIR, LENGTH

THE TRAIN IS A STRIKING example and they wanted to walk inside it like other people in the train car—move their limbs and do headlong whatever occurred to them to do headlong, but they didn't want to look silly. Before this there had been a shop they had stopped in at briefly, where they had admired a bronze sphinx with an upraised paw and an elegant and extremely fine clock on skinny legs. The man is a connoisseur who is generally attracting attention. Physically, he is displayed as a huge adult. Of course, his wife is a tour de force, although she is beginning to get on his nerves.

One of them tried to buy a jug, enameled and gilded. Of course, his wife has a human head. She is a city worker and when the administration changes, they will change her. She does have big hips. She is getting heavy. Her hair is wonderful hair. Very pretty. Very pretty.

The husband undressed at night, carried himself toward his natural bed and the bedclothes. A number of his parts are modern and wide. He looks well made for sustained and undemanding and justified indulgence.

VIRTUE

The woman's comb turned, ready to scratch itself across her skull or to spend a lot of time on the right side of her skull. Like smoke under a fence, the flow of the comb was funny to stare at.

Now, in the hourly slot, the woman and the men sat by the pool with the one child and with Pooky. The woman secured her hairs together in a string. The child ate a doughnut. The woman suggested someone throw a ball to Pooky. For Pooky, the woman fetched the ball, and then the woman fetched the child, and she bunched up a section of his T-shirt, as she bunched up a section of the child, at his neck, and I permitted her to squeeze the demon out of him, because she is so uncommonly nervous, and she is so obedient.

THE USE OF FETISHES

"I was a lucky person. I was a very successful person," said the woman in house slippers who put coral beads on.

She was not entirely busy with her work. She took cups and she took tumblers from her cupboard to prepare a coffee or a tea. She thought, We have some smaller or even smaller.

Her uncle Bill said, "Have you been able to have sexual intercourse?"

The woman said nothing and then she thought, I am going to just talk. I think people like that.

She said, "Yes! And I had a climax, too!"

This idea is compact and stained and strained to the limit.

THE NEWLY MADE SUPPER

The guest's only wish was to see anyone who looked like Betsy, to put his hands around this Betsy's waist, on her breasts. He followed Betsy. He had just lost one.

In front of Betsy, who supports on her knees her dinner dish, you can see the guest approach, then there's their dialogue about the cushion lamb shoulder.

Frankly and honestly, look how she's putting her head up against his hand! She rarely shows up, although she is a good representative. However, she tells a story deceitfully and badly and I am opposed to that. She says her father's name is Louie! She says she has a friend and she has an aunt who explain things to her.

Betsy, in perfect view, takes pains to adequately open her mouth. Some darkening, some shadows. I only wish—

The guest's only wish—well, I guess the guest only barely wishes.

I mean the guest could lean back with some expectation, without one regret.

The host (whose father is an optimist, who believes you can reason with people, although his father does lose his temper a lot) is talking

411

to Frances and he asks her, "Did you get any supper?"
  And Frances answers, "Who is that in the purple shirt?"
  "Did you say purple?" says the host.
  "Yes."
  "That's not purple," says the host.
  "It's—what color would you say that is?" says Frances.
  "Magenta?"
  "No, I have to look up magenta," says Frances.
  "That's magenta," says the host, "that cell phone."
  "No, that's lavender," says another better Frances.

Tear-Down
John Barth

IN LARGE "GATED COMMUNITIES" like our Heron Bay Estates development, obsolescence sets in early. The developers, Tidewater Communities Inc. knew their business: a great flat stretch of former pine woods and agribusiness feed-corn fields along the handsome Mattahannock River, ten minutes from the attractive little colonial-era town of Stratford and two hours from Baltimore/Washington in one direction, Wilmington/Philadelphia in another, and Atlantic beach resorts in a third, converted in the go-go American 1980s into appealingly laid-out subdevelopments of low-rise condos, semi-detached duplex "villas," over-and-under "coach homes," and detached-house neighborhoods ranging from mid- to high-end, the whole well landscaped and amenitied with social/recreational clubs (the Heron Bay Club for golfers, tennis players, and fitness buffs, the Blue Crab Marina Club for boaters, each with restaurant and function rooms), grounds- and gatekeepers, security patrols, and a well-turned-out community newsletter and Web site. The first such development on the Eastern Shore end of Maryland's Chesapeake Bay Bridge, it proved so successful that twenty years later it was not only "built out," as they say (except for a still-controversial proposal for midrise condominiums in what was supposed to remain wood-and-wetland "preserve"), but in its "older" subcommunities, like our Spartina Pointe, already showing its age. In Stratford's Historic District, an "old house" may date from the early eighteenth century; in Heron Bay Estates it dates from Ronald Reagan's second presidential term. More and more, as the American wealthy have grown ever wealthier and the original builder-owners of upscale Spartina Pointe (mostly retirees from one of those above-mentioned cities, for many of whom Heron Bay Estates was a weekend-and-summer retreat, a second or even third residence) aged and died or shifted to some assisted-living facility, the new owners of their twenty-year-old "colonial" minimansions commence their tenure with radical renovation: all-new kitchen and baths, a swimming pool and larger patio/deck area, faux cobblestone driveway and complete relandscaping—all subject, of course, to approval by the HBE Design Review Board.

Which august three-member body, a branch of the Heron Bay Community Association, had reluctantly approved, back in the 1980s, the original design for 211 Spartina Court, a rambling brick-and-clapboard "rancher" on a prime two-acre lot at the very point of Spartina Point(e), with narrow but navigable Spartina Creek on three sides. It was a two-to-one decision: none of the three committee members was happy to let a ranch house, however roomy, set the architectural tone for what was intended as HBE's highest-end neighborhood; two- and three-story "plantation style" manses were what they had in mind. But while one of the committee-folk was steadfastly opposed, another judged it more important to get a first house built (its owners were prepared to begin construction immediately upon their plan's approval) in order to help sell the remaining lots and encourage the building of residences more appropriate to the developer's intentions for that particular community. The third member was sympathetic to both opinions; she ultimately voted approval on the grounds that preliminary designs for two neighboring houses were exactly what the Association wanted for Spartina Pointe—neo-Georgian manors of whitewashed brick, with two-story front columns and the rest— and together should adequately establish the neighborhood's style. The ranch house was allowed, minus the rustic split-rail fence intended to mark the lot's perimeter, and with the provision that a few Leland cypresses be planted instead, to partially screen the residence from streetside view.

The strategy succeeded. Within a few years the several "drives" and "courts" of Spartina Pointe were lined with more or less imposing, more or less Georgian-style homes: no Cape Cods, Dutch Colonials, or half-timbered Tudors (all popular styles in easier-going Rockfish Reach), certainly nothing Contemporary, and no more ranchers. The out-of-synch design of 211 Spartina Court raised a few eyebrows, but the house's owners, Ed and Myra Gunston, were hospitable, community-spirited ex-Philadelphians whom none could dislike: organizers of neighborhood parties and Progressive Dinners, spirited fund-raisers for the Avon County United Way and other worthy causes. A sad day for Spartina Pointe when Myra was crippled by a stroke; another, some months later, when a FOR SALE sign appeared in front of those Leland cypresses.

All the above established, we may now begin this Tear-Down story, which is not about the good-neighbor Gunstons, and for which the next chapter in the history of their Spartina Point(e) house, heavily foreshadowed by the tale's title, is merely the occasion. We shift now across Heron Bay Estates to 414 Doubler Drive in Blue Crab Bight, the second-floor coach home of early-fortyish Joseph and Judith Barnes—first explaining to nontidewater types that "doubler" is the local watermen's term for the mating stage of *Callinectes sapidus,* the Chesapeake Bay blue crab. The male of that species mounts and clasps fast the female who he senses is about to molt, so that when eventually she sheds her carapace and becomes for some hours a helpless "softcrab," he can both shield her from predators and have his way with her himself, to the end of continuing the species: a two-for-one catch for lucky crabbers, and an apt street name for a community of over-and-under duplexes, whose owners (and some of the rest of us) do not tire of explaining it to out-of-staters.

Some months have passed since the space-break above: It is now the late afternoon of a chilly wet April Friday in an early year of the twenty-first century. Ruddyplump Judy Barnes has just arrived home from her English-teaching job at Fenton, a small private coed junior/senior high school up near Stratford, where she's also an assistant girls' soccer coach. This afternoon's intramural game having been rained out, she's home earlier than usual and is starting dinner for the family: her husband, a portfolio manager in the Stratford office of Lucas & Jones, Inc., a Baltimore investment-counseling firm; their elder daughter Ashleigh, a Stratford College sophomore who lives in the campus dorms but often comes home on weekends; and Ashleigh's two-year-younger sister Tiffany, a (tuition-waived) sixth-form student at Fenton, who's helping Mom with dinner prep.

Osso buco, it's going to be. While Judy shakes the veal shanks in a bag of salt-and-peppered flour and Tiffany dices carrots, celery, onions, and garlic cloves for preliminary sautéeing, Joe Barnes is closing his office for the weekend with the help of Jeannine Weston, his secretary, and trying in vain to stop imagining that lean, sexy/sharp young woman at least half naked in various positions to receive in sundry of her orifices his already wet-tipped penis. *Quit that already!* He reprimands himself, to no avail: *Bear in mind that not only do you honor your marriage and love your family; you also say Amen to the Gospel According to Mark, which stipulates that Thou Shalt Not Hump the Help.* "Mark" being Mark Matthews, his boss and mentor first in Baltimore and then, since Lucas & Jones opened their Eastern Shore office five years ago, in Stratford. That's when the Barneses bought 414 Doubler Drive: a bit snug for a family of four with two teenagers, but a sound investment, bound to appreciate rapidly in value as the population of Avon and its neighboring counties steadily grows. The girls had shared a bedroom since their babyhood and enjoyed doing so right through their adolescence; the elderly couple in 412, the coach home's first-floor unit, were both retired and retiring, so quiet that one could almost forget that their place was occupied. In the four years until their recent, reluctant move to Bayview Manor, they never once complained about Ashleigh's and Tiffany's sometimes noisy get-togethers with school friends.

Perhaps Reader is wincing at the heavy New Testament sound of "Mark Matthews Lucas and Jones"? *"Thou shalt not wince,"* Mark himself enjoys commanding new or prospective clients in their first interview: "Why do you think Jim Lucas and Harvey Jones [the firm's co-founders] hired me in the first place, if not to spread the Good Word about asset management?" Which the fellow did in sooth, churning their portfolios to the firm's benefit as well as theirs and coaching his protégé to do likewise. That earlier gospel-tenet of his, however, he formulated after breaking it himself: In his mid-fifties, coincident with the move from Baltimore to Stratford, he ended his twenty-five-year first marriage to wed the striking young woman who'd been his administrative assistant for three and his mistress for two. *"Don't hump the help,"* he then enjoyed advising their dinner guests, Joe and Judy included, in his new bride's presence: "You should see my alimony bills!" "Plus he had to find himself a new secretary," trim young Mrs. Matthews liked to add, "once his Office Squeeze became his Trophy Wife"—and his unofficial Deputy Account Manager, handling routine portfolio transactions from her own office in their Stratford house, "where unfortunately I can't keep an eye on him."

But *"Eew,* Mom!" Tiffany Barnes is exclaiming in the kitchen of 414 Doubler Drive, where she's ladling excess fat now off the osso buco broth. "Even without this glop, the stuff's so *greasy!"*

"Delicious, though," her mother insists. "And we only have it a couple times a year."

"We have it *only* a couple times a year," her just-arrived other daughter corrects her. An English major herself, Ashleigh likes to catch her family's slips in grammar and usage, especially her English-teacher mother's. Patient Judy rolls her eyes. "Dad says I should open a cabernet to breathe before dinner," the girl then adds: "He'll be up in a minute; he's doing stuff in the garage."

"Just take a taste of this marrow," Judy invites both girls, indicating a particularly large cross-section of shank-bone in the casserole, its core of brown marrow fully an inch in diameter, "and tell me it's not the most delicious thing you ever ate."

"*Ee-e-ew!*" her daughters chorus in unison. Then Tiffany (who's taking an elective course at Fenton called The Bible as Literature that her secular mother frowns at as a left-handed way of sneaking religion into the curriculum, although she quite respects the colleague who's teaching it) adds, "*Think not of the marrow!*" Judy chuckles proudly; Ashleigh groans at the pun, musses her sister's hair, and goes to the wine rack to look for cabernet sauvignon, singing a retaliatory pun of her own that she'd seen on a bumper sticker earlier in the week: "*Life is a ca-ber-net, old chum . . .*"

Sipping same half an hour later with a store-bought duck paté in the living room, where a fake log crackles convincingly in the glass-shuttered fireplace, "So guess who just bought that house at the far end of Spartina Court?" Joe Barnes asks his wife. "Mark and Mindy Matthews!"

"*Mindy,*" Ashleigh scorns, not for the first time: "What a lame name!" Though only nineteen, she's allowed these days to take half a glass of wine with her parents at cocktail time and another half at dinner, since they know very well that she drinks with her college friends and believe that she's less likely to binge out like too many of them on beer and hard liquor if, as in most European households, the moderate consumption of wine with dinner is a family custom. Tiffany, having duly helped with the osso buco, has withdrawn to the sisters' bedroom and her laptop computer until the meal is served.

"That ranch house?" Judy wonders. "Why would the Matthewses swap their nice place in Stratford for a run-of-the-mill ranch house?"

Her husband swirls his wine, the better to aerate it. "Because one, Mark's buying himself a cabin cruiser and wants a waterfront place to go with it. And two, by the time they move in it'll be no run-of-the-mill ranch house, believe me. Far from it!"

Judy sighs. "Another Heron Bay remodeling job. And we can't even get around to replacing that old Formica in our kitchen! But a renovated rancher's still a rancher."

Uninterested Ashleigh, pencil in hand, is back to her new passion, the Sudoku puzzle from that day's *Baltimore Sun.* She has the same shoulder-length straight dark hair and trim tight body that her mother had when Joe and Judy first met as University of Maryland undergraduates two dozen years ago, and that Jeannine Weston (of whose tantalizing figure Joe is disturbingly reminded lately whenever, as now, he remarks this about his eldest daughter) has not yet outgrown. He and Judy both, on the other hand, have put on the pounds—and his hair is thinning toward baldness, and hers showing its first traces of gray, before they even reach fifty. . . .

"Never mind remodeling and renovation," he says now. "That's not Mark's style." He raises his glass as if in toast: "Heron Bay Estates is about to see its very first tear-down!"

. . . plus her generous, once so fine/firm breasts are these days anything but, and "love handles" would be the kindest term for those side rolls of his that, like his belly, have begun to lap over his belted trouser top. Men, of course, enjoy the famously unfair advantage that professional status may confer upon their dealings with the opposite sex: Unsaintly Mark, *e.g.*, is hardly the tall/dark/handsome type, but his being double-chinned, pudgy, and doorknob bald didn't stand in the way of his scoring with pert blonde Mindy—and what in God's name is Joe Barnes up to, thinking such thoughts at Happy Hour in the bosom of his family?

Thus self-rebuked, he takes it upon himself to clean up the hors d'oeuvres and call Tiffany to set the table while Judy assembles a salad and Ashleigh pops four dinner rolls into the toaster oven. As is their weekend custom when all hands are present, they then clink glasses (three wines, one diet iced tea) and say their mock table-grace—"Bless this grub and us that eats it"—before settling into the osso buco. *I love you all, God damn it!* lump-throated Joe reminds himself.

"So what do the M&M's intend to put up in place of their tear-down?" Judy wonders. "One of those big Colonial-style jobs, I guess?"

"Oh, no." Her husband grins, shakes his head. "Wait'll you see. You know that fancy new spread on Loblolly Court, over in Rockfish Reach?" Referring to an imposing Mediterranean-style stucco-and-roof-tiled house built recently in that adjacent neighborhood despite the tsk-tsks of numerous homeowners there.

"Ee-e-ew," comments Tiffany.

"Well: This morning Mark showed me their architect's drawings for what he and Mindy have in mind—Mindy especially, but Mark's all for it—and it makes that Loblobby Court place look as humble as ours."

"Ee-e-*ew!*" Ashleigh agrees with her sister: a put-down not of their coach home, which she's always happy to return to from her dorm despite their bedroom's having become mainly Tiffany's space these days, but the pretentiousness, extravagance, and inconsiderate arrogance, in her liberal opinion, of even the Loblolly Court "McMansion," which at least was built on an unoccupied lot.

A month or so later, on a fair-weather A.M. bicycle ride through the pleasantly winding bike and jogging paths of Heron Bay Estates, Judy and the girls and a couple of Tiffany's Fenton classmates pedal up Spartina Court to see what's what (Joe's over in the city with his boss and secretary at some sort of quarterly meeting in the Lucas & Jones home office). Sure enough, the Gunstons' rambling rancher and its screen of trees have been cleared away completely and replaced by a building-permit board and a vast shallow excavation, the foundation footprint of the Matthews's palatial residence-in-the-works.

"A perfectly OK house!" indignant Ashleigh informs her sister's friends. "No older than ours and twice as big, and *wham!* They just knock it down, haul it to the dump, and put up Buckingham Palace instead!"

"More like the Alhambra," in her younger sister's opinion (Tiff's Art History course at Fenton includes some architecture as well).

"Or Michael Jackson's Neverland?" offers one of her companions.

"Dad showed us the latest computer projections of it last week?" Ash explains, with the rising inflection so popular among her generation: "Ee-e-*ew!* And he thinks it's just fine!"

"Different people go for different things," her mother reminds them all: "*De gustibus non disputandum est!*"

"See what I mean?" Tiffany asks her friends, and they seem to, though what it is they see, Judy prefers not to wonder.

"Anyhow," Ashleigh adds, "whatever's right by our dad's boss is fine with our dad."

"Ashleigh! Really!"

Tiffany's exaggerated eye roll suggests that on this one she sides with her mother, at least in the presence of nonfamily. To Judy's relief, Ashleigh drops the subject, and they finish their bike ride.

Over their early Sunday dinner, however—which Joe, as promised, has returned from Baltimore in time for, before Ashleigh goes back to her dorm—the girl takes up her cudgels again. It's one thing, she declares, to build a big pretentious new house like that eyesore in

Rockfish Reach, if that's what a person wants? But to tear down a perfectly OK quote/unquote *older* one to do it is, in her opinion, downright obscene—like those people who order a full-course restaurant meal and then just nibble at each course, leaving the rest to be tossed out. Gross!

"Weak analogy," her teacher-mother can't help pointing out. "Let's think up a better one."

"Like those people who buy a new car every two years?" Tiffany offers. "When their quote *old* one's in perfectly good condition with maybe ten thousand miles on it?"

"No good," in her sister's opinion, "because at least the old car gets traded in and resold and used. This is more like if every time they buy a new one they *junk* their perfectly OK old one!"

"Good point," Judy approves.

"Or like Saint Mark Matthews," bold Ashleigh presses on, "dumping the mother of his kids for a trophy blonde airhead half his age!"

Alarmed Tiffany glances from sister to mother to dad. But Joe, who until now has seemed to Judy still to have city business on his mind, here joins the conversation like the partner she's loved for two dozen years. "Beg to disagree, guys? Not with your analogies, but with your judgment, OK? Because what the heck, Ash: The ranch-house people weren't evicted or dumped; they put their place up for sale and got close to their asking price for it. Seems to me the whole business calls for nothing more than a raised eyebrow—more for the new house's design, if you don't happen to like it, than for the replacement idea itself."

"I think I second that," his wife decides.

"And Mindy Matthews, by the way, is no *airhead*," Joe informs his daughters. "She's sharp as a tack."

"Hot in bed, too, I bet," Tiffany makes bold to add. Her father frowns disapproval. Judy declares, "That's none of our business, girls."

"But what still gets me, Dad," Ashleigh persists, less belligerently, "is the *extravagance* of it! We learned in Poli Sci this week that if Earth's whole human population could be shrunk to a village of exactly one hundred people—with all the same ratios as now?— only thirty of us would be white people, only twenty would live in better than substandard housing, only eight would have some savings in the bank as well as clothes on our back and food in the pantry, and only *one* of the hundred would have all that plus a college education! And you're telling us that this tear-down thing isn't disgraceful?"

"That's exactly what I'm telling you," her father amiably agrees. "We live in a prosperous free-enterprise country, thank God. Mark Matthews—whom I happen to very much admire—earned his money by brains and hard work, and he and Mindy are entitled to spend it as they damn well please. Plus their architect, builder, and landscaper are all local outfits, so they'll be putting a couple million bucks into Avon County's economy right there, along with their whopping property taxes down the line." He turns up his palms. "Everybody benefits; nobody gets hurt. So what's your problem, Lefty?"

This last is a family tease of a couple years' standing. Ashleigh Barnes was in fact born left-handed, as was Judy's mother, but the nickname dates from her ever more emphatic liberalism since her fifth- and sixth-form years at Fenton. It's a tendency that her younger sister has lately been manifesting as well, although apart from their mother and a few of Judy's colleagues, the school, its faculty, and its students' families are predominantly center-right Republicans.

Her problem, Ashleigh guesses with a sigh, is that she just doesn't like Fat Cats.

"Mindy Matthews *fat?*" Tiffany pretends to protest. "She's downright anorexic! Speaking of which," she adds to her father, "at least one person sure got hurt when Saint Mark changed horses: Sharon Matthews." Mindy's predecessor.

Judy looks to her husband with a smile and raised eyebrows, as if to ask How d'you answer *that* one? But Joe merely shrugs and says, "With the alimony payments she's getting for the rest of her life, that woman can cry all the way to the bank. So let's enjoy our dinner now, OK?"

His wife sees their daughters give each other their We Give Up look. She does likewise, for the present, and the family returns to enjoying, or at least making the best of, one another's company.

Later than evening, Ashleigh drives back to campus in her hand-me-down Honda Civic, Tiffany busies herself in her room with homework and computer, Judy takes a preliminary whack at the Sunday *New York Times* crossword puzzle before prepping her Monday lesson plans, Joe scans that newspaper's business section while pondering what Mark Matthews told him that morning en route back from Baltimore in Mark's new Lexus (Mark and his secretary in the front seat, Joe and Jeannine Weston in the rear), and that he hasn't gotten around yet to sharing with Judy—and the new downstairs neighbors' little Yorkshire terrier starts the infernal yip-yipping again that's been driving them batty ever since the Creightons moved into 412 a month ago. They're a pleasant enough younger couple, he an assistant manager at the Stratford GM dealership, she a part-time dietitian at Avon Health Care and busy mother of their four-year-old son. But the kid is noisy and the dog noisier—a far cry from the unit's previous owners!—and although the Creightons respond good-naturedly to the Barneses' tactful complaints, promising to see what if anything they can do about the problem ("You know how it is with kids and pets!"), it gets no better.

He slaps the newspaper down in his lap. "We've got to get out of this fucking place, hon."

"I'm ready." For rich as it is with five years' worth of family memories—the girls' adolescence, their parents' new jobs—the coach home has never really been big enough. No home office space; no TV/family room separate from the living room; a dining area scarcely large enough to seat six. No guest room even with Ashleigh in the dorm; no real backyard of their own for gardening and barbecuing and such. But the place has, as they'd predicted, substantially appreciated in value, and although any alternative housing will have done likewise, by Joe's reckoning they're "positioned," as he puts it, to move on and up. What Judy would go for is one of the better Oyster Cove villas, a side-by-side duplex instead of over-and-under: three bedrooms, of which one could be her study/workroom and another a combination guestroom/den once Tiffany's off to college; a separate family room with adjacent workshop and utility room; and their own small backyard for cookouts, deck lounging, and as much or little gardening as they care to bother with (in all Heron Bay Estates subdivisions except the detached-house neighborhoods, basic exterior maintenance of buildings and streetside grounds is covered by neighborhood association fees). But what Joe has in mind lately is more ambitious: to buy and renovate one of those older detached houses in Rockfish Reach. A dining room big enough for entertaining friends and colleagues in style, as well as Ash and Tiff and *their* friends; a *real* yard and patio; maybe even a pool and some kind of outboard runabout to keep at their own private dock! And they should finally cough up the money to join the Heron Bay Club on a golf membership and take up the game, without which one is definitely *out* of the social scene (so Mark told him, among other things, in the car that morning). . . .

Judy's flabbergasted. "Are you *kidding?* A twelve-thousand-buck initiation fee plus, what, two hundred a month dues? Plus a house to renovate and two college tuitions coming up, dot dot dot question mark?" It's a thing she does now and then.

"Leave that to me, doll," her husband suggests, in a tone she's been hearing him use lately. "I've learned a thing or two from Master Mark about estate building." *Among other things,* he silently adds and she silently worries—not without cause, although "Tennis, maybe, but count me out on the golf" is all she says aloud. "Not this schoolmarm's style."

Amiably, not to alarm her, "Folks can change their style, you know," he says—and then shares with her part of what's been distracting him all day, since Mark announced it on the drive home. Harold Lucas, one of the firm's founding partners, intends to retire as of the fiscal year's end. Mark Matthews will be replacing him as senior partner and co-director of the company's home office (he and Mindy are buying a condo on the city's Inner Harbor to supplement their Spartina Pointe weekend-and-vacation spread). "And Saint Mark's successor as chief of our Stratford office will be . . . guess who? Whoops, sorry there, Teach: Guess *whom.*"

"Oh, *sweetie!*" She duly flings aside her crossword and lays on the congratulatory cries and kisses; calls for Tiffany to come hear Daddy's big news; asks him why in the world he didn't announce it while Ashleigh was there to hear it too, but laughingly agrees with him that the girl will scornfully assign them now to the *crème de la crème* of her hypothetical hundred-person village—and refrains from pointing out to him that the nominative-case *guess who* is in fact correct, the pronoun being the transposed subject of the verb *will be* rather than the object of *guess.* No champagne in the house just now to toast his promotion with; they'll lay some in and raise a glass to him when Ashleigh's next with them. And in their *new* house, maybe he can have the wine cellar he's always yearned for! Meanwhile . . .

"Congratulations, Dad!" cheers Tiffany, piling onto his lap to kiss him. And when Mom and Dad retire not long afterward to their bedroom for the night, Judy gives her crotch a good washcloth wipe after peeing, to freshen it in case he goes down there in the course of celebratory sex. Since the commencement of her early menopause she's been bothered by occasional yeast infections with accompanying vaginal discharge and sometimes downright painful intercourse—not that they go to it as often or as athletically as in years past.

But this night they do, *sans soixante neuf* and such but vigorously *a tergo* and, to her mild surprise, in the dark. Normally they leave Joe's nightstand light dimmed during lovemaking, to facilitate his finding, opening, and applying their Personal Lubricant and to enjoy the sight of each other's so familiar naked bodies. Tonight, however, it's only after he clicks off the light and snuggles up to say goodnight (also to her surprise) that Joe seems to change his mind. He places his right hand on his partial erection and raises himself on one elbow to lift her short nightie, kiss her navel and nipples, and begin fingering her vulva—all the while scolding himself for imagining a certain younger, leaner body responding to his caresses. In the car that afternoon, when Mark broke the big news of his own and Joe's promotions, Jeannine Weston had squealed with excitement, flung her arms around her boss (those fine breasts of hers pressing into his right upper arm), and planted a loud wet kiss on his cheek. Alice Benning, Mark's secretary since Mindy's promotion to wifehood, had then declared to all hands that she'd asked Jeannine earlier whether she'd be interested in shifting to Baltimore to become the hot-stuff new front-desk receptionist for Lucas & Jones, Inc., and that the girl had replied, "As long as Joe Barnes wants me, I'm his." "Tattletale!" Jeannine had mock-scolded the older woman, and squeezed her chief's right hand in both of hers and leaned her head fondly on his shoulder. Mark, winking broadly at the couple in his rearview mirror, had teased, "Don't forget Rule Number One, Joe," and when Jeannine asked what *that* might be, Alice turned in her seat to whisper loudly, "It's *Hands off the help:* a good rule to live by, says I." So "Shoo, girl!" Joe had duly then bade his young assistant with a broad wink of his own—and to his startlement, in the spirit of their sport she had slid laughing back to her side of the car seat, crossed one arm over those breasts, and with her other hand cupped her crotch as if protectively. It is those body parts that Joe Barnes helplessly finds himself picturing now, and that tight little butt of hers, bare and upraised for him to clutch in both hands while he thrusts and thrusts and thrusts and *Ahhh!* . . . collapses atop his accommodating spouse in contrite exhilaration.

Now: This Tear-Down story could proceed from here in any of several pretty obvious directions, e.g.: (1) Joe Barnes "comes to his senses," his love for Judy and the family reaffirmed by that short-lived guilty temptation. While his office relationship with Jeannine Weston retains an element of jocular flirtation, no adultery follows. A year later the young woman is reoffered that receptionist post in the Baltimore office, and this time she takes it. Her replacement in Stratford is a married woman slightly older than Joe: amiable and competent, but not the stuff of lecherous fantasies. Alternatively, (2) somewhat to his own appall, Joe does indeed succumb to temptation and "humps the help," either in what used to be Mark Matthews's office but is now his or in some motel far enough from town for anonymity. The imaginable consequences range from (a) Next to None (adultery goes undiscovered; both parties, ashamed, decide not to repeat it; Jeannine meets and soon after marries a young professor at Stratford College who eventually moves to a better-paying academic post in Ohio), through (b) Considerable (Joe confesses to Judy and asks for divorce with generous settlement. She brokenheartedly agrees to what she condemns as a "marital Tear-Down." Joe and Jeannine then wed and do a modified Mark-and-Mindy, renovating a large house in Rockfish Reach. The girls, both in college by that time, are shocked, embarrassed, and angry, but eventually come more or less to terms with the family's disruption. Judy remarries an estate lawyer from her southern Maryland hometown, and all parties get on with their lives' next chapter, neither unscarred nor, on balance, unhappy), to (c) Disastrous (Judy discovers the affair, goes ballistic, sues for divorce, and bars Joe from the house. Their daughters turn against him for life. The small-town scandal obliges Jeannine to quit her job and Joe to shift, under a cloud, to Lucas & Jones's far-western-Maryland office. "What'd I tell you?" Mark scolds triumphantly. Judy stays on at her Fenton post and in the Blue Crab Bight coach house, where the downstairs dog yips maddeningly on to the tale's last page and beyond).

My personal inclination (George Newett here, Reader, who's been dreaming up this whole story: Tale-Teller Emeritus [but no tale-bearer] in Stratford College's Department of Creative Writing and, like "Joe and Judy Barnes," resident with my Mrs. in Blue Crab Bight) is to go with (3) None of the Above. This being, after all, a Tear-Down story, I'm deciding to tear the sumbitch down right about here, the way people like "Mark and Mindy Matthews" might decide to tear down not only the Gunstons' "old" ranch house on Spartina Court but even the barely started *hacienda grande* that they're in the costly process of replacing it with. Mindy, let's say, has been belatedly persuaded by her longtime friend and fellow Stratford alumna Faye Robertson (now on the Fenton School faculty, Judy Barnes's colleague and Tiffany's Art History teacher) that a mission-style *palacio* in Spartina Pointe will be as in-your-face and out of place as that neo-Neapolitan *palazzo* of Tom and Patricia Hardison's in Rockfish Reach (another story, perhaps, for another time), and that for the sake of Heron Bay Estates' "aesthetic ecology" the Matthewses really ought to have considered a Williamsburg-style manse instead. "Never too late to reconsider," I imagine bold Mindy declaring to her astonished friend with a Just You Watch sort of laugh and then announcing her mind-change to "Saint Mark," who wonders whether *he'd* better reconsider what he's gotten himself into with this woman. Maybe time for a midstream change of horses on *that* front too? But he then decides it'd be an even better demonstration of upscale panache just to shrug, chuckle, and say, "Whatever milady desireth . . ."

You see how it is with us storytellers—with some of us, anyhow, perhaps especially the Old Fart variety, whereof Yours Truly is a member of some standing. Our problem, see, is that we invent people like the Barneses, do our best to make them reasonably believable and even *simpatico*, follow the rules of Story by putting them in a high-stakes situation—and then get to feeling more responsibility to *them* than to you the reader. "Never too late to reconsider," we end up saying to ourselves like Mindy Matthews, and instead of Ending their tear-down tale for better or worse (sorry about that, guys), we pull its narrative plug before somebody gets hurt.

Here's how:

From Scale

A Musical Regression in Five Acts

Will Self

(*There are three playing areas—the interior of the bungalow, the model village, and a third area that does service as the ironmonger's, the bathroom, the carport, an allotment, the median strip of the M40, etc., where indicated. I would prefer the three areas to take up thirds of a revolve, but if necessary they can be laid out across the stage, left to right: the bungalow, the open area, the model village.*

Either around the periphery of the revolve, or downstage and running across its fullest extent, there is a strip of motorway, complete with defined lanes, cats' eyes that glow in the dark, and three large, white-out-of-green motorway signs.

The first of these, which is sited in front of the break between the bungalow and the model village, reads: MODEL VILLAGE *and has an English Heritage rosette symbol. The second—situated between the model village and the open area— reads:* BIRMINGHAM 86, *and the third, either stage right or on the revolve between the open area and the bungalow, reads:* BEACONSFIELD 4. *The signs, where necessary, can be tipped to the horizontal. Needless to say, I would prefer for this motorway to be on an independent revolve.*

There is an orchestra pit that holds a small classical ensemble; either a quartet, quintet, or sextet, depending on what is possible. There is also a singer—preferably a highly mannered soprano. The pit remains sufficiently lit throughout the action of the play for the audience to be conscious of the musicians.

The bungalow is rented by THE AUTHOR, *a jobbing academic-cum-writer in the throes of a major opiate addiction. He is surprisingly straight in appearance: tweed jacket, Viyella shirt, woolen tie, corduroy trousers, etc., but emaciated and quite, quite mad.*

The bungalow reflects his mental state: stage left, against the wall, there is a dilapidated range of kitchen cupboards— Melamine peeling, handles dangling—and below them work surfaces and a gas cooker.

Above the cooker is a small window with diamond mullions that looks out onto the model village. In front of this there is a breakfast bar, equally tatty, at one end of which there are shelves stacked with decorative Tupperware.

On top of the breakfast bar is a Milton sterilizer unit full of some unspeakable brown gloop, this is incorporated—using feeding bottles, pipettes, syringes, etc.—into a bizarre piece of homemade alchemical equipment. Next to this is an anti-quated (1992) clock radio, featuring a large black-on-white digital display. There are a couple of high metal-legged stools at the breakfast bar with painful-looking wickerwork backs.

Downstage there is a circular table with three chairs ranged around it. On top of the table is a still more antiquated (1986) Amstrad word processor and printer. The printer spews a long tongue of paper covered with print. Elsewhere on the table are sheaves of paper, many open volumes, overflowing ashtrays, and other writerly impedimenta.

Stage right there is a sofa backed against the wall and above this a second diamond-paned window looks out onto the open area.

Most crucially: radiating out from the work surfaces of the kitchen, spilling across the breakfast bar and then over the ratty, fitted carpeting, are many, many scores—hundreds even—of the small brown bottles that hold the diarrhea preparation kaolin and morphine. They are all empty.

The overall impression is that the bungalow was rented unpleasantly furnished some time ago, and since then has run seriously to seed.

The model village is just that: a slice of little Little England, including a church, a village hall, and two or three ditsy houses. They are all about shoulder-height and as detailed as possible.

One of these dwellings is hard stage right, so that someone clambering through the window above the cooker in the bungalow can gain direct access to its interior. This dwelling is a plausible version of the bungalow itself—but writ small. (Of course, if a revolve is not possible, there will necessarily be a hiatus when players exit the open area to enter the model village, and vice versa. Hopefully, this can be used to comic effect.)

Downstage of this mini bungalow—and abutting it—is an

older cottage; while upstage and ranging right to left are the church and the village hall. Center stage is a green, complete with miniature oaks, duck pond, benches, etc.

The model village comes complete with discretely positioned model, model inhabitants: a vicar in front of the church, a man washing his car with a dribbling hose, children playing on the green, etc.

It is possible to exit the model village stage left through the village hall and into the open area. The open area has an awning that can be retracted upstage or pulled forward and attached to two stanchions downstage. Downstage there is a lay-by shape carved out from the motorway that runs in front. Behind this there is a steepish rake of artificial grass, if possible forming a tumulus. Vehicles entering the lay-by area from the motorway can either be perceived as pulling off the motorway, or entering—if the awning is pulled forward— the carport of the bungalow.)

*

(THE AUTHOR is younger than you might expect—midthirties—and although disordered, he is attractive and charismatic enough to make his sexual shenanigans plausible. He fronts up well in the presence of authority. That authority figure is

The POLICEMAN who also doubles as the BOROUGH VALUER and the WARDEN of the Nationalist Trust. He is the epitome of straightness and probity in all three guises. A family man of the same age as THE AUTHOR, but clear eyed, purposive, radiating purity of intent. In marked contrast to

The MODEL HEAD who also doubles as the SHAMAN. His garb is a long Hessian cloak, a staff, Hessian puttees that are lashed around his calves and ankles, and also form his footwear. He is bare chested above baggy denim britches and his bald head is embellished with crude Celtic tattoos. He sports a large nose ring and many other piercings. When manifesting as the SHAMAN he affects a curious headdress surmounted by a pair of cat's eyes. He is dirty—in mind and body—an addict of all conceivable narcotics, his mind polluted by every possible superstition. Yet he is young, and beneath his psychic, crazy paving there remains a solid ground. He is without malice.)

ACT ONE

(There is a hiss and a crackle as of a car radio being tuned in. The playing area is in darkness save for a pair of head-lights piercing the gloom. THE AUTHOR *is parading around and around the strip of motorway; he is wearing a panto-mime car: the body is in the region of his middle, sus-pended by shoulder straps. His legs emerge from this in the manner of a character in* The Flintstones. *Occasional flashes from his headlights illuminate the three motorway signs. The overall eeriness of the scene is compounded when the radio is correctly tuned and the voice of* JOHN MAJOR *swells into its full, dweeby, oratorical mode.)*

JOHN MAJOR. *(Unseen.)* . . . For many of you, I know, the heart pulls in one direction and the head in another. There is nothing that can stir the heart like the history of this country. It is part of us. Nothing can change that. But it's a different world now. Our fam-ilies are growing up in a different age. They know we can't pull up the drawbridge and live in our own private yesterday. They know we live in a world of competition—and we can't just wish it away. Change isn't just coming, it's here. I want Britain to mold that change, to lead that change in our own national interest. *(Whoever is listening to the car radio has grown fed up with this and retunes; there is a burst of static that resolves itself into the string ensemble in the orchestra pit sawing away at "Rhythm Is a Dancer" by the popular early 1990s beat combo Snap. The mannered* SOPRANO *begins to sing.)*

SOPRANO. Rhythm is a dancer / It's a soul's companion . . . *(Continues to sing Snap's "Rhythm Is a Dancer," but is cut off abruptly as the radio is once more retuned, and* MAJOR *swims back out of the static.)*

JOHN MAJOR. *(Unseen.)* That's what I mean by being at the heart of Europe. Not turning a deaf ear to the heartbeat of Britain, but hav-ing the courage to stand up and do what we believe to be right. *(*THE AUTHOR *begins to cackle quite loudly over what follows.)* Right for British industry, right for British jobs, right for British prosperity.

During the summer, when I was in Cornwall, a lady came up to speak to me. "Mr. Major," she said, "please, please don't let

Britain's identity be lost in Europe." She didn't tell me her name. But she spoke for the anxieties of millions. She spoke for this country. She spoke for me. So let me tell this conference what I told that lady in Cornwall. (*The hollow laughter increases in intensity, and once more* THE AUTHOR *retunes, so that . . .*) I will never—come hell or high water . . . (*Is lost under a barrage of static to be replaced by the ensemble sawing away at "How Soon Is Now" by the Smiths. This is more to* THE AUTHOR's *taste because once the lyric is encountered he begins to duet with the* SOPRANO.)

THE AUTHOR. I am the son / And the heir . . . (*He becomes more and more raucous as the song continues, but no sooner is this new ambience established than we become aware of a police car, which merges with the motorway from the wings, and passes* THE AUTHOR's *vehicle at speed, before decelerating so that it falls behind. The music is then undercut by a police siren of the demented whip-poor-will sort then (1992) new to Britain.*) Oh shit!

> (*Both vehicles come to a halt upstage, dry ice billows about them, the police car's headlights pick out the bizarre spectacle of* THE AUTHOR *in his pantomime car. Of course, the police car is also of a pantomime sort, but it has two policemen in it, one of whom has a revolving light strapped to his head that casts a blue wash over the dry ice. It is a scene at once eerie and absurd. The ensemble continues to saw away at "How Soon Is Now" in a muted fashion.* THE POLICEMEN *lower the body of their car so one of them can step out. He walks up to* THE AUTHOR *and stands listening, with his ear cocked, for a few moments, before saying:*)

POLICEMAN. It's a rerelease, isn't it?

THE AUTHOR. I'm sorry?

POLICEMAN. The Smiths' "How Soon Is Now?," it's been rereleased. (*As if this statement affirms his authority,* THE POLICEMAN *begins to rock back and forth on his heels, while whistling along—then breaks off.*) Must be, what, '85 or '6 when it first charted, so that's six or seven years—

THE AUTHOR. I hardly—

431

POLICEMAN. Enough time for it to be what you might call an "oldie," no?

THE AUTHOR. Is this why you—

POLICEMAN. Stopped you? Hardly. Although there is a curious, um, contra-flow at work here—if I can be forgiven a traffic-control metaphor—for, as the pace of change in pop music accelerates, so hits, their covers, and their rereleases follow with such alacrity that everything acquires the same, um, patina of the past. Now people experience a sense of acute nostalgia when they contemplate events that occurred a couple of years ago, wouldn't you agree?

THE AUTHOR. I s'pose—

POLICEMAN. It's conceivable that not too long in the future we will have continual, joyful, anticipation of the past that is to come in the very next moment—

THE AUTHOR. (*Who has been cowed like an errant schoolboy, now sees his chance to shine.*) How soon is now?

POLICEMAN. Quite so, which brings us, rather neatly, to you, and to here: the M40 motorway just south of Junction 4, and to now: 12:47 a.m. on a very foggy October night. Can you explain to me, sir, why it is that you have been driving quite so slowly?

THE AUTHOR. Slowly?

POLICEMAN. Under thirty miles per hour, to be precise. (*He turns back to his colleague for confirmation.*)

SECOND POLICEMAN. (*Reading officiously from the display of some radar gizmo.*) An average of twenty-two miles per hour for the past five minutes.

POLICEMAN. Very slow—some might say criminally retarded. Can you justify this leisurely pace: it is foggy, the tail lights on your inferior French car are exceedingly dim, any vehicle traveling at a reasonable pace would be more than justified in squashing you flat, *n'est ce pas?*

THE AUTHOR. Well, I—I mean to—

POLICEMAN. No, no, don't interrupt! (*Quite suddenly he is angry and menacing.*) I don't want to hear any shit out of you! Are you

432

drunk? Are you stoned? Do you have any idea what kind of horrific pileups such utterly irresponsible behavior can cause? Do you know what it's like to spend night after night picking up body parts from the medium strip of the M40? A still-beating heart or a still-wheezing lung skewered on a fucking steel stanchion, the sweet young girl it's been forcibly transplanted from lying only a few feet away, her face a bloody mush! Can you imagine it? Can you?!

THE AUTHOR. Um, you don't think you might be—

POLICEMAN. Exaggerating? No, no I don't. (*Calls over to colleague.*) Am I exaggerating?

SECOND POLICEMAN. Absolutely and categorically not. Why, you and I have patrolled this very road after accidents of such an awful magnitude that the entire thoroughfare, the median strip, and the very embankments have been heaped with dismembered corpses and shattered, burning vehicles. We have had to drive over the dying in our quest for those who might yet live.

POLICEMAN. So, an explanation please as to why you would risk being the cause of such a holocaust?

(*A pause, during which we become insistently aware that no traffic whatsoever is passing by. The ensemble has stopped playing, there is only the night and the fog.*)

THE AUTHOR. (*Shivering.*) S-some people lose their sense of proportion—I—I've lost my sense of scale.

POLICEMAN. Meaning?

THE AUTHOR. I'm driving home from London to Beaconsfield, where I live. It's a drive I've done hundreds of times, but tonight I found myself unable to judge the distance from the last exit sign for Junction 4 to the slip road.

POLICEMAN. Oh really? It's simple enough: there are three exit signs, as you know. The first has three oblique white lines set in blue, the second two, and the third one. By the time you reach the third you should've already begun to appreciate the meaning of the curved wedge, adumbrated with further oblique white lines, that forms—

THE AUTHOR. I know, I know, it's an interzone, isn't it, an unplace, between the slip road as it pares away and the inside carriageway of the motorway, which powers on toward the Chiltern scarp.

POLICEMAN. Beautifully put. (*He becomes creepily emollient.*) So, what's the problem?

THE AUTHOR. The Ministry has cocked up here. There's far too long a gap between the last sign and the start of the slip road. I dunno, I sort of fell into this gap and lost my sense—

POLICEMAN. Of scale, yes?

THE AUTHOR. That's right. You see, I'm writing a work on this very subject: the anthropological significance of modern motorway signs. You can understand why I was so—

POLICEMAN. What are you then, some kind of academic?

THE AUTHOR. Um, no, just a dilettante.

POLICEMAN. (*Menacing once more.*) You're a fucking nutter is what you are. Don't you get it? If you can't coordinate the sequence of these signs (*He gestures.*) with the falling needles on your instrument panel, then you're clearly unable to intuitively apprehend three different scales at once—time, speed, distance—let alone merge them effortlessly into the virtual reality that is motorway driving. You must be pissed. (*Calls to other policeman.*) Stan! Get out the Breathalyzer.

> (*The two* POLICEMEN *go about the business of administering the Breathalyzer test with studious efficiency, while* THE AUTHOR *blathers.*)

THE AUTHOR. No, no, this gap—I think I'm still in it. I think you may be in it as well—

POLICEMAN. Now, take a deep breath and blow into the mouthpiece. It's important that you continue to blow for at least fifteen seconds—

THE AUTHOR. It's not simply a gap, it's also a lacuna—

POLICEMAN. Blow!

THE AUTHOR. (*He blows into the Breathalyzer, then immediately upon finishing continues.*) In terms of my projected thesis, "No Services: Reflex Ritualism and Modern Motorway Signs—

POLICEMAN. Observe that the first light is illuminated, this demonstrates that you have some alcohol in your system—

THE AUTHOR. (with special reference to the M40)"—

POLICEMAN. We will now wait for thirty seconds. If the second light illuminates, it shows evidence that the concentration of alcohol in your bloodstream is greater than .8 milligrams per thousand parts, in which case—

THE AUTHOR. And could be interpreted as an aspect of what the French critical theorists call *délire*—

POLICEMAN. I shall have to advise you of your rights and ask you to accompany us to the station in High Wycombe, where a blood sample will be taken—

THE AUTHOR. Namely that part of the text that is a deviation or derangement, not contained within the text, and yet defines the text better than the text itself.

POLICEMAN. Is that clear?

> (*The three stand motionless for thirty seconds in appropriately hieratic postures:* THE POLICE *martial,* THE AUTHOR *dejected. The dry ice billows.*)

THE AUTHOR. No light.

POLICEMAN. Indeed. You are free to go, sir, with one proviso—

THE AUTHOR. Which is?

POLICEMAN. Drive faster in future, considerably faster. (*He continues as he escorts* THE AUTHOR *back to his pantomime car, and contemptuously observes him as he buckles himself into it.*) Have some consideration for your fellow road users. This is no longer the summer of love—it is a winter of profound and foggy obscurity. You don't want to be in the same position—nothing happening in your life, going nowhere—in another seven years when—

THE AUTHOR. When what?

POLICEMAN. When "How Soon Is Now?" is reissued again. Good evening (*He tips his cap.*) or, should I say, good morning.

> (*The* POLICEMAN *and his colleague walk back to their pantomime car and clamber into it. The ensemble start up with the quavering chords of "How Soon Is Now?" A strobe light flickers through the dry ice. The* SOPRANO *begins her mannered rendition.*)

SOPRANO. I am the son / And the heir . . . (*And continues as the police car herds* THE AUTHOR'S *car off around the strip of motorway that encircles the revolve. The pantomime cars increase in speed. This could either be effected by the revolve turning to create the impression of speed, or the motorway strip revolving, or both counterclockwise. At any rate, as the song reaches a crescendo, the police car puts its headlights on full beam and passes* THE AUTHOR, *almost pushing him off the motorway. His headlights illuminate the sign* BEACONSFIELD 4 *and he pulls into the open area, dumps the pantomime car, and scrambles through the window stage left.*) I am human and I need to be loved . . .

> (*The strobe cuts out; the ensemble swoops down into low, juddering chords, then stops abruptly; the dry ice is evacuated; the lights come on in the bungalow;* THE AUTHOR *does a surprisingly neat somersault through the window and lands sitting on the sofa next to the* MODEL HEAD, *who is entirely wrapped up in his Hessian cloak.* THE AUTHOR'S *impact jolts the* MODEL HEAD *awake, and his jangling face full of rings emerges from the cloak. They leap upright and face one another, shocked (although not quite as much as you'd expect).*)

MODEL HEAD AND AUTHOR. How the fuck did you get in?

MODEL HEAD AND AUTHOR. I came in through the window. (*They gesture to opposite windows.*)

MODEL HEAD AND AUTHOR. I know that!

MODEL HEAD AND AUTHOR. Then why'd you fucking well ask! (*Tiring of the synchrony,* THE AUTHOR *breaks away and begins to pace. He goes to the table and faffs with some papers.*)

THE AUTHOR. You arse, you freaked me right fucking out, what the fuck're you doing here?

MODEL HEAD. (*Aggrieved, babbling.*) I 'ad some deliveries an' that to, as it were, make in the locale. And it's a cold and foggy night— the Wicca Man may be abroad. Or the Bunyip—it makes no kind of sense for the likes of me to be out there, so I thought you wouldn't mind—(*He breaks off.* THE AUTHOR *has stopped faffing and stands shaking with a bit of the computer printout rattling in his hand.*) Whassup wiv you? You look like you've seen a—

THE AUTHOR. I got a pull, when I was coming off at Junction 4.

MODEL HEAD. The filth?

THE AUTHOR. Quite so, blue angels with dirty faces.

MODEL HEAD. But they didn't nick you?

THE AUTHOR. No, no, they didn't nick me—but they pushed me deeper in.

MODEL HEAD. Deeper in? Deeper in to what?

THE AUTHOR. The gap, the lacuna, the un-place, the interzone . . . where I lost my sense of scale.

MODEL HEAD. You're touched, you are—touched.

THE AUTHOR. Touched? Groped—I need a hit. (*He goes to the oven and withdraws a baking tray, which he peers into. The* MODEL HEAD *joins him and they both stare down into the tray.*)

MODEL HEAD. What the fuck is that?

THE AUTHOR. That—or rather those. Those are hard-baked morphine granules. I put them in the oven when I left this morning.

MODEL HEAD. It looks like bleeding Death Valley in there.

THE AUTHOR. (*Scholarly.*) I know what you mean, and observe here, and here (*Indicating.*), where the rime lies in a ruckled surface . . . and over here where it forms a strangely regular pattern of scales like the skin of a moribund lizard.

MODEL HEAD. That's some heavy shit there, that is. What're you gonna do with it?

THE AUTHOR. I'm going to shoot it up.

MODEL HEAD. Oh ma-an, no, that's gross—you can't do that.

THE AUTHOR. Can—and will. (*He scrapes some gray gunk from the tray and places it in a small Tupperware bowl.*)

MODEL HEAD. (*Taking the bowl from him.*) What're those round the rim?

THE AUTHOR. (*Taking it back.*) I think you will find that they are leaping bunnies. I may have vouchsafed to you before, that after my divorce my wife organized the division of the chattels. She took all the adult-size plates and cutlery, leaving me with the diminutive ware that our children had outgrown.

MODEL HEAD. Somehow that makes it worse.

THE AUTHOR. What worse?

MODEL HEAD. Your 'abit.

THE AUTHOR. Well, it couldn't be worse than yours. (*He takes a fold of the* MODEL HEAD's *cloak and pulls it, to reveal the baggy denim breeches, the tattooed chest.*) Anyway, that's not the point. I have no formal training in chemistry, but somehow, by a process of hit and miss (*He turns the queer alchemical apparatus and adds the morphine gunk to the sterilizer, before fiddling with a spigot.*), I have developed a method whereby I can precipitate a soluble tartrate from raw morphine granules. (*He holds up a baby's feeding bottle full of a cloudy yellow liquid.*) The problem with this stuff is that it still contains an appreciable amount of chalk. This is because I obtain my supplies in the form of bottles of kaolin and morphine purchased in sundry chemists.

MODEL HEAD. I dunno why you can't juss score smack like the rest of us.

THE AUTHOR. That would not be seemly for a man of my advanced ideas. Besides, if I leave the bottles for long enough (*He picks up one of the myriad little brown bottles that clutter the entire kitchen area.*), most of the morphine rises to the top. Still, you can never eradicate all the kaolin. (*He expertly pops a disposable hypodermic syringe from a blister pack and marries it to a long blue-collared needle.*) And when the morphine solution is siphoned off (*He employs the hypodermic to draw some of the solution from the feeding bottle.*), some of the kaolin invariably comes as well. (*He holds the hypodermic aloft, depresses the plunger, and a spurt of fluid arcs across the stage.*) Months of injecting this stuff have given my body an odd aspect (*He has moved center stage, he unbuttons his tweed jacket, and throughout what follows: shucks it off, removes his belt with a thwack, unhooks his trousers, and advances upstage to where a full-length mirror is mounted on the wall.*), as with every shot more chalk is deposited along the walls of my veins, much in the manner of earth being piled up to form an embankment for a roadway. Thus the history of my addiction has been mapped out by me, in the same way that the road system of England was originally constructed.

To begin with, conscious of this effect, I methodically worked my way through the veins in my arms and legs, turning them first the tannish color of drovers' paths, then the darker brown of cart tracks, until eventually they became macadamized, blackened, by my abuse. (*He has gained the mirror and stands on a set of bathroom scales in front of it.*) Now, when I stand on these broken bathroom scales and contemplate my route-planning image (*He lets his trousers and underpants fall to his knees; the track marks in his groin and on his belly are so livid that they're clearly visible to the audience.*), I see a network of calcified conduits radiating from my groin.

MODEL HEAD. Oh, fuck, man, that is seriously gross. Totally twisted.

THE AUTHOR. (*Beckoning to him.*) Cummere, look, see. Some of them are scored into my skin.

MODEL HEAD. (*Wonderingly.*) Like underpasses.

THE AUTHOR. Indeed, while others are raised up on hardened revetments of flesh.

MODEL HEAD. Bloody flyovers. (*He breaks away and lurches over to the table, where he sweeps some books and papers off a chair and collapses onto it.*) Nah, nah, I can't be doing wiv this, iss too much, iss creeping me out, man.

THE AUTHOR. Creeping you out? (*He hobbles over, still half naked, and takes another chair.*) Creeping you out? What about me? I've been driven to using these huge five-milliliter barrels, fitted with the blue-collared needles necessary to hit arteries.

MODEL HEAD. Yeah, yeah, I know what that is. (*He waves away the hypo, which* THE AUTHOR *has been brandishing.*)

THE AUTHOR. Do you realize the consequences for my circulatory system if I were to miss an artery? I might lose a limb, and cause tailbacks right the way round—

MODEL HEAD. The M25. Yeah, yeah, you're obsessed by motorways, you are, bloody obsessed, and what's all that about?

THE AUTHOR. It's about this. (*He clutches up an armful of the computer printout.*) My thesis, "No Services: Reflex Ritualism and Modern Motorway Signs (with special reference to the M40)." Once I have my doctorate, everything will change. I'll kick my habit, I'll be able both to support myself and pay the mainte-nance—are you listening to me? (*It doesn't seem as if the* MODEL HEAD *is, because he's withdrawn a jar of some sticky substance from a fold in his cloak, and is sticking his finger into this and licking it.*)

MODEL HEAD. These are ace 'shrooms, man, 'shrooms in honey. You should try some—leave that ugly gear alone, so you should.

THE AUTHOR. (*Waving away the* MODEL HEAD's *sticky fingers.*) If I don't keep up the maintenance, my ex-wife—who is frequently leveled by spirits—will become as obdurate as any consulting civil engineer. She has it within her power to arrange cones around me—

MODEL HEAD. (*Laughing.*) You could always call the Cones Hotline, try and get 'em shifted—

THE AUTHOR. Or she'll insist on the introduction of tolls to pay the maintenance. There could be questions in the bungalow!

MODEL HEAD. You know what, mate?

THE AUTHOR. What?

MODEL HEAD. You've lost your incident room, you have. I've gotta crash. (*He rises, stretches, stashes his honeypot.*) Mind if I use your bed? Coz it looks like you'll be up a while, what with finding an artery an' that. (*But* THE AUTHOR *doesn't answer. He's taking off his trousers and underpants, looping the belt round his upper thigh to form a tourniquet, pulling it tight, holding up the nee-dle to check there are no air bubbles in it, and then plunging it home.*) I'll take that as a yes. (*He exits stage left. The lighting begins to fade to a spot, within which* THE AUTHOR *performs his grisly task.*)

THE AUTHOR. Yes! Yes! Left hand down, harder, harder . . . Oh! And around we go, pinned by g-force into the tight circularity of history. I'm staring . . . staring up, up into the dark, dark blue of a sky . . . (*In fact, he is staring down into the table, he is nodding out.*) that is near to the end of history. . . . (*He slumps forward onto the table, a pathetic and disturbing figure. The hypo clatters from between his legs to the carpet, like a shed penis. Blood drips. The spot continues to shrink, while the ensemble discordantly tunes up and the* SOPRANO *rises to her feet, and, with the ensemble suddenly behind, launches, midsong, back into "Rhythm Is a Dancer."*)

SOPRANO. . . . Oh you can feel it yeah / Oh it's a passion / Oh!

> (*Blackout behind the ensemble, which continues, and when the lights come up again all is changed. The stage has revolved to the open area, the sign reading* BIRMINGHAM 86 *has been tipped to the horizontal. On top of it, now entirely naked, lies* THE AUTHOR. *The scene in the open area is bucolic in the extreme: an expanse of fruiterer's fake grass or Astroturf is being tilled by a small posse of tribesmen, dressed in a more "authentic" form of the* MODEL HEAD's *garb—Hessian breeches, "new primitive" tattoos incorporating motorway signage, wood bangles, and earrings, possibly lip plugs. On the tumulus a pair of young children are tending a small group of extravagantly horned sheep. As the lights come up—very bright—the* TILLERS *are duetting with the* SOPRANO *in time to the wielding of their digging sticks.*)

TILLERS AND SOPRANO. . . . Rhythm is a dancer. . . .

THE AUTHOR. Oh my God! Oh, what a hit! Ah! (*He rolls to the side of the sign/bier and lies drooling over it.*) No, no—I feel claustrophobic, so claustrophobic, like no space is great enough to contain me, not even the involution of time itself. (*The* TILLERS *ignore him, the* SOPRANO *and her ensemble fade out, leaving them to go on with the verse in a subdued, tribal murmur.*)

TILLERS. . . . . I'm serious as cancer when I say / Rhythm is a dancer, etc.

> (*While this has been going on,* THE AUTHOR *has recovered himself and begun to observe the bizarre scene with some acuity, noting the primitive agriculture, the grazing of the mouflon, with a professional detachment. He now sits cross-legged.*
> *The* TILLERS *stop chanting as the* SHAMAN *enters stage left. Clearly this is the* MODEL HEAD *although his garb has been subtly altered in accord with the tribal aesthetic. He sports a complicated headdress, bound into which are a set of cat's eyes that coruscate in the bright lighting. The* TILLERS *hustle forward around him and make obeisance, then, gathering their digging sticks together, exit. The* SHAMAN *advances to the bier and addresses* THE AUTHOR.)

SHAMAN. Well, how you are getting on with decomposing? (*His voice, his demeanor—all suggest that this is the incarnation the* MODEL HEAD *has been waiting for.*)

THE AUTHOR. I'm sorry?

SHAMAN. Decomposing. As a motorway chieftain, your corpse will be laid out here until it decomposes, then excarnated. After that, your bones will be interred in a mausoleum hollowed out from the gigantic concrete caisson of that ancient motorway bridge. (*He gestures.*)

THE AUTHOR. Er, if I'm dead, why are you talking to me?

SHAMAN. As a shaman, it is my sacred duty to converse with the spirits of the departed so that they may enter the afterlife fully aware of what went before—

THE AUTHOR. Forgive me for interrupting, but I note that you observe the *Star Trek* convention—

SHAMAN. *Star Trek?*

THE AUTHOR. You know, whereby even the most outlandish peoples still speak standard English.

SHAMAN. (*Ignoring this sally.*) You must remember as the blue light of your own annihilation bears down on you, how you

442

righteously lived your life as the chieftain of the Junction 2, Cat's Eye clan of the M40, supervising your people as we tilled the thoroughfare and grazed our moufflon (*He gestures to the child shepherds and their little flock.*) on its sacred embankments.

THE AUTHOR. (*Perking up still more.*) Ah, I get it! This is the far distant future, isn't it? This is some neo-neolithic era after the death of civilization. The M40 is grassed over and used for primitive agriculture, and presumably has the same sort of religious significance as the monumental architecture of the old stone age. Tell me, are there still no services?

SHAMAN. (*Again, ignoring the question.*) We do indeed view the M40 as a giant astronomical clock. We use the slip roads, maintenance areas, bridges, and flyovers azimuthally, to predict the solstices and hence the seasons—

THE AUTHOR. Forgive me, but your knowledge of the prior use of the motorway seems to jibe—two time scales are overlaid. How can this be?

SHAMAN. It is true that while we are a simple, agrarian folk, our religion is of great antiquity and complexity. Although we are no longer able to read or write ourselves, we shamans have orally transmitted down the generations the sacred revelations contained in this ancient text! (*With a flourish, he pulls from beneath his cloak a great clutch of computer printout.*)

THE AUTHOR. Let me have a look at that. (*The* SHAMAN *passes it up to him, and the length of it dangles down from the bier, like toilet paper from its holder.*) Stone me! This is my thesis: "No Services: Reflex Ritualism and Modern Motorway Signs (with special reference to the M40)." So I did finish it in the end!

(*Blackout. When the lights come up again, we are back in the kitchen of the bungalow. Morning sunlight streams through the diamond panes of the windows and picks out a peculiar scene:* THE AUTHOR *is slumped where he collapsed into his narcotic reverie the night before, trousers and underpants still around his ankles, while the* MODEL HEAD *sits across from him, looking surprisingly chipper— almost groomed—and reading* The Guardian *while eating cereal. The newspaper headline is* RIO EARTH SUMMIT REACHES AGREEMENT ON CLIMATE CHANGE. *The twittering of birdsong fills the air in a most insistent and, given it was October the night before, unseasonal fashion.)*

(Stirring.) Ga . . . ! Fuck . . . I. Shit. Like Feel.

MODEL HEAD. You oughta have some All Bran, mate *(Gestures with his spoon.)*, it keeps you regular. Your intestines must be blocked up with a traffic jam of crap, what with all that gear you're doing.

THE AUTHOR. Ga, umf, eurgh. *(He rises and adjusts his clothing, finds his belt, threads and buckles it. In a pathetic way he tries to make himself presentable as he limps behind the breakfast bar.)*

MODEL HEAD. *(Calling over his shoulder.)* Any chance of a cuppa? *(THE AUTHOR finds the kettle, fills it from the tap, and puts it on the hob, which he ignites. He snaps on the radio, and the ensemble immediately start up.)*

SOPRANO. Rhythm is a dancer / It's a soul's companion—*(And just as abruptly stops, because THE AUTHOR retunes the radio with a howl of static to—)*

TODAY PROGRAM PRESENTER. *(Unseen.)* -ime Minister's speech to a triumphant Tory party conference. Surprisingly, some of the most commented-on remarks that Mr. Major made were these concerning the lack of service centers on British motorways.

MAJOR. *(Unseen.)* You know, deregulation isn't just about making life better for business. It's about making life easier for everybody. Take the bureaucratic controls, which mean Whitehall decides whether you have the chance to stop off the motorway. Every parent knows what I mean. Next services, fifty-four miles—when your children can't make ten! They've got to go. And so those rules have got to go!

PRESENTER. *(Unseen.)* And here to discuss those bureaucratic controls is Barry Shearman, a spokesman from the Department of Transport. Mr. Shearman, do you think the Prime Minister has a point here?

SHEARMAN. *(Unseen.)* It depends what you mean by bureaucratic—

PRESENTER. *(Unseen.)* It wasn't me who said bureaucratic, but Mr. Major.

SHEARMAN. (*Unseen.*) OK, the Prime Minister then. The point is, without any regulation there would be service center after service center. Many people—not just children—have tiny bladders and there are unscrupulous private operators out there, ready and able to exploit this weakness . . . (*The kettle has begun to boil, and* THE AUTHOR, *who has been lost in the radio interview, summons himself, scouts out a tea pot and tea bags, then pours the boiling water. Over what follows he lets the tea brew, pours a cup, and brings it over to the* MODEL HEAD.) . . . it's up to the responsible agencies to ensure that our motorways don't become too cluttered with retail outlets masquerading as public services.

PRESENTER. (*Unseen.*) But you wouldn't disagree, would you, that the notion that traveling at speed, in a car, with anyone of any age who's on the verge of, ah, urinating, is a miserable state of affairs?

SHEARMAN. (*Unseen.*) Surely we should keep this whole thing in proport—(*The radio is snapped off by* THE AUTHOR, *who stands shaking his head.*)

MODEL HEAD. (*Staring into his tea with frank dubiety.*) What the fuck d'you call that then?

THE AUTHOR. (*Coming back to the table and staring into the cup as well.*) That? That's scale, isn't it.

MODEL HEAD. I know what it is. You expect a few little brownish islands on the meniscus of your morning tea, given the prevalence of lime in the water hereabouts, but not this-this-archipelago of the stuff! (*He sticks his finger into the cup and withdraws it. It is coated in gray-brown gunk.*) Take a look in the kettle. (THE AUTHOR *goes back to the stove, empties the kettle, and removes the lid. He holds it up so the* MODEL HEAD *can see inside as well. It is, indeed, completely choked with scale. He reaches inside and withdraws the furry chrysalis of a descaler.*) Wow! This is the mother of all descalers!

THE AUTHOR. Yes, um, well, I have rather been neglecting things around the bungalow recently. But that can change, that can change. Yes, indeed, um, I tell you what, I'll go and get a new descaler this morning, that I'll do. It will symbolize a new beginning: clean and unsullied. . . . (*He begins to pick up one after another of the little brown bottles, which are standing everywhere,*

445

and holds them up to the light.) . . . I'm right out of K&M as well, so I'll have to visit a chemist—

MODEL HEAD. In Beaconsfield?

THE AUTHOR. No, no, no possibility of that, I'm afraid, none of them will serve me anymore. I have—in junkie parlance—burned them all down. I will have to venture further afield. . . . *(He strikes a pose, holding the furry descaler aloft, and it's worth remarking at this point that despite the excesses of the previous night, he is looking far better than you might expect, almost presentable.)* . . . I shall have to voyage to Tring, to Amersham, or even up the M40 . . . to High Wycombe!

(*Blackout.*)

NOTES ON CONTRIBUTORS

ROBERT ANTONI's most recent novel, *Carnival*, is a Black Cat book published by Grove/Atlantic. It has been translated into several languages, including Finnish and Chinese. He co-edited *Conjunctions:27, The Archipelago.*

RAE ARMANTROUT's most recent book, *Up to Speed*, was published by Wesleyan in 2004. *Next Life* is forthcoming from Wesleyan in February 2007. She teaches writing at the University of California San Diego.

JOHN ASHBERY's new book of poems, *A Worldly Country*, will be published early next year by Ecco/HarperCollins. He has been Charles P. Stevenson, Jr., Professor of Languages and Literature at Bard College since 1990, and is a contributing editor to *Conjunctions.*

JOHN BARTH, a frequent contributor to *Conjunctions*, is the National Book Award–winning author of numerous novels, novellas, and short-story and essay collections, including *Where Three Roads Meet* (Houghton Mifflin), *The Sot-Weed Factor, Giles Goat-Boy* (both Anchor), *Sabbatical* (Dalkey Archive), and many others.

MARTINE BELLEN's newest collection of poems, *GHOSTS!*, is being published by Spuyten Duyvil at the end of 2006. She is a contributing editor to *Conjunctions* and co-edited *Conjunctions:29, Tributes.*

CAN XUE's books in English include *Dialogues in Paradise, Old Floating Cloud, The Embroidered Shoes*, and, most recently, *Blue Light in the Sky & Other Stories* (New Directions).

Among JONATHAN CARROLL's fifteen novels are *The Wooden Sea, Outside the Dog Museum*, and *Glass Soup* (all TOR Books). The excerpt in this issue is the first chapter of a novel in progress. He lives in Vienna, Austria.

CHEN ZEPING, professor of linguistics at Fujian Teachers' University, has published numerous books and articles in his field. He and Karen Gernant are currently translating a novel by Can Xue for Yale University Press.

Recent books by CLARK COOLIDGE are *Now It's Jazz* (Living Batch Press), *Alien Tatters* (Atelos), *Far Out West* (Adventures in Poetry), and *Counting on Planet Zero* (forthcoming from Fewer & Further Press).

BRENDA COULTAS is the author of *A Lonely Cemetery* and *The Abolition Journal*, both forthcoming from Coffee House Press in 2007.

JIM CRACE lives in Birmingham, England. He is the author of nine novels including *Quarantine,* which won the Whitbread Novel Award, and *Being Dead* (both Picador), which won the National Book Critics Circle Award. His first appearance in print in this country was in *Conjunctions:13.*

LYDIA DAVIS's translation of Marcel Proust's *Swann's Way* was awarded the French-American Foundation's annual Translation Prize in 2003. A new collection of her stories, *A Strange Impulse,* is forthcoming next spring from Farrar, Straus and Giroux.

RIKKI DUCORNET's stories in this issue will be included in a forthcoming collection from Dalkey Archive. She is currently working on an exhibit for the Pierre Menard Gallery in Massachusetts, which will open in May 2007. She co-edited *Conjunctions:46, Selected Subversions.*

MARCELLA DURAND is the author of *The Anatomy of Oil* (Belladonna Books) and *Western Capital Rhapsodies* (Faux Press). "Traffic and Weather" was written largely at a Lower Manhattan Cultural Council residency during spring 2006.

JULIA ELLIOTT lives in Columbia, South Carolina. Her fiction has appeared in earlier issues of *Conjunctions,* as well as in *The Georgia Review, Puerto Del Sol, Mississippi Review, Fence, Black Warrior Review,* and other journals.

FORREST GANDER's most recent titles are *Eye Against Eye* (poems, New Directions) and *A Faithful Existence* (essays, Shoemaker & Hoard). His translations of Coral Bracho's selected poems *Firefly under the Tongue* (New Directions) and his translations, with Kent Johnson, of Jaime Saenz's book-length poem *The Night* (Princeton University) are forthcoming.

Among WILLIAM H. GASS's many books are *The Tunnel* (Dalkey Archive), *Reading Rilke* (Basic Books), *In the Heart of the Heart of the Country* (Godine), and, most recently, *A Temple of Texts* (Knopf). He is a longtime contributing editor to *Conjunctions.*

SCOTT GEIGER is currently a member of the Architecture Research Office. The 2007 Pushcart Prize anthology includes his story "The Frank Orison," which originally appeared in *Conjunctions:45, Secret Lives of Children.*

KAREN GERNANT, professor emerita of Chinese history, and Chen Zeping are regular contributors of translations to *Conjunctions.* Other authors they have translated include Yan Lianke, Alai, Zhang Kangkang, Su Tong, Zhu Wenying, Lin Bai, Wei Wei, and Bei Cun.

PETER GIZZI is the author of *Some Values of Landscape and Weather* (Wesleyan), *Artificial Heart* (Burning Deck), and *Periplum and Other Poems 1987–1992* (Salt Publishing). A new book of poems, *The Outernationale,* is forthcoming in spring 2007 from Wesleyan. He is a contributing editor to *Conjunctions.*

Recent books of poetry by the late BARBARA GUEST (1920–2006) include *The Red Gaze, Miniatures,* and *Rocks on a Platter: Notes on Literature,* all from Wesleyan. In 2003 she published two books of prose: *Forces of the Imagination: Writing on Writing* (Kelsey Street) and *Dürer in the Window: Reflexions on Art* (Roof). In 1999 she was awarded the Frost Medal for Lifetime Achievement by the Poetry Society of America.

JESSICA HAGEDORN's novels include *Dream Jungle, The Gangster of Love,* which was nominated for the Irish Times International Fiction Prize, and *Dogeaters* (all Penguin), which was nominated for a National Book Award. She is also the author of *Danger and Beauty* (City Lights), a collection of poetry and prose.

LYN HEJINIAN's most recently published books of poetry are *The Fatalist* (Omnidawn), *A Border Comedy* (Granary Books), and *My Life in the Nineties* (Shark Books). The poems included in this issue are from a work in progress titled *The Book of a Thousand Eyes.* She teaches at the University of California.

MAUREEN HOWARD's books include *A Lover's Almanac, The Silver Screen* (both Penguin), and *Natural History* (Carroll & Graf), among many others. She is currently working on a new novel.

ROBERT KELLY's recent books include *Lapis* (Godine), *Shame/Scham* (McPherson), and *Threads* (First Intensity). Forthcoming are *Mayday* (Parsifal Press) and *Sainte-Terre* (Shivastan). He is a longtime contributing editor to *Conjunctions.*

ANN LAUTERBACH's seventh volume of poetry, *Hum* (Penguin), was published in 2005, along with *The Night Sky: Writings on the Poetics of Experience* (Viking). She is Schwab Professor of Languages and Literature at Bard College, where she also co-chairs the Writing Division of the Milton Avery Graduate School of the Arts. She has been a contributing editor to *Conjunctions* since 1982.

JONATHAN LETHEM is the author of the forthcoming *You Don't Love Me Yet* (Doubleday) and six other novels, including *Amnesia Moon* (Harvest Books), *The Fortress of Solitude* (Doubleday), and *Motherless Brooklyn* (Vintage), which won the National Book Critics Circle Award. He lives in Brooklyn and Maine.

MICHELINE AHARONIAN MARCOM was born in Dhahran, Saudi Arabia, and raised in Los Angeles. She is the author of the novel *Three Apples Fell from Heaven* (Riverhead), which was a 2001 *New York Times* Notable Book. *The Daydreaming Boy* (Riverhead) won the PEN/USA Award in Fiction for 2005. She was a recipient of a 2004 Lannan Literary Fellowship. *Draining the Sea* is forthcoming from Riverhead Books.

VALERIE MARTIN's most recent book is *The Unfinished Novel and Other Stories* (Vintage). Her new novel, *Trespass,* is forthcoming from Doubleday (Nan A. Talese).

EDIE MEIDAV is the author of *Crawl Space* (Farrar, Straus and Giroux) and *The Far Field: A Novel of Ceylon* (Houghton Mifflin). She was the winner of the 2006 Bard Fiction Prize.

RICK MOODY's books include *Purple America, The Ice Storm, The Black Veil* (all Back Bay Books), and, most recently, *The Diviners* (Little, Brown). In May 2007, he will publish *Right Livelihoods: Three Novellas* (also from Little, Brown). A contributing editor to *Conjunctions*, he guest-edited a portfolio of tributes to William Gaddis in *Conjunctions:41, Two Kingdoms.*

EMMA NORMAN is a student at Pitzer College. Her photographs have appeared in *The American Poetry Review* and in a book on Nova Scotia published by National Geographic.

HOWARD NORMAN's books include *The Bird Artist, The Northern Lights,* and *In Fond Remembrance of Me* (all from Picador), among many others. His newest novel, *Devotion,* is forthcoming from Houghton Mifflin early next year. "Scissors-in-Window" is part of a memoir. He is a contributing editor to *Conjunctions,* and guest-edited *Conjunctions:41, Two Kingdoms.*

JOYCE CAROL OATES is the author of numerous works, including *Missing Mom* (Harper Perennial), *We Were the Mulvaneys* (Penguin), *The Falls,* and *Blonde* (both Ecco). She is the Roger S. Berlind Distinguished Professor of the Humanities at Princeton University.

ELIZABETH ROBINSON's father, Bruce Robinson, read Wilkie Collins's *The Woman in White* to her when she was a child. Robinson is the author of eight collections of poetry, most recently *Apostrophe* (Apogee Press) and *Under That Silky Roof* (Burning Deck).

JOANNA SCOTT's most recent novel, *Liberation* (Little, Brown), won the Ambassador Book Award from the English-Speaking Union. Her collection of stories, *Everybody Loves Somebody,* is forthcoming in December. She is a contributing editor to *Conjunctions.*

PETER DALE SCOTT's four books of poetry are *Crossing Borders* and his trilogy *Seculum: Coming to Jakarta, Listening to the Candle,* and *Minding the Darkness* (all New Directions). In 2002 he received the Lannan Award for poetry.

WILL SELF is the author of numerous novels, short-story collections, novellas, and collections of journalism, including *The Quantity Theory of Insanity, How the Dead Live, Great Apes,* and *Junk Mail* (all published by Grove). His latest novel, *The Book of Dave,* is forthcoming from Bloomsbury U.S. in November. *Scale,* which is adapted from his own short story of the same title, is his first play.

REGINALD SHEPHERD's four volumes of poetry, all from the University of Pittsburgh Press, are *Otherhood, Wrong, Angel Interrupted,* and *Some Are Drowning,* winner of the 1993 Associated Writing Programs' Award in Poetry. His fifth collection, *Fata Morgana,* is forthcoming from the University of Pittsburgh in 2007.

CHRISTOPHER SORRENTINO's novel *Trance,* a finalist for the 2005 National Book Award for Fiction, has recently been issued in paperback by Picador.

PETER STRAUB is the author of two collections of shorter fiction and seventeen novels, including *Shadowland* (Berkley), *Lost Boy Lost Girl* (Ballentine), *Ghost Story* (Pocket), and, most recently, *In the Night Room* (Random House). In 2006, he was given a Life Achievement Award by the Horror Writers Association. A contributing editor to *Conjunctions*, he guest-edited *Conjunctions:39, The New Wave Fabulists*.

LYNNE TILLMAN's newest book is *This Is Not It* (Distributed Art Publishers), a collection of stories written in response to twenty-two artists' work. Her new novel, *American Genius, A Comedy*, is forthcoming this fall from Soft Skull Press.

KEITH WALDROP teaches at Brown University and, with Rosmarie Waldrop, is editor of the small press Burning Deck. He has translated, among others, Anne-Marie Albiach, Claude Royet-Journoud, Paol Keineg, Dominique Fourcade, Pascal Quignard, and Jean Grosjean. Recent books include *The Locality Principle, The Silhouette of the Bridge*, which won the America Award in 1997, and *Semiramis If I Remember* (all from Avec). He also recently published a translation of Baudelaire's *Les Fleurs du mal* (Wesleyan).

ROSMARIE WALDROP's trilogy (*The Reproduction of Profiles, Lawn of Excluded Middle*, and *Reluctant Gravities*) is being reprinted by New Directions under the title *Curves to the Apple*. Her collected essays, *Dissonance (if you are interested)*, has been recently published by the University of Alabama.

As the Judith E. Wilson Visiting Poetry Fellow of Cambridge University in 2005, MARJORIE WELISH completed a manuscript, *Isle of the Signatories*, the title poem from which appears in this issue. Her most recent books of poetry are *The Annotated "Here" and Selected Poems* and *Word Group* (both Coffee House Press). *Of the Diagram: The Work of Marjorie Welish* (Slought Books) gathers essays about her practice.

EDMUND WHITE has just finished *Hotel de Dream*, a novel about Stephen Crane and his encounter with an adolescent male prostitute. White's play *Terre Haute* was recently produced at the Edinburgh Festival.

DIANE WILLIAMS's most recent book of fiction is *Romancer Erector* (Dalkey). A new book, *It Was Like My Trying to Have a Tender-Hearted Nature*, is forthcoming from FC$_2$ next year. She is the founder and editor of *NOON*.

C. D. WRIGHT's most recent book is *Cooling Time: An American Poetry Vigil*, and a text edition of *One Big Self* is forthcoming (both from Copper Canyon).

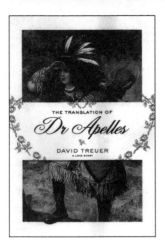
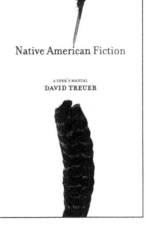

NOON

A LITERARY ANNUAL

1369 MADISON AVENUE   PMB 298
NEW YORK   NEW YORK   10128-0711

EDITION PRICE $9 DOMESTIC $14 FOREIGN

Skinny Dipping in the Lake of the Dead
Alan DeNiro

"You can't help but stop and take real notice."
—Jonathan Carroll (*Glass Soup*)

» A Book Sense Pick: "DeNiro can weld words into some mighty strange configurations."

A passionate, poetic, and political debut fiction collection reminiscent of the work of Aimee Bender & George Saunders. Includes stories from *Fence, One Story, Crowd,* and *3rd Bed*.

$16 · 1931520178
July 1, 2006

Howard Who?
Howard Waldrop

What if the dodo wasn't extinct? What if sumo stars could defeat opponents with the power of their minds? Waldrop's stories are sophisticated, magical recombinations of the stuff our pop-culture dreams are made of. Open this book and encounter jazz singers, robotic cartoon ducks, nosferatu, angry gorillas, and, of course, the dodo.

$14 · 1931520186
Peapod Classics No.3

"Quite as irresistible as ever."—*Booklist*

Mothers & Other Monsters
Maureen F. McHugh

"Gorgeously crafted stories."
—Nancy Pearl, NPR (*Morning Edition*)

"My favorite thing about her is the wry, uncanny tenderness of her stories."—Dan Chaon (*Among the Missing*)

Story Prize Finalist · Paperback has an author interview and essay.

HC · $24 · 1931520135
PB · $16 · 1931520194

The Privilege of the Sword
Ellen Kushner

» A marvelous tale crackling with energy, wit, and wonders, a genuine swashbuckler, an energetic surprise set in a labyrinthine city full of intrigue, secrets, and scoundrels.

"Unholy fun, and wholly fun . . . an elegant riposte, dazzlingly executed."—Gregory Maguire, *Wicked*

$35 · 1931520208

Burning Deck Fall 2006

Erica Carpenter:
PERSPECTIVE WOULD HAVE US

In Carpenter's first full-length collection, dreams, films, foreign countries are entered as so many fields of radiation with the power to mutate the forms of what we know — or think we know.

"this is an excellent, wonderful book... a celebration of subtlety in an age of bluntness"
—Ron Silliman

Poetry, 72 pages, offset, smyth-sewn, ISBN 1-886224-76-5, original paperback $14

Elizabeth Robinson:
UNDER THAT SILKY ROOF

The poems of Robinson's new collection are concerned with the interplay of domestic life — its companionship, its fecundity, its losses — and manifestations of the abstract or, as she puts it, with "the brick floor from which the/kingdom of God extends/or could extend."

"Robinson has reinvented the 'uses of enchantment'"—Ann Lauterbach

Poetry, 80 pages, offset, smyth-sewn, ISBN 1-886224-71-4, original paperback $14

Jean Grosjean:
AN EARTH OF TIME
[Serie d'Ecriture, No. 18; translated from the French by Keith Waldrop]

Written while Jean Grosjean was a prisoner in the Second World War, *Terre du temps*, his first book, was published in 1946, attracted immediate attention and was awarded the "Prix de la Pléiade." Between lyric and meditation on Biblical themes, the poems work up to a personal apocalypse.

The noted author of fiction, poetry and translations (the Koran, books of the Old Testament, Aeschylus, Shakespeare) died on April 10, 2006 in Versailles.

Poetry, 96 pages, offset, smyth-sewn, ISBN 1-886224-79-x, original paperback $14

Suzanne Doppelt:
RING RANG WRONG
[Serie d'Ecriture, No. 19; translated from the French by Cole Swensen]

Juxtaposed with her precise and abstract photographs, Doppelt's prose considers astronomy, weather, the five senses, plant life, the insect world, the nature of time — all in an implicit dialogue with the pre-Socratics. Often funny, often wry, this text betrays an affectionate love for the world.

Some pre-Socratic fragments appear translated into a phonematic language by the composer Georges Aperghis.

Text and Photographs, 80 pages, offset, smyth-sewn, ISBN 1-886224-80-3, original paperback $14

Gerhard Roth:
The Will to Sickness
[Dichten =, No. 8; translated from the German by Tristram Wolff]

Roth burst on the German-speaking scene in the early 1970s with three fiercely experimental novels, among them the present book. It is here that he developed his "objective" prose, aggregates of minute observations with quasi-surrealist effect. "i'm preparing a slow disintegration of the external world inside my head."

Novel, 120 pages, offset, smyth-sewn, ISBN 1-886224-78-1, original paperback $14

Orders: Small Press Distribution 1-800/869-7553, www.spdbooks.org; in Europe, www.h-press.no
www.burningdeck.com

Black Clock

number 6
winter | spring

edited by Steve Erickson
designed by Gail Swanlund

blackclock.org

PUBLISHED BY CALARTS IN ASSOCIATION WITH THE MFA WRITING PROGRAM

NEW DIRECTIONS
Fall 2006 • Winter 2007

CÉSAR AIRA
HOW I BECAME A NUN. Tr. Andrews. Novel. First time in English. "Like García Márquez on LSD!' —Carlos Fuentes. $13.95 pbk. original. February.

DJUNA BARNES
NIGHTWOOD. *NEW* Preface by Jeanette Winterson. Intro. by T.S. Eliot. Reissue of one of the greatest novels of the Modernist era. $12.95 pbk.

ROBERTO BOLAÑO
AMULET. Tr. Andrews. A semi-hallucinatory novel that embodies in one woman's voice Latin America's recent history. $21.95 cloth. January.

INGER CHRISTENSEN
it. Tr. Nied. Intro. by Anne Carson. Now availailable for the first time in English, the Danish poet's masterwork. $17.95 pbk.

JOHN GARDNER
THE SUNLIGHT DIALOGUES. *NEW* intro. by Charles Johnson. Novel. "Large and beautifully written." —*N.Y.Times Book Review.* $17.95 pbk.

JAMES LAUGHLIN
THE WAY IT WASN'T: From the Files of James Laughlin. Ed. by Epler and Javitch. Lavishly illustrated, totally engrossing. $45.00 cl./$25.00 pbk.

JAVIER MARÍAS
THE MAN OF FEELING. Tr. Jull Costa. Now in paper. "Everything that the best fiction might hope to be…" —*The Times of London.* $13.95 pbk. Feb.

TERU MIYAMOTO
KINSHU. Autumn Brocade. Tr. Thomas. Captivating epistolary novel. A "delicately woven tale of romance." —*The Wash.Times.* $14.95 pbk. Feb.

VLADIMIR NABOKOV
LAUGHTER IN THE DARK. *NEW* Intro. by John Banville. The classic novel by the author of *Lolita.* "A cruel little masterpiece."—*TLS.*$12.95 pbk.

GRISELDA OHANNESSIAN
ONCE: AS IT WAS. Autobiography. Illus. and w/letters, and newsclippings. Robert Graves and Laura Riding's sojourn in PA. $13.95 pbk. Feb.

GREGORY RABASSA
IF THIS BE TREASON. Translation and Its Dyscontents: A Memoir. By the English translator of Cortázar, Márquez, Lispector et.al. $14.95 pbk.

MURIEL SPARK
SYMPOSIUM. Novel about high society and low cunning. "A virtuoso performance." —*Time Out.* "A delight to read." —*The N. Y.Times.* $13.95 pbk.

TOMAS TRANSTRÖMER
THE GREAT ENIGMA. New Collected Poems. Tr. Fulton. Finally the collected works of one of the world's greatest living writers. $16.95 pbk.

ROSMARIE WALDROP
CURVES TO THE APPLE. Three pivotal works: *The Reproduction of Profiles, Lawn of the Excluded Middle, Reluctant Gravities.* $16.95 pbk.

TENNESSEE WILLIAMS
MEMOIRS. *NEW* Intro. by John Waters. "A raw display of private life." —*N.Y.T. Bk. Rev.* "Witty, outrageous and brutally frank" —*BOM.*$16.95 pbk.

Please send for free complete catalog.
NEW DIRECTIONS, 80 8th Avenue, NYC 10011
www.ndpublishing.com

KENNETH REXROTH

I write poetry to seduce women and overthrow the capitalist system
...in that order.

Congratulations to
Peter Orner

Winner of the
2007 Bard Fiction Prize

❧

Peter Orner, author of *The Second Coming
of Mavala Shikongo* and *Esther Stories*,
joins previous winners Nathan Englander,
Emily Barton, Monique Truong,
Paul La Farge, and Edie Meidav.

❧

The Bard Fiction Prize is awarded annually to a
promising emerging writer who is an American citizen
aged thirty-nine years or younger at the time
of application. In addition to a monetary award
of $30,000, the winner receives an appointment
as writer in residence at Bard College for one semester
without the expectation that he or she will teach
traditional courses. The recipient will give at least one
public lecture and meet informally with students.

For more information, please contact:

Bard Fiction Prize
Bard College
PO Box 5000
Annandale-on-Hudson, NY 12504-5000

CONJUNCTIONS:44

AN ANATOMY OF ROADS

The Quest Issue

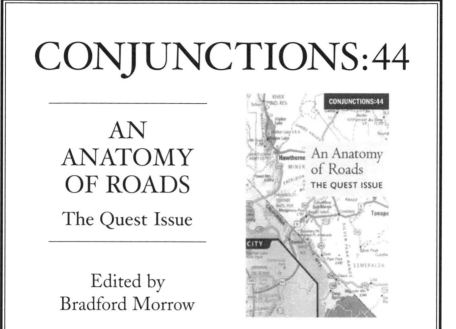

Edited by
Bradford Morrow

New fiction and poetry that undertake journeys of all kinds, ranging from the geographic to those that take place in the interior of the mind. Authors include John Barth, Elizabeth Hand, Jon McGregor, Julia Elliott, Forrest Gander, Jonathan Carroll, Sara Veglahn, Arthur Sze, Robert Coover, David Schuman, Joanna Scott, Bradford Morrow, Rikki Ducornet, Nathaniel Mackey, Susan Steinberg, Toby Olson, Rebecca Curtis, Alai, Joshua Furst, Joyce Carol Oates, Paul West, D. E. Steward, Carol Moldaw, Frederic Tuten, Carole Maso, Robert Kelly, Deb Olin Unferth, and Robert Antoni. Features a portfolio, "A Fiction & Poems by Nine Poets," with new work by William H. Gass, Richard Meier, Martine Bellen, Brian Lucas, Lara Glenum, Elizabeth Willis, James Grinwis, John Taggart, Rae Armantrout, and Rachel Blau DuPlessis.

404 pages. $15.00, shipping included.

To order, send payment to:

CONJUNCTIONS
Bard College
Annandale-on-Hudson, NY 12504
Phone: 845-758-1539
E-mail: Conjunctions@bard.edu

Or, order these and additional back issues online at
www.conjunctions.com.

CONJUNCTIONS:45

SECRET
LIVES
OF
CHILDREN

Edited by
Bradford Morrow

Features new fiction, poetry, and essays that delve into the mystery, trauma, joys, frustrations, and wonderment of childhood. Work by Shelley Jackson, Robert Clark, Melissa Pritchard, Paul La Farge, Rikki Ducornet, David Shields, Karen Russell, Elizabeth Robinson, Joshua Furst, Donald Revell, Emily Barton, Howard Norman, Ben Lerner, Gilbert Sorrentino, Micaela Morrissette, Yan Lianke, Diane Williams, Lois-Ann Yamanaka, Peter Gizzi, Mary Caponegro, Scott Geiger, Brian Evenson, Ilona Karmel, Kim Chinquee, David Marshall Chan, Danielle Pafunda, Julia Elliott, Lucy Corin, Elaine Equi, S. G. Miller, Malinda Markham, Mark Poirier, Can Xue, and Robert Creeley. Includes a "Nuts" cartoon strip by Gahan Wilson and a new translation of Stéphane Mallarmé translated by John Ashbery.

404 pages. Illustrated. $15.00, shipping included.

CONJUNCTIONS:46

SELECTED SUBVERSIONS

Essays on the World at Large

Edited by
Rikki Ducornet,
Bradford Morrow,
and Robert Polito

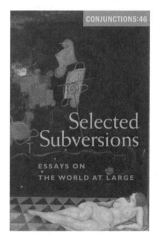

Twenty-four essays that explore a cascade of human experience while rethinking the very nature of essay writing itself. Features new work by John D'Agata, Joanna Scott, Geoffrey O'Brien, Michael Logan, Diane Ackerman, Rick Moody, Robin Hemley, Ned Rorem, Honor Moore, David Shields, Forrest Gander, Rosamond Purcell, William H. Gass, Anne Carson, John Crowley, Eliot Weinberger, Robert Harbison, Sven Birkerts, Martine Bellen, Paul West, Fanny Howe, Matthew Kirby, Kenneth Gross, and Shelley Jackson. Includes a special portfolio, "Ten Unproduced Scenarios," by The Quay Brothers.

408 pages. Illustrated. $15.00, shipping included.

To order, send payment to:

CONJUNCTIONS
Bard College
Annandale-on-Hudson, NY 12504
Phone: 845-758-1539
E-mail: Conjunctions@bard.edu

Or, order these and additional back issues online at
www.conjunctions.com.